ALLAN MALLINSON

Allan Mallinson is a former cavalry officer. Besides the Matthew Hervey series, he is the author of the recently revised and updated *Light Dragoons*, a history of four regiments of British Cavalry, one of which he commanded. He is also a regular reviewer for *The Times* and the *Spectator*, and defence commentator for the *Daily Telegraph*.

For more information on Matthew Hervey, please visit his website on www.hervey.info

www.rbooks.co.uk

THE SABRE'S EDGE

1824: in India Matthew Hervey lays siege to the fortress of Bhurtpore.

*'Splendid . . . the tale is as historically stimulating
as it is stirringly exciting'*
SUNDAY TELEGRAPH

RUMOURS OF WAR

**1826: while Matthew Hervey prepares for civil war in Portugal, he
remembers the Retreat to Corunna twenty years previously.**

*'I enjoyed the adventure immensely . . . as compelling, vivid and
plausible as any war novel I've ever read'*
DAILY TELEGRAPH

AN ACT OF COURAGE

**1826: a prisoner of the Spanish, Matthew Hervey relives the blood
and carnage of the Siege of Badajoz.**

*'Concentrating on the battle of Talavera and the investment of
Badajoz, both sparklingly described, [Mallinson] plays to his
undoubted strengths'*
OBSERVER

COMPANY OF SPEARS

**1827: on the plains of South Africa, Matthew Hervey
confronts the savage Zulu.**

'A damn fine rip-roaring read'
LITERARY REVIEW

MAN OF WAR

1827: at home and at sea, crises loom.

*'As tense, exciting, vivid and gory as we've come to expect
from this master of military fiction'*
SPECTATOR

WARRIOR

ALLAN MALLINSON

BANTAM BOOKS

LONDON • TORONTO • SYDNEY • AUCKLAND • JOHANNESBURG

TRANSWORLD PUBLISHERS
61–63 Uxbridge Road, London W5 5SA
A Random House Group Company
www.rbooks.co.uk

WARRIOR
A BANTAM BOOK: 9780553818628

First published in Great Britain
in 2008 by Bantam Press
a division of Transworld Publishers
Bantam edition published 2009

Addresses for Random House Group Ltd companies outside the UK
can be found at: www.randomhouse.co.uk
The Random House Group Ltd Reg. No. 954009

The Random House Group Limited supports The Forest Stewardship Council
(FSC), the leading international forest certification organisation. All our titles
that are printed on Greenpeace approved FSC certified paper carry the FSC
logo. Our paper procurement policy can be found at
www.rbooks.co.uk/environment

Typeset in 11.5/14.5 Times New Roman by
Falcon Oast Graphic Art Ltd.
Printed in the UK by CPI Cox & Wyman, Reading, RG1 8EX.

2 4 6 8 10 9 7 5 3

CONTENTS

Part Three
U-Shaka!

FOREWORD

Lord Cardigan, who led the Charge of the Light Brigade, was born six years later than Matthew Hervey. But whereas Hervey joined his regiment, the 6th Light Dragoons, when he was seventeen, seeing service throughout the Peninsular War and at Waterloo, the Honourable Thomas Brudenell, as Cardigan then was, did not join the army until 1824, when he was twenty-seven. Brudenell was not entirely without military experience, however, if it could be called that: five years earlier he had formed his own troop of yeomanry cavalry to guard against Reformist demonstrations in Northamptonshire, his family seat (Deene Park). But the troop's purpose and organization gave him a ludicrously feudal attitude to soldiering, which, coupled with an intellect that not even three years at Oxford had raised to adequacy, led with exquisite inevitability to that poetic debacle of the Crimean War.

Cardigan's rise was rapid: cornet in the 8th Hussars in 1824; lieutenant in January 1825; captain in June of the following year; major in August 1830, and lieutenant-colonel, commanding the 15th Hussars, in December that same year. All these promotions were by purchase: using his vast wealth, he literally bribed his way to command in six years. The purchase system was a sort of regulator: it was meant to guarantee that officers had a financial stake in the service of the Crown, after the uncertainties of the Civil War and the Jacobite rebellions and the revolutionary notions which had so disturbed the peace on the other side of the Channel. So the price of a commission was a sort of caution money. And, in truth, the official prices were not so great as to exclude men of talent. The problem lay in the *unofficial* price: an officer in a smart regiment was more or less able to name his own price when he decided to sell, which was often too high for a junior in his own regiment, and so a rich one from another regiment would buy in. There was, therefore, considerable coming and going. But a smart regiment could become non-smart overnight: all it needed was a posting to India, or some other place considered un-convivial (Beau Brummell resigned from the 10th Hussars when they were posted to Manchester). Fashionable officers would exchange with others in home-stationed regiments, and since an officer could live more comfortably on his pay and a smaller private income in the tropics (and, presumably, Manchester), there was no shortage of willing exchangees. There were actually some officers who positively sought out a posting to India, since that offered the best prospect of active service.

As long as all this buying and selling over-price didn't frighten the horses, the authorities were generally content. Periodically there were attempts to enforce the regulation prices, but never very vigorously and always without success. Enforcement was scarcely in the interests of anyone above the rank of cornet who had paid a penny more than the regulation, for he, not unreasonably, hoped to recoup his outlay when he 'sold out'. No one wanted negative equity. Besides, there were always ways for an able but impecunious officer to advance: (free) promotions in the field following the death of his senior, or in reward for some outstanding service; or the system of brevets, and acting and local rank. However, the army was getting smaller, and actual command, as opposed to appointments on the staff, was going to the men with large fortunes – at least in the Guards, the cavalry and some of the better-favoured infantry regiments of the Line; competition for command of the Forty-something Foot on a yellow-fevered island in the West Indies was not so intense. So it all sorted itself out in the end – more or less. But how was the British army to be sure of having capable generals if all that was needed to rise to command of a regiment was deep pockets and aristocratic connections?

Thomas Brudenell, Lord Cardigan, was the most infamous example of the mess into which the army was getting itself during the decades after Waterloo, but there were other contenders for that dubious distinction. Brudenell does not feature in the pages of this latest chronicle of the life of Major (Acting Lieutenant-Colonel) Matthew Hervey, but the man who ordered him to charge at Balaklava, his brother-in-law Lord Bingham, later Earl of Lucan, is remarked on. Bingham had joined the army after Waterloo, straight from school, but before buying command of the 17th Lancers for a record sum, and before he was thirty, he had seen no active service. Indeed, he had spent remarkably little time at actual duty. After command of the Seventeenth, Bingham went on to half-pay – another anomaly of the purchase system, whereby a man could retire from active soldiering, but if he had the right connections could continue to be promoted. Between 1837 and 1854, Bingham went from lieutenant-colonel to lieutenant-general (four ranks higher) without so much as attending a field day.

Today's National Curriculum, with its stress on 'empathizing' in the study of history, would no doubt phrase the exam question thus: 'How would you feel, as a veteran of real fighting, to have men promoted over you merely because they had money?' And doubtless there would be an A* for the candidate who wrote of how wretched he would feel, the victim of aristocratic oppression, but that he could do nothing for fear of the lash or whatever it was that officers were punished with. But the sort of student who gained a top grade in the old 'O' Levels would write something along the lines of 'but there again, the Duke of Wellington's rise had not been so very different from the Earl of Lucan's . . .'

* * *

It is 1828, and Matthew Hervey is thirty-seven. He is major (second in command) of the 6th Light Dragoons, though still nominally in command of a troop on detachment to the Cape Colony; and he has acting lieutenant-colonel's rank for command of the recently raised Cape Mounted Rifles. He has just made a text-book marriage, and his old friend and mentor, Daniel Coates, has left him a deal of money with which to advance himself. He is at a crossroads, a watershed, a pivot point – whichever is the most appropriate word for that magic number thirty-seven – which even in today's army is still the age at which a man's career is best sounded. Matthew Hervey has come a long way since that day in 1808 when the second son of the Horningsham parsonage, straight from Shrewsbury School, joined his regiment. Like Cromwell, he carried with him his Prayer Book on campaign; although unlike Cromwell, his religion was never militant, rather that of the clean young Englishman. Now, in this tenth instal-ment of the Hervey chronicles, the Prayer Book is altogether less well thumbed, though the sabre is no less bloody.

PART ONE

EX AFRICA . . .

I
THE LIEUTENANT-GOVERNOR

The eastern frontier, Cape Colony, April 1828

The spearhead sliced through the blue serge of Private Parks's tunic, driving deep into his chest. The dragoon, wide-eyed at the sudden, silent assault, tumbled from the saddle like a recruit at first riding school, dead before his feet quit the stirrups. He lay with the spear stuck fast, and barely a twitch, at the feet of his troop horse, which stood still throughout as if possessed of the same paralysing shock.

Sir Eyre Somervile, lieutenant-governor of the Cape Colony, fumbled with the cartridge for his cavalry pistol. Serjeant-Major Armstrong's sabre flashed from its scabbard. The covermen closed to Somervile's side, swords drawn, to quieten his excited little arab. Serjeant Wainwright unshipped his carbine, cocked and aimed it in a single motion, more machine-like than human, and fired.

The spearman was sent to meet his Maker with the same rude promptness of Parks's own despatch.

A second *assegai* winged from the thicket, higher than the first (and thus better seen). Corporal Allott, the coverman on Somervile's offside, thrust up his sabre – 'head protect' – just catching the shaft at the binding to deflect it clear of his charge, who then dropped his cartridge ball and cursed most foully.

But the impact knocked the sabre clean from Allott's hand to hang by the sword knot from his jarred wrist. Before he could recover it another Xhosa darted from the thicket and between his horse's legs, thrusting with his spear to hamstring Somervile's arab. Armstrong spurred to his side and cut savagely at the back of the Xhosa's neck as he scrambled from beneath. The razor-sharp blade left but a few bloody sinews joining head to torso. The Xhosa staggered, then fell twitching in a gory, faecal sprawl.

Somervile jumped from the saddle to check his mare's leg.

'No, sir!' cried Armstrong. 'Get back up!'

Two more Xhosa ran in. Armstrong cut down one but the other lunged straight for Somervile. The nearside coverman, Corporal Hardy, urged his trooper forward to get his sabre to the guard, but couldn't make it. An arm's reach from his quarry, the Xhosa lofted his spear. Somervile could smell the animal odour of his fury as he raised his ball-less pistol, and fired.

At an arm's length the blank discharge was enough. Flame and powder grain scored the Xhosa's face, blinding him so that he jabbed wildly but ineffectually with his spear until Corporal Hardy put him out of his frenzied agony with a cleaving slice from crown to chin.

The little arab hobbled a few steps, her off-foreleg held up pitiably as if begging. Hardy jumped from the saddle. 'Sir, here!' He grabbed Somervile by the arm and motioned for him to mount.

Somervile, more exasperated than dazed, made to protest, but Armstrong decided it. 'Get up, sir! Get astride!'

Hardy heaved Somervile's paunchy bulk into his trooper's saddle, as with a deep-throated cry more Xhosa burst from the cover of the bushwillow thicket twenty yards away.

There was no time to front with carbine or pistol; it was for each to do as he could. Serjeant Wainwright, nearest, spurred straight at them, sword and carbine in hand, reins looped over his left arm. He parried the spear on his right a split second before the one on the left thrust through his canvas barrel belt and into his side. He fired the carbine point-blank, taking off the top of the spearman's head like a badly sliced egg, and then carved deep between the shoulders of the first Xhosa with a backhand cut. His trooper halted a few strides beyond, and Wainwright slid helplessly from the saddle, leaving a broad red stripe down the grey's flank.

The remaining spearmen pressed home the attack with a courage and determination Armstrong had not seen in Xhosa before. He turned his mare just in time to get the reach with his sword arm, swinging his sabre with all his strength down behind the nearest shield, all but severing the Xhosa's wrist.

Piet Doorn, burgher-guide, coming back up the trail from checking for spoor, fired his big Hall rifle at fifty yards, felling the tallest Xhosa, but the three others sprang at Somervile and his covermen like leopards on the fold. Corporal Allott, sabre now in left hand, made not even a retaliatory cut, the spear plunging into his gut and pushing him clean from the saddle. Corporal Hardy dived between the little arab's legs to slash at the nearest bare, black heel. The Xhosa staggered momentarily but just long enough for Somervile to urge his new mount forward, tumbling and trampling him like a corn rig.

The last Xhosa hesitated, as if unsure of his target rather than whether to fight or run, in which time Armstrong had closed with him to drive the point of his blade deep into his side, bowling him over to writhe in a bloody pool which spread with uncommon speed. Now Armstrong could risk turning his back on him to despatch Somervile's tumbled assailant.

But the Xhosa had no fight left in him. His hands and eyes pleaded.

Armstrong gestured with his sabre. 'Bind him up, Corp' Hardy. We'll take him a prize.' He turned to

20

Somervile. 'You all right, sir?' he asked in an accent so strong as to sound strangely alien.

But Somervile knew that it was action that revealed the man, and if Armstrong reverted to the Tyne in such a moment, then so be it: without his address they would none of them be alive. Could they *stay* alive? 'I am well, Serjeant-Major. The others?'

Armstrong was already taking stock. 'Corp' Hardy, watch rear, the way we came. Piet, go look ahead, will you? Stand sentry.'

Piet Doorn nodded as he tamped the new charge in his rifle.

Armstrong sprang from the saddle and looked in turn at Corporal Allott and Private Parks, satisfying himself there was no sign of life, before making for where Serjeant Wainwright lay.

'Jobie, Jobie!' he said sharply, shaking Wainwright's shoulder as if it were reveille.

There was no response.

Yet blood was still running from the wound. 'Come on, Jobie, lad – rouse yerself!' said Armstrong quietly but insistently, unfastening Wainwright's barrel-belt, taking off his own neckcloth to staunch the flow of blood.

Somervile was now by his side. 'Brandy, do you think, Serjeant-Major?'

'Ay, sir. Anything that'll bring 'im to,' replied Armstrong, taking the flask.

It was not easy to guess how much blood Wainwright

had lost – in Armstrong's experience it always looked more than it was – but to lose consciousness . . .

He lifted Wainwright's head and put the flask to his mouth, tipping it high to let the brandy pour in copiously.

A spasm of choking signalled that Wainwright was at least fighting. 'That's it, Jobie, lad!' He poured in more.

Another fit of choking brought back up the contents of the flask, and Wainwright's eyes flickered open at last.

Somervile rose, and shook his head. It had been a deuced ill-considered thing, he reckoned. He was not a military man (although he wore the ribbon of the Bath star for his soldierly bearing during the Vellore mutiny), but he knew it to be a sound principle not to divide one's force unless it were necessary. And it had not been necessary: he was perfectly capable of holding his own with pistol and sword! Captain Brereton, the officer in temporary command of E Troop, 6th Light Dragoons, had had no need of sending him to the rear so – into the very jaws, indeed, of the wretched Xhosa reiving party they were meant to be evading! What manner of tactician was this new-come captain?

Sweat poured down Somervile's brow, though the day was not hot. His hat was lost, his neckcloth gone, and his coat was fastened with but its single remaining button. But exhilaration, alarm and anger were in him combined to unusual degree: he was at once all for battle and for retreat. For this was no warfare like that he had seen in

India. This was more the hunting of savage beasts, the leopard or the tiger. Or rather, the *contest* with beasts, for he and his escort had been the prey.

Were these men, these Bantu, Kaffirs, Xhosa – whatever their rightful name – were they cognitive, as the natives of the Indies? Or did they act merely from instinction, as the psalmist had it, like the horse, or the mule, 'which have no understanding, whose mouth must be held in with bit and bridle'? What parley could there be with such primitives, who had not even the accomplishment of writing? Parley, though, depended first on surviving. They had beaten off one attack, but another . . .

It had been his, Somervile's, idea to make this reconnaissance of the frontier. He had wanted to see for himself the country, and the settlers who were often more cause for annoyance to Cape Town than were the native peoples. And of course those very people – Bantu, Kaffirs, Xhosa (it would be so very useful to have these names, at least, unconfused) – about whom he had read much that was contrary, and over whom his friend Colonel Matthew Hervey had lately gained some mastery. But Hervey was not with him. He was on leave, in England, recovering from his wounds and the remittent fever, and about to marry. Somervile had not wanted to undertake the reconnaissance without him, yet he could not wait for ever on his friend's return to duty: it was autumn, and although the winters here were nothing to those of India, the nights could be bitter chill, and the rains in the mountains of the interior could swell the rivers of the frontier into impassable torrents.

And it had begun well enough, in a quiet way – an official progress through Albany and Graaff Reinet, a pleasant ride beyond the Great Fish River to Fort Willshire, where he had inspected the little garrison of His Majesty's 55th Foot (which regiment had so distinguished itself at Umtata with Hervey and the Mounted Rifles a few months before). And he had been most attentively escorted the while by a half troop of the 6th Light Dragoons under the command of Captain the Honourable Stafford Brereton, not long joined from the regiment in England.

Hervey had originally asked for an officer to take temporary command because he was himself occupied increasingly with the Rifles, which corps he had raised, but after his wound at Umtata, and the recurrence of the malaria, the request had proved providential, and Brereton's early arrival a particular boon, allowing him to take home leave with rather more peace of mind. Not that he knew Brereton well, or even much at all. The younger son of the Earl of Brodsworth had joined the Sixth some five or so years earlier, but had not gone out to India, having served first with the depot troop at Maidstone before the general officer commanding the southern district had claimed him as an aide-de-camp.

Brereton had bought his captaincy via another

regiment and then exchanged back into the Sixth. There was nothing unusual in such a progression, although it meant that, a dozen years after Waterloo, and with India experience in short supply, there were many regiments whose officers had never, as the saying went, been shot over. Brereton had certainly not been. He had, however (doubtless in consequence), been keen to get to the frontier, and had been especially glad when the lieutenant-governor had not insisted on any larger escort, and therefore one requiring a more senior officer from the garrison.

Somervile had not been expecting trouble, though. Halting the Zulu incursion at the Umtata River had done much to quell the unease among the Xhosa, who had been so fearful of Shaka's depredations they had been migrating ever closer to the frontier, and frequently across it. But then, when Somervile's party had been returning, a league or so west of the Great Fish River, which marked the border for the settled population of the Eastern Cape, word had come of the Xhosa raid to the north, a much bigger foray than the frontier had seen in some time. It took even the most hardened burghers by surprise, requiring the immediate reinforcement of Fort Willshire and a doubling of the frontier patrols. By the time Somervile's party had re-crossed the Fish into the unsettled buffer tract – 'to see the beggars for myself' – the reivers were back across the Keiskama River into Xhosa territory proper.

But Xhosa raids were by their nature fissiparous affairs, and the proximity of burgher cattle to the Keiskama (against the rules of the buffer treaty), and the leafy cover which the season afforded, as well as the ease of river crossing, had evidently tempted at least one sub-party to remain in the unsettled tract.

Serjeant Wainwright was supporting himself on an elbow. 'There were nothing I could do, sir; not with so many spears.'

'Half a dozen, Jobie; half a dozen,' replied Armstrong, bemused. 'But there were two less when you'd done with them!'

'Noble conduct,' echoed Somervile. 'Finest traditions of the cavalry.'

'Thank you, sir. But what service a shotgun would've been!'

'Indeed.'

Or even one of the double-barrelled Westley-Richards which the Cape Mounted Rifles carried, thought Armstrong; though now was not the time to question why the Rifles were not with them.

'What do we do, Serjeant-Major?' asked Somervile, not afraid to confess thereby that he had no certain idea of his own.

Armstrong shook his head, and sighed. 'I don't want to leave young Parks and Danny Allott for the vultures, or the Xhosa for that matter. They've a nasty way with a blade.'

Somervile was ever of the opinion that a man's mortal remains meant nothing (nor, for that matter, did he believe there was anything *immortal*): the Parsees of Bombay put out their dead so that the vultures could pick the body clean. But he thought not to debate the point at this exigent moment. In any case, he recognized in Armstrong's reluctance the habitual pride of the regiment. A man who bore the numeral 'VI' on his shako plate was not abandoned lightly by another who bore the same.

'Shall we carry them astride then?'

Armstrong nodded. 'We've no chance of making a mile unless we're mounted. Not if those Xhosa don't want us to. We can get Parks and Allott across the one horse, and Jobie here fastened into the saddle. You take Danny's trooper, sir. And I'll have Corp' Hardy get up his carbine, and Parks's.'

'And the prisoner? I should like very much to interrogate him when there is opportunity.'

A bullet through the head would be the most expedient, reckoned Armstrong, but it would not serve; it had not been the way for years, not even with savages. 'I don't see us managing more than a trot, sir: he can keep up on his shanks.'

'Indeed.'

Armstrong offered Wainwright the flask again. 'You right enough for the saddle, Jobie, bonny lad?'

'Right enough, sir,' replied Wainwright, though

shaking his head at the need of help. 'I'll maybe want a leg up . . .'

Piet Doorn came back down the track in the peculiar loping gait that was the Cape frontiersman's – part jogging trot, part native bound. 'No cattle is past this way in two days,' he reported to Armstrong, his English heavily accented. 'But I can smell Kaffir still. A dozen of them maybe.'

Armstrong nodded. 'Will you ride rearguard for us, Piet?'

It was no part of a guide's duty to ride behind, let alone to fight off attackers. But Piet Doorn relished the opportunity to reduce the odds for the burghers of the frontier, as the gamekeeper shoots vermin at every opportunity. 'I will.'

Somervile dabbed at his brow with a red silk hand-kerchief. 'But why do they attack us when there is quite evidently no cattle to be had?'

Armstrong shook his head. 'Don't know, sir. A mystery to me.'

Piet Doorn had a theory, however, though he shuddered at the thought of it. 'They wants our guns. Can be no other.'

Somervile shuddered too. It was futile to suppose they wanted them merely for hunting. But if it were so, did the Xhosa intend them against the Zulu or the colonists?

'Well they're not having 'em unless they sign for 'em,'

said Armstrong, matter of fact. 'And since these heathens can't read or write . . .'

That half his troop couldn't was neither here nor there. What he was saying was that he would part with firearms only – and literally – over his dead body. Others might throw down the weapons, having spiked them first, but these Xhosa, even if heathens and savages, were not incapable blacksmiths, as any who had examined their spears knew: they would soon enough fathom how to put carbines to rights again.

'When do you ride, Serjeant-Major?' asked Piet.

'As soon as I can get Jobie Wainwright into the saddle.' Armstrong turned to Somervile. 'Sir, will you call in Corporal Hardy?'

Somervile nodded, realizing he was less use to Armstrong for the moment than was Piet Doorn. Such things were important for a man to recognize, and he was thankful he had learned the necessity of such humility in his early days in Mysore. 'I had better despatch my mount, too. Is it safe to risk a shot d'ye think?'

Armstrong thought the word 'safe' hardly apt, but he saw no objection to a shot. 'Piet?'

Piet Doorn shook his head, indicating that he too could see no reason to deny the animal a clean death.

Somervile doubled off breathily to recall the remaining able-bodied dragoon, before returning to his stricken mount. The little arab was quietly pulling at a clump of wild ginger the other side of a bushwillow tree, just out of sight of Armstrong and the others, her near fore-leg off the ground, the hamstring severed. Somervile detested the business, always. For a dragoon it was, he supposed (and had indeed occasionally observed), a routine of his occupation; but for him it was somehow a debasement. He held no truck with Scripture (or rather, he admired much of its poetry while disputing its authority), but he took powerfully the responsibility of dominion, and the horse was, to his mind, the noblest of 'every living thing that moveth upon the earth'.

He took off the saddle, and then had to check his pistol (he could not remember whether he had success-fully reloaded it or not), but the little mare stood obligingly. When he was sure he had got the new-fangled percussion cap on the nipple properly, he took a good hold of her reins, short, on the offside, put the pistol muzzle to the fossa above her right eye, aiming at the bottom of the left ear, closed his eyes and fired. The mare dropped like a stone onto her left side, the reins running through Somervile's hands while his eyes were still closed, the off foreleg catching him painfully on the shin.

He returned to the others limping slightly. Armstrong was not inclined to draw too unfavourable a conclusion: he had known old hands botch a despatch, and in any case, Somervile had chosen to do it himself rather than ask another. For that he could respect a man – even one who got himself kicked by a dead horse.

'Well done, sir. Horrible duty to perform. Such a bonny little thing an' all.'

Somervile cleared his throat. 'Indeed, Serjeant-Major.' He had bought the arab for the endurance that the breed was noted for, but also in truth for her looks. There was not a better-looking horse in Cape Town. 'I wonder what to do with the saddle.'

It was a good leather-panelled one, worth a deal more than the military issue, but this was not the time to be changing horses, let alone saddles. 'Sir, I think it best if you leave it be. It might just buy us a minute or so when the Xhosa come on it.'

Somervile nodded.

'Sir, will you lash up Serjeant Wainwright's bridle to lead him? Run a rein through the bit 'stead of the halter, though. If he passes out and the horse takes fright it'll be a deal easier to keep a hold.'

Somervile nodded again, and made to do Armstrong's bidding, for he understood the purpose well enough (whatever his unacquaintance with the particulars of cavalry work, he was no greenhorn when it came to horses).

He unfastened the bridoon rein on the offside, slipped it over the trooper's head and under its chin, then back through the offside bit ring, which would leave Wainwright with the curb reins. He presented himself ready for duty with some satisfaction.

Armstrong, having replaced the compress on

Wainwright's wound and bound the barrel sash even tighter, stood up, turned to Somervile, and sighed. 'I'm sorry, sir, I should have said: would you lead from the *nearside*, please?'

Somervile looked puzzled. 'But I cannot then use my sword and pistol arm so freely.'

'I know, sir,' replied Armstrong, as Corporal Hardy hauled Wainwright to his feet. 'But, with respect, Wainwright here will be able to.'

Somervile's jaw fell. He was being written off as worse than an invalid – all because he dropped the pistol ball.

'It's just, sir, that it's Wainwright's job, this. We're the ones in uniform. We're the escort.'

Somervile could scarcely credit it. Three dragoons, one of them only half conscious, and a burgher, a part-civilian – that was what the escort amounted to. And yet Serjeant-Major Armstrong was insisting on the proprieties as if the entire regiment were on parade. Doubtless were there a trumpeter he would have him sound the advance!

But there could be no argument.

In a quarter of an hour they were ready to move, the bodies of Corporal Allott and Private Parks lashed across the saddle of Parks's trooper, the lead rope in Armstrong's hands, with another around the captive. Then came Somervile leading Wainwright's mount, with Piet Doorn fifty yards behind, and Corporal Hardy scouting the same distance ahead.

It would be scarcely true scout work, though (Armstrong was only too aware of it). In any sort of country, let alone such trappy country as here, the leading scouts needed twice the space to do their work properly. The same went for the rearguard. And there were no flankers. All Hardy would be able to do, at best, was give the others a few seconds in which to take aim or throw up a guard. A few seconds. To Armstrong, however, it was better than nothing: a few seconds might allow him to get to Somervile's side, before turning to fight off the attack. What more to it was there than that?

He raised his right arm and motioned to Corporal Hardy to advance. Turning to Somervile, he smiled grimly. 'Very well, sir, just a couple of miles.'

Somervile nodded.

Serjeant Wainwright's face was bereft of all colour, even the browning of the summer's sun, but he was conscious enough to gather up the reins – no doubt instinctively, Somervile supposed.

The hoofs sounded like so many drums on that parched earth. A little flock of Cape starlings left a nearby kiaat tree noisily. They must have sat out the Xhosa attack, or else alighted soon after, he reckoned; why did they take off now? He was certain that in India the branches would by this time be full of vultures.

A weasel ran across the track between him and Armstrong a dozen yards ahead, its white-striped back arched like a cat at bay.

His trooper stopped dead. 'Just a couple of miles,' he thought, wearily, as he dug in his spurs to get her moving again.

It was strange, this country. Not at all like India, yet so different from England as to make a man wonder powerfully about the nature of Creation. Why was there no native civilization in Africa? There might conceivably be something in the middle of the great dark continent – *ex Africa semper aliquid novi* – but he imagined the place was so vast as to be unexplorable inside a hundred years, even if they set the whole of the Ordnance Survey to the task. Whatever an explorer might find, however, he could not suppose it likely to approach the advancement that India had known even five centuries ago. The savagery of the kind they were seeing here was as primitive as ... well, if Mr Hobbes had wished to demonstrate his theories, he could have found no more brutish state of nature than here. Why, there was not a single road but that was cut by a colonist; even the track they rode along now was made by the beasts of the field. The trouble was—

Piet Doorn's big American rifle went off like a cannon. And then two more shots, less thunderous – his pistols, perhaps.

Armstrong turned to look, without halting.

The rifle boomed again. Armstrong nodded with grim satisfaction: fifteen or twenty seconds to reload – a sure sign that Piet had things in hand (it certainly helped to have a breech-loader in the saddle). Warning shots, maybe?

There was silence for a full minute but for the plodding hoofs. Armstrong cursed he had not a man to drop back to see the business. He could only wait for Piet to canter in and tell him.

Another minute passed. He felt like handing the two lead-ropes – Parks's trooper's and the one binding the captive – to Somervile and going himself. But that would have been asking too much. It was the deucedest luck that this stretch of the track was so thread with trees: he could see nothing to the rear beyond fifty yards.

Then he had his answer. Instead of Piet Doorn, it was Xhosa who came down the trail – warily, almost stealthily, though not concealing themselves. One of them carried Piet's rifle; others brandished his pistols. Had they known how to load them?

Now was the reckoning. Perhaps they could make a run for it; or threaten to put a bullet into the captive's brains? But these savages had shown no sentiment for one another before. And how could they outrun them, making the river without being cut off? There were probably Xhosa waiting for them astride the track even now.

Armstrong got down from the saddle and handed the reins to Somervile. 'If you wouldn't mind, sir? Just for a short while.'

Somervile looked appalled. 'Sarn't-Major, what—'

'Be so good as to hold the reins, sir. That's all.' Armstrong glanced at Serjeant Wainwright as he pushed the captive to his knees and bound his legs and ankles with the rest of the lead-rope. 'Jobie, I want you to take a good deep breath of this fine Cape air and cover me with that excellent firearm His Majesty gave you.'

'I will, sir,' gasped Wainwright, reaching painfully for his carbine.

'This is madness,' said Somervile, beneath his breath, looping the reins of the serjeant-major's trooper round his wrist, trying to work out how he might do as he had been bidden while taking some more active part in the destruction of the enemy.

Armstrong unshipped his carbine from the saddle sleeve, coolly checking it was ready, and began to walk back along the track. The Xhosa halted, as if puzzled – as if it were not at all what they had expected from the men on horses.

At forty yards Armstrong dropped to one knee, took careful aim resting an elbow on his left foreleg, and fired.

It was the limit of accurate shooting for the carbine, but the Xhosa with the rifle crumpled and fell backwards, dead. Two more Xhosa appeared – six now. Armstrong cursed as he bit off the cartridge, took the ball between his teeth, tapped a little powder into the pan, and emptied the charge into the barrel.

Still the Xhosa made no move.

Armstrong spat in the ball and brought the carbine to the aim again without tamping, firing a split second later and felling another of Piet Doorn's slayers.

The five that remained suddenly woke. They began again to close, with the same wary walk, half crouching, gesturing with their spears. Armstrong knew he had one more shot before they would rush him, and then there would be four, and Wainwright would have one of them, and he, the non-commissioned officer in charge of Somervile's escort, would have the other three – one with the pistol at his belt, the other two (if they pressed home the attack) with the edge of the sword.

He fired. Another Xhosa fell. He laid down his carbine to draw his sabre, transferring it to his left hand, then took the pistol from his waist belt with his right and cocked the hammer.

At a dozen yards Wainwright's carbine fired. The biggest of the four Xhosa clutched at his chest, stumbled, then fell.

Armstrong levelled his pistol at the middle Xhosa – twice the distance he wanted, but he needed time to transfer the sabre to his right hand. He pulled the trigger, the hammer fell. There was no spark. Nothing.

The Xhosa checked, but seeing there was no more to fear from the pistol, came on, crouching lower, animal-intent.

Armstrong switched pistol for sabre, coolly weighing the blade as he took stock of the new challenge: three

Xhosa, three spears – odds he would not have faced willingly.

They edged towards him.

He could see their eyes – murderous as the tiger's. He stayed on one knee.

They checked again.

He sprang – left, well left, to the flank of the right-hand Xhosa, cutting savagely, backhand, tearing open his shoulder. He leapt thence at the furthest before he could turn, slicing deep through the back of his neck. The remaining Xhosa spun round and feinted with his shield. But Armstrong knew the ruse. He dropped to one knee and drove his sabre under the shield into the gut with savage force. Two more points finished off the other two, leaving Armstrong on his feet, heart pounding, surveying the bloody outcome of twenty years' drill and gymnasium.

Somervile could not speak, such was his admiration: *Armstrong Agonistes.*

II

REGIMENTAL MOURNING

St Mary Moorfields, London, 4 July 1828

Sweet, white smoke billowed from the silver thurible as the celebrant censed the altar, the deacon and sub-deacon holding aside his black cope to permit of freer movement, they, too, black-vested, the altar frontal black, also. The incense rose like the chantry orisons of another age, refracting the morning light which, though there was no east window, fell on the sanctuary steps in front of the guidon-draped coffin in a warm, sunny pool that seemed to wait-welcome the soul of the faithful departed. There were no wreaths of flowers, these being (except in the exequies for a child) 'alien to the mind of the Church'. But six candles, of unbleached wax, burned bright and hopeful about the coffin.

The smoke drifted from the sanctuary to the nave, into the nostrils of men who would as a rule have reeled at the prospect of ritual – a foreign practice, a thing of those countries which for centuries had contrived to subvert the demi-paradise. But this morning they stood respectful. Hervey, indeed, breathed the scented smoke deep, as if to pay even fuller regard.

The choir sang the introit, plainsong, as the Sixth had often heard through long years in the Peninsula: *Requiem aeternam dona eis, Domine. Et lux perpetua luceat eis.* Some of the officers joined in the final prayer, if *sotto voce*, and two or three of the dragoons made the sign of the cross: *Requiem aeternam.*

The stream of supplication continued: *Deus, cui proprium est misereri semper et parcere* . . . the celebrant's words at once recognizable, yet of another world. What he – what all the Sixth – did, though, was real enough. They were gathered to commend to the Almighty the soul (indeed, to pray for the soul's release, as the regular worshippers of the Moorfields chapel would have it) of one of the goodliest servants of the regiment, whose death and its terrible consequences he, Hervey, could scarcely yet credit: *te supplices exoramus pro anima famulae tuae Catharinae* . . . 'We humbly entreat Thee for the soul of Thy handmaiden . . .'

Tears filled his eyes – the incense smoke, perhaps; but, more likely, for the pity of it, and for those consequences.

Major and Acting Lieutenant-Colonel Matthew Hervey had intended only the briefest of calls on the cavalry barracks at Hounslow. While his new wife drove on to

London to see her aunt (or, more particularly, to see that her aunt's arrangements for the musical entertainment at which she, Kezia, would sing and play – a benefit concert, but a London début none the less – were properly in hand) it was his purpose to speak with the commanding officer of the 6th Light Dragoons on the orders for the recall of the detached troop at the Cape Colony, to which he himself would be returning from his leave of absence in September.

The honeymoon had begun ten days before, in Brighton. Although for Hervey the place held unhappy memories, these were of a dozen years ago and more, and the time had come to lay them to rest. Besides, he knew Brighton and the country thereabout; and his bride had no objection. The town had the merit, too, of some fine houses, with whose occupants Kezia was acquainted, and so there was opportunity for her to practise the pianoforte daily, which, as she had explained to her husband-to-be, she must do, for the entertainment in the Queen's Concert Rooms in Hanover Square was of the utmost importance (the prime minister himself was to attend).

The ten days had not been as they had wished, however; certainly not as Hervey had wished. The glass stood high throughout, and this occasioned Kezia a protracted headache, which her dutiful practice at the pianoforte only served to exacerbate, so that on several evenings she had to take leave of her husband before dinner; and even on those evenings when the headache was not so dispiriting, she had been obliged to retire early. The abandonment of their seaside sojourn was therefore not entirely unwelcome: Kezia would be able to put her mind at rest concerning the arrangements for her music, and for Hervey there was the prospect of an end to headaches.

He kissed his new wife on the cheek, bid her well for the afternoon, said that he would be with her in Hanover Square (where she had lodgings with her aunt) by nine, and got down from the chaise. He watched it pull away, turned to the arched entrance to the barracks, acknowledged the sentry's salute (one of Third Squadron's dragoons, and therefore recognizing his long-absent squadron leader despite his plain clothes), and set off. He walked briskly towards the regimental headquarters beyond the parade-square. He returned several more salutes from NCOs with whom he had long acquaintance, though he was curious as to their rather solemn demeanour in contrast with the customary cheer of that rank. By the time he reached the orderly room he would not have been surprised to hear that the King were dead; except that there was no sign of court mourning.

The adjutant stood as he entered. 'Good morning, Hervey,' he said, with a double measure of surprise.

Hervey smiled at him. 'I know, Malet – appearing at orderly room with but a quarter of the honeymoon spent! The weather at Brighton was inclement. And, you may believe me, I have not the slightest intention of remaining here but an hour.'

The adjutant's brow furrowed. 'You are not come, then, on account of the . . . news?'

'What news?'

Malet swallowed hard. 'Mrs Armstrong.'

Hervey was at once alarmed. 'What—'

'I'm afraid she died yesterday. I sent an express at once.'

Hervey shook his head. 'I did not receive it,' he said, quietly. He sat down. 'How . . . Of what did she die?'

'Poisoning of the blood, I understand. Or rather, I do not understand. That is what the surgeon reported, having it from the man in Hounslow who attended her. She had had a fall. I do not know any more. It was a very sudden business.'

'The children?' asked Hervey, still shaking his head in disbelief.

'Mrs Lincoln has care of them.'

That at least was no cause for concern: the quarter-master's wife was as capable as might be. But Armstrong himself, his serjeant-major, dutifully at his post in the Cape Colony . . .

'Lord Hol'ness is visiting with them now.'

'That is uncommonly civil of him,' replied Hervey, and with complete sincerity, for whatever were Lord

Holderness's weaknesses as commanding officer, they were certainly not of humanity.

'Shall I bring coffee?'

Hervey nodded.

He had known Caithlin Armstrong since before Waterloo. He had known her family, Cork tenants, rack-rented – had stood up for them, indeed, against the magistrate when they faced eviction, setting himself against the military authorities thereby, saved only through the intervention of the young Duke of Devonshire, himself a considerable Cork landowner, at the behest of his, Hervey's, soon-to-be betrothed, Lady Henrietta Lindsay. Caithlin was a scholar of the hedge school. She had good Latin, and he had taught her some Greek. Her marriage to a bruising serjeant, his own serjeant, had come as a surprise to many, but Armstrong had offered her protection, and the rough-hewn decency of his own home and calling, and they had become the best of couples, the parents of . . . four – was it five? – fine children. Hervey had seen the look in Armstrong's eye whenever Caithlin was there – the deepest pride, the most complete adoration, which he supposed he himself had once known, but never could again. He wondered how in God's name he would be able to tell Armstrong of this, how he would be able to see that look of pride and adoration fade, and in its place despair.

Malet came back with a clerk and the orderly-room coffee pot, which was kept permanently hot by a nightlight. Hervey bid the clerk dismiss. The merest nod of the head was all that was necessary in the atmosphere of collective bereavement (Caithlin Armstrong had long run a regimental school, and classes for dragoons who wanted to read and write). He poured a cup for himself, taking neither sugar nor milk. He forced himself to put a hundred and one questions from his mind; in such circumstances it would be easy to become lost in the pity of it all. Two, nevertheless, pressed upon him.

'A fall, Malet: how could such a thing bring about death? Was she unwell?'

The adjutant shook his head. 'Not in the least. She had by all accounts taken a reading class the evening before.'

'Then . . .'

The adjutant sighed, but more with heavy heart than with any impatience at Hervey's incredulity. 'We have seen it ourselves, have we not? A man dead within the day, when all the surgeon does is tend a wound with bandages, while another survives the saw with scarce a fever?'

Hervey nodded, a reluctant acknowledgement of the mysterious ways of God, or of corruption.

There remained his immediate concern. 'What are the arrangements for the funeral? Who has charge of it?'

The adjutant tilted his head. 'The question has vexed me the best part of the morning. The priest from the mission is away for the summer. Serjeant Molloy is devilling about to find what is the form. I confess I know not. I wish there were a chaplain still. Or even that the parson were in his parish instead of . . . wherever it is he's gone.'

Hervey sighed, deeply. The death of a serjeant-major's wife was an unhappy event, but when the widower was half-way round the world, and his late wife's religion strange to all, it became a pitiable thing indeed. 'I think I had better look to the arrangements myself.'

'Are you quite sure?' asked Malet, doubtful but grateful. 'I believe there will be many of every rank who would wish to pay respects; there is a collection already got up in the canteens for the children. But your honeymoon—'

'I will arrange the funeral,' said Hervey decidedly, draining his cup, and rising.

The stamp of the orderly corporal's spurred boots on the wooden floor outside, and 'Good morning, Colonel' announced the return of Lord Holderness, who came into the adjutant's office rather than entering his own directly.

'Ah, Hervey: how glad I am to see you.' The relief was evident not merely in the words themselves. 'I confess I am at a loss to know how to proceed. Come.'

Lord Holderness led him into his office, that which Hervey himself had occupied, albeit in temporary command, for some months the year before. He indicated the leather tub-chair, and sat wearily in the one adjacent.

'I have told Malet that I personally will attend to the arrangements,' said Hervey, sitting perfectly upright.

Lord Holderness looked even more relieved. 'I'd consider it a great favour.'

Hervey shook his head. 'With respect, Colonel, Armstrong is my sar'nt-major, and I've known – I knew – Caithlin Armstrong a good many years.'

'Did you? You will know, therefore, perhaps, how we may inform her people?'

The colonel's solicitousness was heartening (he was, after all, an extract – a man come in from another regiment). But informing Caithlin's people could hardly be by express, reckoned Hervey, and he had no idea who was now in the garrison at Cork, and who therefore might have been able to help.

'I believe it best if we send a cornet, Colonel.'

This was extreme counsel, he knew. Four dragoons, and as many women, had died at Hounslow since January alone, and the practice was that an officer took the ill news, and the lieutenant-colonel's condoling letter, to the family. But to Caithlin's people, in Ireland, beyond the Pale . . .

Lord Holderness smiled, however, if sadly. 'I am glad you are of that opinion, for it is mine too.'

'And one other thing, Colonel,' said Hervey, shifting his feet resolutely. 'Mrs Armstrong should have a regimental funeral. I believe she deserves no less, and that it would be of some consolation to Armstrong. The others, too – the dragoons and NCOs – would want it, I'm sure.'

Lord Holderness nodded: the fifth such funeral in a year – the inescapable business of soldiery.

Hervey now cleared his throat. 'There is, of course, the question of her religion. You would have no objection to . . . to being present at such a service?' He had no idea how his commanding officer had voted in the House of Peers on the various measures for Catholic emancipation; he had certainly not disclosed his views in the mess.

Lord Holderness raised his head, and looked at him frankly. 'I believe a man, or a woman for that matter, has a right to be buried according to the practices of his religion, and that his passing should be mourned with all due respect. I shall instruct that the regiment parades for church on the day, whether a man be Protestant or Catholic.'

Hervey smiled appreciatively. 'Thank you, Colonel.'

Lord Holderness now relaxed visibly. 'Do you happen to know where that church might be?' he asked, nodding his thanks to an orderly who brought in his coffee.

Hervey shook his head. 'I confess I have not yet the slightest idea. I suppose we are not able to have such a service in the parish church here – with a Catholic priest, I mean, not the parson. I think I must seek advice in London. I'll make a beginning at once.'

'And then there is the business of Armstrong. What's

to do? He shall have to come back, don't you think – the children, and all?'

Hervey inclined his head. 'He would not expect to, I think. He would not expect to leave his post just to take up with his children. They're in good hands, after all.'

'But even so . . .'

Hervey thought a little more, and then began nodding his head, slowly. In the normal course of events – in war, India, or wherever – these things were misfortunes to be taken, if not quite in one's stride, then with fortitude, in the place they came. For what other way was there? But not now; not when the nation was at peace, when its army was made up of true volunteers. The Sixth did not treat its dragoons heartlessly; it never had. 'Patrician command and the fellowship of the horse': that was the way of the Sixth, was it not?

He breathed deep. 'I should need to replace him, Colonel. It would not serve with Quilter standing in. He's a sound enough serjeant, but he could not manage a troop.' (He would have been content to have Wainwright do duty, but Wainwright was too junior.)

'Then I'll instruct the adjutant to issue the necessary orders.'

Hervey's mind was already decided, however. 'With respect, Colonel, I should like to take Collins.'

Lord Holderness nodded. 'I have no objection. But why Collins?'

'As a rule, Colonel, I would not try to favour those I

knew best, but Collins, I judge, would serve admirably, and since there is every prospect of trouble with the native tribes before our term at the Cape is up, I should want to be certain of my man.'

'That is reasonable.'

Lord Holderness was indeed a commanding officer whose instincts were reasonable as well as admirable. Hervey did not suppose there was a man in the Sixth who could have complaint against him. Did it matter much that in the exhilaration of manoeuvres, two months ago, a cold immersion in the Thames had induced a fit of epilepsy? (He, Hervey, and the regimental serjeant-major had arranged things with the utmost discretion, so that few others knew of it.) There would always be someone to gather up the reins, so to speak. Was it not more important that the regiment was content, well found – as undoubtedly it was?

He laid down his coffee cup, and rose. 'Thank you, Colonel. And now if you will permit me, I will make haste to London.'

'Of course,' said Lord Holderness, rising also. He smiled a shade broader, and with a touch of wryness. 'How was Brighton?'

Hervey coloured a little. 'It was as ever Brighton is, Colonel.'

'I am glad to hear it!'

* * *

Hervey took his leave a fraction happier, even if his smile concealed its own measure of wryness. He spoke with the adjutant of the agreed arrangements and actions, and was then pleasantly surprised to find that Malet had ordered the regimental chariot to wait on his pleasure.

'Better than sending to Derryman's for a chaise, I think.'

'Indeed,' said Hervey, thankfully (better and a good deal cheaper – half a crown for the chariot man, Corporal Denny). 'I'll send word as soon as I have the day, and then you may arrange things for the parade itself.'

'Of course.'

As Hervey made to leave, Malet handed him a small bundle of letters. 'These were brought from the officers' house for you. There's one with the Horse Guards' stamp.'

'Indeed?' Hervey took them, trying not to show excessive interest (a letter from the commander-in-chief's headquarters could be no occasion for disquiet now that the inquiry into the events at Waltham Abbey was scotched).

'And our respects, of course, to Lady— to Mrs Hervey.'

'Thank you, Malet,' he replied, quietly, putting the letters into his pocket and nodding his goodbye.

Outside the orderly room, Private Johnson was waiting for him. 'Ah didn't think tha were back, sir, till next week.'

Hervey was impressed by the speed at which notice of his return travelled the barracks, though Johnson had always had an ear for comings and goings. 'There were matters to be about.'

'Mrs Armstrong, ay.'

'The most wretched business. Are you able to come with me to London?'

Since only guard duty would require leave of absence of any but his own officer, and since as an officer's groom he was excused such duty, Johnson was able to say 'yes' at once, albeit with a certain reluctance. He was unsure, as he had confided many months before, that Hervey's new bride would welcome his continuance. Hervey had assured him in the most decided fashion that there was no cause for even the slightest unease in that respect, but Johnson fancied he understood the way of new wives. Lady Henrietta Hervey – *Mrs* Hervey, as Johnson had always known her, being perennially unmindful of the correct usages – had welcomed him unreservedly. He would have done anything for her. He thought, still, that if he too had been at Serjeant-Major Armstrong's side that day in the white wastes of America, she might be alive yet, even though once many years ago when he had voiced the same, Hervey, though deeply touched, had told him most unequivocally that he would with certainty have perished by the axe or the arrow. Nevertheless, Lady Henrietta Hervey remained to Johnson's mind the apotheosis of wedded-womanhood.

Lady Lankester – Mrs Matthew Hervey as now was – for all that she was the widow of a regimental hero, was not, to his mind, of the same water.

It was some time before Hervey thought to open his letters. Private Johnson had a good deal to say, and there was the question of how and where to begin on the 'arrangements'. It was the very devil that the regiment no longer had its own chaplain, and that the rector of the parish in which were the barracks, and the priest of the Hounslow mission, were both absentees. His first notion was to send word to his friend John Keble, who would surely know how to proceed, but time precluded it. He knew no clergyman, of any rank, in London. He certainly knew no Catholic. Yet there must be such counsel. A decade or so ago, before the Great Disturber was despatched to his final, fatal exile on St Helena, there had been priests and religious aplenty in London. True, they spoke in French – they were pensioners, indeed, of King George during their temporary exile – but that would have been no impediment. It was an age past, however: he must needs consult, now, with the English Mission.

How he disliked that word – *mission* – as if England were some heathen place, like the Americas of the conquistadores, or the Africa to which he would soon return. It was strange: in Portugal and Spain he had had no resentment of the Pope's religion. He had attended its services, at times even frequently. He liked the air of those churches, great and small, the sense of the living, independent of any actual human presence. In an English church, even in the one he loved the most, his father's in Horningsham, the sense was of something past, gone. In the Peninsula the Duke of Wellington had issued the most particular instructions to the army concerning the respect to be accorded the religion of His Majesty's allies. When the Blessèd Sacrament was carried in procession about the streets, an officer was to remove his headdress, and other ranks were to present arms. And it was strange how this order not only avoided offence to the allies, but also increased the esteem in which their religion was held.

Perhaps his memory played him false, though. He himself had called a good deal of it mummery, and worse, as had others of the Sixth. Yet it was not the same loathing – by no means the same – as that which they sometimes had of the Catholic church in England, where too often it had been the begetter of treachery. Or in Ireland, where contempt for the mean condition of the native population, the ignorance and indolence, was at once extended to their religion, which somehow seemed both the cause and the effect.

But then in Rome, whither his sister had taken him to interrupt the melancholy of Henrietta's death, he had found his way to the English seminary, where the rector himself had greeted him with a warmth that was at once welcoming and yet disturbing. On his knees in the Martyrs' Chapel, tears had welled up at the thought of what he had lost – and what his daughter had lost – and he had found something comforting in that place.

Yes, he would seek out the headquarters of the English Mission in London, and he would do it without hesitation or distaste. He would speak to its chief priest – the bishop, whatever was his style – and ask him how the Sixth might bury the wife of one of its most esteemed soldiers, with all the proper ceremony of her religion. And with all the proper ceremony of the regiment.

'What is that you said, Johnson?'

'Ah said, sir, t'serjeant-major were a good man.'

' "*Were* a good man"? He is still.'

'Ah know, but wi' Mrs Armstrong gone an' all . . .'

'I don't see . . .'

'Ah reckon it'll go bad wi'im.'

'Of course it will go badly with him. How . . .' How did Johnson think that Henrietta's death had gone with *him*?

Johnson could usually be relied on for the blithest of outlooks, but in this case it was not so much insensibility as the conviction that Hervey bore misfortune in some other way. 'Ah reckon 'e'll chuck it for them kinder of 'is. 'E were right soft on 'em.'

Hervey would have reminded his groom that he too had once 'chucked it' – had resigned his commission – except that that was not the material point (Johnson's prognosis somehow stirred guilt in him). 'Then we must pray that he does not. *See* to it that he does not, for his best place is in the regiment; the best place for his children, indeed.'

Johnson had no argument with that. He owned that his own long life to date – half and more of the allotted span – was on account of his wearing regimentals. Corunna, Talavera, Salamanca and many another Peninsula scrape, Waterloo, countless affairs in India: these were nothing compared with the vicissitudes he would have faced in his native county – the silted lungs, the broken back, the roof-falls, the fire-damp . . .

''E'd a'been a right good RSM.'

'Johnson, I don't think I make myself plain. Sar'nt-Major Armstrong's prospects are not diminished. He will return here on long leave of absence, and in due course he will return to his troop – *our* troop.'

'Bet 'e won't if 'e comes back from t'Cape. Them kinder of 'is—'

'He'll return, I tell you.'

'Who's gooin' to do 'is duty at t'Cape – Quilter?'

'*Serjeant* Quilter.'

Johnson huffed, not so decidedly as to require a rebuke, but sufficient to register his opinion.

But Hervey had no need to check the delinquency, not when he could pretend he had not heard, and it was not anyway to be Quilter. 'Sar'nt-Major Collins will do duty.'

Johnson sucked in air sharply. 'That'll go bad wi' t'sar'nt-major. Them's rivals an' all.'

'Rivals? Collins—' (he checked himself, crossly) '*Sar'nt-Major* Collins is his junior. If you're thinking which of them would replace the regimental sar'nt-major there would be no question but that it would be Armstro— *Sar'nt-Major* Armstrong.'

'That's not what they says in t'canteen.'

'The canteen!'

'One o' t'clerks from t'ord'ly room—'

'Damn the clerks! Enough of it!'

Johnson made a 'please yourself' face.

Hervey said nothing.

They sat for some time, the silence broken only by the ticking of the long-case clock in the otherwise empty headquarters room to which they had retreated while the chariot was fetched.

'T'adjutant 'ad a lot o' letters for thee, sir,' tried Johnson, softer, after a while.

Hervey reached into his pocket. 'I have them.' He began sorting through the bundle absently.

There were a dozen and more, some in unfamiliar hands (he would attend to those later). But one, he noted, was from Kat, which pleased him unexpectedly.

'Shall ah be gooin, sir?'

Hervey hesitated. 'No. Stay, if you would.' He opened the letter.

Holland-park, 19th June

My dear Matthew,

(It was written the day after his wedding, and Kat had moderated her salutation, as was only appropriate to his new state. He supposed, too, that it was the correct form for an erstwhile lover to adopt if she were to continue in correspondence.)

I write with news that I am confident you will find most welcome. Today I had occasion to visit with Captain Peto at Greenwich. I found him in the most excellent spirits, despite his most cruel injuries, and I perfectly see why you are so particularly attached to him. He received me with the greatest civility, and when I spoke to him of our acquaintance he was at once all solicitude on your behalf, asking how was the marriage service and expressing his deepest regrets that his situation had not permitted him to attend. I told him that it had been the most perfect occasion and your bride the most perfect picture of contentment, as indeed was the bridegroom. He was, of course, much cheered to hear this, and I was only grateful to have been the envoy of such joyful news. Of his own disappointment he spoke very freely, and of his wish that your sister enjoys the happiness that has lately come to you. In this, I confess, I was truly most moved,

*for such a sentiment, of the very deepest selflessness, is
not commonly to be found, and I resolved at once to
tell him of the offer which I had secured of George
Cholmondeley. Captain Peto was instantly delighted,
for he knows Houghton and admires it, and he
declared that he already felt himself bettering for the
news. And so it has been arranged that at the end of
the month I shall engage a dormeuse for him and
convoy with my own chariot to Houghton, where I
shall remain for a week or such time as there is need of
me, and I tell you this for I know that you shall return
to the Cape Colony before long and that you might
wish to see the place in which your friend will be so
agreeably settled, even perhaps to accompany him
thither . . .*

Hervey smiled in the knowledge that his old friend Sir
Laughton Peto, so grievously wounded at the Battle of
Navarino Bay nine months before, was raised in his
spirits. It had, indeed, been a most handsome scheme of
Kat's. She had, without a word from him save a descrip-
tion of his old friend's situation (an invalid, of what
permanence the doctors could not tell, at the naval
hospital at Greenwich), sought out a protecting billet at
Houghton Hall in Peto's own county of Norfolk – near
where he had taken a lease on a house (in which he
would have lived with Elizabeth if only she . . .). And
Kat had brought the happy news to the wedding, seeking

him out at the breakfast to complete his own joy that day: 'And George' (the new, young Marquess of Cholmondeley) 'has most eagerly contracted to attend to all dear Captain Peto's needs until such time as he is able to return to his own house. Such is dear George's patriotic admiration of his service.'

It had indeed greatly increased his joy, and he had thanked her prodigiously. Indeed, he had declared that he was ever in Kat's debt. And most certainly, if there was the least opportunity, he would go to Norfolk to see his old friend settled. He read on.

> *Perhaps you will communicate with me as soon as may be, so that I might make the arrangements. I shall be at Holland-park, and quite at home to visitors should you find it more convenient to close the matter directly. I write to you $^c/_o$ Hounslow since of course I have no knowledge of where you shall be until you and your bride depart for the Cape . . .*

Hervey sighed, delight and discontent mixed in equal measure. It was, of course, quite impossible that he should go to Holland Park, although it would certainly be most expeditious – and, indeed, a good sight more economical than sending messengers and expresses back and forth. He resolved to write immediately on arriving at Hanover Square, proposing that they tea together at, say, Grillon's, or even that she call on them at Kezia's aunt's (though probably, on reflection, this latter would not be exactly felicitous . . .).

'Good!' he declared, emphatically.

'What is, sir?' asked Johnson, feeling his presence of no great purpose.

'Captain Peto,' replied Hervey, not very helpfully, turning his attention instead to the despatch with the Horse Guards' stamp.

His face fell.

'What's up, sir?'

Hervey handed him the letter.

> *The Horse Guards*
> *19th June 1828*

Major (Actg. Lt-Colnl.) M. P. Hervey
H.M. 6th Light Dragoons

Sir,

I am commanded by the Military Secretary to inform you that the Commander in Chief has been pleased to advance you to the substantive rank of Lieutenant-Colonel, without purchase, and to command of the First Battalion of His Majesty's Eighty-first Regiment of Foot, effective from the First of January next.

I remain, sir, your obedient servant,

Henry Upton,
Colonel.

'That's very nice!'

Hervey made no reply.

'Why's 'e call thee "sir" when 'e's a proper colonel?'

Hervey shook his head. 'It's just the way. Probably to put one in one's place.'

'Ah don't understand . . .'

Hervey turned his head, as if to look from the window.

'But that's right good, sir, isn't it? Tha'll be a proper half-colonel, an' tha won't 'ave to pay for it!'

Hervey turned back to him. 'You don't see, do you? And why should you? If I am appointed to command of the Eighty-first, I can never then be appointed to command the Sixth.'

III

IN PARTIBUS INFIDELIUM

London, later that day

Kezia had retired by the time they reached Hanover Square. The manservant who admitted them explained that her aunt was not expected to return from a firework fête in Regent's Park until midnight. Hervey decided instead that, since he would need to make an early start of the business the next day, his best course was to take a room at the United Service Club. This pleased Johnson: the servants' dormitory at the United Service was perfectly comfortable, and it had the advantage of not being under the supervision of his new mistress. The mixed feelings provoked by the military secretary's letter also doused Hervey's desire for company.

He would have to tell Kezia, of course, and soon, for once these things were gazetted it became the common talk. But Brighton had not quite paved the way for such unexpected news to be sprung at once, and he thought it perhaps best to gain intelligence of the Eighty-first – their station and the like – before broaching the subject with her. Not that he ought to be entertaining his mixed feelings, of course: command of a regiment of the Line, albeit Foot, was a distinction not bestowed on many. And command without purchase, besides being welcome for its economy, was a considerable accolade. There was no doubt his star was bright and rising. He was certain that Kezia would recognize it. Or rather, he was sure he would be able to explain it to her if she did not.

Just for a second – the merest moment – he imagined what Henrietta would have said. And he felt the warmth; and smiled.

Next morning he went early to the Horse Guards. His friend Lord John Howard was already at office, and received him at once. 'I fancy I know why you are come,' he said, rising and offering his hand. 'I must congratulate you on your promotion, though I suspect it is not wholly to your liking.'

Hervey removed his hat, and sat down in the familiar chair by his friend's desk. 'I thank you for your good wishes, but, no, it is not wholly to my liking.'

'You have breakfasted?'

'You somehow perceive that I have not. Nor do I have the slightest appetite.'

'I intended suggesting we repair to White's.'

Hervey half smiled. 'You are ever kind, Howard, but I can't detain you thus. Some coffee, perhaps?'

Lord John Howard rang the bell for a messenger. 'The Eighty-first are a fine regiment, as the Line goes. And it generally goes well, does it not?'

Hervey nodded. 'I don't doubt it. I know it, indeed. I first saw them at Corunna.'

'And I know, too, that Sir James Kempt was pleased to approve the nomination.'

'Kempt is colonel?'

'He is.'

Lieutenant-General Sir James Kempt had commanded a brigade at the storming of Badajoz. Some of Hervey's dragoons had helped carry him to the field hospital. 'I am flattered. Where are they stationed?'

'Canada.'

Hervey had supposed them – for some reason – in Ireland. Canada had unhappy memories, and few opportunities now for an officer to distinguish himself. A look of further disappointment overcame him.

'Have you thought to speak with Irvine?' asked Howard solicitously. 'There may yet be time . . . before it is gazetted.'

Lieutenant-General Lord George Irvine, colonel of the 6th Light Dragoons, had recently been posted to the Unattached List, pending appointment in Ireland. It had long been his wish that Hervey have command of the regiment in which both had served together. But

65

circumstances had contrived to confound him in this – and indeed his predecessor. Money had spoken, for all that the late commander-in-chief, the Duke of York, had tried to moderate the excesses of purchase.

'I have,' said Hervey, nodding firmly. 'But forming any question of him, decently, would not be easy. I can hardly ask how long he expects Hol'ness to remain in command.' Nor, indeed, would an indication of short tenure be necessarily to his advantage. Lord Holderness effectively owned the appointment freehold. In spite of the regulations, he could still name his price. And Hervey, for all that Daniel Coates's legacy provided for him to purchase command at regulation price, could not match some of the figures being bandied.

'You might simply ask what he advises?'

Hervey nodded again, but unconvinced.

The messenger brought coffee.

Howard took his cup and leaned back, as if to emphasize the decidedness with which he would speak. 'I believe I must tell you, truly, from all I see and hear in this place, that your prospects for purchase are lament-able – even *if* Hol'ness were to sell out, that is. You know, do you not, what price Bingham paid for the Seventeenth?'

The transaction had occurred not long before Hervey had first left for the Cape. 'Five thousand?'

He said it with an ironic smile. The regulation price was five thousand pounds. Payment in excess had been illegal for several years. The Grand Old Duke had, indeed, made overpayment an offence before the King's bench. An officer could be fined, or imprisoned, and the transaction cancelled. There had not been a single prosecution, however.

'*Twenty*-five.'

Hervey's mouth fell open.

'And do you know, by the way, what dear old Bacon has done?'

Anthony Bacon – an acquaintance of Hervey's from Peninsular days – had been the Seventeenth's senior major (just as Hervey was the Sixth's). He had confidently expected the command to come his way.

'No.'

'He's sold out, and thrown in with the King of Portugal. A mercenary!'

Hervey could scarce believe it. Anthony Bacon, whom Lord Uxbridge, commanding the cavalry at Corunna and Waterloo, reckoned to be the finest of his officers, and who had married Lady Charlotte Harley, whose father was very probably the King! What chance did he himself have if Bacon were dealt with thus? He shook his head. 'What manner of system do we have?'

He did not expect an answer of his friend, save perhaps, as the old saying went, that hard cases made bad law. The Duke of Wellington was the strongest supporter of purchase. Even Hervey was not so much opposed to the *principle* of purchase (he had seen its beneficent results), as to the abuses. Was it so very difficult to root these out?

He shifted awkwardly in his chair. 'Might . . . d'ye suppose . . . Lord Hill see me?'

Lord John Howard shifted in his own chair as awkwardly. 'My dear friend, you know that I am ever willing to advance your cause, but to arrange an interview with the commander-in-chief, I—'

Hervey stayed his embarrassment with a hand. The notion of an interview on such a matter was preposterous, for an officer could not recommend himself thus. 'I'm sorry.'

His friend sighed. 'See, it would be impossible that you call on him here. But he dines at the United Service this evening, with Lord Hardinge. Were you to encounter him in the hall . . .'

Hervey rose and made to leave. 'Thank you, Howard. You are ever good.'

They exchanged a little general news, before Howard seemed to remember something more pertinent.

'You do know, by the way, there's a new governor for the Cape? Lowry Cole.'

Hervey shook his head, though he knew that Somervile's appointment as *lieutenant*-governor was *ipso facto* of a temporary nature.

'He goes out in the autumn. Another friendly face for you.'

It was true. Sir Lowry Cole had a fine reputation from

the Peninsula. He had commanded the 4th Division for much of it, and had almost certainly saved the day at Albuera. *And* he was a cavalryman. But with Somervile recalled . . . 'Well, no doubt there could be not a better man for the Cape, though I confess it will mean a good deal shorter rein for me.'

Lord John Howard smiled. 'The bit can still remain between your teeth, my friend. But see, I did not ask: how was Brighton?'

Hervey left the Horse Guards and turned right into Whitehall, thinking to make for the abbey, where he supposed there would be someone who knew where was the Roman bishop's house – or rather, as his father would have reminded him (since 'bishop', for a Catholic, could be but colloquial), the *vicar apostolic*. It was then it occurred to him that a hackney driver might know.

There were several cabs near the Houses of Parliament. He walked to the front of the rank, and enquired.

'I can't say I knows, sir,' replied the first. 'There not being the trade, so to speak. But I does know a Catholic shop, close on Grosvenor-square.'

Hervey was unsure what exactly the cabman meant by 'Catholic' shop – whether it was owned by a Catholic, or was like the shops in Rome which sold abominable *articoli religiosi* to the gullible *pellegrini*. Either way he would be making a first footing towards his objective. 'Very well, would you kindly convey me there?'

They drove by the pleasant way of parks – St James's, the Green and then Hyde Park. Ordinarily Hervey would have been much diverted by the sights and sounds, but the mission on which he was embarked was beginning to oppress him. At first he had thought it a fine thing: the Sixth would show everyone how they buried a 'daughter of the regiment'. Now, though, he could think only of Armstrong, and of the devastation the news would bring; and, indeed, the distress of the children. He himself had borne such a loss, of course, but Georgiana had known nothing of it. His serjeant-major's children, all but the very youngest, would know they had lost a mother. And he, Hervey, had had a loving family – still had – in which to contain his grief; Armstrong had none, his people long perished. How might he therefore enjoy such a drive as this, for all its sun and sylvan parks?

But even had he not been bent on his unhappy mission, the business of regimental command overcast the scene like a dark cloud. Was it really come to this: men from nowhere but the vast wealth of their estates, paying fortunes for the mere conceit of a smart uniform and having a regiment wheel about at their command? For the vanity of five hundred men saluting them, officers at their beck and call, the power to make and break any man? How could it come about that a man like Anthony Bacon was passed over for the likes of Lord Bingham, not yet thirty, never having heard a shot fired in anger? Why in God's name did the Duke of Wellington connive at it? And Lord Hill, for that matter?

What was he to do? What *could* he do?

They turned off Park Lane, rolled on through Grosvenor Square and into Duke Street, pulling up outside a bay-windowed shop bearing the sign *Geo Keating, Printer of Religious Books.* Hervey got down from the cab, bid the driver wait, and entered.

The interior was as any bookshop, save for several glass cases in which there were rosaries, crucifixes and other *articoli*, which were somehow less troubling than in Rome for their being rather more discreetly displayed.

The proprietor, an amiable man, received his questions with well-mannered evasion, until an explanation of the purpose in discovering the whereabouts of the 'bishop' set his mind at rest. Indeed, so animated was Mr Keating by (as he put it) the nobility of what Hervey undertook, that he at once volunteered to accompany him to the residence of the vicar apostolic. 'For without a sponsor, His Lordship might feel unable to receive you, and since my business is as printer to the London district I am confident of securing an audience.'

Hervey, amused by the coincidence of episcopal and military terms in 'London district', was pleased to accept the offer, which was not without a trysting feel, as in the dark days when recusants lived in fear of their liberty if not their lives.

They left the shop to the care of an assistant.

'To Holborn, please, driver,' said Mr Keating, as they got into the cab. 'Number four, Castle-street.'

Hervey nodded to him, obliged.

'We amuse ourselves by calling the residence "the Castle",' said his guide, at last allowing himself a little smile.

Hervey gave something of a smile by return, for Holborn was no place for a fashionable.

His guide soon lapsed into respectful silence, however. In truth, Hervey found it curiously difficult to bring himself to conversation. As a rule he found it easy enough to speak with all manner of men, but this surreptitious charge felt most strange.

It took half an hour to negotiate the road to Holborn, during which he began turning over in his mind again the appointment to the Eighty-first. He knew well enough that one day he would have to quit the Sixth (unless he were to become that sad figure, the superseded major, treated kindly but increasingly ignored), but he had not contemplated that it might be so soon. Yet what would happen otherwise, when his temporary command of the Corps of Cape Mounted Riflemen came to an end? Would he have a brevet, or would he have to relinquish altogether the rank of half-colonel? What would be Kezia's thoughts then? She had, after all, accepted him in the prospect of imminent command of the Sixth (he did not doubt that there was disappointment enough already on that count). She would be gratified, or at least relieved, would she not, at his command of the Eighty-first, and would find Canada an agreeable posting? Above all, there was the financial advantage: he would not have to part with a single penny for command, and this meant he would not lose a single penny when promotion to colonel came (as he trusted it would), for an officer forfeited his purchase money on promotion beyond regimental rank. Could he really afford, therefore, to be so fastidious in whether he wore a red or a blue coat in command?

They turned into Castle Street and pulled up outside a narrow-fronted house of three storeys and small windows, shabby but quite evidently respectable. Hervey put away his thoughts of red coats, and got down to pay the cabman while his guide rang the doorbell.

They were admitted by a strange, duenna-looking woman, who explained that His Lordship was not at home, and that his coadjutor was engaged; nevertheless she would see if the vicar-general would receive them. She showed them into the dining room, which served also as an ante-room.

The vicar-general came at once, a pleasant-faced man not much older than Hervey, with an easy manner and ready smile. After due introductions (in which it was explained that Hervey was 'not of our faith'), he declared he was entirely at his visitors' disposal, making much of seeing Mr Keating again so soon after arranging the printing of the recent apostolic letter.

'Mr Keating, as his father before him, is a publisher of most particular standards, Colonel Hervey.'

'You are very gracious, sir,' replied Keating, who turned to Hervey with a look of some pride. 'My father had the honour of printing the bishop's loyal address on the occasion of the victory at Trafalgar.'

'Indeed, sir?' replied Hervey respectfully, but with a note of mystification.

The vicar-general began rummaging in one of several cupboards, until he found what he was looking for. 'Here, sir. Here is a copy of the Trafalgar letter. Keep it, Colonel Hervey. You will find that it speaks eloquently of the loyalty of those of our faith.'

Hervey took it, somewhat abashed. 'Sir, I do not doubt – nor have had any occasion to doubt – the loyalty of His Majesty's subjects.'

The vicar-general smiled disarmingly. 'Well, Colonel Hervey, perhaps you will tell me how we may be of *further* service.'

They sat, and Hervey explained Lord Holderness's intention that the regiment should parade for the funeral.

The vicar-general nodded approvingly. 'Well, Colonel Hervey, may I first say how gratifying is the commanding officer's intention. I foresee no difficulty with the obsequies: solemn requiem in St Mary's church in Moorfields for the soul of the late departed, *praesente cadavere*, followed by interment in the churchyard of St Pancras, which is the new cemetery.'

Hervey noticed the appreciative raising of Mr Keating's eyebrows. Evidently this was a proposal of some distinction. 'And this might be arranged for . . .'

'I believe it could be arranged for Friday next, the fourth.'

'Thank you. May we fix now upon a time? At eleven, say?'

'That would be meet.'

Hervey rose and made to leave. 'Thank you, reverend sir. With whom should the adjutant communicate in respect of the . . . details?'

The vicar-general rose. 'I beg he would communicate with me. In the circumstances, the bishop – if you will permit the word – would wish it so. Indeed, I believe His Lordship would wish to receive you now, before you take your leave. You have no objection?'

Hervey smiled. 'It was my intention in coming here. But I understood the bishop was not at home.'

'Of the London district, no. I meant his coadjutor, the Bishop of Lydda.'

'Lydda?'

'*In partibus infidelium*. You will understand he could have no English title.'

'Mission' . . . 'in the regions of the infidels' . . . words that set these men apart, the suspicion of allegiance elsewhere than to the Crown (for all the fine words, no doubt, of the Trafalgar address). But Hervey did not bridle, for he was convinced that he met here with

sincerity (and, no doubt, Lydda was in Ottoman hands!).
'I am honoured, sir.'

The vicar-general conducted his visitors upstairs to an
old-fashioned wainscoted room. On the walls, smoke-
darkened, were oils of various English martyrs, and over
the fireplace a portrait of Pope Leo, with a crucifix
prominent at the centre of the inner wall. Hervey
examined each as if he were admitted to an exhibition of
curiosities.

The outlandishly beneficed bishop, a man of about
fifty, and wearing black day clothes, came in soon afterwards. Hervey at once recognized him – the spare,
fervent features, the eyes that pierced to the soul, though
the face was even more gaunt than when he had seen it a
decade ago.

'My Lord, this is Colonel Hervey of the Sixth Light
Dragoons.'

His Lordship smiled. 'I believe we have met, Colonel
Hervey, have we not? In Rome?'

'Your Lordship has a good memory,' replied Hervey,
returning the smile. 'There must have been many visitors
to the college.' He bowed.

The bishop, formerly rector of the English seminary in
Rome, held out a hand.

Hervey saw the episcopal ring, and wondered if he
were meant to kiss it (he had once observed the custom
in Spain). But the hand was held at such an angle as to
suggest a more English fashion of greeting.

'I recall that you had left the service at that time,' said the bishop, motioning him to resume his seat.

'I had indeed, but I rejoined immediately on returning from Rome. Are you yourself long returned, sir?'

'Only lately, Colonel Hervey. In point of fact I was ordained bishop but a week ago.'

'And I myself was married but two weeks ago.'

The bishop nodded. 'We are each of us blessed in our respective sacraments.'

'I remember well your kindness that day, Father. I would not have explained, I am sure, that I had then only recently lost my wife.'

'Then you are doubly blessed in the sacrament,' the bishop pronounced gravely.

Hervey bowed again. 'I am.'

The bishop placed his hands together to indicate a change of direction. 'But now, the purpose of your visit . . . most admirable. If there are no objections, I myself will attend the obsequies.'

Hervey looked surprised. 'I am certain I may say, sir, that far from there being any objections, your presence would be an honour. The widower is my own serjeant-major, who is at this time at the Cape Colony. I believe it will be of great comfort to him when I inform him on my return.'

'We shall pray for him as well as for the soul of the faithful departed.'

Hervey nodded. 'I am truly grateful, My Lord.' (He

made to rise.) 'And now I think I must detain you no longer.'

The bishop insisted on seeing him out.

As they came downstairs to the hall, a woman of about Hervey's age, in a day dress of fine brown cotton, with a length of white lace draped loosely about her head and shoulders, curtsied deep.

'Ah, Reverend Mother,' said the bishop. 'I am so very gratified you were able to come.'

The reverend mother looked enquiringly at Hervey as she rose.

'A gentleman from the army come on an unhappy but by no means unrewarding mission,' explained the bishop.

'Mr 'Ervey?' She pronounced his name as would a Frenchwoman.

'Sister Maria?'

'I perceive that introductions are not required,' said the bishop, curious.

Hervey was considerably animated. 'My Lord, my regiment was billeted in the reverend mother's convent after the battle of Toulouse.'

There was a deal more that he might have explained had the circumstances been more propitious.

The reverend mother smiled – an easy smile which spoke of the confidence of both her rank and calling. Maria Chantonnay's father was, or had been (Hervey had no idea if he were alive still), the Comte de Chantonnay, a royalist from the Vendée. Sister Maria, of the Carmelite Order, whose convent had been spared on account of the evident piety and charity of its sisters, as well as its seclusion, had nursed him in his temporary prostration which a French spontoon had occasioned. And, indeed, had helped him sift official papers left behind by Marshal Soult, a convalescent labour imposed on him by the authorities on account of his excellent French.

'May I ask why you come 'ere, Mr 'Ervey? *Vous voulez devenir Catholique . . . enfin?*'

Hervey returned the smile. 'No, ma'am. I am come to arrange a funeral for the wife of one of my non-commissioned officers. Indeed, you may recall my serjeant at Toulouse?'

'I recall him; and your servant.'

'He is with me still.'

The bishop made to close what he imagined might become a prolonged conversation. 'The reverend mother is here on matters touching on the convent at Hammersmith, Colonel Hervey.'

'Ah, yes indeed. Forgive me, sir. I will take my leave at once.'

He was, however, most reluctant to. Much water had flowed under the bridge since he had last seen Sister Maria de Chantonnay, in her father's house in Paris, not long after Waterloo.

He braced himself. 'I thank you again, My Lord – and you, reverend sir,' he added, bowing to the vicar-general.

He took up his hat, caught the eye of Mr Keating, who had waited patiently throughout, and bid good day to the assemblage of priests and religious.

They found a hackney cab, not without a little trouble, and Hervey instructed the cabman to take his companion back to Duke Street, putting him down in Hanover Square en route.

The two had a little more conversation than on the journey out, but in truth Hervey was just as preoccupied as then. So much had happened since Toulouse. Truly, he did not suppose he could begin to recall that time before . . . before Henrietta. Before she had perished (perished on account of his incapability). It had been a vastly simpler age – Bonaparte the enemy, life lived day to day, a distant love; and then a wife, and a colonel not worthy of the name. And then one empty day after another. And the Promethean eagle tearing at his vitals each waking morning.

But that was all over, now. He had a new life, one which he would share with his daughter. For too long he had left her to the care of Elizabeth, gentlest of women though his sister was. Georgiana could not be shut away from him for ever: she had lost a mother; it was not right that her father was lost to her too. And now, of course, she would have a mother – and a practised one – *and* a sister. And there would be the novelty of Cape Town for several months, with its pleasing climate and easy ways. And then, perhaps, Canada.

One thing was certain, however: Elizabeth's most improvident intentions – her breaking off the engagement to his old friend Laughton Peto, and instead her purpose to marry this *baron* of hers – made continued guardianship of Georgiana impossible.

''Anover-square, gen'l'men!'

The cab came to a halt close by St George's church, where but a fortnight ago his own nuptials had been concluded. Hervey got down, thanked Mr Keating profusely for his time, and professed sincerely his hope they would meet again, before paying the cabman and waving them off.

He turned and looked at the steps of St George's, where he had waited to greet the congregants, and he marvelled once more at the pace of events in his life of late. It was but eighteen months since he had sat next to Kezia that night at dinner at Lord George Irvine's. He had just returned from Portugal, much chastened by the incarceration at Badajoz, and was resolved on putting his life in order. That very evening, indeed, marriage with Lady Lankester suggested itself (he saw that, now). And there had been so little time for courtship. What hand of Providence could it have been that placed him in a position, only a few months later, to propose marriage to her – and to have her accept? Why, indeed, *had* she accepted?

Kat had asked him the very same. The question had

first seemed impertinent, even for a lover. Except that, riding together in the green lanes of Chelsea after he had spent the night with her, the question seemed entirely reasonable. He had not been able to answer. As Kat herself had concluded, *le Coeur a ses raisons que la raison ne connaît point*. Did it matter, indeed, what reasons must Kezia have? Were his own reasons so very ... reasonable?

He had concluded that he must marry because he knew there was no health in him in the condition of widowhood. In the condition of adultery, indeed – in disordered, almost casual liaisons, or in the ultimate cruelty (there was no other word) of 'country marriages' such as he had enjoyed in Bengal. Neither was there honour in absentee fatherhood; nor sense in a life at arms which had no secure base. Were these reasons ignoble? Kezia had freely accepted him. She knew he had no fortune, though his abilities were recognized and he therefore had prospects, and she knew there had been too little time for there to have been true romantic love.

And he had desired her. Everything she said or did had seemed to serve its increase as the day of the wedding approached. He admired so much about her, too – her air, her music, that she had once been the wife of such a hero of the regiment – and he was convinced that this, coupled with desire, would in time become the wedded bliss he had once known. And those who thought otherwise (as he knew they did) were quite mistaken in the matter.

Kezia was not at home. Her aunt told him that she had gone to Mr Novello's to buy some sheet music (Hervey did not know of Mr Novello, but supposed that he ought to have), and that she would then most probably call on a cousin in Regent's Park. He declined the offer of solid refreshment, asking merely for coffee and for pen and paper, explaining that he must leave shortly for Whitehall (not caring to specify the United Service Club).

With coffee, pen and paper he sat for half an hour and wrote a memorandum to Kezia of the various and complicated events of the morning, though he explained that he could give no complete account of the offer of the Eighty-first since he was in so many minds about it, and that he would, of course, wish to consult with her before making any irrevocable decision. He ended by saying that, confident it would meet with her approval, he would today send word to Horningsham – perhaps even express – for Georgiana to join them directly, and not at the end of the month as first they had intended.

'You will join us for dinner, will you not, Colonel Hervey?' asked the aunt, as he made to leave.

Hervey hesitated, not least on hearing his Cape rank, for evidently Kezia had described him to her aunt thus (despite his having presented himself before the wedding as 'Major'). 'I . . . I should like very much to, Lady

Marjoribanks. It is possible that I might be detained, however. I have a meeting with the commander-in-chief.'

He knew he stretched the meaning of the word – 'meeting' – but he saw no occasion for a fuller account. And (he would admit) the drive from Brighton had not been all gaiety, which was why he had thought it better not to try Kezia with proposals directly this evening, trusting instead to words on the page. Such a way would not have served with Henrietta (or Kat, for that matter), but it did not follow that there was but the one proper course. He was perfectly aware that women were as different in their natures as were men. And just because he was yet to fathom Kezia's, he would do nothing so crass as to presume there was fault in it.

IV

PRIMIPARA

London, that evening, early

As he entered the United Service Club, Hervey saw one of Kat's footmen conferring with the hall porter.

'George?'

The footman turned. 'Oh, good afternoon, Colonel Hervey. I was enquiring where it might be expedient to deliver this letter to you, sir.'

Hervey took it. 'I am only just returned, and here by chance alone.'

'The porter gave me to understand that you were not expected, sir. But Lady Katherine was most anxious that you receive this, and—'

'Of course, George, of course,' replied Hervey hurriedly, anxious not to have too much rehearsed in front of the porter's lodge. 'Perhaps you will allow me to read the letter and pen a reply as appropriate. I fancy it is in connection with Captain Peto's convalescence.' He did not suppose that it was entirely in that connection, but it served to give respectability to the exchange.

The footman bowed as Hervey withdrew a few paces and broke the seal.

> *Holland-park,*
> *29th June*

> *Dearest Matthew,*
> *I beg you would come here at the first opportunity, for there is a matter of the greatest delicacy to apprise you of, one which I am quite unable to commit to the page. You must believe me when I tell you this, for I would not trouble you in your present circumstances were it not imperative to do so.*
> > *Your ever affectionate,*
> > *Kat.*

Hervey winced at the old familiarity. Such a letter was compromising enough, in his 'present circumstances'. What was it, therefore, that Kat could not commit to the page? Or was it merely a device to have him travel to Holland Park?

No, that was an ignoble thought. Kat had been the best of friends to him; she would not now use subterfuge. And, indeed, he ought not to flatter himself so. In any case, they would, in all probability, meet in Norfolk, when she convoyed Peto there.

'George, do you have a carriage?'

'I do, sir.'

'Then, if I may, I will return with you to Holland-park.'

'Very good, sir.'

'Colonel Hervey, sir, there are more letters here,' called the porter after him.

Hervey took the little bundle and quickly looked them over. There were none in hands he counted pressing, save Somervile's (and there could be no immediate reply to one originating at such a remove). He beckoned to Kat's footman. 'Come then, George, for I must be back here before eight.'

As they turned into the Haymarket, Hervey opened the lieutenant-governor's letter.

Cape-town,
13th May 1828

My dear Hervey,
I trust that by the time you receive this you will be
restored to full health and that all nuptials will have
been completed satisfactorily, for I must ask you, if
you will, to forgo further leave and return here at once,
there being the most urgent need of your capabilities
in the field. But I must first tell you of the events
which compel me to claim your recall.

I took the earliest opportunity, soon after your leaving, of visiting for myself the Eastern Frontier. This progress I made in April, during the course of which I had occasion to fight with the Xhosa in somewhat desperate circumstances, the escort provided by your most excellent corps of dragoons having become divided. In this I digress, but I must next commend to you the conduct of Serjeant-major Armstrong, which was of the most exemplary nature, also that of Serjeant Wainwright who, although grievously wounded, comported himself with the utmost soldierly bearing. I have commanded that a gold medal be struck in recognition of Armstrong's singular service, for he was himself wounded, too, during the course of our escape, and yet so effectually managed affairs as to bring us away with remarkably little loss in the circumstances. I urge that you represent the facts which I lay out in their fullness in attachment herewith to Lord Holderness in the hope that Armstrong might have the proper recognition due to him.

In consequence of the action described therein, I was able to interrogate a captive native who gave intelligence which with other reports received have led me to conclude that a mission at the highest level to the paramount Zulu chief Shaka is a most imperative necessity. I have further concluded, in consequence of my imminent supersession here by Sir Lowry Cole, that I myself must undertake this mission within the third quarter, and therefore that you should return at once to command the escort that shall be required, which must perforce be very much stronger than hitherto . . .

He folded the letter and stifled a sigh. What he would not give to be at the Eastern Frontier this very moment! And then he shivered, though the evening was not cool. He was new-married. Indeed, it was, rightly speaking, his honeymoon still. But to be at the Cape did not mean he must abandon his new wife. Far from it. She would accompany him, take quarters in Cape Town, the house he had found, not far from the Somerviles at the castle. And Georgiana would be with them. Why, therefore, did he recoil from his enthusiasm for being back in the saddle, under arms? It was not escape, nor evasion of his paternal responsibilities, as once it might have been. He was a soldier, was he not? What was a soldier if his instinct were for other than the field and the sound of the guns?

He began turning over in his mind the things he must do preparatory to an early return to duty. He must send an express to Captain Edward Fairbrother in Devon (he could not possibly return without Fairbrother: he was as much a kin of the spirit now as he was a superlative practitioner of frontier war). He must arrange the same passage for Serjeant-Major Collins (no doubt Collins, too, would consider it a mixed blessing, for he himself was newly married). There were all manner of requisites to obtain and accounts to be settled, letters to be written, official and otherwise, work for the War Office to be completed, and not least the business of the Eighty-first to be decided. *And* there was Kezia and Georgiana . . .

Kat's yellow Offord chariot bowled through St James's and then Green Park, through the Piccadilly bar past Apsley House, the residence of the Duke of Wellington (now prime minister), where Hervey had first met Kat, and along the fashionables' drive through Hyde Park, past the Knightsbridge Barracks, Kensington Palace, and into Holland Park, to the elegant but not large establishment of Lieutenant-General Sir Peregrine and Lady Katherine Greville.

Sir Peregrine, he knew, would not be at home. Indeed, he would not be in London, nor even England. He would be in the governor's residence on Alderney, which position he had occupied largely unaccompanied but with the greatest satisfaction for many years. The fishing off Alderney, and indeed Sark, which island was also within his commandery, was infinitely diverting to him, and now that all threat of hostile landing from France was gone, the appointment allowed him a life of complete ease.

There were many years between Sir Peregrine and his wife. Kat was forty, or there about, yet she possessed the blush of a much younger woman. Her many admirers, of whom the Duke of Wellington was merely the most elevated (not counting the King himself, whom Kat had never found herself able to flatter with much conviction), admitted her one of the handsomest females in London. Hervey, though several years her junior, shared their opinion. Although now he would place Kezia alongside her. Their looks, their whole demeanour, were, however, so unalike as to puzzle him: the attraction of two women so markedly different.

Kat. He had, perhaps, treated her ill. He had courted Kezia (if 'courted' were the right word for something so ... extemporary) without first speaking with her of it. And then he had gone to Holland Park to tell her the news of his engagement, and she had been hurt (without doubt hurt) by the manner of his telling her as much as the news itself. And then he had not returned that night to the United Service Club; he had stayed at Holland Park, as he so often had.

He shook his head, for what had followed, on the eve of his wedding, was too shameful to contemplate. And afterwards Kat had been so understanding. She had maintained every expression of cordiality, she had come to his wedding, she had troubled herself no little over the convalescence of his great friend Peto. What a woman she was! He could not regret what they had been to each other, for all that he had broken the Seventh Commandment (as Elizabeth had reminded him with such devastating effect). Except perhaps that last time. For that had been unworthy.

The chariot turned into the little forecourt, and Hervey woke from his thoughts. 'Well, George . . .' He had insisted the footman travel inside with him.

George descended from the offside door and went round to lower the carriage step, but an under-footman came out to attend, so that he was able instead to assume the position due to him at the door of the house.

Hervey got down, straightened his neck cloth, and went inside.

'Colonel Hervey, m'lady,' George announced at the door of Kat's sitting room.

Kat did not come out to greet him, however, as invariably she had. Hervey thought perhaps it was the more appropriate to their new respective situations.

He entered the sitting room, and smiled. 'Kat, how very agreeable it is to see you.'

But Kat did not return the smile, nor move to kiss him. 'Matthew, thank you for coming so promptly.'

Hervey's brow furrowed. 'Kat?'

She made no reply, turning instead to the window, distinctly uneasy.

He moved to her side. 'Kat, what is it?'

'How was Brighton?' she asked, distantly.

He shook his head rather dismissively. 'It was . . . very agreeable.'

She seemed not to hear. She did not, at least, make any response.

'Kat, what is it? What were you not able to say in the letter?'

She turned back to him, and with a look quite cast down. 'I am with child, Matthew.'

The shock – the horror indeed – upon her lover's face was too much for her. She turned back to the window, her eyes moist.

He stumbled with his words. 'Kat . . . I . . . who . . . ?'

She turned again, blazing. '*Who? Who*, do you say! Matthew, how could you ask such a question?'

Hervey now felt a rising panic. 'I . . . that is . . . how . . .'

Kat looked more astonished still. '*How*, Matthew? You ask *how*? Or do you suggest my years make it impossible?'

That was not what he meant. He knew well enough how. Indeed, he knew *when*. He struggled not to take her hand, and then gave way. 'What are you to do?'

She sighed deeply, and gave him a sort of resigned, pitying smile. 'Do not worry, Matthew; it is taken care of.'

He looked at her, puzzled.

'Sir Peregrine.'

He looked at her quite horrified.

'He was in London when I learned of it. He . . . he has no reason to suppose he is not the father.'

'But you said he was incapable of . . .'

'And so he is. But the dear, kind old booby had no memory of his incapability after two bottles.'

Hervey shuddered.

'The child is yours, Matthew, and although Sir Peregrine shall be the proud father – and I shall tell no one to the contrary, not even my sister – I must have you know.'

Thoughts raced in Hervey's mind as if from a legion of criers. Who might *he* tell of it? What should be his duty to Kat? What might he say to Kezia . . . 'Kat, I am so very sorry.'

'And so am I, Matthew.' Tears filled her eyes again. 'And yet . . .'

He looked about, as if for salvation.

There was no salvation, however. Kat was now sobbing.

He embraced her. But when Henrietta had told him she was with child, and he had taken her in his arms, he had felt such a warming in his vitals. Now only rats scrambled in the pit of his stomach.

He pulled her closer, yet with a distance that came from the horror of the very wretchedness he was trying to allay.

But Kat's dejection was too much to be tempered by what she knew was transient. She knew she would no more enjoy his attention. Her place in society would be gone, too. There would be no more beaux to flatter her. Motherhood would not at all become her. Her tears were many-coloured.

* * *

He left Holland Park much later than he had intended, so late as to conclude that returning to Hanover Square would be inconvenient to the occupants. And in truth he had no desire to. Not in his own state of wretchedness. He went instead to the United Service, arriving a little after midnight, and in the smoking room, to his surprise, he found the commander-in-chief still, and a little gathering of officers, all in plain clothes but some of whom he recognized.

His inclination was to bow and then retire, but Lord Hill saw him first.

'Hervey!'

'My lord,' he replied, with a less formal bow than he would have made had it not been in his club, where notions of a certain gentlemanly egality applied.

'Come, join us. We were talking of affairs in the Levant.'

Hervey nodded.

'Now, you may know, I imagine, Generals Burt and Richardson, Colonel Cowan and Major Hawtrey.' Lord Hill indicated each in turn.

It was a gracious way of introduction, for Hervey knew only the two generals, and those by name alone.

'Gentlemen, this is Colonel Hervey, lately returned from the Cape, where he has been raising a corps of mounted rifles.'

There was no shaking of hands, merely the usual bows of acknowledgement.

'And also lately of the gunpowder mills at Waltham Abbey, do I not recall?' said General Richardson.

'Yes, General,' replied Hervey, somewhat indifferently since attitudes to the action at the mills were, he knew, mixed.

'Sit you down,' commanded Lord Hill, but benignly, as befitted his nickname among the troops – 'Daddy'.

Hervey took the remaining tub chair gratefully. The evening, the whole day, had drained him of resource to an extent he would not have imagined.

'Colonel Hervey is to have command of the Eighty-first in Canada next year,' Lord Hill told his party.

There was a general murmur of approval. Hervey shifted awkwardly in his chair, the matter yet undecided in his own mind.

'When do you return to the Cape?' asked Lord Hill.

'I have just had a letter from the lieutenant-governor hastening it, my lord. I believe I shall sail within the fortnight.' He realised too late that by mentioning haste he might be inviting the commander-in-chief to enquire into the necessity for it, and since Somervile's position was somewhat precarious, and the expedition to the territory of the Zulu doubtless an enterprise without sanction from the Secretary for War, he might well have jeopardized his old friend's initiative.

But Lord Hill's concerns were not with so distant a place about which the Horse Guards knew very little. The situation in the Eastern Mediterranean was what occupied His Majesty's ministers, and was consequently the concern of the commander-in-chief. 'And when do you relinquish the commission with the Rifles?'

'The date is uncertain, my lord, but I believe it will be before the end of the year.'

'Mm.' Lord Hill appeared to be turning something over in his mind.

The smoking-room waiter brought Hervey his brandy and soda.

'How is your French, Hervey?'

'I fancy it is very adequate, sir,' he replied, rather startled by the turn of questioning. His French was entirely fluent, as was his German.

'You have no Russian, I imagine?'

Hervey's brow furrowed, curious. 'No-o, General.'

'Well, French would be perfectly serviceable. What say you to an attachment to Prince Worontzov's headquarters?'

Hervey had no very precise idea who was Prince Worontzov, or where his headquarters might be, but with the Russians now at war with the Turks it could be supposed that it was in the Levant (anything more precise was hardly necessary at this stage of enquiry). 'I am all enthusiasm, my lord, but I believe I must return to the Cape, at least for a month or so – to make proper arrangements for the corps, and indeed for the return of my detachment of dragoons.'

Lord Hill nodded. 'That is understood. Indeed, it

works to advantage. George Bingham is to go at once, but he will have to return by the year's end to take command of the Seventeenth.'

Hervey had to check his instinct to agree to the commission at once.

'Think on it a while,' said Lord Hill, rising to leave. 'Let my military secretary know before you embark for sunnier climes.'

Hervey rose with him, and smiled. 'I will indeed, sir.'

'And, by the bye, I should have mentioned it before. I saw the notice of your marriage. Hearty congratulations, my boy! Ivo Lankester's widow, is she not?'

Hervey shifted a little awkwardly, forcing something of a smile. 'I suppose it will be some years before she is referred to as wife rather than widow, my lord.'

Lord Hill returned the smile. 'Just so, Hervey, just so. I stand rebuked. Mind you don't make her a widow again in that uncivilized colony of yours. The Eighty-first will be looking to welcome you both in due course.'

'Thank you for your sentiment, my lord.'

The commander-in-chief and his party took their leave, and Hervey sank down gratefully into his tub chair again. He now felt sicker in his stomach than he had even at Holland Park.

Another brandy and soda settled him somewhat, but it required a considerable act of will to rouse and make to leave. He really could not in all decency stay a second night at the United Service; especially when he had sent no communication to Kezia to say even that he might return late to Hanover Square.

He went out into the hall and asked the porter to hail him a cab.

Alone, now, he had the sudden and profoundest desire to speak to someone. But who? Fairbrother? Fairbrother was the only one of his military companions that he could possibly conceive of speaking to. And it was strange, because Fairbrother was not as the others: he neither wore the 'VI' on his shako plate, nor was he even an Englishman. Not in the usual sense. For much of the time Hervey had no notion that Fairbrother was any different in birth or upbringing from any in the Sixth, for his manners were entirely those of the gentleman, his speech likewise, with but the faintest accent of the plantation. Nor was the colour of his skin so markedly different, especially in the summer months, when the sun in Spain and India had made of the Sixth a fraternity of half-castes.

But he could not speak to Fairbrother, for even had his friend been at hand, these were waters too deep. The Reverend Mr Keble, perhaps, would have given steadfast counsel, but could he face such a man as John Keble? Would that admirable, saintly curate truly be able to understand his situation? Elizabeth should have been his confidante, but although his sister had for so many years been his support (without her, indeed, he did not know what would have become of him after Henrietta had died), he had never spoken his innermost thoughts. And now that there was this . . . estrangement between the two of them, any such course was out of the question. He was not certain, even, if she were in London or in Wiltshire (this improvident engagement with her German widower had made her lose all sense of judgement).

One person only did he imagine might help him: Sister Maria. For a few short weeks in 1814 they had been intimate in the easy manner of their conversation, touching on things spiritual that were never the subject of discourse with any other of his acquaintance. It had been helped no little by her calling, the otherworldliness of her habit. And yet, though she had not worn the habit that morning (the law forbade it in public), he was certain that if she were here now he would be able to tell her all.

He sighed, giving way for the moment to the greatest sense of hopelessness. Which would occasion the greater alarm at two in the morning: pulling on the doorbell at the Hammersmith Convent, or at Kezia's aunt's in Hanover Square?

He woke to the sound of piano scales. He looked at his watch; it was not yet seven. He sat up and looked about: a good-size room, with fine hangings and paintings; he had not taken it in by the light of the candle when the manservant had brought him to it in the early hours (he hoped he had not woken too many of the household, for there had been a noisy drawing of bolts). He rose and poured water from the decanter by his bed into a washing bowl, supposing it a little early for hot water to be brought, even though there was piano practice. He shaved, then dressed.

He went downstairs to the music room. Kezia was now begun on her arpeggios. He bent and kissed her forehead. 'Good morning, my love,' he said boldly.

'Good morning,' she replied, without interruption to her practice. 'Evidently priests are not easy to find these days in London.'

He smiled. 'I'm sorry. I was detained by all manner of things yesterday. And some I must speak with you about as a matter of urgency. I saw Lord Hill, and he has proposed I go to the seat of the Turkish war for six months – not immediately, but in the new year. And Eyre Somervile wants me to return forthwith to the Cape. And I have been offered command of the Eighty-first.'

Kezia continued playing, if perhaps less complex chords. 'On what particular do you seek my attention?'

Hervey's brow furrowed. 'On all of them! We might begin with the Turkish war.'

She threw him an indulgent smile. 'I am perfectly aware that the wife of a soldier must bear such absences.'

'And the early return to the Cape?'

'I cannot think but that the lieutenant-governor has good reason.'

Hervey was finding the easy acceptance a shade disconcerting. 'And the Eighty-first?'

She smiled indulgently again. 'I cannot know the reputation of every regiment of the army. Where are they stationed?'

'Canada.'

'*Canada?*' She mis-keyed, and looked vexed with herself. 'I cannot be expected to go with you to Canada!'

His mouth fell open. If she had gone to India with her late husband, what possible objection could there be to Canada?

'Are you inclined to accept the command?' she asked, taking up the exercises again, speaking in an indifferent manner, not that of wife to husband.

He put a hand to her shoulder. 'I am not strongly minded to, no; and your disapproval reinforces me in that position.'

She stopped playing, momentarily. 'I thank you for consulting me in the matter.'

'The fact is, my love, I may not get a better offer. It is without purchase too. Lord Hol'ness shows no sign of selling out, and when he does, the price may be too high. John Howard told me the Seventeenth went for twenty-five thousand!'

'To whom? Who would pay such a sum just to sit in front of five hundred other men on horses?'

Hervey was rather put out by this dismissal of the

honour of command, even though he supposed she spoke with irony. 'Lord Bingham.'

'Oh, then that explains it. George Bingham will merely rack-rent his miserable tenants in Mayo all the more.'

Hervey frowned again. 'I don't know George Bingham in that particular – or, indeed, any – except that he is to go to the Russians meanwhile. Lord Hill wishes me to take his place when he goes to his regiment.'

Kezia increased the dynamics of her exercises as if to underscore her disapproval. 'I know George Bingham perfectly well enough. He is not a cultivated man.'

Hervey could not see the relevance of what he had no reason to doubt was a perfectly apt judgement of Lord Bingham's character to the price of the Seventeenth; but he was intrigued that his wife should claim an acquaintance with their new commanding officer. 'How old would you say he was exactly?'

'He is my age, perhaps a little more. He attended the balls in the year I was out.'

Hervey cursed silently for being inclined to dislike a man he had never met. He had no knowledge of Bingham save that he was too young to have seen service in the French war, and to his almost certain knowledge had not been to India. 'But the Cape, my love: we must needs take passage by the month's end.'

Kezia stopped playing, her hands poised above the keyboard, her face all astonishment. '*We?* Matthew, I cannot possibly go by the month's end. You know I am to play at the benefit concerts. It is quite impossible!'

Hervey was likewise dismayed. 'But I cannot leave you here. I cannot return to the Cape without my wife!'

Kezia laid her hands in her lap, and turned her head to him with a pleasant countenance despite the evident dis-agreeability of the subject. 'Matthew, you yourself have said that Eyre Somervile wishes you to return forthwith. Manifestly he has urgent need of you, and I do not suppose that he has need of you at his office, do you? I have no desire to sit at Cape-town while you and he hunt tiger or whatever it is that you do. And then Lord Hill wishes you to go to the Turks or the Russians, so we would not be at the Cape for more than six months, in which case, where is the sense in my undertaking two voyages and enduring the intervening months of separation? And would you wish it, too, for your daughter and for mine?'

Hervey pulled a chair nearer to the piano and sat down, taking her hand. 'But we should be making those voyages together, and the work that Somervile has in mind would not, I'm sure, take me from Cape-town for all the months in between. Besides, if I am to replace Bingham in the Levant I shall be gone a further six months or more, and it will scarcely be possible for you to accompany me then.'

Kezia withdrew her hand. 'Matthew, all that matters not, for as I have said already, I am beholden to my aunt.'

Hervey shook his head in disbelief.

'Matthew, you of all people must know the calls of duty.'

He was about to say 'yes, but duty of *substance*' when he thought better of it. Perhaps it was expedient to leave the matter, for the moment. It was early, they had not breakfasted, and he had interrupted her practice.

V
A HUNT

Hounslow, afternoon, the same day

Hervey gathered up the reins as the commanding officer came on parade. He turned in the little finger of his right hand as far as he could and saluted, hoping that Lord Holderness would not notice that the seam of his glove had unaccountably split. In the scheme of things it was not perhaps of the greatest moment: a broken stitch even on a piece of saddlery was not unknown, but it suggested less than the sharpest eye for maintenance. And Hervey knew his eye had been elsewhere than on such things these past weeks (neither had Johnson been given opportunity for the usual making and mending). But if Lord Holderness noticed, he did not show it. He returned the salute cheerily, without greeting (they had taken lunch together in the mess), and Hervey closed to his side, his borrowed mare whickering her own salutation to the colonel's charger.

It was an unexpected as well as a pleasant diversion. He had gone to Hounslow in the morning to place the details of Caithlin Armstrong's funeral in the hands of the adjutant, and Lord Holderness had asked him to ride out with him in the afternoon. 'I hope you will both be able to dine with us at Heston before you sail,' he said as they passed the sentries presenting arms at the barrack gates (he and Lady Holderness had taken the lease on Heston House, a mile or so away).

'A pleasure, Colonel,' replied Hervey, adding with something of a smile, 'though persuading Kezia to leave her pianoforte is not easy at present. She has several bene-fit concerts.' He could not help thinking how eagerly Kat would have accepted.

Lord Holderness nodded, and smiled indulgently. 'A prodigious talent, I understand.'

They rode on in silence, accompanied by a trumpeter, an orderly and the picket officer, who had all reined in, respectfully, to allow the colonel and the senior major to converse in private.

The sun shone, but it was not too hot a day. Blackbirds were still singing – mellow, fluting song despite the hour; swifts in great numbers screamed this way and that; and, high above, a red kite circled effortlessly. Hervey watched as suddenly a crow flew up at it. A nest to guard, perhaps? But he had only ever observed a kite pick at carrion; he did not think it hunted like the hawk or the buzzard. Did the crow not know one bird from another?

Or did it suppose that the kite might forget itself? He recalled the service of the vultures at the Cape, how Fairbrother had detected the movement of the Zulu by observing their flight. How he missed Fairbrother's easy company now. He wondered how he was enjoying Devon, and the relicts of his family there.

Lord Holderness shifted his left leg forward and began tightening the girth on his hunting saddle. 'Now, we have made no mention of it – the Eighty-first. What is your inclination?'

Hervey tried to keep one eye on the kite, which evaded its impertinent assailant by leisurely flexions of its deep-forked tail. He had, of course, intended telling Lord Holderness of the offer of the Eighty-first, this afternoon possibly, for he had not supposed he knew of it.

Lord Holderness sensed his discomfiture. 'I should add that I believe I alone know of it in the regiment. It was given to me upon most particular honour.'

'Of course, Colonel. Thank you.'

Lord Holderness had, in fact, made personal representation to the commander-in-chief, further to a letter he had sent to the general officer commanding the London District after the manoeuvres at Windsor. But he would never speak of it. If Hervey were promoted, he did not wish it to be thought of as being other than through merit recognized in the usual way. 'You will, I imagine, be disappointed that it is a regiment of Foot.'

Hervey held up his reins, as if to say 'see what my hands are accustomed to', and smiled.

Lord Holderness acknowledged with a sigh. 'A perfectly ridiculous supposition that it could be otherwise,' he added, his smile the equal of Hervey's.

'In truth, Colonel, I don't know what to think. I have not had opportunity to tell you, either, that last night Lord Hill asked if I would go to the Russians for a few months, when Lord Bingham returns.'

'Did he? By then, of course, I should be quite used to having no major!'

Now Hervey sighed. 'I know, Colonel. It is most unsatisfactory. I must declare my intentions soon, for all our sakes.'

'Oh, worry not on my account, Hervey. Malet's a good adjutant.'

Hervey nodded. 'But all the same . . .'

They came to the London Road. Ordinarily there was no check to their crossing, but this afternoon they had to take a good hold.

''Pon my word, what a sight!'

Beyond the hawthorn hedge, on the high road, 'Salmanazar's Travelling Menagerie' (according to the emblazon on the side of the caravan) was making its way east, waggon after waggon, a vast train, like the baggage of the army in Spain, but tarpaulin-covered. Except the waggon next in line, whose occupant could not so easily be roofed over.

'A cameleopard, no less!' exclaimed Lord Holderness, as delighted as a child. 'You might think yourself back at the Cape already, eh, Hervey?'

Hervey was just as astonished. In fact he had not seen the beast, live, before. 'Extraordinary. I recall a speculation as to whether its neck was elongated so that it could eat the leaves at the top of the tree, or whether it ate the leaves thus because its neck was long.'

'Now that is a question of the deepest natural philosophy!' agreed Lord Holderness.

His horse now began running back, which only a deal of urging could check. 'Good God, man, it is but an elephant!'

An elderly Indian bull tramped along behind a haywain, the tip of his trunk curled round the mahout's wrist, walking beside him like a led child.

Hervey's mare, backing and snorting likewise, tried to take the bit, but the picket officer, whose charger was perfectly composed, grabbed her bridle and gave a settling lead.

'Well done, Hawkes,' said Hervey, when he had managed to get his temporary charger back in hand. 'Quite like first parade in Bengal.'

'I was thinking more of Trebia – Hannibal's surprise of the Romans,' said Lord Holderness, whose gelding was now settled. He gazed intently at the lone terrifier of cavalry. 'Livy brought quite to life!'

'Just so,' replied Hervey, his poise recovered.

110

'I never saw an elephant before, except by the taxidermist's art.'

But before Hervey could make reply, there was a loud splintering, the breaking of an axle on the next but one waggon.

The front offside wheel disintegrated before their eyes, canting the load and driving the pole into the quarters of the nearer of the team. The horse, already frighted by the noise of the shattering axle, began to rear, rocking the high-sided waggon so violently that it turned over in the road. The terrified team broke loose, and bolted.

The tarpaulin fell away, revealing a cage and its content.

''Pon my word,' exclaimed Lord Holderness again, thoroughly enjoying the impromptu carnival of animals. 'I declare that we might indeed be at the Cape!'

'Just so, Colonel,' replied Hervey, taking a firm grip of the reins once more. 'Though I confess I never saw its like there either.'

But the cage was no longer fast. The locking pin had sheared, and the door fell open noisily on the road. The occupant, a big, maned lion, half dazed, stepped from his confinement, turned to look at the debris of his transport, and snarled.

No one in the commanding officer's party moved. The horses were turned to stone.

'The picket, Colonel?' suggested Hervey.

'Better had.'

111

'Have the picket turn out under arms,' said Hervey to Cornet Hawkes. 'And move away slowly. Don't alarm the beast.'

'Sir!'

Hawkes did as he was told. The lion showed no interest.

'A magnificent thing, don't you think?' Lord Holderness was contemplating the scene as if he were watching hounds at a covert.

'Indeed, Colonel – magnificent,' replied Hervey, wondering what they might do if the object of their admiration rushed them.

Did lions rush in so? Did they pounce? He was sure they did. He had seen pictures.

Where were the keepers? He looked about. Those not occupied with their own charges had taken high refuge. The lion was free to make good its escape.

He wondered if they should try to arrest it, but how? The picket would show in five minutes, and with carbines. If it became necessary, the animal could be subdued by bullets. Could they not corral it somehow, tempt it back into its cage with meat or some such?

The lion sniffed the air and looked about once more, seeming to study the commanding officer's party. Then, as if with disdain, it began walking away in the direction of the drilling ground.

'A cool customer,' said Lord Holderness, looking to right and left for some sign of address in the keepers, but seeing none. 'I think we had better go after him, if only to observe what Prall makes of it when the beast comes on his troop!'

F Troop's new captain, recently bought in from the Tenth, was having his dragoons out for the first time on the drilling ground, and Lord Holderness had wished to show his interest, for the troop had not been out in some months, having been doing duties in penny-packets here and there, and the officers largely absent on leave.

Hervey was much taken by Lord Holderness's coolness, not to say amusement at the thought of F Troop's new captain being put to such a test. But he had no reason to suppose the owner of the menagerie kept the lion on short rations; and in any case, had he not read that it was the lioness which hunted, not the male? Deprived of the female's efforts in his favour, however, the male did not simply lie down and starve? Had he not seen somewhere the picture of several males – or lions with manes (perhaps some females were maned?) – leaping onto some other beast to drag it down?

The drilling ground, a mile or so square of heath, lay just the other side of the London Road, masked by a line of elms in full leaf. As they closed with them, Hervey became anxious: might the lion have taken post in the branches, waiting his moment to pounce? He knew that leopards did – he had seen it for himself in India – and tigers too. 'Have a care, Colonel,' he said, searching the nearest trees as best the leaves allowed him.

'No, he's yonder. See?'

Hervey peered in the direction Lord Holderness pointed.

There indeed, fifty yards away, was the lion, all but concealed in a patch of gorse. 'Perhaps he will discover a thorn in his foot?'

'Well, I for one shall not play Androcles if he does!' declared Lord Holderness, but as composed as before. 'See, he lowers his tail, like a cat before it pounces on a mouse.'

'I hope to God it's not intending to run in on the troop,' said Hervey, wishing he had his telescope.

'Not on the troop, I suspect. Look yonder, to the left, a furlong – one of Prall's videttes. Most tempting to a lion, don't you suppose?'

Hervey saw. 'I'd better tell them.'

'I believe we ought.'

'I think, with respect, Colonel, it would be better if you stood your ground here. If the lion backs . . .'

'I concur.'

Hervey spurred into a trot, taking as indirect a route as he could, keeping to the tree line until he was at the shortest point from the two mounted sentries. He now put his mare into a brisker trot (thinking that any faster pace might encourage the lion to run in at him) and made straight for them.

'So-ho, F Troop!' he called from fifty yards, believing they had not seen his approach.

But another sentry, dismounted, stepped from behind a clump of gorse and raised his hand to challenge. 'Good afternoon, Major Hervey, sir!'

Hervey wore the regimental undress of a major, content to leave his acting rank behind in the colony. 'Doolan, isn't it? How far distant did you observe me?'

'Saw you come out from the trees, sir!' Doolan, being from Liverpool, elongated the 'sir' (which he pronounced 'sair') more than any man in the Sixth.

'And do you perceive anything else?'

'Sir?'

'Look yonder,' (he pointed) 'two hundred yards, standing by itself, a large bush of gorse. D'ye see?'

'Sir.'

'The other side of it, there crouches a lion.'

'Sir.' Doolan had experience of such schemes. He knew it was his duty to relay whatever information an officer gave him. And then the officer would judge the address with which the corporal acted in response. It mattered not that the information was preposterous.

'No, Doolan: it is no play. There is a lion escaped and it has taken refuge on the drilling ground. Go tell Captain Prall at once. My compliments, and ask him to form line to try to turn the creature back should it try to go further onto the common. The picket has been sent for, with carbines, and the colonel is in the field.'

'Sir!'

Hervey acknowledged the salute, reined about and put

his mare for the trees again. Doolan might be a delinquent (if only of a pay night), but he knew him to be sharp enough to alert the Troop.

By the time he got back to Lord Holderness the picket was coming up. 'F Troop will form line to back him if he tries to go further, Colonel. Is there any sign of a keeper?'

Lord Holderness nodded in the direction of the road.

Hervey saw two men folding a net, and another with a noose on a pole about twenty feet long.

'They say the beast's harmless enough. Tame, almost. He's been sitting by yonder bush since you left.'

'What would you have me do now, Colonel?'

Lord Holderness smiled and shook his head. 'Watch the entertainment before us! I suppose you might have the picket take post and load.'

Hervey reined about and told the picket officer to get the ten men into line just in advance of the trees. 'And make ready.'

Cornet Hawkes saluted, and turned to the picket serjeant, who had heard the orders well enough. 'Carry on, Serjeant Henry!'

'Sir!' The picket serjeant smiled ruefully. *Carry on* – as if he had any particular expertise in lion hunting!

At last the keepers were ready with the net. They advanced confidently into the open, calling the lion by name – 'Samson!'

Serjeant Henry motioned to the picket to follow.

'Keep your distance, mind. Give 'em room to work. Fifty paces; no closer!'

'A regular bandobast, Hervey!' Lord Holderness pressed his charger to the walk.

Hervey nodded. It did indeed have the appearance of a tiger shoot, or a hog hunt. All they needed was the elephant and its mahout and the scene would be complete.

As the keepers closed on the gorse, the lion at last stirred itself, getting to its feet and turning round to face them, with a look not unlike a boy caught in an orchard.

'Come, Samson, my lad,' called the chief keeper, with not the slightest trepidation.

When he got within reach he began gently playing out the pole. The lion raised a paw and swiped at the noose – not violently, more as if it were a mild irritant, like a fly buzzing too close to his face.

The keeper tried again. The lion swiped at the noose once more.

But the keeper was patient, and the lion showed no inclination to make off one way or the other. Ten minutes passed in an almost playful attempt to snare the runaway.

At length, however, the keeper judged he was beat. 'Net, then, lads,' he told the other two.

The assistants came alongside him, almost as fearlessly, and readied themselves.

'A good bold cast, mind. Ready?'

'Ay.'

He tried again with the noose, to distract the animal. 'Now!'

They cast high, the weighted corners spreading the net perfectly. But the lion sidestepped and the net fell across its back and quarters.

The keepers at once knew the game was up. But before they could move, the lion, frighted by the thing that had leapt on its back, sprang.

The chief keeper jabbed furiously with the pole as the beast tore at the downed assistant's shoulder.

Dragoons ran in to take aim.

But Lord Holderness was already out of the saddle, sabre in hand. He ran at the lion, driving the point into its flank. The animal roared in pain, freeing the wretched keeper, and made to leap at its attacker.

At that instant the chief keeper managed to thrust the noose over its head. 'Don't shoot! Don't shoot!'

'Don't shoot!' echoed Lord Holderness.

Hervey, too, was now out of the saddle, sabre drawn. 'Will it hold?' he shouted.

'It will! Just don't alarum 'im. He's a good old soul.'

Hervey looked at Lord Holderness. 'Colonel?'

'Let him be. Let him walk him back to the road. The picket can follow. Such a magnificent creature. I never thought I should come as close to the king of beasts!' He looked at the blood on his sword with evident dismay.

Hervey, bemused, turned to the savaged keeper. The

118

man was already sitting up, dragoons showing him consideration. His shoulder was badly torn, but he would live – as would the lion. 'Shall we leave the picket officer to carry on, Colonel?' (there was only so much a senior officer should do).

Lord Holderness appeared reluctant . . . 'Yes, Hervey, I think we might go and tell Captain Prall he may stand down his troop.'

Hervey was relieved. Care of Lord Holderness was becoming an altogether hair-raising business.

When they were done with F Troop, Hervey and the commanding officer turned for the barracks. 'Come then, Hervey; we can resume our conversation,' said Lord Holderness cheerily, as if nothing of any moment had occurred. 'I would have your opinion on this Russian business. The talk at White's is that we shall be drawn in.'

Only the trumpeter accompanied them now as they gave the menagerie a wide berth, and Hervey felt himself free to speak. 'I think that had Lord Palmerston been in the cabinet still, we would be at the Russians' side, think you not, Colonel? But after Navarino, the duke will surely have no truck with interference? He's recalled the troops from Portugal quickly enough.'

'That much is true, certainly, but I wonder how free a hand the duke might have. This treaty over the Greeks is still a deuced entangling thing.'

Hervey nodded. And the irony was that the Duke of Wellington had been in no little measure responsible for it, for Mr Canning had sent him to Russia two years before, and out of that visit had come the treaty with the Tsar and with France for the expulsion of the Turks from Greece (during the course of which, at Navarino, Peto had been so grievously wounded). 'I wonder that we appear to know so little of what Austria may think?'

'Ah, indeed. We should—'

Lord Holderness ducked to avoid a branch. When he raised his head again he seemed to sway, and began to shake; then he slumped forward.

Hervey moved to support him in the saddle. 'Close up!' he called to the trumpeter.

Lord Holderness was now struggling, his eyes closed, his mouth frothing.

Hervey knew: the exact same as the night of the river crossing.

Corporal Meade closed on the nearside, reaching for Lord Holderness's reins. 'What 'appened, sir?'

'The colonel's unwell, that's all. We'll ride straight for Heston.'

VI

THE KING'S GERMAN

London, a few days later

Georgiana contained her disappointment admirably, thought Hervey, for he had all but promised her their new quarters.

She had been looking forward to a sea passage. It would, indeed, have been her first sight of the sea. And she had looked forward even more to the mysterious prospect of the Cape Colony, in the company of her father and her new stepmother. But she could not very well go with him alone, even if he were to engage a travelling governess. She had tried her hardest, when first he had told her of the change in the 'arrangements'. After all, the express had hastened her to London for the very purpose of an early passage. She had pressed her case; but if her stepmother could not accompany her father, then it was certain that she could not. She did not fully comprehend why her stepmother could not sail directly; perhaps it was that her half-sister was too young? And then there had been the question of where, in her father's absence, she would stay.

On the one hand it had seemed to him only right and proper that Georgiana should be at her new family home (though there was none, yet; only that of Kezia's family); on the other, his own absence would be for so short a time that it seemed prudent to continue with the present arrangements. Except that the present arrangements were fast becoming objectionable. Indeed it would be quite impossible for Elizabeth to act as guardian if she were to persist in her design to marry her German.

And so he had set the question to one side this morning, choosing instead to spend a little of the day with his daughter in the most agreeable way they might – no talk of his going away, no talk of where she might live, no talk of Elizabeth's intentions.

'Your aunt is engaged for the day, so I am at your disposal,' he said, smiling over a breakfast cup in the dining room at Grillon's Hotel in Albemarle Street, where Georgiana and her Aunt Elizabeth were staying.

Georgiana had of late grown quite tall for her age, so that she occupied the chair opposite him less as the child he was used to contemplating (or, rather, imagining, for he had in truth spent little time in her company) and more as a replica of her mother. Indeed, seeing her now put him in mind of the portrait which stood at the studio of Sir Thomas Lawrence (and which still awaited his instructions for carriage), with its raven lustre of ringlets, and large and happy eyes.

Georgiana contemplated the offer very seriously. She was ten years old, yet somehow she presented a picture three times that age (doubtless, thought Hervey, the influence of his sister). 'I think that I should like to see a lion. I should like to know how big is one, and then I might picture in my mind more faithfully your fight with him at Hounslow.'

Hervey smiled. 'You misunderstand. It was not I who fought him, but Lord Holderness.'

'But you were by his side, were you not, Papa?'

'I was, but as I explained, Lord Holderness acted with such address that the lion was quite subdued by the time I was able to dismount. And glad of it I was, too, for I do not in the least mind admitting that a lion is a most troubling beast to be so close to.'

'May we see one, though, Papa? Can we not seek out the menagerie?'

'That, or another, yes. But first, there's a museum of curiosities only five minutes' walk from here. It has preserved lions and tigers. And there is something else I would show you – a lion *hunt*.'

'A lion *hunt*, Papa?'

He smiled again. 'A *petrified* lion hunt.'

'How so?'

'At the British Museum there is a frieze, carved out of stone – a lion hunt in Mesopotamia, or somewhere like.

It is very ancient. And there are the zoological gardens, not long opened.'

Georgiana agreed enthusiastically to all his proposals.

And so for the rest of the morning they roved London in search of lions, first to Mr Bullock's 'museum of natural curiosities', and then to a travelling menagerie in St James's Park, where a lioness paced her cage restlessly, and occasionally snarled, to the squealed delight of the female onlookers; and from here they took a hackney cab to Bloomsbury for their study of the art of lion hunting. The adventure was as thoroughly diverting to Hervey as to Georgiana.

They lunched at a large and noisy chophouse, took a ride on a 'catch-me-who-can', and then walked back to Grillon's by way of Bond Street, where he bought her some silk gloves, and Piccadilly, where at number one hundred and ninety, Mr Hatchard the bookseller's, he made to hand over a guinea for *Mrs Teachwell's Grammar Box*, which he had ordered at Kezia's recommendation.

'It will instruct you in every point of English grammar,' he explained to Georgiana, who was much taken by the woodcuts of various animals which were to serve in the construction and parsing of sentences. 'Such as what is a noun and a preposition and the like.'

'Oh, but I know what are nouns and prepositions, Papa. And verbs and adjectives – and all the other parts of speech. Aunt Elizabeth has taught me.'

'Has she indeed,' he replied, with irrational

disappointment, and putting the guinea back into his pocket. He was naturally grateful to allay the expense if it were not necessary, but this further evidence of Elizabeth's admirable qualities he found singularly unwelcome.

Georgiana mistook his manner for displeasure that his generosity and thoughtfulness had been ill received. 'I am sorry, Papa. I did not wish to display ingratitude, only that ... I am sure a grammar box would serve always.'

He smiled at her, benignly. 'No; evidently I under-estimated your aunt's address in teaching, and your own in learning. Better, I think, that we save the guinea.'

They browsed instead among the titles in that part of the shop set aside for 'the young entry', settling on *Fables in Monosyllables*, also by Mrs Teachwell. Hervey felt that Kezia's recommendation of the author boded well, and so they each left the shop contented, if for different reasons.

They were not long at tea when Elizabeth returned, but accompanied. Hervey rose, and a shade awkwardly.

'Brother,' she began boldly. 'May I present Major Heinrici.'

Hervey bristled: Elizabeth had humbugged him. Yet the honour required of one soldier to another demanded nothing less than civility. He bowed. 'Major Heinrici.'

Major Baron (more properly, *Freiherr*) von Heinrici zu Gehrden was ten years Hervey's senior, but an inch or so shorter. He braced himself in military fashion (though he had not served with the colours in some time) and returned the bow. 'Colonel Hervey.' The accent was apparent but not pronounced.

There was a moment's awkwardness, when no one spoke.

'May we join you, brother?' asked Elizabeth, looking away from him and at Georgiana.

Hervey cleared his throat. 'By all means.' He nodded to one of the Grillon's waiters.

They sat down.

'Have you had an instructive day, Georgiana?'

Georgiana's face lit up. 'Oh, yes indeed, Aunt Elizabeth. Papa told me all about a lion which had escaped at Hounslow, and how he captured it, and so we have been to see more lions.'

'Indeed?'

Hervey cleared his throat again. 'It was not I who caught the lion but Lord Holderness.'

'I am sure you would have caught the lion, Matthew, if Lord Holderness had not first done so.'

He was not entirely sure if his sister teased or not. He chose to ignore the remark. 'We have had a most enlightening day: lions carved out of stone, lions stuffed, and lions living – or rather, *one* lion living.'

'Though it was only a female lion,' added Georgiana, with just a measure of disappointment.

Major Heinrici leaned towards her, and with a smile

that even Hervey was forced to recognize as most genuinely kind, said in a conspiratorial voice, 'But, *mein gnädige Fraülein*, it is the lioness who hunts!'

Georgiana returned the smile, and with obvious warmth.

Hervey saw. 'Indeed,' he tried, allowing himself a smile too. 'I should not wish to choose between the lion and the lioness.'

Tea was brought, and Elizabeth busied herself thankfully in directing the waiter.

'When do you return to the Cape Colony, Herr Colonel?' asked Heinrici, easily, as he reached for a piece of gingerbread.

Hervey was still uncomfortable with the degree of intimacy which Elizabeth had contrived, yet he could not show it. And besides, it was difficult not to be civil to so patently agreeable a man as Heinrici; especially when he knew him to have been an officer of cavalry in the King's German Legion. 'At the end of next week. There is a steamship leaving Gravesend.'

'And how long is the passage?'

'It depends of course on the weather, but nothing in excess of eight weeks – barring calamity.' He realized he should not perhaps have used the word calamity, and he looked slightly anxiously at Georgiana and Elizabeth. But neither of them appeared troubled.

'Matthew, when we are married, Major Heinrici is to take me to Paris and then to Brussels, and thence to Hanover to see his people, and as we travel to Brussels we shall visit the battlefield at Waterloo.'

Hervey shifted in his chair. Before he could say anything, Georgiana spoke her mind.

'Oh, Aunt Elizabeth, how I too should like to see the battlefield at Waterloo! I should find it so much easier to imagine Papa's doings that day. And of course Major Heinrici's!'

Hervey was now thoroughly discomfited. Whether or not mention of the battle was yet another ploy on his sister's behalf he could not tell, but the appeal to the fellowship of Waterloo was always a powerful one. How ran the canteen ditty?

> *Were you, too, at Waterloo?*
> *'Tis no matter what you do,*
> *If you were at Waterloo.*

It was not the absolute truth, of course, but many a flogging had been commuted when a man's record of service was read out, and the words 'present at Waterloo'. And many a magistrate had passed a lighter sentence on some beggar in red who wore his Waterloo medal in court. Yes, the fellowship of Waterloo was a powerful one. As, too, was the fellowship of 'the yellow circle', which extended even into the enemy's lines. But Hervey knew also that Heinrici was not just *any* cavalry: he was of that elect, a light dragoon – and a light

128

dragoon of the King's German Legion. That admirable corps of men from the electorate of Hanover, the late King's German realm, had made their way to England when Bonaparte overran the Rhineland. He began to feel himself ashamed.

'If only you might come too, Papa!'

That did it. He cleared his throat, intending, civilly, to take his leave.

But Georgiana had not quite finished. 'You have never said, Major Heinrici: did you see Papa that day?' And then she turned to her father. 'And you, Papa: did you see Major Heinrici?'

Heinrici smiled. 'I saw him, yes, but I did not know it was he, not until your aunt told me of what he did. You see, my dear, your father's regiment came into the middle of the field, where my own corps was, towards the end of the battle, and they lost a good many of their officers, so that when it came the time to charge, your father was in command of them – and he but a cornet! I remember their charge most well, and seeing the officer who led them.'

Georgiana looked at her aunt, and then at her father. 'Papa, Aunt Elizabeth has not told me this. It is true?'

Hervey raised an eyebrow, and smiled very slightly. 'It is.'

'And did you see Major Heinrici?'

'I saw his brigade – General Dornberg's.'

'*Ach, ja! Lieber Willy!* What a man was he!'

Hervey was now warmed to his subject. 'I rather fancy that we in Lord Vyvyan's brigade had an easier time of it on the left flank, for when we moved to the centre towards evening, the sight of Dornberg's brigade, and so many others, filled us with foreboding. I never saw such a thing, so many lying dead about the place, and those still afoot or astride as black as their boots!'

'Black, Papa?'

'From the powder smoke.'

'And you recall the advance of the Imperial Guard, Hervey,' added Heinrici, enthusiastically. 'And how your Guards beat them off, and then the Duke of Wellington raising his hat and beckoning the whole line to advance. *Quelle affaire!*'

Hervey was quite overcome with the memory. And it was as if the scales were falling from his eyes, for what did Elizabeth's indiscretion matter when here sat one of Dornberg's men? He leaned forward, offered his hand, and spoke the words exactly as Prince Blücher had at the inn *La Belle Alliance*, when the duke and the old Prussian marshal met on the field at last, the battle run: '*Mein lieber Kamerad: quelle affaire!*'

Fairbrother arrived next morning. Hervey met him at his club quite by accident, for he had not returned to Hanover Square the evening before, whither his friend's express had been sent, on account of the most convivial dinner with Major Heinrici and Elizabeth (and

130

afterwards, when Elizabeth had retired, prolonged reminiscences with Heinrici himself over Teutonic quantities of port). He was glad to sit down with Fairbrother now, and copious coffee, to relate all that had occurred in his friend's absence in the West Country.

Fairbrother looked well, even for his long journey by mail coach. He had been taking the opportunity to visit with distant family of his natural father, for he had not wished to be any encumbrance to either bridegroom or bride, and he had not felt sufficiently at ease, yet, to take up the several invitations to stay in Wiltshire which his new acquaintance with Hervey's people had brought. The distant family being two elderly female cousins, he had been able to spend his days riding on the moors, or swimming, and the evenings in their not inconsiderable, if antique, library.

Hervey envied him, indeed. That is to say, he envied the contentment that his friend's sojourn (albeit fore-shortened) had evidently brought him.

There was no one else in the smoking room, but an observer might have remarked on how alike were the two men (allowing a little for complexion, and rather more for features). There was nothing but a year or so between them. They were of about equal height and frame, so that they could wear each other's clothes if needs be. An observer might not at once be able to judge that their natures were agreeably matched, but he might begin to suspect it before too long. In some of the essentials they were the same, and in those in which they were not, there was a happy complement.

Hervey deferred to no one in matters of soldiery except where rank emphatically demanded it (or, exceptionally, when rank and capability were unquestionably combined). Excepting, that is, in those matters on which only service in the ranks gave true authority, so that he deferred always to the likes of Sar'nt-Major Armstrong and RSM (now Quartermaster) Lincoln. But in Fairbrother he recognized a wholly exceptional ability, a sort of sixth sense for the field which was not merely acquired, there being something, he reckoned, that came with the blood – that part of his friend's blood which came from the dark continent of Africa. For his mother, a house-slave of a Jamaica plantation, was but one generation removed from the savagery of the African tribe – the savagery *and* the wisdom. When the two friends had faced that savagery together, at the frontier of the Eastern Cape, it had been Fairbrother who had known, unfailingly, what to do. And, further, he had been able then to slip from the lofty strategy of the saddle, so to speak, and take to his belly and better the savage at his own craft.

And, too, such were Fairbrother's cultivated mind and manners that his company would have been sought by gentlemen of the best of families. Only a certain weariness with life (although not so much as when they had first met a year or so ago) stood between him and Hervey, which the latter chose largely to ignore rather than understand. Fairbrother was not a willing soldier in the way that Hervey was; he had not thought himself a soldier from an early age. His father had purchased a commission for him in the Jamaica Militia, and thence in the Royal Africans (a corps which more resembled the penitentiary than the regular army), and then on the best of recommendations Hervey had sought him out from his indolent half pay at the Cape to accompany him to the frontier as interpreter. Their first meeting had been unpropitious. Indeed, Hervey had very near walked from it in contempt of the man. But now this handsome, half-caste, gentlemanlike, disinclined soldier was rapidly becoming his paramount friend. *La vie militaire*: it was the deucedest, strangest thing!

When his friend was done with his uncharacteristically enthusiastic account of the countryside and seashores of Devon, Hervey told him of the offer of command, and of the Russian mission, and why they must return early to the Cape. He told him that Kezia and Georgiana would not be able to accompany him (hiding his disappointment, he thought, adequately). He said that it grieved him to leave poor Peto, and how he had wished to see him settled first at Houghton, but he trusted that Lord Cholmondeley, with Kat's continuing interest, would see his old friend right. He did not speak of Kat herself. He told him of Caithlin Armstrong, and observed his friend's real and considerable dismay. Lastly, he told him of Lord Holderness's relapse, although the epileptic seizure was not so debilitating as had been the one at Windsor, when he had nearly drowned as a consequence. He said that Lady Holderness had expressed her alarm that her husband had suffered another bout so soon (they did not normally recur within six months); and he confessed he had told the adjutant that the colonel had a cold and would not appear at orderly room for a day or so. That had been in the middle of the preceding week, he explained, and Lord Holderness was now restored and at office. He himself was therefore free to make the arrangements for their return to Cape Town.

'Is there anything I might do on your behalf?' asked Fairbrother.

Hervey thought for a moment. 'There is, but not today. Tomorrow will do perfectly well. I should like you to go to the War Office and inform them that I am soon to return to the Cape, and enquire if in consequence there is any commission they wish of me. Explain that I must attend at Hounslow; hence my not coming in person.'

'Very well. You will give me a letter of introduction or some such?'

'I will, though John Howard might best conduct you there. And I beg you will forgive me if I ask that you dine here alone – just this evening – for Kezia and I are obliged to her aunt.'

Fairbrother raised a hand. 'Think nothing of it. I

would not dream of intruding on the honeymoon. You have not said, by the way: how was your Brighton?'

Lady Marjoribanks lifted her head high when she addressed her new nephew by marriage. 'It is most unfortunate, Colonel Hervey, that you will not be able to hear your wife sing. You are quite certain, are you, that you must leave for Africa so early?'

And the tone was distinctly more accusatory than sympathetic. Hervey had to resist the desire to re-phrase the observation so that the misfortune was Kezia's in not being able to accompany her husband in his duties. 'I fear I must return next week, yes, Lady Marjoribanks.'

A footman poured more wine, which gave him just enough cause to avoid the gaze of his hostess. Hervey was by no means entirely discomfited by Kezia's aunt, but on the subject of his return to the Cape there had already been a sufficiency of objection. He was in any case reconciled, however reluctantly, to returning unaccompanied.

Lady Marjoribanks watched as another footman served her fish, a pause which Hervey hoped would be followed by a change in the direction of the conversation. 'Your wife's voice stands comparison with that of any professional singer, you know, Colonel Hervey. It is truly inopportune, this early return. The presence of the husband at this first concert in London is most desirable. Indeed to my mind it is unthinkable that it should be otherwise.'

Hervey would not have conceived it otherwise had there not been the imperative of Somervile's mission. He began to resent this – to his mind – inversion of the usual order of things. It was simple enough, was it not? He was a soldier, a soldier was under discipline, and he had received orders. Or, if not exactly orders, then a request; and a request from a senior officer was always to be considered an order (even though Somervile was not a senior officer). 'It is a deprivation that we shall all have to bear, Lady Marjoribanks, and it will be the easier in knowing that it is on His Majesty's business that I am bent.'

'Mm.' Lady Marjoribanks raised her head again, sounding unconvinced.

Hervey was wondering, too, if Kezia herself might not make some intervention on his behalf. He had after all withdrawn his objection to her remaining in England, and that was surely no little thing. He had likewise put in abeyance (in his mind at least) command of the Eighty-first: if a wife had objection to so great a thing as command of a particular regiment (or, more expressly, a particular station), then a man must take very careful account of it. And she knew, did she not, that he did so? He was at something of a loss, therefore, to know why she did not speak up for him now.

He looked at her.

'Shall you bring Georgiana here tomorrow?' was all that Kezia asked.

He was glad nevertheless of the change of subject. 'I shall have to go to Hounslow tomorrow. The day after, perhaps.'

'Where does she stay?' asked Lady Marjoribanks.

'At Grillon's hotel, in Albemarle-street.'

'Ah, Grillon's,' she replied, somewhat enigmatically, so that Hervey was tempted to ask if there was something he ought to know of it.

But instead he would be blithe. 'My family stayed there for the wedding. It appears a very agreeable place. It is convenient, also, for my sister.'

'Mm.'

The dinner continued in much the same fashion for a full hour. Lady Marjoribanks asked a good many questions but gave little by reply to any which Hervey was able to put to her in return. Kezia said next to nothing other than in direct response to an enquiry from her aunt. The proceedings were, indeed, so laboured that Hervey believed he had sufficient of the language to translate them simultaneously into Hindoostani or even Portuguese. Just after nine they rose, and Lady Marjoribanks announced that she would retire.

Hervey and Kezia took their coffee on the garden terrace. The evening was warm, the light only now beginning to fail.

'You said little at dinner, my love. Is all well?'

Kezia smiled thinly. 'All is perfectly well, yes, thank you. I am sorry if I was dull.'

Hervey frowned. 'I did not mean to imply . . . I merely remarked that you seemed a little . . . Perhaps you are tired. This heat . . .'

Kezia put down her coffee cup. 'I am a little tired, yes. And this weather brings on my headaches so. I think, if you will permit me, I shall retire, too.'

Hervey put down his own cup. A confusion of dismay and anger welled up within. He had to fight hard to suppress it, for the wine was freeing the reins. A contrary image of Kat then danced into his mind. He did not summon it, nor even wish it; he pushed hard against it, in fact, for together with the wine it only served to aggravate his frustration.

Kezia turned. For all the distance in her manner, she was as striking in the perfection of her form and features as that day at Sezincote when he had first understood how much he desired her. She threw him a parting smile; but it spoke of sadness.

Hervey's confusion was now the greater, to the point of despair, almost; but some instinct to protect overtook him, so that his frustration gave way instead to gentleness. 'I am happy to retire early,' he said, quietly. 'For I must be at Hounslow by ten.'

Kezia smiled thinly again. 'You must do as you will, my dear. But please try not to wake me when you come up.'

She kissed his cheek before he could find her lips, and left him to the tray of brandy and water.

* * *

Hounslow did not, in the event, detain him long, for Lord Holderness was returned to muster, and there had been no regimental defaulters in the brief hiatus of command. Hervey made his farewells before midday, certain that taking lunch in the officers' house would protract his stay overlong, there being old friends at duty. But he did not intend returning directly to London. He had resolved to call on Sister Maria, and although he did not know anything about conventual routine, he supposed that the early afternoon, as with any household, was the appropriate time to visit without appointment.

He therefore made his way to Hammersmith, enquiring of several passers-by where was the convent, until a drayman was able to give him authoritative directions. To his surprise, he found that he had passed it each time he had come and gone from Hounslow, but so high was the wall that there was no clue to what lay beyond.

He dismounted from the roadster, one of Kezia's aunt's, and rang the bell at the great double gates which fronted what he could now see was an establishment of some size. After not too long a time, an oldish man answered. He held a trowel in one hand, and he stooped, but he evidently possessed the authority to admit callers, since Hervey had given but his rank and name before one of the gates was opened to him. The man was at home with horses too, taking the reins willingly, and nodding to the gravel path between trimmed box, which led to the door of the convent.

Hervey advanced cautiously in these hallows, more so than ever he had in Spain. And he knew why, for in the Peninsula the convent was an entirely native thing; here, if not exactly in London then close enough to be counted a suburb, it was altogether alien. The high walls did not help, of course: doubtless they were supposed to make for seclusion, but they spoke also of secrecy. And the whole appearance – purporting to be a sort of gentleman's residence, *incognito*, so to speak, whereas in Spain and Portugal a convent *looked* like a religious house . . .

He came to the door, which was at least arched like a church's. He took a deep breath, and pulled at the bell. He heard it ring, distantly. There was now no going back.

One of the sisters answered. She wore a black habit, like many of the Spanish and Portuguese nuns. Hervey was a little surprised, though, for having seen Sister Maria (the Reverend Mother Maria, as he must remember she now was) in a day dress at the bishop's house, he had assumed that the sisters kept the custom at home. It was, after all, the law of the land. But then, why should an Englishwoman not wear what she pleased in her home? And in truth, alien though the habit was, he was strangely pleased to see it, for at once it ordered, and therefore made easier, their intercourse – exactly as did the soldier's uniform.

He took off his hat and cleared his throat. 'Good afternoon, Sister. Might I speak with the reverend mother?'

The nun, not quite as old as the gardener-gatekeeper, peered at him through ivory-framed spectacles. 'Which?'

Hervey cleared his throat again. 'The reverend mother, ma'am.'

'*Which* reverend mother?' she repeated, and somewhat testily.

He should have known, for he had not supposed that Sister Maria was likely to be superior of *this* convent. He smiled, he hoped pleasantly. 'Reverend Mother Maria,' he answered. And then, to be absolutely certain (for Maria could not be an unusual name for a nun), he added 'de Chantonnay.'

'Come,' she replied, briskly and with no flicker of curiosity.

Hervey assumed it to be an extension of the confidentiality of the confessional, except that he was not come to make his confession. Well, not in the strict sense. Nor, he knew for sure, could a nun pronounce absolution.

The floor of the inner hall was flagstone, the hall itself rising to the third storey by a broad, scrubbed oak staircase. There were pictures of male and female religious on the walls, a niche with a crucifix, and another with a statue of the Virgin, but other than a tall long-case clock, there was no furniture of any kind. It was cool despite the heat of the afternoon, and silent but for the movement of the pendulum. Although the paintings were not those that would grace the walls of the gentry, the place might have been a friendly old manor house in Queen Anne's day.

He was shown into a small receiving room.

'Please wait.'

The sister had been of few words, but he thought he detected an accent of the Low Countries. That was nothing surprising; so many priests and religious had taken refuge in England during the late war. Indeed, Parliament had paid many a stipend to foreign Catholics in holy orders. He smiled. The irony of it: Parliament, fount of the penal laws and yet paymaster to the clergy of Rome!

In the receiving room there was a crucifix on the wall, three chairs, and nothing else. He thought he might as well sit down since he expected that Sister Maria would be at prayer or study or some such, and therefore not immediately to be disturbed.

In this he was wrong, however, for scarcely had he sat but he was on his feet again, and bowing.

'Colonel 'Ervey, this is a most pleasant surprise!'

Sister Maria wore a habit the colour of the day dress she had worn at the bishop's house – brown, like some of the Franciscan friars he had seen in Spain. Evidently the other nun and she were of different orders, unless her position required her to wear a different colour (in

France she had worn white, but, as he recollected, it was an overmantle). He did not suppose it was of importance.

Her manner was not in the least like that of the other sister, however. Here was the same easy welcome of the bishop's house, and of all those years ago at Toulouse (though he did recall that at first their meeting had been stiff).

'Sister Maria, it is very good of you to receive me. I should have sent notice, but . . .'

'That would only be necessary if you wished to be certain that I was here. But it is so very rare that I am not. Please, take a seat, Colonel. Oh, may I bring you water?'

It intrigued him how much of her pleasant disposition was revealed in her general air, for the wimple exposed so little of her features. Perhaps the severe framing of the face drew attention more directly to the eyes, which were ice blue and had lost none of the ability to pierce. And the years since Toulouse had been kind to her (kinder than to him). There, he had thought she was his senior; now, he thought it the other way round.

He shook his head. 'No, thank you, Sister. Or – forgive me – do I call you "Reverend Mother"?'

She sat down. 'That is the more correct. I am prioress of my carmel.'

'And you are here . . . temporarily?'

'I am.'

Since she did not volunteer any more information, and since it was no part of the reason he was here, Hervey curbed his curiosity. 'Colonel Holderness has written to you thanking you for your assistance with Mrs Armstrong's funeral. You may have received it already?'

'I have, and I was most touched by it, for I did but a very little.'

'I regret I did not see you that day; there was much to be about.'

'Of course. I did, however, see you, with, I imagine, your wife. And I should most certainly have presented myself had I not been in attendance on the bishop.'

Hervey nodded. 'The bishop's presence was a considerable honour. It ought to go well with Serjeant-Major Armstrong when I am able to tell him of it. Some little comfort, at least. You know that he is at the Cape of Good Hope, and that I return there shortly with the ill news.'

'I understood that, yes.'

He fell silent.

'And so, Colonel, what is it further that I may do for you?'

He shifted a little in his chair, clenched his fists and cleared his throat. 'Reverend Mother, I am troubled by a particular . . . event, and I seek your counsel.'

Sister Maria smiled beatifically. 'Colonel 'Ervey, would that counsel not be better had from a priest?'

144

'I cannot judge, Reverend Mother, but I recall your good counsel in Toulouse.'

'I recall that I gave you a *vade mecum*, the Spiritual Exercises of St Ignatius.'

'You did indeed. And they were of use.'

'Are they of use still?'

If he had followed the Spiritual Exercises still with any degree of faithfulness, there would be no cause for his coming to Hammersmith. But he could not frame his reply thus. 'I regret that it is some years . . .'

'Well, you are here now.'

He nodded, gratefully. 'I am.'

'Then let me help you begin. Perhaps it would serve if you told me, as much or as little as pleases you, of your life since that day in Paris, after Waterloo, when last I knew anything of you?'

Hervey was a little surprised at Sister Maria's wishing to reach so far back, when quite evidently the event to which he alluded must be recent. Nevertheless he was also curiously relieved, however daunting was the prospect of recounting his life thus. Had he been content with mere pardon, as a man who, in the words of the Prayer Book, 'cannot quiet his own conscience herein, but requireth further comfort or counsel', he might have gone instead to some chaplain, 'or to some other discreet and learned Minister of God's Word, and open his grief; that . . . he may receive the benefit of absolution, together with ghostly counsel and advice'. And but a hundred yards from the house of Kezia's aunt, at St George's church, he would have found a willing curate for 'the quieting of his conscience, and avoiding of all scruple and doubtfulness'.

That indeed would have been the way of his own church. But he feared that its ghostly counsel and advice would be more by formula than true understanding of his predicament. Not that he expected other than dismay in Sister Maria when he told her of his cause for unquietness. Yet in her counsel he felt certain there would be some understanding of his conscience, and that without such understanding the counsel might not be . . . complete. He expected no undue allowance, but he was sure he would be better able somehow to do what was commanded by Scripture if the counsel came from so particular a sister of Carmel.

And so he told her everything. He told her of his marriage with Henrietta, and he spared not her blushes in describing their short-lived bliss (though she did not in the least blush on learning of it), and of Georgiana. He told her of his own part in his wife's death, his guilt, the subsequent resignation of his commission, his time in Rome, his reinstatement, his time in India, his feelings there for Vaneeta, how he and Kat had become lovers, his ill-starred sojourn in Portugal and his resolution to put right his life, not least his neglect of Georgiana and his trespassing on the infinite good nature of his sister (and, indeed, his unreasonable treatment of her of late), of his courtship and marriage with Kezia (which Sister Maria could not fail to recognize was couched in greatly less animated form than that for his first marriage), his indecision over command of another regiment, his return to the Cape alone . . .

So long was his account that the bell began tolling for the afternoon office. Hervey looked at his watch – a quarter to three – and then at Sister Maria, anxiously: he had yet to say what was the urgent cause of his disquiet.

She nodded encouragingly. 'God calls me to hear you, Colonel 'Ervey. Please continue.'

He steeled himself. 'Reverend Mother, Lady Katherine Greville is with child, by me. And her husband believes that the child is his.'

Having braced himself, he sank back into his chair – or so he felt, for the chair was entirely upright and to an observer he barely moved a muscle.

But the look of horror in his confessor's face, in expectation of which he had so resolutely screwed his courage to the sticking post, was entirely absent. There remained the same aspect of benevolence, infinitely patient, wholly serene. For a moment he wondered if he had explained himself clearly enough.

After some considerable measure of silence, Sister Maria spoke. 'Colonel 'Ervey, there is a great deal in what you have told me which calls for remark, not solely that which you suppose is the present cause of your troubled mind. But let us address that which you perceive is the greatest sin. I mean, of course, the adultery with Lady Katherine Greville.'

Hervey shifted slightly, but continued to look his confidante in the eye, as if not to do so were somehow a sign of evasion.

Sister Maria remained perfectly still, her hands clasped. 'Your sin is a matter for reconciliation with God. You are Protestant, and you are therefore minded to speak directly to Him. If you were Catholic you would know that in such circumstances the offices of a priest would be the most efficacious.'

His father had never called himself Protestant, but this was not a thing to be debated now. Hervey nodded to acknowledge the point.

'The teaching of the Church is plain in this regard, following as it does from the unequivocal commandment against adultery, and so you cannot have need of words from me. The question now is what is the right course in the matter of truth.'

He nodded again. It was precisely the question, and that to which the examination of his life for the better part of an hour had been prelude.

'Since you are not Catholic, Colonel 'Ervey, I am – ironically, as you say – at liberty to give what counsel I will.'

Not for the first time in that hour, Hervey marvelled at Sister Maria's command of English. She had once told him that she had learned it from an English governess, but such precision (and indeed elegance) of phrase must have been perfected by much reading – the advantage, perhaps, of an eremitical life?

'I am grateful, Sister.'

'Colonel 'Ervey, in addressing the right course in the matter of truth we leave the realm of moral teaching and enter that of prudence. And since I know you to be a *prud'homme*, it will not be a realm unknown to you.'

He nodded again, doubly grateful for the accolade.

'Prudence, Colonel 'Ervey, is one of the cardinal virtues. It does not itself perform any actions, concerned as it is solely with knowledge, yet all other virtues must be regulated by it. As a *prud'homme*, you will understand perfectly, for example, that to distinguish when an act is courageous, instead of merely reckless, or cowardly, is an act of prudence.'

'Indeed.'

'Prudence is to apply one's mind in affairs of this world to discern what is virtuous and what is not, and how to address the one and avoid the other. Its intention is to perfect not the will but the mind in its practical decisions, seeking where the essence of virtue lies.' She smiled, as if the search for virtue were pleasing in itself. 'But it is not enough simply to will the good which it discerns. Prudence bids us do three things: to take counsel to discover the means of securing the virtuous end, and then to judge soundly the fitness of those means;

and, finally, to command their employment.' She laid emphasis on the word 'command', as if knowing it would strike a chord.

He nodded again.

She rose.

Hervey rose too, but in some despair: his own prudence had led him to do its first bidding – to seek counsel – and he trusted he knew how to command; what he wanted now of Sister Maria was to know the means.

She clasped her hands together, and looked grave. 'The end of all moral virtues, Colonel 'Ervey, is human good. I must first ponder on the matter, and pray, before giving such counsel. Are you able to return tomorrow, at this time?'

'I am.'

She smiled again, though with a suggestion of disquiet. 'And now I must say another thing, but briefly for the vespers bell cannot be long away. It distresses me to see such confusion of mind over your opportunity for promotion and command of this new regiment. It is not a matter of prudence in the sense that I have just spoken of, but I believe it to be of the first importance in the proper ordering of your affairs, which itself is at the heart of the virtuous life. You are a soldier, Colonel 'Ervey. I understood that perfectly at Toulouse.'

He smiled by return. 'It is a matter to which I am giving the most particular attention, I assure you, Sister.'

'Then I think that before you return to the Cape of Good Hope we might speak of these – and other matters – too.'

It was a most generous invitation, and one which he had not supposed he might receive. 'I should be ever grateful, Sister.'

She made to lead him from the room, when another thought occurred to her. 'I should like very much to meet your wife, Colonel 'Ervey. Do you think I might call on her?'

He was surprised by the question, not so much alarmed, for they had spoken under what he knew as the seal of the confessional, but rather that Sister Maria imagined meeting with Kezia might in any degree inform their intercourse. 'You may call at your liberty, Sister.'

'Then I will do so tomorrow morning.'

He put on his hat.

Sister Maria sighed, and looked at him in a sort of frowning perplexity. 'Colonel 'Ervey, I full well understand what are your travails, but I am truly saddened that there is no joy in you, as once I recall there was. The gift of a child, even if in unfortunate circumstances, is a matter for rejoicing. *Sursum corda*: lift up your heart!'

He smiled, if not wholeheartedly, then thankfully. 'I will indeed, ma'am.'

The vespers bell began chiming. It was nearing five o'clock. Holland Park was but a mile away: he could call on Kat, and begin to prepare the ground. And he could return thence to Hanover Square before the evening invited too much intimacy.

He took his leave, and for all his earlier despair, he rode from Hammersmith with a heart that was indeed beginning to lift.

PART TWO

THE GATHERING STORM

VII

INDEFINITE LEAVE OF ABSENCE

Cape Colony, early September

The great paddle wheels began churning in the swell off Robben Island, whither the colony's worst miscreants were banished. The noise, like a giant blanket, smothered all conversation on deck.

Hervey braced himself to the vibration of the engines, which took a minute or so after firing to reach their full speed. The *Enterprise* had not had much recourse to them during the passage. The wind had been favourable. The engines' purpose, explained her captain, was to get them in and out of port against contrary airs (they would have been waiting at Gravesend, still, so strong had been the south-westerlies). The captain was very decided in his opinion, and although a man of scientific bent, he was certain that the wind would ever be the motive power of the high seas, for it failed only rarely, it was health-giving (no one, not even Peto, who was convinced there was more to steam than they saw at present, would laud a sulphurous chimney stack) – and it was free.

Hervey was gladdened by the sight of Table Mountain. It had been fifty-four days only – faster than he had first come out with *Leviathan*, but slower than his return home six months ago. The *Enterprise* would continue on to Calcutta in a day or so, another six weeks, perhaps, making the India passage in fourteen, a good month quicker than the rule, especially at this time of year before the south-west monsoon was come.

For a moment he wondered how he would feel if he were going on too, back to Bengal, to take command of the Eighty-first – had they been there and not Canada. Did he wish that they were? He had spent the better part of seven years in India. They had been extraordinary years, impossible to explain to any who had not set foot in that land. But it had been, as it were, a parade which was marking time, waiting interminably for some part of it (which he could not see) to come into line, and only thereafter the order 'Forward!'

And while they had been marking time in Bengal, the ranks had thinned. Some had fallen nobly, like the commanding officer, Sir Ivo Lankester (Kezia's husband), leading his men in battle. More – *many* more – had died of the cholera, or of any number of strange diseases which defied the surgeon's learning. Some had died by their own hand, to lie in everlasting dishonour in the suicides' corner of the cantonment cemetery. And yet, no matter how they met their end, they would all be but bones now – the ultimate comradeship of the regiment, of every one of the dragoons who had died with the colours in four continents:

Behold, I shew you a mystery;
We shall not all sleep, but we shall all be changed,
In a moment, in the twinkling of an eye, at the last trump:
For the trumpet shall sound, and the dead shall be raised
    incorruptible,
And we shall be changed.

And he wondered, as often he did, how, when the trumpet sounded, they would all be mustered.

No, he did not wish the Eighty-first were in India, for all the country's easy pleasures and the thrill of its warfare. He was glad – at least for the time being – that the regiment slept in their beds at Fort York. Canada would be a painful return for him, of course, the place of Georgiana's birth. But then, when he had told her, she had been animated by the prospect. And if Georgiana was content in going to the place whence her mother had marched for that fatal reunion, then he must be too – for all that it might remind him of a bliss too great.

For now, however, there were other things to disquiet him: *Sufficient unto the day is the evil thereof.* Before long, he would see Serjeant-Major Armstrong. And an evil it most certainly would be. He had tried to imagine how he would tell him of Caithlin; but there was nothing he could with confidence settle on.

The crew were shortening sail. The wind seemed to be a point or so east from south, but he always found it difficult to judge these things. And for all that Peto had attempted to instruct him in the science of sailing, in the setting and trimming of sails his old friend had merely shown him a mystery.

Yes: he had a high regard for the naval profession, even when it was made easy by steam engines and paddle wheels.

He cupped a hand to his mouth. '*Ngathi kuza kunetha*,' nodding to the threatening cloud.

Fairbrother screwed up his face and shook his head. The cloud was too high; it would not rain today – '*Akuzi kuna namhlanje!*' He clasped a hand to Hervey's shoulder, and then looked down at the water. '*Siyacothoza*.'

Hervey had to think before he could compose a worth-while reply: the ship was indeed running in slowly, but . . .

For six weeks his friend had instructed him daily in the language of the Xhosa. Hervey did not expect that he would stay long in the Colony (the troop had orders to return to England in the new year) but Somervile's letter had prompted him to acquire what in India they called a 'scouting tongue' – enough of the language to enquire the way ahead and what it held. In fact, Hervey had acquired rather more than the scout's portion: while he could hold no discursive conversation, his vocabulary was broader than the here and now. He had in fact found the language of the Xhosa, while not easy, surprisingly rich and subtle. He would have chosen to learn that of the Zulu instead, had there been the means; but the two were close enough, as he had discovered in the prelude to the affair at the Umtata River.

In another quarter of an hour the crew had taken in all but the topgallants as the *Enterprise* turned to larboard and, with the wind abeam and the cold Benguela Current no longer directly opposing her, picked up speed.

Hervey smiled to himself. How effortless this all was. How different it would have been aboard one of Peto's ships: all hands on deck, alternately making and shortening sail, the activity constant. And then they would have had to anchor out in the bay and come ashore by lighter, and boats would ply to and fro all day with supplies. Yet inside the hour, the *Enterprise* would moor in Cape Town, and they would descend by gangway to the quay. Here, most certainly, was the future. At least of merchant ships: he did not suppose you could make war with a paddle wheel.

'*Ubusika abufuni kumka,*' – winter does not want to go away – said Fairbrother, pulling his cloak closer about him.

Hervey nodded. He too felt the chill in the air. But it was *eyomSintsi*, the month when the coast coral tree flowered: summer was not so very far away. Indeed, as he took up his telescope to observe the landmarks of the Cape, there on the slopes of the Table Mountain he thought he could make out the yellows and whites of early spring. He took a deep breath, but it was the sea air only; there was nothing to be smelled of the land yet. He would never forget that first time, with Peto, when he had stood on the quarterdeck of *Nisus*, the fleetest of frigates, and the scent of Coromandel had drifted across the still, Indian waters.

Peto – would he ever venture with him again? No, it could never be. For his old friend was as much an invalid, now, as those of the lower-deck who limped and coughed their way about Greenwich. If ever there was a man with whom to hazard, and then to share a table, it was Peto. Long years at sea, in daily battle with elements that would overwhelm his wooden world if he were once to nod, and periodically with the King's enemies, who sought more particularly to destroy him, had made of Peto an officer in whom boldness and discretion were admirably combined. Fairbrother's brilliance was of an altogether different nature; and Somervile, although he would shoot tiger with him, as the saying went, was not a soldier or a fighting captain. Somervile was first a man of letters; his love of powder smoke was like that for tobacco, to be taken up or put down as occasion had it. Somervile was a good, and old, friend; Hervey looked forward eagerly to seeing him again. Doubtless there would be some beating up and down in Kaffraria (and he would be first to admit, from painful experience, that the warriors in that place could fight), but it would not be the same as India with Peto.

But if he had to keep his cloak tight closed now, it was indeed *eyomSintsi*, and with the flowering of the coral tree would come warmer weather. It would soon be the time to begin the mission to Shaka Zulu, before the summer's parching heat made the cattle thin and thirsty, and Xhosa and Zulu, and all the others of Kaffraria and Natal, in no humour to parley.

'Hervey! Capital, capital!' Sir Eyre Somervile, lieutenant-governor of the Cape Colony, rose from his desk to meet his old friend with outstretched hand.

Hervey took it, smiling. It was, indeed, good to see him, truly one of his most constant friends, his company ever enlivening. And he looked so much better than when he had seen him last. The spreading girth, the result, no doubt, of the ample table of the Court of Directors of the East India Company, and the scarce provision of exercise in the City, was very much reduced, and the claret-complexion was no longer so pronounced. In fact, he looked quite his old self of ten and more years ago, when first they had met in Madras. 'It has evidently been a lean winter!'

Somervile patted his stomach, convinced it was no

longer any handicap to exertion. 'Indeed, indeed. After the contest with those infernal Xhosa reivers I deemed it expedient to reduce my store. I trust I am campaigning fit!'

Hervey nodded. 'You have every appearance of it, I assure you.'

Somervile glanced over Hervey's shoulder, and seeing Fairbrother waiting, threw up his hands and made noisily for the door. 'My dear sir! Forgive me: come in; come in!'

They shook hands. And Hervey noticed how much less guarded was Fairbrother now. His manner was ever unhurried, in contrast to Somervile's, but before the two friends had gone to England, Fairbrother had always seemed watchful, almost resentful (if there could be resentment in languor). Perhaps his friend might at last recognize that the lieutenant-governor held him in nothing but the best of opinion.

'Good morning, Sir Eyre,' he replied, taking his hand freely.

'Now, are you just landed? I had not yet had word of a ship. And the fortunate Mrs Matthew Hervey, and Miss Georgiana Hervey: are they gone directly to the residence?'

Hervey tried not to look too uncomfortable. 'We came by the *Enterprise*, yes. Kezia and Georgiana remain in London, however. In the circumstances I thought it best. Fairbrother and I came at once when we were landed to let you know of our return, though I have a sad and urgent duty to perform elsewhere.'

'Oh? Sit you both down. Some coffee?'

'Thank you, yes.'

Somervile nodded to his clerk.

'Armstrong,' said Hervey, his voice lowered. 'Caithlin Armstrong died two months ago.'

The joy at once left Somervile's face. 'Oh, great gods!' he groaned. 'He was of most excellent bearing at the frontier, as I told you in my letter. I owe my life to him. It is as simple as that.'

Hervey shook his head slowly. 'These things . . .'

Somervile shook his head too. 'You know that if there is anything at all that I or Emma may do . . .'

Hervey nodded. 'Thank you.'

'The children – how many? – they are taken care of, I imagine?'

'They are. The quartermaster's wife, Mrs Lincoln – you remember?'

'How could I forget? Such a wedding.'

'There are five.'

'And what will Armstrong do, therefore?'

'Return at once to England. There's an Indiaman which leaves tomorrow. I have brought Sarn't-Major Collins with me to do duty instead.'

Somervile nodded. 'A capital fellow, too, as I recall.'

'I was half minded to have one of the serjeants stand

the duty, but if we are to take to the field I want a head such as Collins's with me.'

Somervile placed his hands together, as if to beg indulgence. 'It is not my business, but I might add that Serjeant Wainwright's conduct was as noble as the serjeant-major's.'

'So I read in your letter, and so I would have expected. Were he not so junior a serjeant, and were the troop to remain in its lines until we sail for home, I would give him the fourth stripes for the duration.'

A bearer brought coffee.

'Something fortifying to accompany it?' asked Somervile, glancing at one and then the other.

Hervey certainly felt the need of fortification, but he had resolved to face Armstrong with a clear mind and clear breath. He shook his head.

Fairbrother nodded to the offer of Cape brandy.

Hervey composed himself. 'What must I needs know this minute about your intentions for the frontier?' he asked, taking a good sip of his coffee before resting the cup and saucer in his lap. 'I would give preparatory orders to Brereton and Collins. It will be best that the troop is active as may be when Armstrong takes his leave of them.'

Somervile sighed heavily. 'Ye-es; *Brereton.*'

Hervey's brow furrowed.

'Forgive my civilian interference, Hervey, but it is my opinion that the peril which beset us at the frontier was the direct consequence of Brereton's incapability. And, I might add, his conduct in the face of the Xhosa stands poorly in comparison with Armstrong's and Wainwright's.'

If Hervey had had the least indignation at 'civilian interference' it was wholly dispelled by the knowledge of Somervile's own zeal in the field. His friend wore the same ribbon at his neck as he, and for deeds with sword and pistol, if twenty years ago. If his deeds frequently showed more impetuosity than true capability, it scarcely mattered here.

He glanced at Fairbrother, a touch uneasily, for this was regimental business of the most intimate kind. 'Are you saying that he wants courage?'

Somervile hesitated before replying. 'No, I am not. I saw nothing that could be construed *only* as want of courage.'

'It is true that he wants for experience. He himself was eager to come to the Cape to remedy that.'

'I believe I made due allowance on account of that. It is merely that . . . judgement is not exclusively a matter of experience. I fear that his instinct is faulty.'

Hervey raised his eyebrows, and sighed in his turn before draining his coffee cup. 'I shall observe him carefully. And speak to him. And to Armstrong.'

Somervile finished his brandy and held up his hands. 'It is, as I believe I have made clear, entirely your business, Hervey. I make no formal complaint.'

'Thank you.' Hervey laid aside his cup and saucer, and made as if to rise. 'And by way of a preparatory order?'

Somervile nodded. 'Very well. We leave for Port Natal in five days' time. There is the *Reliant* transport at hand, and a tow-steamer making repairs. Are you able to furnish fifty sabres?'

Hervey rose. 'I cannot say, for I have not been to the lines yet. But I should be dismayed if we could not. The *Reliant* is evidently big enough?'

'Serjeant-Major Armstrong believes so.'

'Then you may believe it.'

Somervile now rose. 'Dine with us this evening, Hervey. And you, Captain Fairbrother.'

'Thank you,' said Hervey, taking up his cap. 'But . . . May I first see what Armstrong wishes?'

Somervile frowned at his own insensibility. 'Of course, of course.'

The lieutenant-governor had bid one of his dogcarts come for them, and Hervey quit the Castle of Good Hope directly for E Troop lines, taking Fairbrother en route to his quarters near the Company's gardens. They made arrangements for the evening, and then Hervey steeled himself to his duty.

He had not had to do its like before. After Waterloo he had travelled to Norfolk to condole with the widow of his former troop leader, and lately commanding officer, Major Joseph Edmonds; and thence to Suffolk to give an account of the heroic death of his serjeant-escort, Strange, to his widow. But both women had known already of their loss. Some weeks indeed had elapsed between receipt of the news and his visiting, so that there was some measure of joy in being able to recount happy memories (and in the case of Mrs Strange he had been able to arrange for her to take charge of his father's school, a position she held still).

The lines were all activity when he arrived. It was late morning, the horses had been exercised, and the hour before the second feed was a time of making and mending. Hervey noted the improvements in the appearance of the lines, and not merely the new application of paint: the roofs were now well thatched, both barrack and stable, and the water troughs served by pipes rather than buckets. He would at least be able to commend Captain Brereton for his address in administration, though he had no doubt that the improvements would have been chiefly by Armstrong's efforts.

The picket corporal came doubling as the dogcart drew up. 'G'mornin, Col 'Ervey, sir!' he yapped as he halted at attention and jerked his right hand to the salute. 'Trust you's well, now, sir.'

Hervey smiled. Sad duty or no, it was therapeutic to be back with dragoons, especially dragoons under his orders. 'Wholly restored, Corporal Battle. But more to the point, how is E Troop?'

'Gradely, sir, gradely.'

'The sar'nt-major?'

'He were poorly for a bit after us fight wi' them Kaffirs, but 'e's in right fine fettle now, sir.'

Hervey saw 'Bugle' Roddis emerge purposefully from the orderly room to sound the midday watering call. Roddis had been a recruit when they came out to the Cape, but he was troop trumpeter now, since Corporal Dilke's death by the Zulu spear.

He watched him take post like a veteran. The man was not yet twenty, but he had been uncommonly steady in his first action; he had blown accurately when the lives of many had depended on it. And the dragoons had christened him, thus, 'Bugle', for the bugle rather than the trumpet was used for mounted calls on account of the carry of its extra octave.

The noon gun fired from the signal hill a mile to the north-west, though it sounded closer in the giant bowl that was Cape Town. Roddis began the call – by no means an easy one with its low 'G'.

Hervey had no great ear for music, but he knew the difference between a good and an indifferent call; and 'Bugle' sounded it well, with not once a cracked note. Here was efficiency, he marked with satisfaction. Somervile's strictures were not wholly deserved.

The troop mustered by divisions in front of their stable blocks.

'Parade state, Corporal Battle?'

It was not strictly the picket corporal's business to

have the morning parade states to hand, but Battle took out his notebook. 'Seventy-five rank and file on parade, sir, and six officers. Fourteen rank and file sick. Total ninety-five, sir.'

Hervey nodded. Not too bad a muster.

'Sixty-eight troop horses and five chargers fit for duty, sir. Thirteen troopers sick. Total eighty-one, sir.'

That number again: *eighty-one*! A world away from *Six* . . . 'Thirteen sick?' he forced himself to ask.

'Sir. Nought special, though.'

By which Hervey knew he meant nothing too life-threatening. 'End of winter . . . It could be worse. Thank you, Corporal Battle. Dismiss.'

'Sir!' Battle sprang back to attention and saluted with the same vigour as before.

Hervey returned the salute less formally, and smiled to himself. Battle, he knew, wanted his third stripes more than most dragoons wanted a drink after stand-down. It must daily go hard with him to have a man five years his junior – Wainwright – give him orders. But Battle, for all his cheeriness and capability, had liked a drop or two as a younger man, and occasionally a drop too many. And so the stitches of his single tapes – always a lonely and precarious badge of very limited authority – had been unpicked two or three times before finally he had mastered his temper long enough to gain a second, which substantive authority had then induced in him a determined ambition.

Watering was not a formal parade, more a count of heads. Every man knew his duty, which did not as a rule vary from day to day, and so there was no call for the snapping and barking which characterized the morning muster. It was an occasion for the officers to speak words of encouragement or impart news. They were not on parade, but attended by custom, and Hervey now saw the little group of lieutenants and cornets, and Captain the Honourable Stafford Brereton, come out of the orderly room. They were deep in confabulation.

And then from behind the nearest stable block appeared Armstrong, marching briskly in his direction. Hervey smiled. It amused him to think how, in the space of mere moments, Corporal Battle had found and alerted the serjeant-major to the return of the officer commanding. For a second or so it made easier what was to come.

Armstrong halted and saluted – sharp, but not the exaggerated manner of Battle's. 'Good afternoon, sir! Leave to carry on, sir, please!'

'Carry on, Sar'nt-Major,' said Hervey, nodding his greeting by return.

It was good to be able to say that again, knowing that this old NCO friend (of more years' close acquaintance than most officers now with the regiment) would carry on whatever that duty – like Bathsheba's husband, faithful unto death. Except that that was the least apt of comparisons, Bathsheba and Caithlin Armstrong, for Caithlin's life had been without blemish.

He shook himself: Brereton and the officers approached.

He returned their greetings with as easy an air as he could manage, though he found himself searching Brereton's face more intently than he might normally.

There were the usual exchanges, and then Brereton said, 'It is well that you are back, Colonel. We hear rumours of a campaign.'

'Not so much a campaign as an expedition,' replied Hervey, wondering if Brereton's tone revealed disquiet. And the honour 'Colonel' discomfited him, too. It was correct enough, in that he held the rank of acting lieutenant-colonel, but the rank came with his appointment to command of the Mounted Rifles, and thereafter the substantive rank would be with the infantry; he would not now, *rightly*, hear the honour on the lips of a dragoon.

But what was all this compared with the calamity that was about to befall Armstrong? From the corner of his eye he could see him, watching like a hawk as the dragoons dismissed to their watering duties. Armstrong was master of his world; and in a few minutes that world would be no more. He could hardly bear the thought of what he must do – like going to an old horse with a peck of corn in one hand and a pistol in the other.

'Brereton, I would speak quietly on a matter with the sar'nt-major, and then perhaps you would be good enough to join me in the officers' house?'

'Of course.'

Hervey left them and made his way to where Armstrong stood eyeing the farrier's struggle with one of the stallions, which needed twitching to take the tooth rasp.

'He's got his work cut out has Blackie Patch, sir.'

'Evidently so. A new entry?'

'Ay, sir. Bought from Eerste River not long after you went back. Not what *I* would have fetched, but . . .'

'Mm. Sarn't-major, can we walk? There is something I would tell you.'

'Of course, sir. The mission in Zulu-land?'

Evidently the sar'nt-major was more comfortable with the notion than was Brereton, but that was neither here nor there. 'That, yes, and . . .'

They walked via the huttings towards the parade ground.

'By the way, sir, we saw the notice in *The Times*. We're all very glad for you and Mrs Hervey.' He said it in a tone at once respectful and brotherly.

Hervey had to swallow hard. 'Thank you, Sar'nt-Major. It is most thoughtful.'

'And did you see my bonny lass at Hounslow, sir?'

He could hardly speak the words. 'I did.'

'Ay, well, just another few months . . .'

Hervey stopped, and turned to him. 'Geordie, there's . . .'

'Sir?'

172

He took a breath as though he would dive deep in a pool. 'Caithlin . . . Caithlin is dead.'

Armstrong started like a man struck by a ball.

Hervey steadied him with a hand to the shoulder. 'Come, I'll tell you all.'

'Them bairns . . . them poor bairns.'

'Don't distress yourself on that count, Geordie. Quartermaster and Mrs Lincoln have them fine.'

'Ay, sir, but . . .'

Hervey knew the 'but' well enough.

They sat on a bench at the edge of the parade ground, and Hervey told him all that he knew. Caithlin had fallen – the merest thing, but a poisoning of the blood had resulted. There had been the seemliest of funerals – with all the proper Catholic rites, and a bishop, no less, and the whole regiment willingly on parade. And the children wanted for nothing – well, nothing that could be provided for them; some of the dragoons had even been fashioning toys and the like.

But instead of reassurance, with each word Armstrong appeared diminished, like a doll whose stuffing was picked from it bit by bit. In twenty years (for it was two decades since the greenhorn cornet had first encountered this pocket Atlas from the Tyne), Hervey had never seen Armstrong thus.

'Them bairns,' he repeated, shaking his head. 'An' my lass.'

Hervey stole a glance: a tear dropped from

Armstrong's right eye, and then another began running down his left cheek. The serjeant-major was a man defeated; and Hervey felt suddenly as helpless.

They sat in silence a good while.

At length Armstrong made to rise. 'I'd better gan a yon stables,' he said, with a resignation that sounded neither convinced nor convincing, wiping his eyes with his sleeve. 'Feed off, an' all.'

'There's no need of that,' said Hervey, putting a hand to Armstrong's forearm to stay him. He cleared his throat for the next part, which he knew would be every bit as painful to his comrade as it might be welcome. 'Geordie, there's a ship leaving for Falmouth tomorrow, and I've arranged passage for you. Indefinite leave of absence.'

There was only silence.

Hervey tried again in a minute or so. 'The troop'll be returning to Hounslow in the new year. Just routine. Even Battle could arrange things.'

Armstrong continued to gaze into the distance. 'And what about this affair with the Zulu?'

Hervey took another deep breath. 'Geordie, I've brought Jack Collins back with me.'

The informality – familiarity, indeed – of the absence of rank would have surprised many (dismayed them, perhaps); but these were circumstances wholly without the ordinary. For the circumstances were a suspension of natural justice. A man who placed his life at the service of the nation might well make a widow, but for a much younger wife to die of a fall, and five children to be made half-orphans (and to Armstrong's mind, orphaned of the better half) – that was not how it ought to be.

'Jack Collins taking my troop...' He sighed, shaking his head.

'Only until we return to Hounslow. I would not have done it were there not this expedition to the Zulu.'

Armstrong rose, slowly but resolutely. 'Well, I suppose I'd better go and tell 'im what's what.'

Hervey rose, too, and replaced his forage cap. 'I'd like you to come and stay at the castle tonight. Easier for the ship tomorrow.'

Armstrong thought for a moment, and then shook his head. 'No, sir; that's not the way. I'll have my work cut out handing things over to Collins. And I'll take my leave prop'ly – at muster tomorrow.'

The lump in Hervey's throat grew so large that his reply was inaudible.

VIII

AMOUR EN GUERRE

Later

At five o'clock, Hervey went wearily to his quarters in the castle. He could have – ought perhaps to have – dined with the troop officers and stayed in the lines, but his need of retreat took precedence. And there was, after all, the business of the Zulu to discuss.

In driving back he had passed the house which he had engaged as his married quarters, a pleasant place with its window boxes in spring bloom. Tomorrow he would have to go and find the owner, and surrender the lease – and he had cursed at the need to do so, and wondered if he ought to have done more to persuade Kezia; or, indeed, brought Georgiana by herself, and a governess. But the days before his leaving London had been full of affairs, with little time for thinking. Even when he thought he might have half a morning or a part of an afternoon to spare, he had invariably found himself detained at Hounslow on regimental business, or in seeing to Caithlin Armstrong and her children. Kat he saw but once more after that Hammersmith evening, at a drawing room. He had even had to send word to Sister Maria, deferring another meeting until his return from the Cape, so that her counsel had been left, so to speak, in the air. The turning of the paddle wheels at Gravesend had been a welcome thing.

He found Private Johnson in the servant's room, saddle-soaping the leather that had hung unused since March.

''Allo, sir,' tried Johnson, cheerily.

Hervey nodded.

'It's not bad at all – only a bit o' mildew 'ere and there. Tea, sir?'

'Yes, please . . . if you would.'

Hervey went back into his sitting room, sank down into the low armchair next to the unlit fire, and closed his eyes.

In barracks, Johnson served tea in one of two ways: on a tray, with linen and silver, and the china which Henrietta had bought; or in an enamelled mug. His choice depended on what was convenient to him, and his perception of Hervey's indifference. This afternoon – or evening, for the light was fast failing – he was in no doubt, and he returned with a steaming mug of the strongest brew.

'Si-ir.'

Hervey opened his eyes, smiled gratefully and took it.

''Ow was Eli, sir, an' Molly?'

'The veterinarian says they're well. I'm afraid I had not the heart to go in.'

''E's a good'n is young Toyne.'

'He is.' Private Toyne had looked after the chargers while they were gone.

Johnson had brought in the second spare bridle, and he now resumed his saddle-soaping.

It was, perhaps, a strange place to be cleaning leather, but Hervey was glad of it, for the smell of saddle soap was always pleasing, and the company welcome.

There was a few moments' silence, and then Johnson put the question he really wanted to ask. ''Ow were t'serjeant-major, sir?'

Hervey sighed, took a big sip of his tea again, and then rested the mug on his foreleg. 'I never saw a man so broken by anything, I said. Nor, I believe, any man so broken by ill news.'

'Will 'e be gooin back?'

'Yes. Tomorrow. And it's as well that I brought Collins. The sar'nt-major was dismayed at first – the thought of handing over the troop to another – but it couldn't be to a better man, and he said as much. And Collins will keep watch tonight, which I admit was occupying me rather. I wish there were someone to go back with him; it will be a hard thing to make that passage with no one to speak to.'

'Mebbe 'e's better off by 'imself,' said Johnson,

reattaching the reins to the snaffle he had been polishing. 'Don't reckon ah'd be wantin anybody, and ah'm not a serjeant-major.'

Hervey nodded: perhaps Johnson was right. 'Well, let us pray it is so.' He took another sip, and frowned. 'I don't complain, but this is uncommonly strong.'

'Ah thought ah'd make thee a good mashin', sir, but a'may've put in a bit too much. It's gunpowder ah foraged from Mrs Somervile's.'

Hervey smiled resignedly. He had long given up teaching Johnson correct form. What did it matter if no one were accorded their title: there would always be tea. 'Johnson, would you send word to Captain Fairbrother to come at eight? And I would sleep for an hour, and then write a letter for tomorrow's sailing . . . and then a bath, if you will.'

'Right, sir.' Johnson looked suddenly contented. He *was* contented, for the uncertainty that was his position in Hervey's new domestic establishment (he was sure that Kezia would give him his *congé*, as the officers called it) was several thousand miles behind them. The old routine was returned.

Fairbrother came carefully upon his hour. They drank whiskey brought with them from London, and Hervey listened while his friend recounted the intelligence he had gained in an afternoon with his barber – and with his housekeeper, M'ma Anke.

M'ma Anke: she was round, her thick curls were white and she walked with a rolling motion, but somehow she combined the qualities of mother, aunt, sister and housemaid in ideal proportion. How fortunate his friend was in having such a good soul as she to keep house! When Hervey had first called on Fairbrother's little establishment by the Company's gardens, he had formed the distinct impression that without her, his friend would rarely have bestirred himself, content as he seemed to spend his day with books and wine, living comfortably on bank drafts from Jamaica in exchange for a very modest effort in commerce. Indeed, if the man whom Somervile had superseded, Lord Charles Somerset, had not recommended Fairbrother's employment as guide-interpreter (although Fairbrother was convinced of the governor's contempt for him, and therefore reciprocated the supposed emotion), then Hervey would have turned on his heels early, dismissing him as a mere idler, jealous in honour, too sudden and quick in quarrel. It had been M'ma Anke's evident regard that had made it otherwise. Hervey had much to thank her for. His life, in truth, for if Fairbrother had not been with him at the frontier, the Xhosa would have had the better of him. He was certain of it.

The talk on the Rialto, said Fairbrother, greatly warming to both his whiskey and his role of intelligencer, was of the new governor and the necessary, or rather, unnecessary expense that such an august figure as Sir

Lowry Cole would occasion them: a military man such as he would expect to see an impressive order of battle. While Somervile, it seemed, was held in some regard for his economies. The talk in the bazaars, on the other hand, was of Somervile's repressive new restrictions on the control of powder, too much of which was being sold to the Kaffirs in an unregulated fashion (as well as much grumbling about taxing Malays whose income was in excess of fifteen shillings a week).

Hervey drew the same conclusion as his friend, that the situation of the colony was unremarkable.

The one thing that surprised him was the evident absence of anxiety with regard to the eastern frontier and the Zulu beyond, and he could only suppose that Somervile was in possession of very particular and secret intelligence which impelled him to his mission, and their early recall.

The sentry at the steps of the residence, a mere stroll across the courtyard from Hervey's quarters, presented arms as they approached. The garrison battalion, the 55th (Westmoreland) Regiment of Foot, had been accorded the privilege of mounting single rather than the usual double sentries for the castle guard. Somervile had been much moved by the reports of their steadiness at the battle at Umtata River, the first occasion since Waterloo (by common reckoning) that one of His Majesty's battalions of infantry had formed square in the face of the enemy. 'In square my battalion could not be broken,' their commanding officer had said when asked if they should give battle at the ford; 'and in line it could not be resisted.'

Chief Matiwane's Zulu had come on that square like a great wave upon a beach, falling to the Fifty-fifth's disciplined volleys, or impaling themselves upon their bayonets, until the Westmorelands' colonel judged it the moment to turn the tide. Extending then into the line which could not be resisted, they had driven Matiwane's warriors back across the river, and with renewed volleying finally put them to headlong flight. Hervey could picture it as if yesterday. How he had cheered the legionary infantry, where only a day or so before he had come to think them of little or no use in this country except for close garrisons and parades!

He returned the salute smartly.

Inside the residence, candles and lamps burned bright. Jaswant, the khansamah, and others of the Somerviles' Indian servants, as well as black faces, were got up in reds and blues, as if for a levee.

'Good evening, Colonel sahib!'

Hervey smiled by return, and gave his hat to a khitmagar. 'Good evening, Jaswant. How good it is to be back, and to see you.'

'Mehrbani, Colonel sahib,' replied Jaswant, bowing. 'And good evening also to you, Captain Fairbrother sahib.'

Fairbrother returned the salutations with rather more ease than he had formerly been disposed to.

'There are others to dine?' asked Hervey, nodding to the finery. He had expected it to be just the four of them.

'Sahib. Colonel Bird and his lady are here, and Major Dundas, and Colonel Mill. And Colonel Smith and his lady.'

The names he was well acquainted with (Bird the colonial secretary, Dundas the military secretary, Mill the Fifty-fifth's colonel), except the one. 'Colonel Smith?'

'He is new deputy quartermaster-general, Colonel sahib.'

'General Bourke, and Colonel Somerset – are they not here, too?'

'General Bourke-sahib is gone home to England for leave, Colonel sahib, and Colonel Somerset-sahib is being in Graham's-town.'

That was pleasing to Hervey's ear. He held Bourke in due regard, but the presence of the general officer commanding would always tend to circumscribe conversation with his old friend the lieutenant-governor, for all that Somervile did not feel himself obliged to observe the usual distinctions of rank. And although after Umtata there was a certain respect between Colonel the Honourable Henry Somerset (the former governor's son), commander of the eastern frontier, and he, Hervey would not yet choose his company without necessity.

'We had better go in,' he said to Fairbrother. 'Say nothing of the Shaka mission unless Somervile first makes mention.'

'Of course, Colonel sahib.'

Hervey pulled a face.

Jaswant announced them, not to the room but to Lady Somervile, who was standing talking to Colonel Mill, splendid in the scarlet coatee of the 55th Westmoreland, with its distinctive dark green facings.

Emma turned, all smiles.

Hervey at once forgot his cares. He had known Emma for as long as he had known Somervile, since before the two were married. He supposed he might tell her anything. He supposed he might spend any amount of time in her company without regret. She had a keen mind. She was a most pleasing-looking woman, not yet Kat's age (for all he knew, she was his junior; it was just that he had always found her sensibility superior to his), and the fierce Indies sun, and now that of the Cape, had served only to increase her attraction rather than wreak its more usual havoc. She had kept her figure, too, in spite of children and her husband's inclination to the pleasures of the table. And, ever important, she enjoyed his, Hervey's, company in like degree. He kissed her, smiling broader than he had since leaving England.

Fairbrother bowed.

'How delighted I am to see you returned – *both* of you.'

'Eyre's letter was most persuasive.' Hervey's smile was now mock rueful.

'I hope it did not suspend any pleasure that cannot be recovered,' said Emma, her look now mock indignant.

'I am certain it has not.'

She turned to the Fifty-fifth's colonel. 'You are all three well acquainted, so I have read.'

'Indeed we are, Lady Somervile,' said Colonel Mill, bowing in return to Hervey.

'The fellowship of black powder?'

They all shared her smile.

'Eyre would give anything to be admitted a full member,' she said, shaking her head. 'I am certain of it. He is increasingly fretful at office.'

As a rule, Emma Somervile gave nothing away except to those she counted the surest of friends. Hervey detected more than jest in the remark, and so concluded that Colonel Mill had gained the Castle's confidence. And he was glad of it, for Mill was an officer of un-impeachable fighting record – the West Indies, the Peninsula, Waterloo; and now Umtata.

'I should have thought the recent affair at the frontier enough to satisfy anyone, at least for a while,' said the Fifty-fifth's colonel, looking like a man who considered such things occupational hazards rather than sport.

Emma sighed. 'I fear it has merely whetted his appetite.'

A khitmagar advanced with a tray of champagne.

As Hervey took a glass, Emma turned to him, confidentially. 'I am so very sorry to hear about poor Caithlin Armstrong. Most distressed, indeed. The loveliest of people. And the serjeant-major . . . You have told him by now, I suppose?'

Hervey nodded.

'I simply cannot imagine what will now be the fate of those children. Shall they go back to Ireland, do you think?'

Hervey's sigh echoed Emma's. 'I don't know. For the time being the Lincolns – you remember? – have charge of them, but I fancy it can't be too long an arrangement. The elder boy will go to the Duke of York's school, and the second one in a year or so. The girls . . .' (he shook his head) 'Armstrong has no family.'

'Shall he have to leave the service?'

Hervey's eyebrows rose. 'Great heavens, I hope not. The service is exactly what he needs to bind himself to after such a thing!'

Emma was a little taken aback at Hervey's surprise, for he himself had quit the service in like circumstances (not that it was a course she approved of). 'Well, he is fortunate in having such friends as the Lincolns. And, I might add, you.'

Hervey swallowed. What friend might he be in Canada with the Eighty-first?

'And now,' said Emma resolutely, squeezing his arm, 'I must introduce you to our new arrivals.'

'Colonel Smith?'

'And his most intriguing wife!'

But Emma's guests scarcely needed introduction. Although 'Smith' was a commonplace of the Army List, and Hervey had not seen the colonel's lantern-jaw in many a year (and certainly not since Waterloo), he would have known him anywhere. As for the arresting Latin features of Mrs Smith, a Peninsula-bride of just fifteen, his acquaintance was entirely by repute. But everyone in the army knew Harry and Juana Smith.

'May I introduce Colonel Hervey, who commands the Cape Mounted Rifles,' said Emma.

The colonels bowed, and Mrs Smith curtsied.

'Hervey, I fancy we must have met?' said Colonel Smith confidently.

'We have. I think at the Bidassoa.'

Colonel Smith was perhaps half a dozen years Hervey's senior, and wore the dark green of the 95th Rifles, in which corps he had risen largely by field promotion in the thick of the fighting in the Peninsula and the two Americas. 'I fancy it must have been,' he replied. And then, breaking into a wry smile, added, 'You, however, would have kept your feet dry, I imagine?'

The army had crossed many rivers in Spain, but the Bidassoa had been a considerable splash. 'I imagine I did,' conceded Hervey, content on this occasion to allow the infantry its customary sense of superiority in bearing privations.

But Colonel Smith was no conformist in that regard. 'I read of your exploits of late at Badajoz. An extraordinary business.'

'You could call it so, yes. I had not thought to see the inside of that place again.'

'Indeed.' Colonel Smith turned to his wife. 'My dear, Colonel Hervey was made captive by Miguel's men last year, and had to cut his way out of the castle.'

Juana gave a little gasp. '*Madre mia!* You must tell me of it, Colonel.'

Emma was quick to oblige. 'I have placed you together at table, my dear Mrs Smith. Colonel Hervey will be able to tell you all. It is, in truth, a most thrilling story!'

The Somerviles were yet maintaining their Indian habit, observed Hervey as they went into dinner. On the table were grapes and jujubes, pawpaw, oranges peeled and dusted with ginger, finger-lengths of sugar cane, and slices of coconut and Bombay mango. It troubled some, he knew – Kezia was one of them – to begin a dinner with such sweet things, but in truth he was never much bothered with the precise progression of tastes. He recognized, certainly, the culinarian art when at its highest, but he did not fret for the want of it. Indeed, a dinner had to be of the most pronounced indifference – the meat rank, perhaps, the side dishes salty as sea, the bread very stale, and the sauces utterly congealed – before he would admit any remark. How might it be otherwise after years at Shrewsbury and then on campaign?

'And so were you long kept in Badajoz, Colonel?' asked Juana, her accent in large part gone but still with the exaggerated aspirates of her native tongue.

'A few weeks, ma'am. Not long, but it seemed longer.'

She shook her head sympathetically. 'It is a *place formidable.*'

Hervey did not feel much inclined to speak of his own discomfort at Badajoz, but knew he must be patient with one so well acquainted with the fortress-town. 'It was all a most distressing affair, concerning as it did two former allies.'

'Oh, but I trust not just *former* allies,' said Juana, raising her eyebrows as she took a pleasurable sip of Sauternes, which was chilled so much as to bring a mist about the glass.

Indeed, Hervey was not sure if she raised her eyebrows at his remark or the wine, but he would say 'amen' to her optimism. Perhaps it was for this reason that the Duke of Wellington, as soon as his new office had given him the power to do so, had recalled the force of intervention which Mr Canning had sent to Portugal the better part of two years ago, for trying to secure a peace between the two factions was as likely to end in the alienation of the victorious party as in earning its gratitude. And whatever the outcome of the Portuguese imbroglio, Spain would not be unmoved. 'Let us say that I should not like to have the Spanish *guerrilleros* on any side but my own!'

Juana appeared to study him for a moment. 'You do know, Colonel, that I too am Spanish?'

'Indeed I do, ma'am.'

'And I claim a connection with Badajoz, for it was there that I met my husband.'

Hervey smiled. He had wondered when, and quite how, it would out. 'Madam, I do not believe there is an officer in the old Peninsular army, nor many a private man either, that does not know of the circumstances of your meeting.'

Juana returned the smile. 'You flatter us, Colonel Hervey. But tell me, were you at Badajoz – at the time of the siege?'

Hervey nodded, gravely. 'I was. And – I speak plainly – I was never more proud of the bravery of our troops, nor yet so grieved by their conduct afterwards. I fancy you do not like to recall it much, either. An infamous episode.'

He decided, however, that he would tell her the whole story of his part in the siege a decade and a half ago, and its 'Androclean' outcome but eighteen months ago.

She listened, rapt. He told her how he had followed the storming divisions through the breaches and over the walls, how every regiment seemed to be without its officers, who had fallen in the van of the assault, and how some diabolic blood-lust then overcame those men, so that they fell upon the town and its wretched people like wild beasts. He told her how he had had to shoot a Connaught soldier who had despoiled a girl and slit her throat and had then tried to kill him, and how last year, when he had been taken prisoner in the confusion of the incipient civil war in Portugal, he had escaped from the fortress of Badajoz by the help of that very girl's father.

He related all this knowing, too, that Juana's own rescue had been scarcely less dramatic. The protecting arms of a captain of Rifles, as Harry Smith then was, must indeed have been welcome, and marriage to him, within days, sweet. Well, it was *amour courtois; amour en guerre*. Except that seeing Juana and Harry Smith now, the looks between them, their mutual ease, it was evident that what might at first have been *mariage urgent*, was now a marriage of the very deepest affection. And he was at once both warmed and discomfited by it.

After a plate of ackee, which neither of them had tasted before, Hervey turned to the wife of Colonel Bird, the colonial secretary. They were not unacquainted. He liked Bird, a shrewd and gentle man, to whom Colonel Somerset had frequently taken an open dislike (it was said partly on account of Bird's being a Catholic).

Mrs Bird, a woman in her fifties, and of maternal disposition, laid a hand on his forearm. 'I am sorry Mrs Hervey was unable to accompany you, Colonel. Her society would have been most welcome, especially now that Lady Somervile is to leave.'

Hervey smiled indulgently. He understood how Mrs Bird must find Cape society somewhat confined and unvarying. In Bengal it had been different: although there the conventions were perhaps a good deal stricter, the society itself was also a good deal larger. 'I am afraid the fault is all mine, ma'am. My return here was somewhat precipitate, and it was not expedient for my wife – or indeed my daughter – to sail with me. And, you may know, my own assignment here with the Cape Rifles, and my troop of dragoons, will come to an end in the new year. So I am afraid it would not serve for them to make the passage at all, now.'

'Well, my dear Colonel Hervey, I shall pray that you are all three restored to each other soon and in perfect health. Bird and I have had the great good fortune to spend the better part of our days in each other's company. It does not do, you know, to become too accustomed to these absences, although it is of course the lot of any of my sex that marries a soldier.'

Hervey shifted awkwardly in his chair at the marital contentment on his either hand. He might have replied to Mrs Bird that it was the determination to accompany her husband that had killed his first wife, but he could not be so cruel (to her nor himself). 'Just so, ma'am,' he replied softly, instead.

'And what do you do then, on return to England, Colonel?'

He brightened at the opportunity to change the

subject, before realizing he would be giving further evidence of marital imprudence. 'I go to the Levant, to observe the war with Turkey.' And then, as if a plea in mitigation, he added, 'But I do not suppose the war will last beyond the spring.'

Mrs Bird nodded, and smiled understandingly. 'You are a young man, Colonel Hervey; you need to hear the sound of the guns. Bird was long ago reconciled to his calling with the quill.'

After two curry dishes (fish and mutton), a *bêche de mer*, a savoury of guinea-fowl, Constantia wines of very fine vintage, and easy conversation, the ladies retired and the officers congregated at the head of the table. Port and brandy were brought, and then Jaswant ushered out the khitmagars and the Hottentots.

'Well,' began Somervile, lighting a cigar with the silver grenade which Jaswant had placed on the table before himself retiring. 'This is a most felicitous gathering.'

Hervey fancied he knew precisely what his old friend meant. General Bourke was absent on leave, and Colonel Somerset was absent on duty. There was therefore no impediment to his gathering together those he could trust for, if not exactly a council of *war*, then a council of something most hazardous. He supposed that Somervile might have had qualms about the presence of Colonel Smith, an upright, professional officer whose responsibilities as deputy quartermaster-general at the Cape would have him look to Bourke, the general officer commanding, rather than to the lieutenant-governor. Indeed, as the general's chief of staff, Colonel Smith was in a position to refuse all military assistance to the venture, and it occurred to Hervey that the Shakan conception might well be stillborn this very evening. He shrugged, pushed his chair back to extend his legs, and lit a cheroot.

Somervile, having sent a small cloud of cigar smoke ceilingwards, gestured with his glass to the colonial secretary. 'Colonel, will you be good enough to tell these gallant officers assembled what it is that you and I have contemplated these past weeks – the cause of it, I mean.'

Colonel Bird, sitting erect and with neither cigar nor glass to hand, bowed. 'I will, Sir Eyre,' he replied, crisply. 'Gentlemen,' (he glanced at each in turn) 'I first came to the Cape in eighteen hundred and seven, and in every year since then there has been trouble with the Kaffirs in the eastern settlements. Not ten years ago there was a most savage, if mercifully short, war – there is no other word to describe it – with the Xhosa. As a result of which the frontier was more thoroughly delineated, and to the advantage of peace. For a year or two the frontier was indeed quite settled, but it has of late – as I hardly need tell you – been troublesome.'

Somervile interjected by waving his cigar at the assemblage. 'For which I will admit that the land grants in the Eastern Cape have been part cause. The settlers there in late years have too frequently been of a low sort; they have not abided by the terms of the grants, and there's cattle beyond the Great Fish River, where there should be none.'

'Just so,' said Colonel Bird, nodding slowly but emphatically. 'The presence of cattle at the frontier, though no justification for the Xhosa raids of course, is a definite cause of the nuisance. Now, if I may address what might be the perfectly reasonable deduction that if we enforce the terms of the land grants, and rid the frontier of cattle, we will eliminate the Xhosa threat . . . Firstly, such a course would be difficult in the extreme. I do not say that it cannot, or should not, be done, but it would bring the government here in Cape-town into a most invidious and possibly bloody quarrel with the colonists – on whom we rely for militia service, I need hardly add. It would be bound to exacerbate, too, the already brittle relations with the burghers.'

Somervile thrust his cigar out again. 'And the whole Dutch question is of course one that must constantly exercise the government here.'

'The second reason,' (Colonel Bird's tone of voice changed to suggest something more discursive) 'is that it might be argued that the terms of the land grants were too restrictive in the first instance. Parliament cannot on the one hand encourage emigration to those wild parts, and on the other restrict the means of subsistence. It is the considered opinion of the lieutenant-governor that the terms are contrary to natural justice, and that they must soon be formally set aside.'

'It is,' echoed Somervile. 'And although I cannot of course speak for Sir Lowry Cole, I confidently expect that very shortly I shall receive authorization from the War and Colonies Office to rescind the terms.'

Hervey took another sip of his brandy. It seemed to him only right that a farmer be allowed to decide for himself what best to do with his land. But what was the object of all this? It appeared that Somervile intended a course which would bring the Xhosa to a fight. Did he wish to enlist Shaka's support?

Somervile suddenly struck the table with his hand. 'Now, to the meat of the matter! It is my opinion, formed of the no little intelligence received, and' (he smiled) 'personal reconnaissance, that the cattle reiving is what I might call a constabulary affair – of no great moment, though undeniably vexing. It poses no threat to the general peace, nor is it necessarily prelude to hostilities of the kind Colonel Bird describes of ten years ago. No, gentlemen, that is not where the threat to the King's peace lies. It lies further east, towards Natal, and with the ambition of Shaka. *He* is the true cause of the unrest in Kaffraria.'

And for close on an hour, Somervile expounded on his 'colonial stratagem', and his design for the embassy to King Shaka Zulu.

IX

A GOOD JUDGE OF HORSEFLESH

Next morning

A fresh south-easterly was whipping up a swell as Serjeant-Major Armstrong descended to the lighter waiting to take him to the East Indiaman *Surat*. In this wind, she would get out of the bay without a steam tug, and with not too much work with canvas. Hervey was glad of it; a laboured farewell would be yet another trial for his old NCO friend.

Armstrong turned to look back one more time. Hervey touched the peak of his forage cap, and then Armstrong braced himself, and set his eyes resolutely to seaward, as the lighter cast off.

Hervey watched until it rounded *Surat*'s stern, and out of sight, before turning back for the castle.

Colonel Smith was standing a few feet away.

Hervey saluted in the gentlemanlike manner of

officers of the same rank – not so very different from the way he had said farewell to Armstrong.

Colonel Smith returned the salute, and inclined his head. 'Tell me, Hervey; I am intrigued.'

'My serjeant-major. His wife died when I was in England.'

'Your bringing him to his ship tells me much.'

'We have been in the same troop since I was a cornet.'

Colonel Smith nodded.

'And you?'

'To say farewell to a King's messenger, an old friend.'

'Ah, yes; he was in the lighter too.'

Colonel Smith hesitated. 'What do you do now?'

'I . . . I think I shall probably go and see what maps there are in the castle. Of Natal, and the Zulus' country.'

Colonel Smith was a severe-looking man, but his face softened just perceptibly. 'I am going to a stud near Eerste River to see a saddle horse. If you would spare me the time, Hervey, I should esteem your advice – a second eye and such like. And there are certain matters touching on what the lieutenant-governor spoke of last night. I would likewise have your opinion.'

Hervey scarcely needed to consider it: the diversion would be welcome. 'I shall be glad to. But I will join you there, if I may. I must first see Edward Fairbrother on a pressing matter.'

* * *

The pressing matter was the extension of Fairbrother's commission, his accompanying them to Shaka's country. It was concluded with more despatch than Hervey had expected, however, for Fairbrother said at once that he wished to remain with the Rifles until his 'good friend' returned finally to England. Hervey was much touched by the gesture. Indeed, he was touched and surprised. They had spoken only a little of his serving on during the voyage south. He had supposed that Fairbrother's attachment to soldiery would not long survive their return to Cape Town, for he knew there was much-neglected business of his father's to attend to. He had asked him, just the once, if he would consider coming to Canada with him, but his friend had all but scoffed at the notion. But now (and this much Hervey found characteristic of his contrariness), Fairbrother expressed himself surprised that his friend had doubted he would want to ride east with him.

And so Hervey was able thence to ride to Eerste River, fifteen miles or so east of Cape Town, by the mid-morning, and in good spirits, arriving at the stud farm not long after Colonel Smith himself.

The farm was well set up. There were some handsome buildings, all of one storey, whitewashed, with the distinctive Cape Dutch gables. The fences were solid, straight, pleasing as well as serviceable. And beyond was pasture as green as he would find in his own corner of Wiltshire. Here was a place to foal remounts.

Colonel Smith was admiring a good-looking blood.

'A handsome fellow,' said Hervey, coming up on them unseen.

'Indeed, Hervey, but we would say in the Rifle Brigade that handsome is as handsome does.'

'A phrase I have myself used. A blood might be needless fire, and an entire altogether too . . .'

'I thought the same.'

The breeder became anxious. 'I have another, three-quarter bred,' he tried, his English thick with the accent of Cape Dutch. 'A gelding. I will have him brung, sir. And I have any number of Cape horses.'

Colonel Smith said he was obliged. 'You know these Capers, Hervey?'

Hervey told him how they had lost so many troopers to the *perdesiekt* when they arrived that they had been forced to buy Capers, though not from this breeder. 'There's much to be said for them, since they're salted.'

'How so?'

'In truth I can't say. They haven't all had the sickness. Our veterinarian, an excellent, scientific man, believes it to be some sort of . . . immunity, so to speak, passed from dam to foal. In the blood.'

Colonel Smith looked at him cautiously. 'Very well, Hervey, since you are a colonel of mounted rifles and I merely of the pedestrian variety, perhaps you will tell me what it is that *you* look for in a horse.'

Hervey checked himself for a moment. Colonel Smith

bantered with him, but a man did not lightly admit himself the inferior judge of horseflesh. 'You will know as I that a chain is but as strong as its weakest link, and it is that link which I always endeavour to discover. Mind, if a chain is not tested to the utmost, that link may not fail. Do you intend working the horse hard?'

'I do not see my duties especially requiring it.'

Hervey nodded. 'It's as well to determine these things first.'

One of the breeder's men trotted up the three-quarter bred, a second man behind it with a whip.

'A handsome gelding, Kuyper,' agreed Colonel Smith. 'And he moves well.'

Hervey recollected himself again, for if it were the old trick (and he felt sure it was) it would not do to suggest that his companion fell for it too easily. 'I think we might see how he goes at the walk.'

The breeder bid his men do so, sounding a little piqued.

'I thought it was the *trot* which revealed the most in a faulty action,' said Colonel Smith, but quietly.

'I don't dispute it,' replied Hervey, likewise lowering his voice (the breeder stood closer than he ought). 'But I doubt the action is true. There'll be a severe bit in his mouth, and the whip cracking behind makes him go forward, and the leader then checks him sharply, so the animal's knees go up because his progress is arrested and the impulse is all from behind.'

The leader walked the gelding up to them, and then away again.

'He looks to me straight and level, Hervey,' said Colonel Smith, doubtful.

'I've seen many worse. Yet to me the action is not free enough. He raises his knee too much. And see how he winds his foot. A horse with such an action tires early, and is prone to stumbling. And – here's the thing – I'm certain it's not his *natural* action.'

Colonel Smith frowned. 'How so? There's no whip behind him now.'

'I'll warrant that if we see inside yonder stable there'll be a set of heavy shoes taken off this morning, and a couple of shot-bags which have been fastened round his fetlocks.'

'Ah.'

'And quite probably for no good cause, for the horse to me does not look as if he should be otherwise excessively flat.'

'Then we ought to leave at once; find another dealer,' said Colonel Smith decidedly.

Hervey shook his head. 'It doesn't follow that his horses are unsound. He'll have learned the English like a showy action, and that's what he's producing. Neither may he know exactly – strange to say – that it's not how high a horse picks his feet up which causes him to stumble, but how he places them *down*. Let us see his Capers.'

To the breeder's evident disappointment they dismissed

the gelding and asked to see instead his *Boerperds* (which would command only half the price of the bloods).

Five minutes later he brought out half a dozen, in-hand, all much the same to look at in height and general conformation. The Hottentot stable-lads began walking them and then trotting in a large circle about the manège.

'You see, they all move true,' said Hervey after studying them a minute or so. 'No bridle, just a halter – no tricks.'

'But rather slighter than I had imagined for myself,' replied Colonel Smith, in a way that suggested he agreed but with some reluctance still. 'You think them up to weight?'

'Try the grey,' said Hervey (the mare with pronounced iron dappling looked the most active of the bunch). 'I fancy you would weigh in at fourteen stone' (he meant with saddle) 'and there's plenty of arab in them. They'd carry eighteen without complaint. And that black mane will go well with Rifle facings,' he added a shade drolly.

'I think I might.'

'But let's first see her run free.' He asked for the mare to be loosed in one of the turnouts.

The breeder seemed reluctant.

'Come, man; let her have her liberty.'

When the halter was off, the mare trotted confidently to the middle of the turnout – dusty even at this time of year – and began to roll. She got up, shook herself, looked about, and then walked to the far side.

'Would you call her, please, Menheer Kuyper?' asked Hervey, pleased so far with what he saw.

The breeder barked an order to one of the Hottentots, who cupped a hand to his mouth. 'Kuni!'

The mare turned her head.

'Komm, Kuni, komm!'

She began trotting back to the gate. The breeder looked pleasantly surprised.

Hervey smiled. 'Well, Colonel, if she's as well mannered under saddle, I would say that there is your hack.'

And to the breeder's evidently even greater surprise, the mare then went well in a simple snaffle. After five minutes of serpentines, Colonel Smith handed her back with an approving nod, and expressed himself pleased. 'Well, Hervey?'

'I find no fault.'

'Nothing at all?'

'If you were to press me, I might say she were a little cresty – more stallion-like than mare – but that is mere taste. Handsome is as handsome does; and she does well. And she is by no means ill-favoured. No, quite the contrary.'

'Nothing more?' Colonel Smith had not expected to buy a country-bred, and he would be certain of his decision.

'Again, if you were to press me, I might say that her pasterns are long – I've never cared for length below the fetlock – but I myself would not be disobliged by such a fault in country such as this. Were we back in the hills of the Peninsula, I might prefer them shorter, but here you will have no trouble in it, I'm sure.'

Colonel Smith nodded. 'I am glad you say so. I liked her.' He turned again to the breeder. 'Very well, Menheer . . .'

They settled on a price which pleased them both (for the mare showed more quality than either of them had expected), and with assurances of a full month's warranty, the breeder received the promise of a further visit, this next time for a saddle horse for Juana. They parted, if not exactly as friends, then as trusted men of business, the Hottentots assembled in a line, like a guard of honour.

'I will say that I am much taken with the Cape-bred, Hervey,' declared Colonel Smith as they drove away in his whiskey, Hervey's hack following on a long rein. 'And I thank you heartily for your counsel.'

'Think nothing of it. I was glad of the diversion, and in truth it was instructive. I'm not as a rule so interested in these things, but I should like to see Kuyper's stud books, or whatever he calls them. I think there's a deal more blood in his horses than I supposed.'

The sun was now high, and both men were glad of their wide-brimmed straw hats. Hervey sat back, content to take his ease with another at the reins. Neither of them spoke for half a mile, the distant views and the Cape's invigorating air wholly diverting.

At length Colonel Smith's thoughts turned to Somervile and his expedition. 'I have a mind to take charge of the governor's escort myself for this affair of his,' he said, out of the blue.

Hervey cleared his throat. It had become a habit of his when faced with something unpalatable and which required a considered but instant response – rather as he would check a horse before a fence. 'Indeed?'

'Yes. I see both opportunity and trouble ahead.'

So did Hervey, but he did not want the complications of an officer his senior on the expedition. Besides aught else, he reckoned he would have considerably more influence – restraining influence – on Somervile than would another (even General Bourke). 'But would your duties at the castle permit it?'

'These things can always be arranged. What escort do you propose?'

'Fifty sabres, and a section from the Rifles,' he replied, and somewhat grudgingly. 'With Welsh, their admirable captain, who was at Umtata with me.' (He hoped that mention of the battle would remind Colonel Smith of his 'native' credentials.) 'I don't know the *Reliant*'s exact capacity, but if she can't ship them all, and the chargers and bat-horses, I shall reduce the number of sabres to accommodate the riflemen.'

'As I imagined. But landing at Port Natal with such a

force will need some herald, will it not, lest Shaka take fright?'

'Somervile has sent word to Natal to prepare the way. *Voerlopers*, our Dutch friends call them.' Again, Hervey thought that a little display of local knowledge might give his companion second thoughts.

They were rounding a blind corner by a craggy outcrop, and the driving horse shied suddenly. The whiskey lurched to the left, and the nearside wheel-spokes splintered painfully against the jagged granite.

'Damnation!' spat Colonel Smith, recovering his balance.

Hervey had already jumped down to take hold of the horse, which stood stock-still in surprise, but which otherwise showed every sign of bolting. 'We'd better unhitch him. We can't change the wheel with him between the shafts.'

Colonel Smith got down, patting the gelding on the neck encouragingly. 'He's no shier, as a rule.'

'They never are,' replied Hervey ruefully. 'Could have been anything – snake, probably.' He began unfastening the harness.

A falling rock made them turn.

'Perhaps that was it,' said Colonel Smith, anxious only to get the gelding from between the shafts before there was any more damage.

Hervey looked back again. A black face atop a crag thirty yards off ducked down into cover.

'Indeed it might have been. See,' he said, gesturing. 'Yonder, the rocks with those yellow flowers.'

Colonel Smith looked, but saw nothing.

'There was a Kaffir.' Hervey let go the harness and cupped his hands to his mouth. '*Wenza ntoni apho!*' he called.

There was no reply, nor sight of the man.

'Curse them! Two or three backs to the wheel would serve nicely.' He turned again to the harness.

Neither of them heard the Hottentots edging their way behind the crags towards them. Only the whiskey-gelding, who whinnied in vain.

'Steady,' growled Hervey, unfastening the last buckle.

The gelding shied suddenly. Hervey jumped clear, cursing.

But now he saw them – spears, blades, clubs. 'Christ!' he gasped, drawing his sabre as Colonel Smith lunged for his own on the whiskey's seat.

He ran straight at the nearest, sword levelled. Before the man could guard or parry, the point was four inches in his chest.

Hervey withdrew – 'on guard' – for the split second it took for the Hottentot to crumple, then lunged at a second.

A third rushed him with a nailed club. Hervey gave point again – this time above the breastbone.

A fourth faltered, then turned and ran. The rest took flight with him, making for their craggy fastness as suddenly as they'd come.

Hervey turned to see Colonel Smith, sword drawn.

'What in the name of God . . .'

'We were lucky,' said Hervey, grimly. He did not add that he reckoned himself careless for having to count on it, for he should not have allowed himself such an ambush.

The Hottentots had died so quickly that Colonel Smith's blade had not been needed. He shook his head in admiration as he returned his sword. 'I don't recall I ever saw such sabre-work. My compliments to you, sir.'

Hervey raised his eyebrows. 'The warrior's trade. Yours, as mine.'

'Just so; but all the same . . . Were they bandits?'

Hervey was yet making sure that those at his feet were not feigning death. He threw the clubs into the scrub, and a rusty cutlass. 'Maroons,' he said, sighing at having to use his sabre thus. 'That's what Fairbrother calls them, at least. Wretched creatures. See the brand on this one?'

He wiped his sabre on a patch of moss before sheathing it.

'Wretched indeed,' said Colonel Smith, examining the mark – and the shackle scars about the ankles. 'But I shall have the burghers form a posse to apprehend them. I've no craving for chasing runaways, but if they threaten the peace so . . .'

'They keep well to the north, as a rule. A regular little band. They must have thought us merchants, easy pickings.'

'I'd've given 'em silver to change the blessèd wheel,' rasped Colonel Smith, turning back to the whiskey.

And then he turned again, as if he had come to some particular resolution. 'Hervey, I will say it here, without ceremony. I would that you keep the lieutenant-governor out of harm's way in like manner. In Natal, I mean.'

'Do you doubt that I might?'

Colonel Smith shook his head. 'I mean that yours shall be the entire responsibility.'

'Depend upon it.'

'No, Hervey: I mean that you shall command the escort. I shall remain here.'

Hervey thought to turn the tables a little. 'Ah, so duties at the castle do not permit of riding with us after all?'

But Colonel Smith was not to be baited. 'There's no question of it. With Bourke away I mayn't so much as come out to buy a horse without wondering what I shall find on return.'

'You have my sympathies in that regard.'

A smile came to Colonel Smith's lips, broadening by degrees until his whole face was creased.

'Evidently not all is care,' said Hervey, drily.

'My dear fellow, I suggested I might take charge only to see what was your rejoinder.'

Hervey was, if in the smallest measure, put out. It was not as if he knew Colonel Smith well, or even that the colonel had shown any predisposition to pranking. 'Occasioned merely by sport, or some particular purpose?'

Colonel Smith continued to smile, but rather less broadly. 'You know, Hervey, with Bourke away I must act in his name. If I considered something to be ill founded – or, indeed, if I were to be convinced that the general would consider it to be thus – I should have to object.'

By which Hervey knew that if the general's deputy objected, there would be no expedition. It was, of course, perfectly reasonable that Colonel Smith should wish to test the mettle of a man in whom he would be placing such confidence. 'I trust you do *not* believe the expedition to be ill founded.'

'No. Your assurance in the matter is everything. Had you somehow welcomed a superior, I should have been uncertain.'

Hervey smiled, but thinly, for his self-assurance had more often than not stood to his disadvantage. There was no need of reply; he simply nodded.

'And for my part, be assured you will have my very best support at the castle.'

X

A MOST AGREEABLE THING

That afternoon

'I have been pondering on Sarn't-Major Armstrong's situation,' said Hervey, trying not to grimace at the rank coffee which Captain Brereton's man had brought them.

Brereton shifted slightly in his chair, but only to let his sword hang a little freer. The troop office was not the best of places for such a conversation, Hervey knew, but the officers' house would have been altogether too cosy.

'It is certainly a very sad one.'

And Brereton said it in such a way as suggested true compassion. Hervey did not doubt that Stafford Brereton, for all that he was an extract, had formed the highest regard for his – their – serjeant-major. What *affection* there might be was another matter; such things came only with time, perhaps.

'I mean that I was wondering what recognition might be had for his conduct at the frontier. The lieutenant-governor is certain he owes his life to the sarn't-major's address.'

This was something of a challenge to Brereton (as Hervey knew full well), for if Armstrong had saved Somervile's life, it had been Brereton who had first placed it in jeopardy by his decision to divide his force. When Hervey had spoken to him of it yesterday, but briefly, Brereton had given him a plausible enough explanation of the decision; but since the action had not achieved its object, and the lieutenant-governor had almost died (not to mention the dragoons), the decision was hardly vindicated.

'I had heard that Sir Eyre has commissioned a gold medal.'

Hervey had not known the intention was out. 'Indeed. But I meant something rather more elevating than ribbons.'

The point was a little unfair, and again he knew it: neither promotion nor the grant of seniority was within Brereton's gift. And so lately come to the acting command of a troop, he was scarcely in a position to press the matter with Lord Holderness. In any case, Brereton had written a full account of the action and had forwarded it to Hounslow, as Hervey knew because he had already told him.

'I feel sure the commanding officer will take all due note of his conduct. Is there anything you believe I myself might do, Colonel?'

'I think . . . if I were to see a copy of your report . . .' Hervey checked himself, for he was otherwise close to imputing dishonour. 'There might occur to me something.'

He had nicely reached his objective. He had given E Troop's captain the reassurance that he wished to read the report for a reason other than that he doubted either his actions or his frankness in relating them. He paused to study Brereton's reaction, before adding a further emollient: 'I think it behoves us to look at everything.'

'Indeed. I will have the clerk fetch it,' replied Brereton, making to rise.

'Later,' said Hervey, equably, raising his hand to stay him. 'Let us first speak of the arrangements for the Shaka expedition. There's a good deal to consider.'

They spoke for an hour or so, and then went to evening stables. Hervey was glad to be back among faces he knew by name, and so many of which he counted friends: they had been in scrapes enough together in India, and the odd old hand in the Peninsula, to be too particular in recalling the occasions for rebuke or punishment.

He knew he would miss them. He knew he would miss *it* – the fellowship of the stable – when he took up command of the Eighty-first. *If* he took up command. In command even of a company he would have felt the distance between the ranks, let alone of a whole battalion. Lord John Howard had once said to him, in jest, but with just such a measure of possibility as to sound true, that in going on parade he could never recognize which was his company unless the serjeants were posted. Here, in the formal but shabby ease of the evening stables parade, a man would touch the peak of his forage cap in salute, with a smile of recognition and an 'evenin sir' in greater or lesser degree according to his length of service. And he, Hervey, could return that greeting with an intimacy which defied the understanding of all but an insider. Yet on parade, in the field, in the face of the enemy, he could give the same man an order to charge – even unto death – knowing that it would be obeyed without question.

Obeyed not through fear of the lash (for the Sixth did not flog) but through trust that a man's life was not thrown away merely because his rank was lowly; and, too, that no one – officer or NCO – would ask a man to do a thing which he himself would not. Trust, mutual trust, was the secret of light cavalry discipline. This he had learned, before ever seeing a dragoon, from his old and late friend and mentor Daniel Coates, sometime Trumpeter-Corporal Coates of His Majesty's 16th Light Dragoons (and now in death his magnificent benefactor). And that trust he had cultivated throughout the years of the Peninsula, and since. It would be deuced hard to exchange it all for the world of the serjeant's half-pike and the cat-o'-nine-tails. Likely as not, he would never speak directly to a private man again . . .

'Sir?'

He snapped to. 'Sar'nt-Major.'

Collins was standing at attention in front of him.

Hervey recollected himself as best he could with a 'How do you find things?'

Collins took his whip from under his arm and moved to Hervey's side, ready to continue the progress through the lines. 'Just as I expected, sir.'

Which was indeed exactly as Hervey himself expected, for both Armstrong and Collins had been raised in the same school – RSM Lincoln's.

'Every last item in the ledger accounted for, all of it in good condition, and a satisfactory store of *backshee*.'

The regiment had picked up the word in India, where the native regiments used it to describe those items held in excess of what the ledger specified – the 'working margin', as the quartermasters and serjeant-majors more usually officialized it. Except that as a rule none would ever declare the existence of *backshee*, since by rights any excess belonged to the superior account holder.

Hervey nodded, perfectly appreciating the candour: Collins wanted him to know that Armstrong had run the troop exactly as it should be run. 'I trust that Sar'nt-Major Armstrong will be able to report the same in due course,' he added, though in truth with no certainty, now, that Armstrong would indeed take back his troop (Private Johnson's conviction that he would 'chuck it' for the sake of his children seemed no longer impossible).

'Evenin, sor!'

Hervey was taken aback. 'Corporal McCarthy!' (He had last seen him in the quartermaster-serjeant's office in Hounslow.) 'It is *still* "Corporal" isn't it?' he enquired, with mock severity.

'Sor!'

'What do you do here? The stores not to your liking?'

'Sor, they was askin for men for E Troop, sor, an' I thought as I might volunteer. Sor!'

Hervey tried hard not to smile, which he always found difficult when dealing with this irrepressible Cork man. 'What happened to the principle of "never volunteer for anything"?'

'I make an exception, sor, in connection with E Troop.'

Hervey recalled well McCarthy's special devotion: on one occasion in India it had cost him the stripes on his arm, when he had broken the nose of a pug from another troop who had impugned E Troop's honour. 'I'm sure you are very welcome.'

He moved on to the next stall. The dragoon was bending with his back to him, but Hervey had known the man's thick, black curls for ten years. 'Corporal French!'

The NCO rose and turned, bringing his hands to his side in salute. 'Good evening, sir.'

French was almost a gentleman. Indeed he *was* a gentleman by the usual measure; the 'almost' was the regiment's customary form of allowing him a kind of halfway status between other rank and officer, though he

217

answered to a serjeant as any other. He was a gentleman by birth, a son of impoverished Welsh gentry and the parsonage, but he lacked any means to support himself as such, and had been a counting-house clerk before enlisting. Had he been five or six years older he would almost certainly have had a free commission in a battalion of the Line, for the ensign ranks of the Peninsular infantry had suffered sorely. With peace come, however, and with it retrenchment, there were sons enough of the gentry who could pay their way. But Corporal French had always appeared content with his situation; and he was liked by all ranks.

'I was thinking, sir,' said Collins quietly as they moved on. 'With Wainwright still poorly, French would be a good coverman.'

Hervey nodded. 'In any case, with Wainwright now serjeant he shouldn't be covering.' And then he remembered. 'But the troop's under Captain Brereton's orders, Sar'nt-Major. I shouldn't be making these decisions.'

'No, sir,' agreed Collins. He said nothing for a few paces. 'But if you are content on French, sir, I'll arrange it.'

Hervey nodded again. 'That would be the way. Thank you.'

And he found himself nodding to dragoons in turn as if for the last time, looking at each with an eye almost paternal. Most of them he had first seen as green recruits; some he had himself enlisted; a few were old sweats, Peninsular veterans who remembered *his* arriving. He would miss them – more than he had imagined. But he thanked God there was this one last ride together: if not actually a campaign, then an expedition promising something unusual, something to remember, even if it were only the face of this intriguing chief, Shaka.

But there must be no sentiment; it did not serve. 'Have you *seen* Wainwright yet?' he asked, to be more purposeful. 'I must say he looks in better condition than I'd dared hope.'

'I saw him last night, sir. He'll mend right enough.'

Hervey smiled to himself. He might have known that Collins would lose no time in calling on a brother NCO. 'Anything more?'

Collins sighed. 'Quilter.'

Hervey sighed too. Serjeant Quilter looked the part, but he had risen more by seniority than merit. He was not an E Troop man: he had come on promotion from B. At eighteen years' service he was one of the oldest corporals to be made serjeant, and for the two years since then he had never looked at ease in the rank.

Collins, who had known him many years, shook his head. 'He does his best, mind.'

Hervey raised his eyebrows. 'That in its way is discouraging.'

'Ay, sir. Even if I decided everything for him, he'd still make a muddle of it. Armstrong said as 'e was fed up with putting him on report. And what with Wainwright on box rest, it makes things twice as bad.'

'You would prefer Corporal Hardy to stand duty, I imagine.'

'I don't know Hardy well enough to say, sir, but Armstrong rates him.'

'He did well in the skirmish at the frontier, by all accounts – very cool-headed, and economical with the sabre.' Hervey nodded slowly. 'I'll speak with Captain Brereton. And we should have someone slated for rear details – Quilter, I mean. I can't have him in the field. Though in fairness I should say he did not disgrace himself at Umtata.'

When they had walked the huttings, Hervey dismissed Collins and took his leave of Brereton, telling him that he would dine in the officers' house, but that first he must call on the lieutenant-governor. He went then to the charger stables, which was hutting no different from the troop lines, but with the usual extra space for loose boxes rather than standing stalls. Here he found Private Toyne, his second groom. Toyne, a quiet-spoken Westmorland man who had learned horses at the gypsy fair in Appleby, had joined the Sixth in India. Hervey had liked him at once, as (more importantly) had Johnson; he felt confident always of leaving a horse in his charge.

Toyne greeted him as if he had seen him but an hour ago. 'Both of 'em's doin' right, sir,' he added, nodding to Hervey's two mares.

Hervey had not doubted it would be so; not, at least, as far as husbandry was concerned (the *perdesiekt* was another matter). He looked into Eli's box. Eli – Eliab – was Jessye's foal, nine years old, fifteen hands three, a pretty bay and now a handy charger, with all her dam's sturdiness, and a fair bit of bone. She was a 'good doer', as the saying went: she did not lose condition quickly when her rations were changed or reduced. But he had yet to take her into the field. Gilbert had been his battle-charger, a fast and seasoned one, and for the foray into Kaffraria he had taken Molly as his second, for Eli had coughed once or twice the day before, and he had decided not to risk it. But now Eli was his second, for he had had to put a bullet in Gilbert's brains when an aneurysm brought him down only yards from the Zulu.

Eli turned at his voice, and whickered. She came up to the door of the box and put her nose out to him. Hervey took her head in his left hand and rubbed her muzzle with his right. 'Well, my girl, how good it is to see you. I hope you still have your sea legs.'

'She'll 'ave em, sir, right enough. I 'eard we were goin, an' I've been puttin Stock'ollum on 'er feet.'

Hervey nodded approvingly.

'And on Molly's,' added Toyne, turning to the adjacent box. 'She went lame a bit when you were gone, sir, but it were nothin' really – just a week's box rest an' she were back on t'road soon enough.'

Molly did not immediately turn, finding the hay rack

altogether more compelling than her master's voice. It was in any case not nearly as familiar to her as it was to Eli, for Hervey had bought her only just before leaving England, and although she had carried him faithfully at Umtata they were not yet truly acquainted. Molly was nearer black than dark bay (she had certainly looked so in her summer coat and a good sweat), and stood half a hand higher than Eli. She had been an officer's charger, in the Tenth, a good five years before coming to him, and at rising twelve she was a sound prospect for what lay ahead.

He watched her calmly grinding the hay. 'I've a hack from the castle, but I shall take him back tonight, and then tomorrow I'll take her out,' he said, reaching forward to pat her quarters.

'She'd like that, sir.'

Hervey nodded again. Would she like it? Would she know it was he riding her? Eli would; and Jessye would have, certainly ... Would he take Molly with him to Canada? And Eli? Would he take Toyne with him? It could be arranged, no doubt. Johnson would most definitely come with him, although he had not really told him yet. That is, they had not discussed it. Johnson had so much reckonable service that he could have his free discharge at any time, and he could easily re-enlist in the Eighty-first if there were any administrative objection to his transfer. He would promote him corporal, too. Johnson had always refused promotion on the grounds that it brought 'responsibility' (by which he really meant the scrutiny of the RSM) without any benefit save a few shillings a week. But without rank, in the Eighty-first he would not have the standing.

As he left the charger stables, Hervey began wondering again who else he might be allowed to claim for his new command. Would he be able to tempt an officer or two? There again, what would it profit them? The only ones he knew well enough to be sure of – sure in his estimation that they would be better than those with whom they might exchange – were two or three of the captains, and why would they exchange a troop for a company, the spur for the gaiter? For they were all of sufficient means to be comfortable in Hounslow. It was not as if there was the prospect of any action in Canada.

Somervile was not returned from office when Hervey called at the residence. Jaswant showed him to Emma's sitting room.

'Matthew, what a pleasing surprise. Shall you join us for dinner?' she asked as they kissed.

'No, forgive me, Emma; I must dine with my officers. I came but briefly to speak with Somervile about the arrangements for Natal.'

'I expect him in an hour. He sent word that he was receiving someone from the frontier. Will you have some wine?'

'Thank you, yes.'

Emma nodded to the khansamah.

'I much enjoyed the table last night,' Hervey said, taking a chair at Emma's bidding. 'The ship's fare was a little unvarying. And I was most engaged by Colonel Smith and his wife.'

'Oh, indeed yes; they are a most welcome adornment to the Cape. I quite wish we were to stay longer.'

Hervey had almost forgotten the Somerviles were to leave the colony in not many months. Or rather, he had failed to imagine all the consequences of it. 'I did not ask: Eyre will return to the court of directors?' Somervile was principally a servant of the Honourable East India Company. The two of them had first met in Madras, ten years before, and renewed their friendship in Calcutta when the Sixth had been posted to the Bengal presidency; and they had continued it on return to London.

Emma looked surprised. 'He did not say? We are to go to Canada.'

Hervey brightened, like a child given a present. 'Canada!'

Emma looked at him a little strangely. 'Ye-es. Eyre is to be lieutenant-governor, minister, or whatever it is called there, in Fort York.'

Hervey smiled broadly. 'My dear Emma, you will forgive me if I ask you to keep this to yourself – I mean, I will tell Somervile of course – but I too am to go to York. I am to have command of the Eighty-first there.'

Emma positively beamed. 'That is wonderful news,

Matthew! Wonderful! I know now that I shall have agreeable company. You and Kezia . . . the *most* agreeable thing!'

Hervey was tempted to tell Emma that to this date Kezia had set her mind against Canada, but . . . it would not help him, nor would it please her. And there was every chance that Kezia would have a change of mind in the matter.

But they had known each other too long, and his face betrayed something of his unease. 'What is it, Matthew?'

He cleared his throat. There was no point in pretence. 'Kezia is not yet persuaded to go . . . But I have every hope she will change her mind in the normal course of things, and especially once she knows that you will be there.'

Emma looked dismayed. 'You mean that you will otherwise go alone?'

Hervey shifted in his chair. Jaswant returned with wine (for which he was now especially grateful). 'I . . . That is . . . She has not said that she will *not* accompany me to Canada, merely that, when I spoke with her about the offer of the Eighty-first, she did not wish me to accept command.'

Emma's brow was now deeply furrowed. 'But you have said yes to command – have you not?'

'I have. These things are always somewhat provisional, of course.'

She shook her head, uncomprehending.

'I had but little time before returning here.'

'Not the time to speak with your wife?'

He shifted again. 'No.'

Emma studied him carefully. 'Matthew?'

He looked away, and raised an eyebrow the merest fraction.

It was enough, however. Emma rose.

'Matthew, I must go to the children; it is the nursery hour. Perhaps you would come tomorrow morning, when you have spoken to Eyre?'

That night, after an unusually abstemious dinner in the officers' house (he had felt an unaccountable reluctance to give way to the pleasures of the cellar), he retired to the little room that was permanently made up for him, and seeing there was pen and paper as well as brandy and water on the table (in proper regimental fashion), he sat down to write a few lines to Kezia. He knew he ought to have done so a day or two out from the Cape so that Armstrong could carry them back – as he had with letters to his family (and, if truth be known, to Kat) – but somehow the words had evaded him. He had, after all, written not many days out from England, and then again off the Azores, and the letters had been transferred to passing merchantmen, so he was not wholly to be thought inattentive in the matter. It was just that . . .

He picked up the pen.

My dear wife, he began. And then he put the pen down again.

Such an inadequate salutation, that. He could not quite recall why he had used the form in his first letter. Was it, somehow, that he was reminding himself of his status; reminding Kezia, too? After all, they had hardly begun things in the best of ways. So unlike the month – months only – that he and Henrietta had enjoyed. In truth, the marriage was barely consummated.

But to change the form of salutation . . . what might he write? *My Dearest*? It seemed too contrived.

He must, however, tell her of his decision to take command of the Eighty-first, and butting no further delay, for it was bound to be out soon. How much more agreeable it would have been had she been Kat – he meant had she been *like* Kat – who seemed to delight in his progress always.

He picked up the pen again and wrote his news, fast.

When he had finished, he read it over. He felt a twinge of unease as he did so, for he had couched the news as if he had only now made the decision, and after a great deal of thought. Kezia might believe that he had had to make his decision at once, without being able to discuss it with her. She might perceive there were other matters which she herself could not know. She might accept that he had decided with reluctance but in good faith, and that since he was unable to communicate with her in coming to the decision he must – as *paterfamilias* – act

227

as he saw best. She might. But it was not the truth. He had made the decision almost defiantly, before leaving England, and he had not told her because . . . Well, he knew there would be the strongest objections, and if he waited there might come a more propitious time to break it to her. And so, in all honesty, he ought to tear up this half truth before him and begin afresh. But he was tired, and there were other matters pressing on him, matters of considerable moment, and if he waited for an opportunity tomorrow he would miss the Indiaman which was due to sail at midday . . .

He laid aside the sheets for the ink to dry. He would rise early and write another letter in its place.

XI

THE CONSEQUENCES OF INACTION

Next morning

Hervey had slept soundly. He rarely slept ill, but the second night in a bed instead of a hanging cot was perfect repose. A Malay bearer woke him with tea.

He lay listening to the morning: a native voice here and there, collared doves calling peaceably, the labouring of the water carrier. He turned and looked at his half-hunter on the bedside table, and cursed. He rose at once, but it was later than he intended.

The bearer came back with hot water.

And then a knock at the door announced the picket commander. 'Sir?'

'Is the camp under attack, Corporal Hardy?' asked Hervey, with a mock frown.

'Sir, sorry, sir, but this message just came from the castle, and the hircarrah said as it was urgent, so I

229

brought it myself rather than give it the picket officer. Sir.'

Hervey smiled. In that briefest of explanations Corporal Hardy had revealed so much of what he esteemed in the Sixth. Would the picket commander of the Eighty-first have acted upon such initiative? Likely as not he would have waited until the serjeant had come, and then the serjeant would have sought out the picket officer . . . Perhaps he was being unfair.

'Is the hircarrah waiting on a reply?' he asked, as he opened the despatch from the lieutenant-governor's office (hircarrah, like *backshee*, was another word the regiment had brought back from India).

'No, sir.'

Hervey read the hand he knew well from many years' acquaintance: *Would you be so good as to come hither post haste, and with you Captain Fairbrother. There is ripe intelligence from Natal . . .*

'Corporal Hardy, have Toyne bring Molly, if you please, and my compliments to Captain Brereton but I shall not be able to attend first parade.'

He shaved, dressed, and set out without breakfasting for the castle, but via Fairbrother's house by the Company's gardens.

An old Hottentot was watering the window boxes there; another was sweeping the *stoep*. For a moment, Hervey imagined how Georgiana would have loved it.

The door was open.

Inside, Fairbrother's housekeeper greeted him warmly as an established friend of the quarters.

'Is he awake, M'ma Anke?'

'He was after I'd waked him, Colonel.'

'I perceive that you believe him not to be awake now. Perhaps you would bring coffee for me to take in to him?'

'I will, Colonel,' she sighed. 'He did ask for me to wake him early, but this morning he said as he wished he hadn't because he had stayed late at his desk.'

Hervey smiled.

'Not as I sees any sign of what kept him there,' she added, with a pronounced roll of her eyes.

Hervey sat down to await the coffee. On Fairbrother's writing table was a vase of flowers, blue and yellow. They were fresh, placed there this morning. What sort, he did not know, only that it was a woman's touch, delightful – the estimable M'ma Anke. A most agreeable fusing of native and colonist was she. But in what combination or sequence, Fairbrother said, not even she knew. Hervey wished he might find another of her capability, for his own establishment – saving Johnson's protests, of course (and, perhaps, Kezia's).

He stood up as she returned with a small basin of steaming black arabica. 'We must leave for the castle as soon as he's dressed, M'ma Anke. I know he's indifferent to breakfast.'

'Not so much indifferent as contrary, Colonel.'

Hervey smiled. She most certainly had the measure of 'the master'.

The house was on one floor only, Fairbrother's room on the east side. Hervey opened the door without knocking, and was surprised to find the curtains drawn back, the window full open and his friend sitting up in bed reading the *Jamaica Courant and Public Advertiser*.

'Good morning,' said Fairbrother without taking his eyes from the newspaper.

'My dear fellow, I believe I shall drink this coffee myself, for you evidently have no need of it. Come; we are bidden to the castle.'

'In good time,' he replied, intent on his news.

Hervey knew that hurrying him was fruitless. He put down the coffee and found himself a chair. 'What detains you there?'

Fairbrother lowered the *Courant* a moment or two later. He appeared lost in thought. 'News of my father.'

'Not ill news, I trust?' Besides comradely concern, Hervey had formed a high opinion of his friend's father, evidently a plantation owner of enlightened views and kindly disposition: to have raised a bastard son as his own must have been no small thing in that confined society. He hoped one day they might meet.

'Not of him, no. Quite the opposite, if one is to take the humane view.' He pulled back the bedclothes and made to get up.

Hervey reached for the discarded *Courant*.

'See the report regarding "Treatment of a Female Slave".'

'I have it.'

'Read it – aloud, if you will.'

Hervey began:

At a Council of Protection holden this 11th July 1828 in conformity to the 25th clause of the Slave Law now in force, before the Honorable Henry Fairbrother, Custos Rotulorum, and others, Justices and Vestrymen of the parish of Saint Ann, – Kitty Hilton, a Slave belonging to the Rev. G. W. Bridges, was brought forward in pursuance of a written order. The several parties having been duly served, the Council of Protection proceeded to investigate the said Charge.

Kitty Hilton, sworn; stated, – That she belongs to the Rev. Mr. Bridges, Rector of Saint Ann's. On Friday, after breakfast went to her master in the library, and asked, what he would have for dinner, who asked what witness had done with all the turkeys; had the turkey killed about two o'clock, p.m.; when he saw it killed, master was angry; took her into the pantry and nailed witness against the dresser in the pantry, and kicked her with his foot. Witness begged not to be kicked so severely, as she would buy another turkey and have it for the Sunday's dinner. Being asked, if any one was present? – she said, Miss Moreland; – Was kicked for upwards of an hour; master said he wished he could see her a corpse, as he hated her so. Called old Charles to pick up the largest bundle of bamboo switches he could find, which he did. Master followed her and old Charles to the cow-penn, and had her laid down. He was standing over witness, beating her with a stick, and telling the man to cut all the flesh off her. When master had done flogging her, and witness rose up, the blood was running down her heels. He ordered old Charles to run her down to the pond; and went as ordered, washed her skin, and the blood off her clothes. Did your master follow you? – No, he stopped at the cow-penn: That on her return from the pond her master was pelting her up to the house with stones; the pond can be seen from the house; it was about two o'clock in the day; was struck by her master at the cow-penn; on her return from the pond to the house, her master was following her with a stick, but as he could not catch her, he continued pelting her. On her return to the house, the blood gushed out as bad as ever. Her mistress called for a kettle of water, which she went to take up: she met her master, he gave her a kick, and told her to go out and change her clothes. He followed her into the washhouse and beat her there with a stick.

'This is abominable, Fairbrother. Do you know either of the parties?'

'I know the Rector of St Ann's, yes. An odious fellow, his religion distinctly Christless. Read on.'

Hervey took up the paper again.

Dr. Stewart, sworn. States the witness had two black eyes when the woman was sent to the workhouse. Witness examined her, and saw severe marks of punishment. W. T. Harker, sworn. Saw the woman on the morning of Wednesday; had heard a report of a woman being severely flogged; examined her, – her eyes were black, as if she had received a severe blow; her posteriors were very much cut up; on the inner part of her thigh, on each, there were several black marks. The Hon. Henry Fairbrother, sworn. Kitty Hilton came to witness to complain against her master, Mr. Bridges; she was very much injured; saw her bruises, evidently switching from the nape of her neck to her posteriors; her face and thighs dreadfully bruised. Has never seen any thing so severe of this kind; in consequences ordered her before the Council of Protection. Miss Steer, sworn. Was at Mr. Bridges on the 2d of April. The dinner was shamefully cooked, and a part of it was obliged to be sent away; Mr. Bridges told her, he should remember her. On the following day she killed a turkey, saying to Mr. Bridges she had been ordered to do so, and Mrs. Bridges told her, it must have been a mistake. Heard she was to have been punished; switches were sent for; and she was sent to the watchman for punishment. Saw Mr. Bridges on the top of the hill. Question to Mr. Colen, by Mr. Bridges. Had I any other negro than Charles, or any other coloured person about me, to punish the woman? Replied – No. The Justices and Vestry having heard the Evidence on behalf of Kitty Hilton, and the Evidence on behalf of the Reverend Mr. Bridges; on its being put to the vote; whether Mr. Bridges should be prosecuted or not, it was carried, by a majority of thirteen to four against the Prosecution.

'A most objectionable business indeed. I am astonished at the verdict.'

Fairbrother had begun his ablutions with unusual address, working up a vigorous lather on his shaving brush. 'Just so. I have it from my father that as custos he has made protest to the governor.'

'It does him credit,' replied Hervey, sitting back in his chair. He would indeed like to meet him.

'But it will go ill with him. He and the governor are of different minds when it comes to the matter of the Slave Act.'

'Is that what troubles you?'

'Do I appear troubled?' asked Fairbrother, without taking his eyes from the mirror as he applied the soap.

'Shall we say that you are not, as a rule, so active this time of a morning?'

'Let us say that I am roused by that account.'

Hervey smiled at the pun, for all that he too was sickened by the account. 'I perfectly understand it. And I trust your father will see justice done without excessive vexation for himself.'

'I must depend upon it,' said Fairbrother, in a way that told Hervey the affair touched him deeply (and not merely because of the discomfiting of his father). He finished lathering his face and took up the razor.

Hervey in his turn took up the *Courant* again to see what manner of business occupied this other of the Crown's colonies. He perused the court notices, the shipping and transactions in silence, allowing his friend to shave with due concentration.

When the first soap was scraped from his cheeks, Fairbrother began again. 'There's another piece in the *Courant* worthy of your attention – under "Foreign Intelligence". General Jackson is likely next president of the United States.'

'The hero of New Orleans?' replied Hervey, his tone suggesting neither great surprise nor dismay. 'Do we fear that this will bring some difficulty with that country? And I think we might have read it first in *The Times* if it were true.'

Fairbrother frowned, before lathering again. 'You mistake matters, Hervey, if you think Jamaica is the last to hear things: recollect that it's but a cruise from Washington to Spanish-town. And see the date, too – a fortnight after we sailed.'

'I stand rebuked. And in truth I suppose I ought to take more cognizance of affairs in Washington if I am to go to Canada.'

'*If?*' Fairbrother turned to look at him accusingly.

'Merely the subjunctive mood. My mind is still quite made up.'

Fairbrother returned to his shaving. 'I am glad to hear it.' After a minute or so, he took a towel and began dabbing at his face. 'Fine fellows, Americans. D'ye know, they now have their own dictionary?'

'What nonsense are you trying?'

Fairbrother nodded to the *Courant*. 'See there, a notice: a man called Webster's got up a dictionary of American words.'

'Truly?'

'Not content with sending the old King packing, they now disdain the King's English!'

'The devil!' Hervey found the report.

'Fine fellows. I should very much like to see the country,' declared Fairbrother, laying down the towel and picking up the bowl of coffee. 'Hervey, my good friend, if your offer still stands, I should like to come with you to Canada.'

Hervey's surprise was marked.

Fairbrother ignored it. 'You're sure an exchange can be arranged?'

Hervey stood up, and with a look not merely of satisfaction but of admiration. 'Of course the offer stands. And I'm sure the agents can arrange an exchange with no difficulty. As I told you, these things are perfectly easily done when it is known how.'

Fairbrother cast off his robe, though the door was full

open, and took up the clean linen laid out on a chair next to the press.

Hervey observed the sinews of an athlete, and wondered, again, how his friend kept such condition when he took no exercise and chose his food and drink entirely at will. It could only be, he concluded, some blood-gift of his mother's line. *Ex Africa . . .*

There was Madeira and seedcake on a sideboard in the lieutenant-governor's ante-room, a breakfast for which both Hervey and Fairbrother were grateful.

'Sir Eyre-sahib will be coming shortly, Colonel Hervey sahib,' Jaswant assured them.

They were soon joined by the colonial secretary, Colonel Bird.

'I am sorry we had no opportunity to speak last evening, Hervey,' he said, taking coffee rather than Madeira. 'These are singular times, are they not? Who would have supposed that Jackson would be president of the United States?'

Hervey was somewhat taken aback by this early corroboration of his friend's superior intelligence gathering. 'Quite so.'

'Or, for that matter, the Duke of Wellington prime minister?'

'Who indeed.' Hervey helped himself to more cake, wondering what the supplementary question might be, for he knew Colonel Bird to be as shrewd as he was gentle.

'And that he, of all people, should champion Catholics?'

The cadence suggested that this was Colonel Bird's material interest, and the omission of the definite article before 'Catholics', though not determinative, served nevertheless to remind Hervey of Bird's own religion (and of the consequent animosity, it was said, of some in the colony).

'Shall the emancipation measure be carried, do you suppose?'

Hervey took a deep breath. In truth, emancipation was not a matter in which he was given to much thinking. Catholics or slaves, he was uncertain how the country had come to deprive them of their liberty in the first place. He concerned himself only with the practical questions arising – the murky affair of the gunpowder mills, the obsequies of his serjeant-major's wife. 'I think I would say that there appear to be two types of Catholic: the Irish and the English. I had occasion to attend a requiem mass in London, the whole regiment indeed, and it seemed no more remarkable than if we had been in Lisbon. Well, perhaps a little more so. The Irish, on the other hand ... Let us say that if the emancipation bill is passed, and the parliament in Dublin restored – and that is their object, is it not? – it would be a Catholic parliament.'

Colonel Bird looked doubtful. 'That is assuming the franchise were extended. I cannot suppose that even the duke wishes the demands of Reform to be extended so far.'

Hervey raised his eyebrows. He knew (or supposed he knew) that the duke had little time for Reform in any part of England, let alone Ireland.

'It seems to me all of a piece – Ireland or Jamaica,' remarked Fairbrother drily from a corner, and between sips at his Madeira. 'Free the devils and they'll next want the vote.'

His friend had cast a fly on the water, so to speak, and Hervey was resolved not to rise to it. He returned to Colonel Bird. 'You must understand that I speak not for myself in this.'

'Of course, my dear Colonel, of course,' replied Bird, with a positively benign aspect. 'Captain Fairbrother's comparison with slavery, though I suspect he spoke with tongue in cheek, prompts me nevertheless to recall that Shaka has remarked unfavourably on the British as a consequence of it.'

Hervey frowned. 'I wonder at Shaka's moral pertur-bation in light of his marauding. How, indeed, does he know of the practice? The slavers never took from his part of the country.'

'No, but he will know well enough of the slaves here.'

'Brought by the Dutch, not by us.' But even as he said it, he knew what must be Fairbrother's rejoinder.

But Fairbrother surprised him. 'Whence comes this intelligence?' was all he asked.

'From one of the British trading party at Port Natal. You doubt its accuracy?' The question was genuine rather than challenging; Colonel Bird had a high regard for Fairbrother's independent mind (which many another in Cape Town thought merely resentful).

Fairbrother shrugged. 'Since when has any native chief been opposed to the trade? And Shaka has crushed so many tribes he would not have hesitated to sell them off to the slavers, just as he took their land and cattle. *Vae Victis!*'

Hervey cleared his throat. 'Somervile speaks of ripe intelligence from Natal . . .'

Colonel Bird smiled. 'I see what you are thinking, Hervey, but the intelligence on which the lieutenant-governor is pondering is of a more substantial kind than this sort of speculation.' He then appeared to recollect himself, becoming quite grave. 'Shaka's kingdom is, I fear, in a condition of desolation, and no good can come of it.'

Hervey was about to enquire further when Colonel Smith appeared, with Jaswant.

'Good morning, gentlemen. The lieutenant-governor awaits us.'

They all voiced their 'good mornings' and made to follow, Colonel Bird laying aside his cup, Hervey draining his glass, and Fairbrother pouring a further measure with which to wash down the remaining seedcake.

Jaswant led them with his usual insistent formality to the state study.

Somervile, smoking a strong cheroot, rose to greet them. He shook hands in the way of men transacting business, and then took a chair in the circle of five beside the east window. 'Thank you, Hervey – and you, Fairbrother – for coming so promptly upon the summons. Sit you down, gentlemen; sit you down.'

Major Dundas, the military secretary, who was already in the room, took his seat at a table in the corner, where pen and paper lay ready for his minute-taking.

'I have asked Dundas to make a record of this meeting for the purposes of a despatch to Huskisson at the War and Colonies Office. You are at liberty, of course, to peruse the record before it is complete. I would have this adventure properly minuted to London in case, shall we say, of any mischance and subsequent misunderstanding.'

Hervey nodded. It was principally to him that Somervile appeared to be directing his remarks.

'And so, let me begin by telling you of what we have just lately learned respecting Shaka. Some weeks ago there arrived at Port Elizabeth emissaries, several Englishmen who trade from Port Natal, and some of Shaka's dignitaries. They were conveyed by an officer of the Royal Navy – or former officer: his status is yet wholly unclear to me – in a country-built and un-seaworthy vessel. I regret to say that the mission does not appear to have been met with any great address. Indeed it was botched; but that is by the bye. As soon as I learned of their parlous condition yesterday evening, and of their wish to return to Natal forthwith, I despatched the *Helicon* to Algoa Bay with presents for Shaka, to convey the embassy back to Port Natal with the declaration of our intent to visit with him.'

'They bore messages as well as gifts, I imagine, this embassy?'

'Nothing in writing, of course, but an assurance that Shaka wishes to live in peace as long as we do not provoke him.'

Hervey thought this curious, and glanced at Colonels Smith and Bird, but they appeared to know of it already. 'Provocation is rather more a question of judgement than fact, is it not? Does he mean, I wonder, that the affair at Umtata was provoking? Is that why he sent the embassy?'

'Strange to relate,' said Somervile, blowing a great deal of smoke into the circle: 'Shaka denies there were Zulu at Umtata.'

Hervey's brow creased. 'Then Umtata was not a provocation. Unless, of course, he thinks we believed we were seeking to bring on a battle with him there.'

'Black men look very much the same when they're feathered and carrying spears,' said Fairbrother.

'A *little* droll, Captain Fairbrother,' suggested Somervile.

'I stand rebuked, Sir Eyre.'

'Not rebuked, sir. Not at all rebuked,' Somervile

insisted, taking a particularly satisfying draw on his cheroot.

'May I ask a question?' continued Fairbrother, recrossing his legs and folding his arms.

'By all means.'

'The presence of Shaka's men in Algoa Bay will not have escaped the notice of the Xhosa. What do you propose to do to reassure their chief that our intentions are unchanged, that we have no design to make alliance with Shaka against them?'

Somervile nodded. 'I have instructed the officer commanding the frontier to send word to the Xhosa of Shaka's embassy, and of my intention to make an embassy in return. For the greater safety of the frontier and for the Xhosa.'

Fairbrother bowed.

'May I, Sir Eyre?' asked Colonel Smith, indicating that he wished to question Fairbrother.

'By all means.'

Colonel Smith turned, distinctly hawk-like. 'Captain Fairbrother, I would hear your view of the Xhosa unrest, its cause and so forth. You will know there are contrary opinions.'

Fairbrother shifted not at all in the chair, his legs remaining crossed, for all the world looking as if these matters were to him an open book. 'It does not follow that all these opinions must each be worthy of consideration, Colonel.'

Hervey winced: his friend had a most unfortunate pre-disposition to assume hostility on the part of others.

But Colonel Smith took no offence. Or, at least, he did not show it. 'I am proceeding on the supposition that yours is worthy, however. Continue, if you please.'

Fairbrother nodded. 'My opinion is very easily given.' (He spoke with just a trace of the emollient.) 'The late irruptions into the east of the colony by the Xhosa do not stem from any ambition on their part, but are occasioned by Shaka. His cohorts press in from the north-east of the Xhosa's territory, and they in their Archimedean turn are displaced towards the south-west and over the frontier. The reiving is to all intents and purposes, therefore, a Zulu peril.'

Colonel Smith asked upon what evidence he had formulated this opinion, to which Fairbrother replied that he had spoken with several Xhosa elders, who had also expressed their belief that Gaika, the paramount chief, and others could be persuaded to resist the Zulu if they were given military assistance – which had indeed been the case before Umtata. He expressed himself certain that, from all he knew of the Colony and beyond these past ten years, Shaka would not give up his predations. At best he would push the Xhosa from their land, and they in turn would cross the frontier and make war with the Colony. But at worst Shaka might sub-jugate them by battle, or otherwise coerce them, and then the Colony would be obliged to fight an alliance of both Xhosa *and* Zulu – and for that matter, every Kaffir tribe east of the Keiskama.'

Colonel Smith remained thoughtfully silent for some moments.

'The implication of what you say is that, one way or another, Shaka is a menace to the peace of the Colony.'

'It would be folly to rely on a line on the map when Shaka does not read or write. Besides, the growth of such a power to rival ours could not but have an unsettling effect.'

'You are not persuaded, Colonel?' asked Somervile, taking the cheroot from his mouth and leaning forward in his chair.

'I have been at the Cape but a month, Sir Eyre; and while I have been aware of the conflicting opinion as to the native menace, I have not been able to form any view of the consequences of *inaction*. My instinct, I must confess, is to delay until matters are clearer, for although I would always urge the boldest strategy – and the swiftest – it must be directed towards an objective which is unequivocally defined.' He spoke in a measured way, seeming to weigh his words with great care, as if still trying to come to a conclusion. 'This mission from Shaka, poorly handled as it was, is encouraging; it implies that war is perhaps avoidable. Which is as well, for our military strength is not great. Even if the government in London were to agree its increase, it would be a year at least before there was the means to undertake a campaign. The Zulu – what do they number?'

Somervile raised his hands. 'We have no number. We have no clear notion, indeed, where Shaka's domain ends.'

Colonel Smith shook his head. 'You will know what is my duty in this, Sir Eyre. But I do say one thing: there can be no military objection to an *embassy* to Shaka. I am perfectly clear in my mind in that regard.'

Somervile was grateful. He was by no means certain that General Bourke would have come to that determination.

Colonel Smith had one more question, though the ease of his expression no longer boded ill. 'You spoke of extra intelligence.'

Somervile smiled, but grimly. He leaned back in his chair and drew long on his cheroot before laying it aside and clasping his hands together in a gesture of resolve. 'On the death of his mother, by the name of Nandi, in October of last year, Shaka slaughtered a good many of his own people for reasons that are unclear, which may indeed be some manifestation of insanity, and ordered a year's mourning in which there was to be no cultivation of the soil, nor milk taken, nor conjugal activity – on pain of death. Indeed, any woman found with child suffers death with her husband.' Somervile spoke in an entirely detached way. He had seen things as cruel and senseless in India, though not on such a scale as this, if the reports were to be believed. 'Shaka has most brutally enforced these prohibitions, say our intelligencers, to the point that there is now talk of plots against him. It is well, therefore, that we meet with Shaka as soon as may be.'

All was silent. Fairbrother spoke the first. 'It is said that Shaka has never impregnated any of his harem. Did your intelligencers make remark on who is the rightful heir?'

Somervile took up his cheroot again to re-light with a safety match. 'It is supposed that it is the elder brother – half-brother – Dingane.'

Fairbrother made no reply.

'There could arise at any time a claimant, of course, for it seems scarcely possible that Shaka has not fathered a child. And that would be the very devil of a business to become entangled in.'

They all nodded.

Having succeeded in getting his cheroot lit once more, Somervile brought their deliberations to a point by blowing a prodigious cloud of smoke towards the ceiling. 'So you see, gentlemen, in consequence of the intelligence of active plots against Shaka, I am resolved on this embassy by the very greatest necessity. It is no longer, to my mind, an expedition of discovery but a prelude to action. Perhaps, even, an armed reconnaissance, as you *militaire* call it. I am persuaded that – to use Colonel Smith's words – the consequences of inaction are now too perilous to leave until the arrival of Sir Lowry Cole. Put plainly, it is the very safeguard of the Colony on which we embark.'

PART THREE

U-SHAKA!

MAP OF
NATAL
AND
ZULULAND

KwaWambaza

Ezi-Kleboni Hto

R. Thukola

Mountains
u.Khulamba

Nonoti

Duluza

R. Umgeni

Port Natal

N

0   10   20   30   40   50
Miles

XII

THE PLACE OF KILLING

Port Natal, towards the end of September

Hervey folded the cotton sheet, and shook his head. It was without doubt the most featureless map he had ever taken to the field with, a mere sketch of the hills and ridges, the rivers and winter bournes of that part of the Zulus' country which the British traders at Port Natal had noted ('surveyed' would have been too exact a term for the exercise). He had had a dozen copies made, drawn in an indelible ink by the troop clerk, and he had been able to commit every detail to memory. He tucked the map into an inside pocket of his dolman, confident that when he next took it out it would be to add to it rather than to consult.

It was in refastening the black buttons of the dragoon-fashion coat that he became conscious of the occasion: the expedition was the last time he would wear the green of the Rifles. Next he would exchange the blue of the

Sixth for the scarlet of the infantry. He would thereby leave behind the world of semi-independence that was the light dragoon's (and in large measure the mounted rifleman's too) for the close order and volleying of the Line. And he thought to savour it one last time. He certainly had no intention of trying to re-form the 81st Foot in the image of the Sixth, for he had seen for himself the effect of volleying often enough. He had begun to doubt the musket, thinking it a thing of antiquity, for the rifle was more accurate and had the greater range. Single, aimed shots were surely the future? But then at Umtata, even against a foe as active in using ground as any he had seen, Colonel Mili's double rank of red (six volleys in every minute) had been as solid a wall as on that day in 1815 when the cream of Bonaparte's Grande Armée had tried to break its way through to Brussels. The shock of so many muskets firing as one was ever great. 'They came on in the old way, and we saw them off in the old way!'

The Zulu selected their lines of advance with cunning, using the folds of the ground to conceal their approach (in the prelude to Umtata he had twice found himself all but surrounded), but they fought shoulder to shoulder. Fought with the utmost courage. Rarely had he seen an opponent persist in the face of such volleying as the Fifty-fifth's. Then again, it had been the first time they had even seen a wall of red, let alone felt its fire.

How intelligent were these Zulu? Shaka, by all reports,

was a warrior whose instinct for battle had forged the entire Zulu nation. Hervey could not but imagine that he would be thinking even now how to recast his army, in light of the reports of Umtata. Whatever Somervile might gain from this expedition by way of a treaty, he himself had but one object beyond the lieutenant-governor's safety: to discover how Shaka meant to fight if it came to war.

Reliant dropped anchor. Port Natal was but a sandy bay, with only a wooden jetty, though a fair haven; and a very fair prospect. Hervey thought he had never spied so pleasant a spot – the still blue water, the breakers beyond the sand bar, the wide, white beaches shimmering in the spring sunshine; and the rolling green hills, with here and there a red scar where the earth was scraped bare by the hand of nature or those of the settlers, few that they were. It was a land well watered, fertile, rich with game. He perfectly saw why its native tenants would be jealous of any that might threaten their title, although Shaka had been generous in welcoming the white man, making a gift of the bay, indeed.

Why, then, did Shaka wish to take the territory of the Xhosa? It was not nearly so abundant. Whence came the impulse for this *difaqane*, as the Xhosa called it, this crushing and scattering of every neighbouring clan and tribe? Could it really proceed from some urgent need of the Zulu for land? Or was it from something within Shaka himself? By all accounts he was no mere savage, rapacious, as any predatory beast. It seemed to Hervey that the self-made king of the Zulu perceived the situation of a nation without natural borders – the necessity for an active policy of war rather than waiting only on the defensive – as perfectly as had Frederick the Great himself . . .

Fairbrother, who had been observing the shore from the other side of *Reliant*'s quarterdeck, came across to where Hervey stood, by the starboard shrouds. 'Well, Colonel Hervey, what emotion is masked by that countenance of command?'

Hervey turned. 'I was contemplating the relative draughts of our ship and of the *Severus*. *She* went in unchecked, and yet we scraped our bottom a good minute on the sand bar – and she with a deck of twelve-pounders and all.'

It was true that *Reliant* had followed exactly the course of the accompanying brig, but Fairbrother was disinclined to believe that nautical details were occupying his friend's mind at this time. Nevertheless he humoured him. 'I had half hoped that we would be grounded, for I wanted to see what the steam tug would do. She's been of no use since we set sail.'

That was to be applauded, however, for they had had favourable airs since putting out of Cape Town. They had, in fact, made the passage in five days: a steady nine knots.

Hervey shrugged. 'I fancy if she had grounded we

could have lightened her by swimming the horses ashore, and she would have refloated of her own accord. I swam my best mare further at Madras, and that through breakers twice as big as those yonder.'

He had expected they would have to swim them ashore here too, but the *Reliant*'s master reckoned on getting close in – a hundred yards, he had promised. And he was as good as his word, for *Reliant* was now swinging round on her bow anchor, so that they would be able to get out the horses from the larboard entry port, but a stone's throw from the beach.

The master's words of command interrupted their speculation. 'Let go!'

The stern anchor dropped to arrest the swing.

At once Serjeant-Major Collins began mustering the dragoons. They would land by boat to be ready to catch the troopers (he had already chosen the lead horses, those good to call, so that the more wayward animals would herd-to in the shock of finding themselves in the water).

'A boat for yourselves, gentlemen?' asked the bosun.

Hervey looked about for Somervile, for it was his decision. 'I don't see the lieutenant-governor, Mr Caute.'

'I believe I saw him go to his cabin as we came in the bay, sir.'

'Mm.' A letter to write, perhaps – a despatch for the returning tug to take. 'I myself am content to stay aboard until the horses are ashore.' There was little he could do until his own chargers were disembarked; and in any case, he wished to observe what Captain Brereton did.

Somervile came on deck five minutes later, by which time the first of the boats was in the water and pulling for the beach. Another was pulling from the shore and making for *Severus*. 'Our welcoming party, I perceive,' he said, observing its white-faced occupants. 'Not unreasonable for them to suppose we are aboard the brig.'

'Especially not as one of them wears the uniform of the service, Sir Eyre,' replied Fairbrother, his telescope lighting on a dark blue jacket. 'Mr King, I imagine.'

Somervile looked content. 'Our expedition begins well, then.'

Some moments of contemplating the prospect followed until Fairbrother broke silence. 'Ah, the boat is now bound for us,' he reported, seeing it striking out again from *Severus*.

Somervile nodded. 'Captain Fairbrother, would you be so good as to go and receive them?'

'Of course, Sir Eyre.' Fairbrother touched the peak of his shako to take his leave.

'We are not, after all, in a Crown colony,' added Somervile, when he was gone. 'We do well to recollect it.'

'Just so,' replied Hervey, wondering why Somervile supposed he needed reminding. 'Though it would be as well to discover Lieutenant King's exact situation. Is he one of His Majesty's officers still, or does he act principally in Shaka's interest?'

'I was of a mind to discover that, certainly, but in truth I think it matters not in the end. All I require of him is that he leads us to the fellow, and tells us faithfully what he says. He might, of course, have every appearance of a King's officer and yet be in Shaka's pay.' Somervile looked grave, before adding wryly, 'Such things are not impossible.'

They waited in silence as the boat closed to *Reliant*'s larboard, and then the coming aboard of her party, and Fairbrother's courtesies at the entry port. In a minute or so the visitors were climbing the companionway to the quarterdeck, led by the man they supposed might just possibly be in Shaka's pay.

Lieutenant King, in the remnant of his naval bicorn, climbed the ladder wearily. His appearance was shocking – jaundiced, fevered even. He put his feet together in front of Somervile, although he could not have recognized him, and saluted. 'Lieutenant King, sir, at your service.'

Somervile raised his straw hat in return. 'I am glad to make your acquaintance, sir. Somervile, lieutenant-governor of the Cape.' He held out a hand, and felt the cold clamminess of King's as he took it.

'Forgive, me, Sir Eyre; I have been unwell these late days. My liver . . .'

'Then you must see my surgeon at once.' Somervile turned to Fairbrother.

Fairbrother went to find him.

'Perhaps you should sit down. Here, on the lockers.' Somervile gestured to the stern rail.

Lieutenant King was pleased to take the seat.

'A little brandy, perhaps? And then you might be so good as to introduce the rest of your party?'

'Brandy would be most efficacious, Sir Eyre,' replied King, supporting himself with a hand to the locker beside him. 'May I present Mr Nathaniel Isaacs, who has been here these three years, and John Ross, my clerk.'

The two had removed hats on coming onto the quarterdeck. Somervile returned their bows. 'Gentlemen.'

There followed a little conversation about the anchorage and the provision for the horses, before the surgeon, and brandy, came on deck.

The surgeon took King's pulse. 'I should wish to make a proper examination,' he said, with some asperity.

'Of course,' replied Somervile. 'You are at liberty to take Mr King below just as soon as I have a general report as to Chief Shaka's situation.'

The surgeon bowed, if reluctantly, and nodded to Somervile's steward to authorize a replenishment of the brandy glass.

King took it, and it appeared to revive him, for he let go the locker lid and removed his hat to wipe his brow. 'I beg pardon, Sir Eyre. It comes and goes, the fever, though I must admit the pain is much worse this time.'

Somervile nodded. 'There is no cause for apology, I

assure you. But, pray, are you able to say anything of Shaka that might be of help at this time – before Mr Fernyhough takes you below to his dispensary?'

Lieutenant King coughed a little (the stimulus of the brandy, Somervile supposed). 'Shaka is presently engaged on a campaign against Soshangane, Sir Eyre, a chief whose country lies just to the south of Delagoa Bay. In the autumn he crushed the Pondo—'

'The Pondo – to the south, you mean?'

'Yes. Shaka had long had it in his mind to crush the Pondo. He sent his spies there in the summer, and they reported favourably. Besides subjugating the clan, Shaka declared it would serve as the mourning hunt for his mother.' He began coughing again, and had to breathe deeply for a while before resuming. 'They call it *i-hlambo*, and every warrior must wash his spear in blood. And for his mother, there had to be a great washing of spears.'

Hervey shook his head.

Somervile appeared merely to be absorbed in scholarly discovery. 'And I take it that once this "washing of spears" is done, Shaka will declare that the country shall return to its normal condition? We have heard of the depredations on his people on account of Nandi's death.'

'I believe that was to be so. But when the army returned, with a great number of cattle, Shaka became restless again, fearing his warriors became soft, and so he ordered them to march north against Soshangane.'

Somervile looked disappointed. 'Where is Shaka now – in the north?'

'No, at his kraal, Dukuza, two days' ride north of here, but he's called a meeting of the elders towards the end of the month, at his capital, Bulawayo, the same distance beyond.' He began coughing again.

'I think, Sir Eyre . . .' tried the surgeon.

'Yes, Mr Fernyhough, a moment or two more,' replied Somervile, testily. He turned back to King. 'I am much obliged to you, sir. We must make every effort to see Shaka before he leaves for . . .'

'Bulawayo: "the place of killing".'

Somervile grimaced. 'The place of killing?'

'The Zulu regard the act quite differently from us.'

'So I am coming to conclude, Mr King.' He nodded to the surgeon. 'But see now, you must go below and take Fernyhough's medicine, and then we may speak of Shaka's philosophy at more leisure.'

The lieutenant rose unsteadily and replaced his hat, clasped the point in salute, and left with his companions in the surgeon's charge.

'I hope we shall not be too long detained by his fever,' said Somervile when they were out of earshot. 'I would strike out for Dukuza the day after tomorrow, at the latest.'

Hervey saw no reason to delay the entire party. 'Might I ride ahead, with Fairbrother, so that Shaka knows you are coming?'

Somervile had already considered the idea. 'I imagine Shaka will know by nightfall that we have arrived, do you not suppose? Let us wait for the surgeon's art to work its beneficial effects with Mr King. Since Shaka entrusted him with the mission to Port Elizabeth, he evidently has high regard of him. The time will be well spent if we address – as you have it – our interior economy. I want to parade before the great chief of the Zulu with all the appearance of superiority.'

The landing proceeded without mishap. Indeed, it was done with ease, and the deconfining made for a degree of skylarking by horses and men alike. Many a dragoon had not set foot on a beach before, and gave way to the pleasure of warm water and sand. It was not long before they were catching fish, climbing trees, pointing animatedly to the dolphins beyond the sandbar, taking shots at seabirds, hauling a turtle from the shallows . . .

Content that the Rifles had the landing securely picketed, Hervey decided he too would take his pleasure. 'A bathe, Somervile?'

'By all means,' replied his old friend, readily. 'But you will excuse me, for I must press King to a question or two more – if the surgeon hasn't dosed him too severely.'

Hervey could not believe there would be much to have from King before the morning, whatever the surgeon's medicine, but he would not debate it.

He turned to Fairbrother. 'Shall you take the waters?'

It was not his habit to take exercise for the pleasure of it, but Fairbrother reckoned there was purpose in accompanying his friend. 'Very well.'

They stripped and swam ashore.

And as they dried themselves by one of the driftwood fires, which the dragoons lost no time making, and waited for the jolly-boat with Johnson and their clothes, Fairbrother observed the evident delight of the troop in their recreation. 'What are you thinking of?' he asked, seeing his friend in thought.

Hervey smiled. 'That it would indeed be pleasing to remain here for several days. Such a pity that Shaka is to leave his kraal, and that we therefore have to make haste.'

Fairbrother looked at him quizzically. 'Remain here for a mere several days – not more?'

'Ha! If we were not engaged upon official business, I believe I could pass many a happy week here – months, even. I hazard there'd be no shortage of volunteers from the troop for outpost duty. Or even to have their discharge. See how agreeable they find it!'

Fairbrother smiled, ironically. 'Just so. Happy colonists. And have you thought: Shaka may come to that same conclusion?'

XIII
METTLE ENOUGH

Next morning

The surgeon came onto *Reliant*'s quarterdeck a little after six, and with a weary look. 'I regret to inform you, Sir Eyre, that Lieutenant King is dead.'

Somervile sighed heavily.

Hervey put his coffee cup aside. 'Not of any contagion, I trust, doctor?'

The surgeon shook his head. 'I cannot be certain, but I believe it to be poisoning of the liver. Not any contagion, however. Nothing that need dismay.'

Somervile huffed. 'Except that King was to be our interlocutor with Shaka!'

'Isaacs speaks his language as well as did King, so I understand,' said Hervey, encouragingly.

'Isaacs? A rough sort by the look of him. Not the man I would choose to engage for diplomacy.'

Hervey bridled, rather, at the harsh judgement. His

old friend had invested a great deal in this venture, his reputation, indeed; but all the same . . . 'Rough *and* ready, Somervile.'

'If I might add, Sir Eyre,' tried Fairbrother, who had likewise laid aside his breakfast cup: 'Isaacs may yet be a more faithful interpreter, for he does not enjoy Shaka's confidence in the way King did, and therefore will be obliged to render the translation without, shall we say, his own estimation.'

Hervey said nothing, but he agreed with him. And besides, the principal means of gathering the intelligence that *he* required would be from observation.

Somervile began nodding, slowly. 'Thank you, Fairbrother. I'm obliged.' He thought for a moment or two more. 'We have, in any case, no option but to proceed.'

Lieutenant King's body was sewn into a hammock. Somervile instructed that it be transferred to the brig, HMS *Severus*, and thence taken for burial at sea, beyond the bar, following the traditions of the service. At the last minute, however, the lieutenant's native servant had sought out Fairbrother and told him of his master's most particular request, that if he were to die in this place he should be buried on the bluff overlooking the anchorage. And so, a little after seven, a party of seamen took the body ashore, and Hottentot bearers dug the grave.

In the absence of a chaplain, Hervey read the service.

Afterwards, he and Fairbrother walked down from the bluff together.

'It marks well what we spoke of last night, does it not?' said his friend, the sun now strong enough to oblige them both to replace their hats. 'This is a country in which a man might happily put down roots.'

It was just that, Hervey conceded. And he was happy to acknowledge its bounties. But he confessed that his thoughts were with the more practical details of the days ahead. He had urged Somervile to discount too great a setback in losing King's good offices with Shaka, but there was first the question of seeking Shaka out. Isaacs had assured them that he knew the way to Dukuza: it was but a *trek*, as the Cape Dutch had it, north for a day and a half, perhaps two, following the coast. But without King, Hervey was uncertain how they would make their entry. Would Shaka receive them, indeed? But Isaacs had been confident in proposing himself, albeit in some dejection at the loss of his friend. Shaka, said Isaacs, had told them that he had moved his kraal to Dukuza from Bulawayo to be nearer his English friends – *friends*, not merely Lieutenant King. And although Isaacs did not have King's rank, and therefore quite Shaka's esteem, he assured Hervey he would be received as an honest man of trade.

A little after nine o'clock, the embassy to the Court of Shaka left Port Natal for Dukuza. Welsh, the Rifles' captain, had enlisted half a dozen *voerlopers* from the settlement, native and part-native men of whom Isaacs spoke well, to range ahead and read the country. The military scouting proper was given to a section of eight dragoons under the command of Lance-Serjeant Hardy, Isaacs riding with them, and the section of mounted riflemen following as advance guard.

Somervile, at the head of the main body (the half troop of light dragoons and the thirty bat-horses), was animated to an unusual degree. Africa was not India, as he had been at pains to point out on every occasion they had been drawn to make comparison, but something of India evidently stirred within, the same impulse of many a gallop across the plains of Madras or of Bengal. '*Ex Africa semper aliquid novi!*' he declared at length, shaking his head slowly in wonder.

Hervey smiled. His friend was a considerable classical scholar, if a repetitious one. 'Pliny again? Most apt. I have always thought of you as formed in Pliny's mould.'

Somervile nodded gravely. 'The comparison is favourable. Pliny was an assiduous observer.'

Hervey smiled the more. He was not given to flattering to advantage, but if ever he had the inclination . . .

'But perhaps I should add "*novi omnes dies*", for certainly Pliny never saw such sights as these.'

Hervey frowned at his old friend's proposal to gild the lily. 'Recollect, Sir Eyre, that assiduous observation was in the end the death of him.'

Somervile scowled. 'Not only do you tempt the Fates, you betray a want of comprehension. Recollect that it was not the volcano that killed Pliny; he was found with not a mark upon him. He was by that time a corpulent man, and almost certainly placed a strain upon his heart wholly in excess of its capacity.'

Hervey smiled wryly, and raised an eyebrow, glancing at the spread (if undoubtedly diminished of late) that was the lieutenant-governor's waist. 'Just so.'

Somervile appeared not to notice, intent as he was on a green-backed heron that flapped low and awkwardly between them and the scouts. 'It was a heron that crossed our path the first time you and I rode together,' he replied absently.

Hervey did not recall it. 'At Cape-town?'

Somervile looked at him, puzzled. 'At Guntoor. A pair of them, indeed. The day we rode to see what ill the Pindarees had done.'

Hervey shook his head: Madras was an age ago. 'You astound me, Somervile. I remember the Pindaree depredations, but . . .'

'Do you not recall my quarters at Guntoor? I have a clear recollection of your being greatly discomfited by the house snakes.'

'I have no recollection of them, no, although I do remember your quarters,' he replied warily, for he was invariably discomfited by snakes, despite his years in India.

'They were night herons at Guntoor, however. I wonder if the species is to be found in these parts . . .'

A big black bird the size of a turkey, with a huge curved bill and vivid red face, scuttled out of the scrub a dozen yards ahead of them and made for the haven of a nearby thorn bush. Somervile's horse protested at the effrontery, resisting its rider's attempts to close with the bush for a better look, until shortened reins, and spurs, did the trick.

Hervey did not feel inclined to follow so eagerly; he had never been as keen an observer of the bird kingdom as Somervile (except birds of prey). They would surely see more if they stood off a little?

Johnson took the opportunity to come up alongside him. 'What were Mr Somervile sayin – liquid an' Africa? An' thee abaht dyin, sir? Ah couldn't catch it right.'

Hervey was long past protesting that being overheard was one thing, but having to repeat himself quite another. 'Latin, a saying by a general called Pliny: "There is always something new out of Africa." And *I* said that Sir Eyre should remember that Pliny's curiosity was the death of him, because, when the volcano erupted, he went to take a closer look, and was killed.'

'But there aren't no volcanoes 'ere, are there?'

'None that I can see. I meant in the general sense, that care killed the cat.'

'What?'

Hervey turned in the saddle, and thrust his hand out.

' "What, courage man! What though care killed a cat." '

Johnson looked at him strangely. 'Tha's chirrupy this mornin', sir.'

'Shakespeare, Johnson! "What though care killed a cat, thou hast mettle enough in thee to kill care." '

'What? Shakespeare talked like that?'

'Like what?'

'Like me.'

Hervey looked at him quizzically. 'Now that you mention it—'

But Somervile had closed with him again, and so Johnson fell respectfully back a length.

'Some sort of hornbill, as I never saw before. What was that you were saying?'

'About Guntoor?'

'No; Private Johnson.' He looked over his shoulder and nodded, to Johnson's satisfaction. '*Much Ado About Nothing*, was it not?'

Hervey had to think for a moment. 'It was.'

' "Thou hast mettle enough in thee to kill care." And thou dost indeed, Hervey. And I am depending on it.'

Hervey scowled back. 'It is for that dependability that His Majesty pays me, Sir Eyre.'

Somervile affected no notice. 'You know, Hervey, this infantry command you are to take up . . . I am not so certain it is second best. There may perhaps be the greater opportunity for distinction.'

Hervey looked at his old friend, curious. 'What makes

you say that? What greater distinction might there be than to make history with the lieutenant-governor of the Cape Colony?'

The sun's increasing warmth had brought out the horseflies – bigger even than those in Bengal. Somervile's charger was beginning to object to their attentions, and Hervey's Molly the same. 'Before I address that, I propose we trot a while to see if we can shake these beggars off.'

Hervey signalled to the column, though he doubted they would leave the flies behind at a mere trot; and he did not consider it wise to allow a canter just yet in country he did not know (bare country that it was, as poor grassland as the great plain in Wiltshire).

'And so: *distinction*?' he prompted, raising his voice a little as they bumped along.

Somervile looked pleased. 'There's much to be done in Canada. Not an affair of arms, of course – or rather, I trust not – but of consolidation, with the Americans, the border, the native Indians and the like.'

They had spoken only a little of Canada since Emma had told Hervey the good news. Both were of the view that contemplating the next posting was the besetting sin of the too-ambitious man.

The prospect was appealing, though; it did not do to be forever taking up arms. 'And when is it, you say, that you go?'

'To be decided. Indeed, I ought to repeat that the

appointment is yet to be approved, but if Huskisson manages to stay at the Colonies Office the position will be mine. I did not mention, too, that it is upon the most agreeable terms.'

Hervey checked his mare, for she was beginning to force the pace. 'I am excessively pleased. When I was last—'

But the sudden activity of the scouts half a mile ahead stayed his recollections. Hervey's hand was raised even before Somervile noticed.

The column fell back to a walk, and then halted. Out came the telescopes.

'What do they signal, Hervey?'

One scout was circling around a second, anti-clockwise, in a twenty-yard radius, his horse on a long rein.

The movement contained all the information Hervey needed. 'Zulu, on foot, between one and two dozen, stationary.'

'Scouts, perhaps?' suggested Somervile, trying to keep his horse still enough to train his telescope.

'I would think so,' said Hervey, searching the ground to left and right. 'We expected them, did we not?' They had been marching for two hours and more – long enough for Shaka's standing patrols to have learned of the column's approach.

All Serjeant Hardy's scouts were now observing the Zulu from the crest of the hill.

Hervey was keen to close with them to make his own reconnaissance. 'Hardy's orders are to halt on first contact. Shall we take a look?'

Somervile was already so active in the saddle that Hervey was certain what his answer would be. 'Why do we wait?'

'Proprieties,' replied Hervey – and a shade impatiently, turning in the saddle to look behind. 'The scouts are under Brereton's command.'

He strained to see what the officer in acting command of E Troop did.

But Brereton appeared to be doing nothing other than observe.

Hervey saw Serjeant-Major Collins come up from the rear, halting beside his troop leader, and the brief conference which followed.

Cornet Kemmis now left the column and cantered forward, saluting as he passed the head of the column.

Hervey sighed.

'Is something amiss?' enquired Somervile.

'If Brereton had wanted an officer's patrol instead of scouts then he ought to have arranged it so at the beginning. There's scarce point in sending a cornet back and forth like a fly shuttle.'

'Why do we not follow him?'

'Because that would be to disparage Brereton in front of the troop. I wonder what Collins was thinking to allow it.'

Somervile looked at him oddly. 'You expect a serjeant-major to trump a captain?'

'I expect Collins to know what is what!' He almost said 'Armstrong would have!'

They sat silent, if not exactly patient (or even still, for both horses were now fidgeting), until Kemmis returned, at a fast canter, to report to his troop leader. Hervey kept himself in check while the cornet relayed the scouts' intelligence to Brereton, just beyond his hearing.

And then, to his surprise, Kemmis and not Brereton rode back up the column towards them.

'Sir Eyre,' he began, while looking directly at Hervey (the custom of the service being to proceed as if addressing the most senior officer present), 'there is a party of Zulu half a mile or so ahead of the scouts, not many, a dozen perhaps, though the ground might conceal more. They stand in the open, observing, and make no move. Mr Isaacs says they are from Shaka's guards regiment.'

Hervey suppressed his irritation as best he could: he would speak with Brereton later, for the intelligence was nothing but that which Serjeant Hardy himself could have brought – or even the corporal. Kemmis had evidently not observed anything for himself, and knowing Kemmis, it was because there was nothing more to observe.

'And, Colonel . . .'

'Yes, Mr Kemmis, what is it? Do not try my patience.'

'No, Colonel. Mr Isaacs is unwell.'

'What do you mean, "unwell"? Do try to give a full account of things, Kemmis, else we waste no end of time.'

'No, Colonel. I mean, he's shivering, really quite violently, and he can't see clearly.'

Hervey frowned. 'How then can he tell which regiment the Zulu are from?'

'Serjeant Hardy described to him what he observed, Colonel.'

Hervey nodded approvingly.

'The same as King, d'you suppose?' suggested Somervile, wearily.

Hervey suspected not; he knew the symptoms right enough. 'We'd better have Fernyhough come with us.'

He told Kemmis to call the surgeon up. He almost told him to summon Brereton, too, but thought better of it.

Somervile raised his telescope once more. 'Hervey, do you suppose—'

But Hervey was reining round, intent on speaking to E Troop leader.

Brereton was by now riding forward, however.

'At last,' muttered Hervey.

Brereton saluted. 'Colonel, your orders?'

Hervey forced himself to speak as a colonel to a captain. 'To proceed with caution. I shall go forward to the scouts, to see for myself with Sir Eyre. And the surgeon.'

'Very well.'

'And, Brereton . . .' (he lowered his voice) 'do not have us converse through a cornet again.'

'No, Hervey. Thank you; I realized—'

'Proceed with caution, then. I'll get the scouts moving, and then wait on yonder crest for you.'

'Yes,' replied Brereton, quietly, saluting and turning about.

Hervey and his party cantered to the ridge where the scouts had halted, the lieutenant-governor so intent on his first sight of the famed Zulu that he would have given his gelding its head if Hervey had not insisted otherwise.

Serjeant Hardy saluted as they pulled up. 'Sir!'

'At ease, Sar'nt Hardy. The lieutenant-governor wishes to see what the Zulu look like. I fancy much as we saw them last summer?'

'Ay, sir, but about one in ten thousand as many,' he replied drily, his Cotswold vowels notably more pronounced than those of his fellow-countryman Collins.

They crested the rise together, where Isaacs was sitting hunched on the ground.

Hervey and the surgeon dismounted. 'Shaka's scouts, you say, Isaacs?'

'See for yourself, Colonel,' managed Isaacs, but weakly.

Somervile was already observing.

'I will,' replied Hervey. 'But first let the surgeon take a look at you.'

'There are but a very few,' Somervile called from the saddle, sounding disappointed.

'There might be hundreds more you can't see,' Hervey called back, hoping to silence his old friend for a few moments while the surgeon made his examination.

'There isn't any others, Colonel,' said Isaacs in almost a whisper. 'I know this country like the back of m'hand. You sees all there is, here. Not even a Zulu could 'ide 'imself. Not till we gets the other side of the Umhloti.'

'Tell me, how are they revealed as scouts?' asked Somervile, lowering his glass after several minutes' intense study. 'Either Serjeant Hardy's telescope is greatly more powerful than mine, or else something eludes me.'

'You observe what they carry?' Hervey tried his best not to sound exasperated.

'I do: the short spear, exactly as you described it.'

'Anything more?'

'No-o. Only a very small shield. Like a toy, indeed.'

'Exactly so.'

Isaacs insisted on answering for himself, if with the greatest difficulty. 'That's Shaka's way of saying 'e 'as no fear of us. The spear an' small shield belongs to the warrior; the war shield belongs to Shaka.'

'Should we speak with them?'

'No, Sir Eyre.'

The surgeon tried to stay him, but Isaacs insisted.

'They'll not let us within reach. Their job's to tell

Shaka we're 'ere and when we comes to Dukuza, so's Shaka can look 'is best.'

Somervile nodded. 'Very well. There can be no objection in that. It shows that he does expect us.'

Hervey drew him aside, leaving the surgeon to his dosing. 'Not a sight to awe. But then, as a rule scouts are not meant even to be seen.'

Somervile raised a hand to acknowledge. In any case, he had wished only for a peaceful glimpse of a Zulu: his acquaintance with the Xhosa had been so fleeting and violent that he had not been able to form any impression of them from, as he put it, an 'ethnological' point of view. 'You know, Hervey, I am by no means certain that Shaka is waiting with equanimity at his kraal.'

Hervey shrugged. 'There could scarcely be certainty of anything in these parts.'

Somervile nodded. 'But *beyond* that: if his army has been fighting the Pondo, might he not believe that this has occasioned alarm in the Colony, and that we are harbingers of war?'

'He might. And with the bulk of his army in the north, he might be, shall we say, nervous?'

'Quite so. It is ironic, is it not, that our advantage would lie in Shaka's army being at Dukuza!'

Hervey frowned. 'Somervile, from what I have learned of the Zulu, Shaka will not have the entire army away either in the north or the south. We place ourselves as hostages to his good will either way. I must remind you that our safety rests ultimately in the speed of the horse.'

' "A horse is a vain thing for safety. Neither shall he deliver any by his great strength." '

'I have always considered that the psalmist must have had other things in mind. We must trust differently.'

Somervile nodded again, but gravely. 'You know, Hervey, there is a line in that play of yours – I mean the *Malfi* – when one of the courtiers, an old and wise lord – do you recall, Castruchio? – is discussing with the duchess's brother whether a prince might also be a soldier.'

'I recall it.'

'And Castruchio says that while it is fitting for a soldier to become a prince, it is not fitting that a prince descend to be a captain.'

' "That realm is never long in quiet, where the ruler is a soldier." '

'Well remembered. Do you not think it apt?'

'I thought it our design in coming here.'

'It is. But look at the condition of Isaacs: how might we take the measure of Shaka, prince *and* soldier, without him? Without Mr King it was unpropitious enough! I confess I shall count as much on your judgement, now, as I do on your sword.'

Hervey would have sighed as heavily as his old friend, had he not just been placed upon his quality so. 'These fevers – the malaria – two or three days, that's all. Isaacs will be well. And Fairbrother has enough Xhosa for our purposes. We know it to be not so very different from the Zulu.'

He hoped he sounded more certain than he was.

XIV

ERROR'S CHAIN

Later

Marching across grassland was always a tedious affair. The dragoons stumbled when they were leading on foot, and there was nothing to mark their progress by, dismounted or mounted. Hervey lapsed into ruminatory silence.

They rested in the afternoon, not long, for it was by no means hot. But Fairbrother was able to rejoin them. His gelding had twisted a shoe just before they set off, and he had wanted the new one hot-fitted. Hervey asked him if he would ride with the scouts in place of Isaacs.

Towards four o'clock they saw the first of distant kraals, if modest sized: *umuzi*, single homesteads, with small herds of cattle tended by youths and boys. It was a pastoral landscape that once more put Hervey in mind of the Wiltshire plain.

He started singing, beneath his breath:

From Greenland's icy mountains,
From India's coral strand,
Where Afric's sunny fountains
Roll down their golden sand,
From many an ancient river,
From many a palmy plain,
They call us to deliver
Their land from error's chain.

He had known the author of those words, Bishop Heber of Calcutta. True, he had tended to avoid his society, but he did respect the evident sincerity in wishing to share the gospel with a country that, in the end, had been the death of him – martyr to a climate his constitution was not equipped to brave. But 'India's coral strand' was at least half welcoming to mission (India, after all, had heard the gospel before England), whereas 'Afric's sunny fountains' and 'palmy plains', from all he had seen so far, appeared decidedly less so. He had certainly heard no one calling to be delivered from 'error's chain'.

His thoughts began to range again as they plodded on.

'Galloper guns,' he said suddenly, out of a silence of a quarter of an hour. 'That is what we must have here. I can't think why we ever did away with them in India.'

Somervile, though startled by the sudden martial turn (they had previously been observing on the habits of egrets) was nevertheless quick to the point. 'I fancy it

283

would not be beyond the capability of the foundry at Cape-town.'

'In such country, seeing how sharp the Zulu move, a galloper would have capital effect, especially with explosive shell, or shrapnel. I for one would trade weight of shot for celerity.'

He wondered that he had not thought of it after Umtata. But then, such thoughts did not always spring from the theoretical contemplation of a problem, or else the men at the Board of Ordnance would have no need of field service; and in any case, the battle at Umtata, after the skirmishing which preceded it, had been as set-piece an affair as any in Spain.

'I will see to it when we return,' he said decidedly, and then he lapsed once more into consideration of 'error's chain'.

Late in the afternoon they reached the southernmost of the Fasimba kraals. Isaacs struggled to the front of the column, despite Somervile's assurance that there was no need. Fasimba, he told them, 'haze', was the name of the regiment of guards – 'Shaka's Own'.

This royal kraal – *ikhanda* – was bigger than they had seen so far. Isaacs said it was the headquarters of a Fasimba general, and the barracks of the unmarried youths who reported for training there – the *inkwebane*. It was by no means a great *ikhanda*, some fifty or so huts, whereas at Dukuza there were a thousand, but the cattle byre had been enlarged to pen the booty-cattle of the Pondoland campaign. He said it would not be prudent to pass by without acknowledging Shaka's man, the *induna*.

'Isaacs, your devotion to duty is admirable, but . . .'

Isaacs waved a hand, protesting.

Somervile shook his head. Isaacs was not fit to be in the saddle, yet how might they proceed without him – here, especially, the kraal of Shaka's guards? But he had to concede, and he did so with an esteeming smile. 'I am most excessively obliged to you.'

Hervey sent back the order for a close escort of six dragoons, and then with Somervile, Fairbrother and Isaacs, set off down the half-mile of gentle slope for the kraal.

Only as they came close did they see the 'sentinels' flanking the *sango*, the ceremonial entrance.

Hervey groaned. 'Good God!'

Somervile was as quick to the recognition, but quicker to the necessity for composure. 'Eyes front, I think, Hervey.'

'One of them's a woman!'

'I am able to determine that for myself. Nod to the guard of honour forming up for us.' He cleared his throat. 'Or I *imagine* it's a guard of honour.'

A dozen *inkwebane* in ceremonial dress, a single red-lory feather in each head-ring, the distinction of the Fasimba, were mustering outside the *sango*. They carried the short, stabbing spear, the *iklwa*, and black war shields, and appeared oblivious to the impalings under which they paraded.

Somervile raised his hat to return their salute. Hervey and Fairbrother saluted in the usual fashion, for although a salute was meant for the senior officer, and therefore returned by him alone, it seemed prudent to err on the side of unequivocal respect.

'I've a mind they were alive when they were hoist,' said Hervey, trying to keep his stomach down, for the stench of corruption was almost overpowering.

'Seven days ago, I'd say,' opined Fairbrother, not to Hervey's mind very usefully.

They rode through the opening in the great thorn stockade and halted inside the empty cattle byre, the herds grazing in an adjacent valley. The *inkwebane* followed, silent, and ranged in a half-moon behind them, closing off the *sango* so that Somervile's escort remained outside; though whether or not it was their intention to exclude them, Hervey could not tell.

'What is the meaning of that butchery, Isaacs?' asked Somervile as they reined to a halt, intent on remaining in the saddle for both his dignity and safety.

Isaacs was now barely able to sit upright. He gasped rather than spoke his reply. 'I'm fearful you'll see many another. They'll 'ave broken Shaka's mourning orders. Like as not the woman was with child.'

This much they had learned in Cape Town; but to see it for themselves . . . 'Bestial!' hissed Somervile.

'And no crops planted, no milk drawn – only to be poured on the earth.'

'Madness!'

'That is Shaka. When you meets 'im, you'll understand.'

An older warrior, wearing the otter-skin head-ring, the privilege of the married man, advanced on them.

'One of the gatekeepers,' said Isaacs, only with the greatest effort. 'Pay 'im no honours unless 'e crouches – which 'e won't.'

The warrior turned to face them squarely. He carried the *iklwa*, like the guard of honour, but a smaller shield.

'*Wozani!*'

'He wants us to follow 'im.'

'To the head man?'

'Can't be certain; but they're expecting us plain enough.'

'In that case we will dismount – once we have our horse-holders.' Somervile turned in the saddle and beckoned forward the escort. 'Since we're bidden, the guard'll have to let them in.'

Hervey prayed they would.

At the keeper's nod, the *inkwebane* parted left and right, making an opening just large enough to allow the escort to enter in file.

Hervey beckoned Trumpeter Roddis to him, reckoning a bugle preferable to the best swordsman. Then the five of them struck out behind the silent old warrior, across the byre towards the *isigodlo*, the private quarters of Shaka's man, the *induna*. Isaacs was now so fevered that he needed Fairbrother's support.

Another thorn fence, smaller than that of the outer perimeter of the kraal, enclosed the *isigodlo*, a collection of seven or eight beehive-shaped huts made of tightly woven grass. They passed through a narrow gate guarded by a single warrior, and made for the largest of the huts.

The *induna* himself greeted them. His smile, if equivocal, was easy none the less. He bid them enter.

Inside were calf skins spread on a clay floor. The *induna* gestured for his visitors to sit. Three serving-girls, their breasts bare, brought hollowed gourds filled with beer.

Isaacs, whom the *induna* appeared to know, began speaking. With the very greatest effort, and periodic gestures towards the others, Somervile in particular, he began to explain their coming here.

He spoke of 'Um Joji', as Shaka called King George, which appeared to establish the party's importance. Indeed, the *induna* seemed more flattered by the minute with the visitation (although Hervey could not but suppose that he had hourly expected them, and knew precisely their status).

Gradually, the *induna* allowed himself more ease. He was especially intent on Fairbrother, and when the latter spoke to him in Xhosa he narrowed his eyes as if to gain a sharper resolution of his features. With only a little help from Isaacs, Fairbrother explained that he had spent many years at the Cape and had made it his business to be fluent in the tongue of his nearest neighbours.

This brought nods of approval.

And half an hour passed agreeably. Somervile had not expected to learn anything (nor had Hervey); his principal concern was with how long he would be required to sup here before he could decently take his leave. However, the *induna* told them that half the booty-cattle were to be returned to the Pondo king, Faku – a gesture of peace on Shaka's part. And ripe intelligence.

A gesture of peace, or a sign of weakness? Somervile pressed him for more. 'Ask how the campaign went, and now that against Soshangane.'

But Isaacs could barely summon the breath.

Fairbrother tried instead.

It took a little longer, but he was confident of his ability. 'The *induna* says the Pondo fought hard, but that Shaka crushed them, as he has crushed all his enemies. There is no news yet from the north, but Soshangane will be crushed like Faku.'

Somervile looked at the *induna*, and bowed. 'And what of the clash at Umtata, with Matiwane's warriors?'

There was an even longer exchange, Fairbrother pressing the *induna* hard.

'It is as we heard, Sir Eyre. He says that Matiwane had

been no vassal, or even friend of Shaka's. I could not exactly follow all he said, but it seems that Shaka's keen to know how Matiwane's warriors were brought to defeat by our fewer numbers.'

Hervey did not doubt it. Shaka could hardly be indifferent to the defeat of an army trained in the manner of his own. 'Does the *induna* suppose we were there?'

'I believe he does.'

The serving-girls brought more beer, but before they could pour much of it, the older warrior returned, and with a graver expression than when he had greeted the visitors at the *sango*.

He whispered into the *induna*'s ear.

The *induna* looked perturbed. He questioned him urgently, *sotto voce*, and then gave way, for the briefest moment at least, to a look of dismay, before masking it with resolution, and rising.

He bowed to his guests, who rose with him, and from a loop fastening by the door of the hut he took his ceremonial staff.

Somervile motioned to Fairbrother.

With no time to think how he might phrase his question, Fairbrother asked simply if they might be of help.

The *induna* hesitated, as if unsure whether or not he had a right to speak, and then turned back to him. Twelve youths and boys, tenders of the royal cattle at Dukuza, had been sent to him for punishment, he explained. Shaka suspected them of *kleza* – squirting the milk from the cows' udders into their mouths – contrary to the mourning orders. Shaka had questioned them, they denied it, and he had directed them to take the usual oath, to swear 'by Shaka'. This, knowing their guilt, they had refused to do, and so Shaka had ordered them to come here, to the Fasimba kraal, where in a year or so they would have been enrolled as *inkwebane*, and tell the *induna* that Shaka had ordered them to be put to death.

Somervile looked at Isaacs, who nodded that this was a fair translation.

The *induna* watched, as if somehow fearful of their opinion.

'Hervey, we must prevent this,' said Somervile, decidedly.

Isaacs looked alarmed. 'Sir, there's no way on earth as we can prevent it. We'd be cut down at once – before yon bugler could play a note!'

Hervey took hold of Somervile's arm. 'You cannot think otherwise but as Isaacs says!'

Isaacs gasped for breath even more. 'He said the youths'd come 'ere without escort, solely on their honour. That's Shaka's power!'

'And Shaka knows we'll be here,' suggested Fairbrother, in a sinister way. ' "My name is Shaka, king of kings: Look on my works, ye mighty, and despair" . . .'

Somervile, if not exactly despairing, was agitated nevertheless. 'I have no desire to look upon his bestial works, yet we can do no good inside this hut.'

Hervey was not so sure. 'What say you, Isaacs?'

'Will make no difference.' He sank back to the floor, the sweat running freely down his face.

'Come,' said Somervile, striding for the door.

A dozen youths and boys stood in the middle of the cattle enclosure, in line, facing the *isigodlo*. The same cadets of the guard of honour, but without their finery, stood in line behind them.

The *induna* strode angrily across the byre, berating Shaka's consigned.

Somervile followed as close as he thought safe.

'What does he say, Fairbrother? I can't make out a word.'

Fairbrother raised an eyebrow. 'A Zulu general's ranting, Sir Eyre – I doubt even the wretched boys know.'

But slowly, as the *induna* stopped his railing and began speaking in more measured terms, though angry still, Fairbrother was able to catch some sense of it.

'He asks them if it's true they did *kleza*, and that Shaka sent them to say that he'd ordered them to be put to death.'

There was a murmuring among the condemned youths, with here and there a stronger voice seeming to admit it was so.

The *induna* raised his stick and swung it down furiously. '*Ni ngama qawu* . . . You are heroes – and as men and heroes you shall die by the spear, and not by the felons' club!'

The words were spoken so clearly – for the hearing of all in the enclosure – that Somervile and even Hervey were able to understand.

The young heroes had ranged themselves in age, so that on the right of the line, the place of honour, was the eldest, a youth of about Hervey's own height, and sixteen years, perhaps.

Somervile grew restless. 'My God, Hervey: those boys at yonder end are but eight or nine!'

Fairbrother spoke sharply. 'Close your eyes, Sir Eyre. That, or keep your counsel – with respect.'

Isaacs, who had struggled to join them on the arm of the older warrior, sealed the business. 'It's Shaka's will, and none of us'd be worth a spit if we crossed it!'

Somervile shook his head in unhappy resignation. Hervey stayed his own hand from his sabre only with the fiercest resolve.

And then, removing his shako, Fairbrother stepped forward. '*Mnumzana* . . .'

At this formal style of address by one of the visitors, the *induna* turned. There were tears on his cheeks.

Fairbrother struggled to express their objection, trying to combine in his voice and manner not only the imperative to stay the executions, but the deference necessary to keep *them* alive too. '*Mnumzana* . . . Sir, it is displeasing to the religion of King George, of whom Sir Eyre Somervile here is the personal representative, to have the blood of common felons shed in his presence, although undoubtedly they are brave men. King Shaka cannot know how brave these youths and boys have been, only that they disobeyed his command. Although King George knows that all Zulu are brave, would not King Shaka wish to know of their especial bravery, and might therefore wish to spare them?'

Only once did the *induna* need Isaacs's help to explain.

Hervey watched, tense, ready to draw his sabre. If he had to, he would tell Somervile to dash for the *isigodlo* while he warded off the *inkwebane*, and then would fall back with Fairbrother to the entrance. There they would make their stand there until the escort, and the rest of the column, answered Roddis's bugle. It was at least a plan, if a forlorn hope.

The *induna*, impassive despite his streaming eyes, turned away and beckoned the old warrior. He spoke quickly, insistently, but not in a voice that carried to the visitors.

When he was finished, the warrior nodded his head, once, in a gesture of resolve. '*Yebo, baba!*'

Fairbrother stepped rear, to Somervile's left side, sensing they would soon have to make a dash for it.

'We fall back to the hut if they turn,' whispered Hervey, on Somervile's right. 'I'll take the headman.'

'And the other dozen spears?' whispered Fairbrother. 'Keep praying, my friend!'

The keeper now spoke quietly to the *inkwebane*.

Hervey was on the point of drawing his sabre when the cadets divided, marching round either flank of the youths and halting in front of them, so that each of the condemned could look into the eyes of his executioner.

'Good God!' spluttered Somervile. 'What a monstrous ceremony.'

'Easy,' whispered Hervey. 'There's not a thing we can do to save them. When I give the word, run like Hades for the hut!'

The old warrior raised his spear. '*U-Shaka!*'

The *inkwebane* thrust their spears forward. '*U-Shaka!*' they roared.

None of the condemned, not even the youngest, flinched. '*U-Shaka!*' they cried back resolutely.

The *inkwebane* braced, spears now inches from their deadly work, waiting the final order.

The youths and boys, their chins high, stood motionless.

The old warrior turned to the *induna* for the order.

The *induna*, his tears replaced by a look of intense pride, stepped between the errant youths and their executioners. '*Nihambe kahle!*' he growled – 'You must go well' (the Zulu parting) – and then repeated his praise: '*Ni ngama qawu* . . . You are heroes. *Sobonana futhi* . . . We shall see each other again!'

They steeled themselves visibly for the point of the spear.

'*Hlezi!*' he commanded.

The boys hesitated.

'*Hlezi!*'

They sat, crestfallen at the indignity of meeting the spear in any attitude but on their feet.

'Be done with it, man!' muttered Somervile.

Hervey grasped his arm, fearing his old friend would not be able to contain himself.

The *induna* turned, and nodded – sharp – to the old warrior.

The warrior gestured with his spear to the senior of the *inkwebane*.

The cadet marched up to his general.

'*U-Shaka!*' roared the *induna*.

The cadet thrust the spear into his general's chest, and Shaka's liegeman died with not a sound but that of the *iklwa* as it withdrew – the very sound that gave its name to the spear.

The cadet turned, his hands to his side. The old warrior nodded to the second of the *inkwebane*, who stepped forward and thrust his spear beneath his senior's breastbone.

Hervey and Fairbrother drew their sabres. 'Get ready, Somervile!'

The warrior barked another order.

Before Hervey could say 'Go!', the *inkwebane*

turned and began marching back towards the *sango*.

Somervile gasped. 'I never saw nor heard such a thing!'

Hervey sighed with the most prodigious relief.

'A noble savage,' said Fairbrother, but with a touch of irony. 'See how his courage would let him kill himself, and another, rather than face Shaka's wrath.'

XV

HE WHO IS EQUAL TO A THOUSAND WARRIORS

The following morning

They made camp that night a league to the north of the Fasimba kraal, on the round top of a little hill which afforded good observation, and with plentiful water in the stream below. The moon was near full, and the sky clear, which allowed the pickets to lie in rather closer than they would otherwise have been able to do. But without cloud, the night was cold; and dawn, when it broke at about five-thirty, was doubly welcome. They had stood-to half an hour before, in unusually wary expectation, and Hervey had kept them under arms for another half-hour after daylight while mounted patrols cleared out to rifle range and beyond. There was no sign of Zulu, however, other than smoke from the home-steads on distant hills.

They were within a morning's march of Dukuza, and Somervile had begun turning over in his mind how they would make their entrance to the royal kraal. If Shaka *were* in some way deranged – and he was beginning to believe it possible – was there, indeed, any future for his embassy? He had read of the work of an eminent French physician, who postulated a sort of 'insanity without delirium', in which a man acted without restraint or remorse, and yet with none of the common manifestations of derangement; it was only in scrutinizing a man's actions, therefore, that the insanity was manifest, as if some demon were working clandestinely within. He had every expectation, yet, of a civilized exchange of courtesies with Shaka, and at least the preliminaries to a proper accord if not a full-blown treaty, and he was certain that this could be more enduring than any made with the Xhosa, for Shaka exerted an absolute power in his kingdom. But to negotiate with a man who was insane . . . It was wholly without his experience.

Hervey's thoughts were no less troubled. He had not the slightest doubt (nor Fairbrother) that news of what had happened at the Fasimba kraal would by now have reached Dukuza. And, like Somervile, he feared that Shaka might perceive it that his will had been thwarted, and ascribe it to the malign intervention of the visitors from Cape Town. His mind was therefore occupied in thinking how to deploy his little command to effect, hoping as Somervile for a 'civilized exchange of courtesies', but preparing meanwhile for the worst. It certainly did not augur well that Isaacs was now too weak for the saddle, and that they would have to leave him here until the fever was sweated out. But Fairbrother's capability at the Fasimba kraal had been encouraging, so that the suggestion of delaying the march received no more than a passing moment's consideration.

The column, when it set off just after seven, was distinctly more subdued than on the day before. Though none but the five who had entered the *isigodlo* had seen the death of the *induna*, and of his executioner in turn, word had got about camp. Word always got about camp. Comprehending this full well, Hervey had spoken with the officers and serjeants so that the least lurid and speculative accounts were likely to circulate. Nevertheless, at stand-to, Private Johnson had told him that the slaughter did not bode well with the dragoons, and that they were swearing 'no quarter'.

In consequence, Hervey rode the first mile or so with Brereton, and then with Serjeant-Major Collins, to explain his design for disposing the column when they encountered the Zulu. The force would divide into three. The lieutenant-governor's party would be no more than a dozen: Corporal Battle would be Somervile's coverman, Corporals McCarthy and French would be his, with Corporal Brayshaw covering Fairbrother. He would need Trumpeter Roddis, too, for he must be able to rely on the best of calls to communicate his orders to the other two groups, as well as Johnson and three of the most experienced dragoons. This would be the group that would enter Shaka's kraal. The second would be a supporting group, Captain Welsh's Mounted Riflemen. These would attempt to position themselves so as to be at the immediate support of the first group. Bearing in mind what had happened at the Fasimba kraal, Hervey explained that he wanted the Rifles to be but one fence from them at all times (Isaacs did not know how many stockades there were at Dukuza, but he thought there were at least two). The third group, the rest of the dragoons, under Brereton's command, would remain outside the kraal to be able to judge how best to support the groups within, and to have a free hand in doing so.

Brereton said he understood perfectly, but in a manner that made Hervey uneasy, for he seemed not to receive it with the same relish that he himself would have. And so he rode with him a little longer, rehearsing the various exigencies and how they might deal with them. He would have liked Collins to hear, too, but that would have been to undermine Brereton's own authority – and not least his confidence. In any case, he knew he could trust to Collins's 'cavalry eye'. Exactly as he would have been able to trust to Armstrong's.

'Upon my word, did you ever see such a sight?' Somervile was standing in the stirrups, shielding his eyes against the sun, taking in the sheer size of distant Dukuza. 'And not a thing but that might be taken down like canvas. Not a stone – nor even a nail, I'll warrant. A metaphor, perhaps: the true nature of Shaka's power?'

Hervey was not much amenable to metaphors this morning. The here and now of a hundred or so men and horses was amply engaging him. He took out his telescope, and tried to humour his old friend nevertheless. 'I am reminded of stout Cortez.'

Somervile arched an eyebrow.

They were halted on yet another of the hilltops which afforded an outlook of half a mile or so to the next; except that now before them was the seat of the king of the Zulu. The kraal was vast, encompassing both valley and hillside. How many huts were contained within its enormous perimeter, he could not estimate (Isaacs had said a thousand, but he could have believed it twice that number). In the centre lay the great cattle byre, empty at this time of day, but five times, at least, the size of that at the Fasimba kraal. And beyond, on the highest point of the hillside, like the dome of the Roman Pantheon, was Shaka's *ndlunkulu*, palace-hut. The whole kraal, indeed, radiated a brooding regal presence – something in the scale of it, the enclosing, subduing, of so immense an area of wilderness, and yet where Nature should be the pre-eminent savage force. Hervey had seen many a place where the walls were taller, wider, longer, but they did not stand out as remarkably as here, because even in the empty tracts, in India, or Spain, they stood in a landscape which belonged unquestionably to man. The very primitiveness of this place made it somehow more powerful.

' "And Joshua and all Israel made as if they were beaten before them, and fled by the way of the wilderness." '

'I mark well enough the passage, Hervey,' replied Somervile, sinking back into the saddle. 'But I would put no store by Joshua's stratagem here. Shaka would not be tempted from such a fastness, I think.'

'I fear that if we are drawn into its depth...'

'Surely your spirit is not failing you, Colonel?'

'It is not. But neither is my reason.'

There was another cause of his disquiet, however. Hervey's scheme required some degree of adroitness on the part of Brereton in holding his troop aloof but in contact with the Rifles. With Welsh's men drawn deep into the kraal, it would be hard enough for the best of officers to judge this rightly.

Somervile was not inclined to see much hazard in entering. Indeed, he saw their vulnerability as a positive advantage, for was not this Shaka a king? He would receive a delegation from a fellow king with the utmost correctness. They would have ample time to withdraw if he showed displeasure, and under the natural laws which protected such a delegation; for not to allow them such rights would surely risk undermining his own status in the eyes of his people?

Hervey conceded the logic, and was by no means

reluctant in doing so; all that he had heard did indeed suggest that Shaka could behave with the most kingly decorum. Supposing, that is, that Shaka was not insane. 'Might we not first test the water, so to speak: draw up the troop and have Shaka inspect them – but outside the kraal?'

'I think not, Hervey. I see that it might serve, but if we are bidden to the royal quarters then we have no alternative but to accede. It would be folly otherwise, even to hesitate, for that might show us fearful, or give mortal offence. I am persuaded that we must trust to the normal usages of diplomacy.'

Hervey, sighing deeply but to himself, acknowledged the order with a touch to his shako peak.

Dukuza, regal as it appeared from that first vantage point, took on a meaner aspect as they came closer. It was not merely that its construction was so primitive, lacking fine craft and ennobling colour, it was the abounding image and odour of death. The whitened bones of all manner of beasts, the carcasses of slaughtered cattle and game picked over by the scavengers of the bush, lay scattered for a quarter of a mile, and the skulls of elephants, on poles, marked the processional way to the *sango*. But the true horror was human, not animal: the impalings, hundreds of them, like crucifixions along the Appian Way. Hervey had seen much carnage, and every dragoon had seen the gibbet at the crossroads, but here was a veritable religion of death. The column fell into a deep silence.

A furlong from the *sango*, Hervey held up a hand. 'This will serve.'

Somervile reined to a halt. He surveyed the ground, and sighed. 'The heathen in his blindness!'

'What?'

He turned to his old friend. ' "From Greenland's icy mountains", Hervey. You were singing to yourself, were you not?'

Hervey looked at him, almost perturbed. 'Beneath my breath, or so I'd thought.'

'We have known each other for a long time.'

'Indeed.' He broke into a smile.

Somervile shook his head as he turned once more to the prospect before them. 'A charnel house. Was there ever such a processional! I confess it troubles me.'

'You are not contemplating withdrawal?'

Somervile paused before answering. 'I am not. I am merely contemplating the meaning of it.'

Hervey was accustomed to the frequent ellipses in his old friend's manner of speaking. Ordinarily he was not troubled by it, but in the face of a potentially hostile multitude, he was not inclined to humour him long. 'Do I have your permission to deploy the troop into line?'

'Do you need it?'

Hervey sighed again, and with some consternation. 'I do not need it when it is a matter of military necessity, but I see no cause to deploy if you are to tell me you have no intention of proceeding!'

Somervile did not answer immediately, looking long at the kraal. 'I do not wish you to come in with me,' he said abruptly. 'Eggs, baskets . . .'

'Insupportable,' replied Hervey at once.

The lieutenant-governor turned to him. 'I need hardly add that I may make it an order. You shall have it in writing if that is what troubles you.'

Hervey blinked. 'Somervile, you're speaking to *me*, not to someone new-come from the Horse Guards!'

'I know that,' replied his old friend calmly. 'That is why I cannot have you come into the kraal with me. If anything should happen . . .'

'May I remind you that it is on the assumption that something might happen that you are furnished with an escort, which I have the honour of commanding. And strictly speaking, I'm not sure that any but General Bourke could relieve me of that duty.'

Somervile began to look resigned. 'I had merely thought . . . I have Emma, and the children, you are but new married, and . . .'

Hervey cursed. Did Somervile not imagine that he, too, had such thoughts from time to time? But then he chided himself: Somervile had so often shown both appetite and aptitude for the soldier's art that it was too easy to imagine he was of the profession.

'Come,' he said, resolved. 'Let my dragoons make a bit

of a splash along this ridge, and we shall walk under their gaze into the lion's den.'

Somervile turned and looked at him, studiously. 'The lion's den?'

Hervey returned his gaze, but quizzical. 'A not uncommon figurative expression. And that is what his name means, does it not? *Shaka* – lion?'

Somervile's brow furrowed beneath the peak of his straw hat, but his eyes displayed his incredulity just as surely. 'Where did you learn that?'

'I don't rightly recall. I . . .'

'I'm disappointed, Hervey. As a rule you have such a facility with native tongues.'

Hervey sighed, conceding his error. 'Evidently not in that of the Zulu. *Shaka* is not a word for "lion"?'

'Intestinal beetle.'

He laughed. Campaigning was a hard business, but not always grim. '*Beetle?*'

'Shaka was born out of wedlock, which many believe to have been his driving shame – that and the harsh treatment of his mother. When Nandi appeared to be with child she protested that it was merely *I-Shaka*, the beetle which suppressed the menses.'

'I wonder he did not change his name to something nobler.'

'He had no need. The Zulu have a custom – *hlonipa*, which, if you do not know it,' (he said this with a certain wryness) 'means "modesty" – whereby they devise

307

another word for the everyday where it is also the name of a warrior of rank.'

Hervey shook his head in mock disbelief, and in admiration of Somervile's learning. '*Huzoor*, do I have your leave to carry on?'

'Carry on.'

He turned in the saddle to see where was Brereton, but he was not in his place at the head of the troop. He beckoned forward Cornet Kemmis instead. 'The troop leader?'

'He fell rear, Colonel; to speak with the sar'nt-major.'

Hervey frowned. There was nothing so very wrong in Brereton's falling to the rear, except that if he wanted to speak with the serjeant-major he could as well have summoned him forward. And when they halted, he ought to have come forward again at once in expectation of orders . . . 'Have the troop form line. We shall make our approach from here. You understood the design?'

'Perfectly, Colonel.'

Hervey nodded, then turned forward in the saddle again. Kemmis's answer was confident, and one in which he, Hervey, at once had confidence. A cornet not long out of the military college possessed of a more natural air of command than his captain, ten years his senior – these things were unaccountable.

Up came Welsh. 'Riflemen all ready, Colonel.'

By which he meant loaded. The dragoons, on the other hand, would have more time to make ready their carbines, and so Hervey intended keeping them unprimed; there was no more damnable a business than having to draw unused charges, or risking accidental discharge (this was no time for a spark in the brushwood, literally or otherwise).

He gave the executive order.

The troop fronted with impressive speed, and the riflemen formed skirmish line at the foot of the rise, dismounting and standing steady, waiting for the lieutenant-governor's party to begin their procession to the *sango*.

Hervey nodded, well pleased. He reckoned that *any* observer would be impressed by the handiness of his little force. The Zulu had their regularity, the feathers, the animal skins, the cowhides of the war shields, but a line of blue coats and white-covered shakos: altogether different. And if they had heard of Umtata, how they must respect the rifle, the sabre, and the fleetness of the horse.

Somervile's party advanced without speaking.

The skulls of two gigantic bull elephants atop crudely carved baobab pillars marked the saluting point. A guard of honour – Fasimba – lined the swept path to the entrance.

Shaka's chamberlain, Mbopa, shorter by head and shoulders than any of the Fasimba, and markedly stouter, came out from the kraal.

The party dismounted.

Fairbrother, with only a little assistance from Mbopa's interpreter, a man of indeterminate but very mixed blood, presented the King's respects, and explained that they brought with them but small tokens of that esteem in advance of many more substantial ones.

Mbopa assured them that Shaka was aware of the King's respect, and that they would enjoy his hospitality for as long as they wished it. They would first eat and drink, and then be brought into his royal presence.

Somervile spoke a few words in return, all politeness, intending to convey the dignity of the Crown and the confidence of the embassy, and presented Hervey as the King's military representative.

Mbopa bowed, and indicated the Fasimba to left and right, witness to his own king's esteem for his visitors.

Hervey took advantage of his newly exalted status to request that his 'royal guards' (the riflemen) be allowed to accompany them.

'It would be our honour,' Mbopa replied.

The kraal was half a mile and more across, and by Hervey's rapid estimate there were as many huts in its outer circle as there were men in a battalion of the Line – eight hundred at least, ample quarters for two thousand warriors and for all the husbandry necessary to the life of Shaka's headquarters. In turn, these encircled the central cattle-fold and another, lower palisade. At the far end of the kraal, as in the Fasimba *ikhanda*, were the royal quarters, the *isigodlo*, hedged around by the thickest thorn. Here was Shaka's *ndlunkulu*, larger even than the great council hut which stood outside.

As they made their way there, Hervey saw that the warriors' huts were empty. Perhaps he might have expected it (why else would Shaka send the herd boys to the Fasimba kraal to be executed?), for the campaign against Soshangane could not be waged without warriors, and even Shaka's legions were not limitless. He suddenly felt less like a fox among hounds, and more like a cock which enters the pit with a fighting chance.

At the entrance to the *isigodlo* the guards held up their spears in salute. Hervey told Welsh to form here with his riflemen, and then Mbopa led the rest of the party through the opening in the thorn fence and into one of the smaller huts.

This, beehive-shaped like the others, was a dozen yards in diameter, and well lit by oil lamps. Inside were several of Shaka's serving-girls holding earthen basins, his 'sisters' as he called them (or 'harem lilies' as the warriors, less reverently, knew them). The party washed their hands and then seated themselves on the rush mats in the middle of the clay floor; or rather squatted, for Isaacs had told them that to sit would give offence to their host.

More serving-girls appeared with hollowed gourds of beer, and then others with wooden trenchers and spoons. Bowls of boiled maize were brought, and sweet potatoes, mashes of pumpkins, fermented sorghum, clotted milk. Evidently, whispered Somervile, the mourning hunt, *i-hlambo*, the washing of spears, was over, even though the warriors were not yet returned.

They ate respectfully.

When the remains of the honoured meal were cleared away, the serving-girls (six of them, festooned with beads which expertly covered their modesty, unlike those at the Fasimba kraal) assembled in line opposite the door, as if waiting on the party's further pleasure.

'Are we to dismiss them, do you suppose?' asked Somervile.

Fairbrother shook his head. 'I think it best to wait for Mbopa to return.'

The serving-girls dropped suddenly to their knees, eyes lowered, anxious.

Shaka's silent presence was so compelling that the party rose as one.

And they were, as one, taken aback, for Shaka stood taller than any man Hervey had seen since coming to the Cape – a towering column of sinew and muscle. Even Somervile was without a word.

It was Mbopa who at length broke silence. '*Baba! Unkosi! Ndabezita!* . . . Father, King, Illustrious Sir, these are the men who have come from Um Joji.'

Somervile made a deep bow, deeper than he would have made even to King George, for he did not wish any misunderstanding on so simple a business as the courtesies due to rank. 'May I present Colonel Hervey, chief of my Guards,' he began, in the little Zulu that Isaacs had been able to give him. 'And Captain Fairbrother, his aide-de-camp.'

Shaka remained wholly impassive. Hervey searched his face for something of his character, but saw nothing. The eyes, though large, were no window on what lay within. His features were regular and strong. His cropped hair was flecked with grey, which only increased the impression of hard-willed power. There was no mark or blemish to his skin. He wore a claw necklace and a skirt of leopard tails – nothing more, as if to say that in this simple garb of the warrior was all there was to know of him: no sumptuary was required to proclaim the supremacy of Shaka Zulu!

Mbopa spoke. '*Si-gi-di* ... (He who is equal to a thousand warriors) accepts these cordial greetings, and bids you take your ease before feasting with him this night, when his brothers, whom he has only moments ago received, shall be present also.'

Somervile needed only the briefest words of clarification from Fairbrother before bowing once more, and returning his answer. 'Be pleased to inform He who is equal to a thousand warriors that King George's embassy is honoured to accept.'

Mbopa's interpreter spoke quickly and surely.

But Shaka did not wait on further words, turning instead, and without letting his eyes meet any, leaving with the same air of brooding power.

The serving-girls remained on their knees even when he was gone, as if fearful that the 'Great Crushing Elephant' (one of Shaka's many praise-names) would reappear and find their temerity in rising too quickly an affront, and their lives thus forfeit.

'I think I might have a cheroot,' said Somervile, as if he were at a drawing room, taking out a silver case from his pocket and offering it to the other two.

None of them was certain of the propriety, but they soon filled the hut with tobacco smoke. The serving-girls seemed to find it pleasant, and certainly amusing.

Somervile blew a perfect ring, which rose intact to the roof. 'Fine-looking fellow, Shaka. Can't but wonder what he'd make of our own esteemed sovereign.'

Hervey had expected something rather more ambassadorial by way of opinion. He smiled nevertheless. 'We must hope he is not acquainted with the portraitist's art of flattery.' One of Shaka's presents was a print of Sir Thomas Lawrence's portrait of George IV, which Hervey knew, from direct observation at Windsor only six months before, was no longer – if it had ever been – a faithful likeness.

'It would not do for Shaka to be put in mind of his fat half-brother,' said Fairbrother.

Isaacs had spoken much of Shaka's half-brothers during yesterday's ride – their character and which of them would succeed to the throne. Dingane thought of nothing but women, a milksop; Mhlangana was a fine warrior but no statesman; Mpande was fat and self-indulgent; Ngwadi, Nandi's son by a commoner, was beloved of Shaka, but lived many miles distant, and had a lesser claim on the throne than any. Was there truly no son, a son of which even Shaka might be unaware? To which Isaacs had replied that if there were such an heir, and his name were to become known, his life would soon be at an end, for Shaka had a most unnatural fear of sons, and the inevitable challenge of the young buck. And even if his identity were to escape Shaka's knowledge, he would not long survive Dingane's spears.

Mbopa now returned, and with him a woman of about Hervey's age, tall and severe, though handsome. The serving-girls paid no formal respects, except for their glances, one to another.

'Pampata?' suggested Fairbrother, his voice lowered confidentially (Isaacs had spoken of – warned them of – Shaka's favourite).

They rose.

Unlike the serving-girls, Pampata wore the *sidwaba*, the longer, hide skirt of the betrothed or married woman, with a necklace of plaited cow-hair and feathers between her high, unsuckled breasts. Her hair, like Shaka's, was cropped, and stood proud. Her eyes were bright, active, intelligent. She spoke in a slow, measured way, lower in pitch than a white woman. Her bearing was one of dignity, if not authority, and at once commanded all attention.

Mbopa's interpreter said that she wished to greet them, and that Shaka, despite saying nothing directly to them, was much pleased by their arrival.

Somervile bowed, saying that he perfectly understood the king's greeting, that it was most gracious of him to leave his *ndlunkulu* to come to them at this hour, when affairs of state must be pressing (he presumed the visit of the brothers to be such), and that they waited on his pleasure with complete ease.

Pampata turned and spoke to Mbopa in a way that denied them hearing. His face betrayed disquiet. He spoke some words by return, but Pampata was insistent.

He stepped back, gave her a long and searching look, and then withdrew, followed by the interpreter and the serving-girls.

Hervey moved to Somervile's left side, allowing himself a free hand to draw his sabre. Somervile merely smiled encouragingly.

Pampata looked each of them in the eye, searching perhaps a little longer in Fairbrother's, and then addressed Somervile directly. How she knew that any of them would understand, Hervey could not suppose, save perhaps that she had been observing them discreetly.

'Shaka is a great man and a great king,' she began, almost defiantly. 'You are, I know, repelled by the sights of death all about.'

Fairbrother made sure that Somervile and Hervey had understood.

Hervey had, but again he wondered how she knew their minds. Perhaps, though, she too was repelled by the sights of death.

'But let not your unknowing of our ways deceive you: without Shaka there is no nation, and with no nation there is no peace. When Shaka accomplishes his purpose, which will be soon, there will be peace throughout all the land. Without Shaka there will only be war.'

This took longer for Fairbrother to translate, and he was not sure that he did so entirely faithfully, but the essence of it at least was clear – as much by the speaker's inflection.

Somervile felt able to reply, if in a distinctly unpolished mix of Xhosa and Zulu. 'Madam, why do you say "without Shaka"? By what means would the nation be without its king?'

'I do not fear the white man.'

Somervile narrowed his eyes, and looked at her intently. 'I would not have you fear us, madam. Who is it that you do fear?' He glanced at the door to suggest what he meant, his voice lowered.

Pampata stood proud, despite the peril in her words. 'I fear Shaka's brothers. They are not his true brothers but only the sons of his father. And I fear Mbopa. None of this I fear for myself but for Shaka and his people.'

'Why do you speak with such . . . ?' He could not find the word, and turned to Fairbrother: 'Urgency?'

Fairbrother looked at Pampata, shaking his head. '*Sheshile?*'

She nodded. 'Because the people are tired, they do not understand why they must mourn for Nandi so much, and Shaka's brothers would take advantage of that. Even now, as we speak.'

Somervile realized that here was a course he had not considered. What was His Majesty's interest in such an eventuality as Pampata was suggesting? His India instinct was to see advantage in the overthrow of a ruler who did not wholeheartedly support the Company. 'What do you wish me to do, madam?'

'Shaka sends his guards away, believing himself to be in no danger, as if tempting a hand to move against him, so that he himself might stay it. While his brothers are here he is in the greatest danger. You have warriors enough to protect him from harm.'

Hervey struggled to understand the exchanges, needing Fairbrother's whispered translations, but he caught the essence of what Pampata wanted, and he reeled at the thought of it. 'Somervile, I must counsel—'

His old friend shook his head; he had understood her well, and would have her reveal more. 'Who is Shaka's legitimate heir?' he asked, his voice lowered almost to nothing.

Fairbrother had to try several constructions before he was certain she understood.

Pampata glanced at the entrance, and then turned back to Somervile. 'There is a child, a boy-child,' she replied, almost inaudibly. 'Nandi has called him "Little Bull-Calf".'

'Your child?' whispered Somervile.

She shook her head, seemingly with a most intense disappointment. 'I cannot say more now.'

Somervile nodded. 'But if Shaka will not have his own warriors guard him, he will surely not permit us to?'

'You are here in the *ikhanda*, already.'

'But—'

Mbopa returned. They fell silent.

He eyed them warily. 'Lady, *Si-gi-di*, He who is equal to a thousand warriors, commands your presence.'

Hervey wondered how much he had overheard. Did he use that praise-name to warn them that their own little force was ineffectual?

Pampata ignored him for as long as she dare, her eyes on Somervile still, almost beseeching.

Somervile held her gaze for as long as he dared, rapidly turning over in his mind this new intelligence. At length he bowed. 'Madam, we are your servants.'

XVI

THE MOUNTAIN FALLS

Next day

'Bugle' Roddis sounded reveille at the first intimations of daybreak, the little darts of sunlight that shot up in the eastern sky like fireworks at a fête.

They had camped a quarter of a mile from the kraal – on favoured ground, said Mbopa. But it was to the west, so that the rising sun was in their eyes. Hervey had not supposed that this was coincidental. Half an hour before reveille, therefore, as the troop and the riflemen quietly stood-to-arms, a dozen of the most trusted dragoons, with Fairbrother, had slipped out in pairs, beyond the pickets, to scout for any Zulu using the shadows and the favourable light to make a stealthy approach.

But as the sun's full face slowly revealed the ground to the watching dragoons and riflemen, Hervey saw not warriors but women and children. They had gathered as spectators, just as the Spanish and Bengali peasants used to gather. A camp of soldiers was a thing of universal fascination.

They might have been decoys, even innocent decoys, to distract them from the manoeuvring of the warriors around the flanks. But it was to detect such manoeuvring that he had sent out Fairbrother and the picked men. Had he truly expected to be attacked? To a soldier the question was pointless: expectation and possibility required the same precautions. But if he had been asked, he would have said 'no'. The threat to Shaka's life, which Pampata had pressed upon them, had proved empty: his brothers had left Dukuza for their own kraals before nightfall, and Shaka himself had walked peaceably abroad, observing his visitors from a distance in the manner of one who was merely intrigued by the appearance of something new. The discipline of the field, however, the stand-to-arms dawn and dusk (which too many of his acquaintance derided as slavishness), was a rule of life as that of any religious.

And he thought of Sister Maria. She would be on her knees at this hour. How he wished he had been able to return and speak with her. She had pointed the way at their convent meeting, but there was so much he would have asked about the twists and turns of the path he knew he must take. Nothing had been resolved, but it had, at least, been a beginning. When he was returned to England he would be able to take up these things again. There had been nothing he could do about Kat; there had been nothing he could do about Kezia – nor Georgiana, nor Elizabeth – but he knew his relief on embarking for the Cape had been almost indecent.

'Leave to stand-down, sir?'

He woke; he had not seen Brereton come to his side, with the captain of the Rifles. He cleared his throat, and made a show of putting his telescope under his arm. 'By all means. General parade at . . . ten.'

It was a generous allowance for breakfast and mustering, but Hervey saw no reason to put on a display any earlier. In any case, they waited on Shaka's word for what would happen next.

Somervile now appeared, looking discomposed. 'My servant did not wake me. Why did not the picket officer?'

Hervey kept his smile to himself. 'My dear Somervile, there was no need of your presence. Your sleep is more valuable to us than your pistol.'

'Yes, yes, that's all very well; but I am quite put out. You must not take these things upon yourself so.'

Hervey frowned. 'If I am not to take the simplest of decisions, how do you expect me to take the important ones? I must, with the very greatest of respect, remind you that I command your escort.'

Somervile looked at him with a combination of dismay and affront.

But Hervey was adamant. 'It simply will not do if you insist on being the soldier. I cannot have the responsibility.'

Somervile shook his head. 'I wished only to see the sun come up on the kraal. I had no intention of usurping your command.'

'Then I will be sure to call you tomorrow.' Hervey knew he traded on their long years' acquaintance, but he was certain of his point: he could not discharge his duty if Somervile were given leave to range.

Private Johnson came up, saluting both of them. 'Would tha like some more tea, sir?' He addressed his remarks to Hervey, who had enjoyed his first at stand-to. 'An' you an' all, Sir Somervile?'

Whether Johnson's incorrect form was intended or not (he could be distinctly perverse in such things), neither Hervey nor his friend thought fit to remark on it. Hot tea was ever worth a breach of etiquette.

A steaming brew of best Bengal filled their canteens.

Hervey's brow furrowed as he drank, in no measure of distaste, rather of mystification.

'Summat up wi'it, sir?'

'Johnson, there's milk in this tea. Where did you get it?'

'From one o' them 'erd boys, last night.'

'Which herd boys?'

'When you were in wi' t'king.'

Hervey tried hard to keep his countenance, for the sake of regimental pride. He certainly had no desire to inhibit Johnson's legendary skills in 'progging'. The executions at the Fasimba kraal were so fresh in his mind, however, that he could not but shiver at the thought of how dearly they might be taking milk with their tea. It was one thing to drink sour curds in Shaka's kraal. 'He gave it to you?'

'I gave 'im some beads for it.'

Somervile could no longer forbear. 'Admirable diplomacy, Private Johnson. Admirable.'

''E said 'e'd bring some more this morning an' all, sir. That'll be 'im there now.' Johnson nodded to the crowd of women and children advancing on them gingerly.

Hervey turned, with no little anxiety, to look for Brereton and Welsh. He saw Collins instead, and pointed to the visitors. 'Sar'nt-Major, pass the word to be civil to them, but to be on guard. *Sharp* on guard.'

'Sir.'

In an instant, Collins had his corporals relaying the orders.

'I don't suppose they're any different from those who swarm round a camp of soldiers anywhere, but in the circumstances . . .'

'I don't imagine they are,' agreed Somervile, 'save that they may tell us a great deal more about matters than would your average peasant.'

He was soon proved right. With the babble of women and children was Pampata.

They received her warmly, offering her a camp-chair, and tea, which she drank with surprised pleasure, before she in turn presented them with a gourd full of honey.

Somervile had no difficulty making himself understood, or understanding, albeit the conversation was of a straightforward kind. Hervey grasped the essentials well enough. And Pampata appeared perfectly at ease and in no measure fearful. But yet to him she was . . . preoccupied.

At length she revealed her purpose. 'The king has sent for reports from the armies in Pondoland and in the north, against Soshangane. He is displeased with the *impi* in the north, for they have not pressed our enemies with determination. But I know there are some in the army who fear Shaka's wrath, and are therefore intriguing with Dingane and Mhlangana. Those two will come again to see Shaka this evening, to hear the despatches from the armies. I believe they will do him harm.'

Somervile asked Hervey if he had understood.

Hervey thought he had. 'Is it not but a reprise of her previous fears?'

'It is, but with more reason. You heard her say there were malcontents in the army?'

Hervey frowned. 'There are always malcontents in an army.'

Somervile waved a hand. 'Yes, yes, but we are not speaking of the odd case of insubordination.'

'I suppose not.'

He turned back to Pampata. 'Why, madam, does Shaka not take the necessary precautions himself? He has the means to do so, does he not?'

Pampata had been expecting just such a riposte. 'He will not believe they would do him harm. He says that just as he could not raise a hand against one of his father's sons, they could not also.'

Somervile made sympathetic noises.

Hervey looked at him for enlightenment.

His old friend repeated what she had said, adding, 'There is either a nobility among the Zulu people which surpasses all others – or Shaka is as deluded as Hamlet's father.'

Fairbrother had now joined them, fresh from the folds and hollows; enlivened, indeed. Johnson placed a canteen of tea in his hands as he took the remaining chair.

'Shakespeare, again, Sir Eyre? I believe he might have written a good play here.'

Somervile nodded. 'You come most carefully upon your hour.'

'But not to see a ghost, I hope.'

Somervile explained what Pampata had told them.

'And what did you say by reply? I believe I heard you tell her we were the king's good friends.' (He was careful not to use 'Shaka'.)

'Exactly so.'

Hervey leaned forward, lending emphasis to a look of some concern. 'But surely you are not contemplating intervention on our part without the king's express will? I must say that I consider her fears' (he was equally

326

careful not to use 'Pampata') 'tend to ... frankly, an hysteric passion. I cannot imagine that one such as this king, who has raised his nation by the most barbarous of acts, is about to hazard all by refusing to take the most elementary precautions!'

Somervile did not at first answer, appearing to weigh his words. 'What say you, Fairbrother?'

For a few moments, Fairbrother merely continued to sip his tea. 'Sir Eyre, in the febrile condition of this wretched country I would hazard no guess at what might happen. I attempted to read the face of yon Othello, and saw nothing but the tyrant's hubris.'

Somervile raised his eyebrows. 'Upon my word, we seem embarked on some tragedy!' He looked again at Hervey.

Hervey was reluctant to doubt his friend's instincts (they had served him well of late), but also his own. 'I confess I find her convincing in her sincerity, but without cause other than her evident charms. She might equally be a spy. There is precedent.'

Somervile nodded once more. 'We must treat her with the very greatest courtesy, nonetheless. She is the king's favourite, and evidently holds sway – as the deference of that wily chamberlain of his demonstrated.'

And so they treated her attentively, and gave her little presents – horsehair, tunic buttons, a looking-glass and a silver whistle. She stayed with them for an hour and more, until the others she had come with were ready to return, and she took her leave with them, as if she shared their simple curiosity in a camp of soldiers, and no more.

The routine of the morning passed unobserved except by the odd herd boy. The general parade drew no admirers, neither did the midday bring out those with things to trade, so that Somervile began to wonder if he should not make his approaches once again. Heavy clouds had begun rolling in from the east, however, and so instead they occupied themselves in making shelter (amid a good deal of grumbling in the ranks that with many an empty hut inside the kraal, it was needless to take a drenching).

Late in the afternoon, bearers arrived at the kraal with heavy portage.

Fairbrother, who had been talking with some of the youthful drovers by the watering place beyond the collecting byre, came back into the camp soon after.

'Izi-Yendane – Natal men,' he said. 'Skins and feathers, from the Pondo.'

'More booty?' Hervey was still observing their progress with his telescope.

'They won't have hunted, themselves. The Zulu say they're fit for nothing but fetching and carrying.'

Somervile joined them. 'Quite a procession, I see. Are they auguries?'

'I can't say, Sir Eyre. But I've just been speaking to some of the herd boys, and uncommonly free with their opinion were they. The *impi* gone north against

Soshangane are deeply troubled. They're tired from the fighting in Pondoland, and Shaka sent them north without so much as a night in their own kraals. And he's now recalled the *u-dibi*, the bearers, to form into a new regiment, and told the rest – the officers as well – they must carry their own baggage.'

Somervile pondered the intelligence. 'Shaka makes malcontents of the warriors, but the *u-dibi* happy. And they are youths, are they not?' He smiled. 'The eternal contest of young and old buck!'

Hervey took a less sanguine view. 'I for one would be reluctant to alter the terms of service in the middle of a campaign! Most perilous, I should say.'

'Mm.' Somervile turned and took up his telescope again. 'Do you suppose Shaka intends feeding us, as he promised, or does he make a show of his power by this delay?'

'Both, I'm sure,' said Hervey.

'Mm. Fairbrother, do you think you might discover when these brothers will arrive? That way we shall at least know not to dress too early.'

Hervey hid his smile.

'I'll go back, of course, Sir Eyre,' said Fairbrother. 'A few buttons and those boys will be as good as on the strength.'

'I am excessively grateful. And now I think I will take a little exercise. Shall you accompany me, Colonel Hervey? We might ride to the north a little way and see how the ocean looks. Yon clouds are heavy, but there's no sign of their decanting onto us.'

Sometimes there was nothing for Hervey to do but be diverted by his old friend's archness. 'Delighted, Sir Eyre.'

And as Fairbrother went to find beads and trinkets for the herd boys, Somervile confided that he was pleased beyond all expectations that Hervey's friend was of such good service, for although his own facility with the language was better than he had dared suppose, once the true business of 'diplomacy' began he would need more than a merely serviceable knowledge of Xhosa. 'But beyond that, his ease with the country is a pearl of special worth. If anything should happen to prevent my doing so myself, I trust that you will ensure so singular a fellow has due recognition and reward.'

Fairbrother left them as they were getting into the saddle. With perhaps a couple of hours' full daylight left (some of which the blackening clouds might claim), he made his way on foot to the collecting byre. The herd boys were once again pleased to talk to him. Shaka's brothers Dingane and Mhlangana had come into the kraal by one of the entrances on the far side reserved for the king and his officials, they said. Mbopa had met them, and taken them to his hut, while Shaka received the Izi-Yendane, the 'mop heads' from Natal, and examined the skins and feathers they had brought from Pondoland.

Fairbrother gave them the beads and other little charms. He felt almost as if he bargained too easily: herd boys, thought nothing of by the men of the kraal, would always learn more than they ought; and, being boys, they would always be keen to prove they knew more than was supposed. He drank fermented milk with them, and listened as they spoke keenly of becoming *u-dibi*, and in due course *inkwebane*, and one day warriors, and how they would go then to where the sun goes, and make all before them submit to Shaka.

And what of their friends, who had been sent to the Fasimba, he asked them.

The herd boys shrugged. Shaka had said they were not to drink milk, and they had defied him. If they had been dutiful they would have been drinking it today, as much as they pleased, for Shaka had now declared the mourning to be over.

And then one of them sprang to his feet and pointed excitedly. 'Look! It is Shaka!'

They got up from their haunches to see better where he pointed.

Fairbrother saw. 'Where does he go? And by himself.'

'To Kwa-Nyakamubi,' they all said.

'Kwa-Nyakamubi?'

'The other side of the hill. Shaka goes each evening to watch his special cattle being driven in for the night. Soon, *we* shall be herders of Kwa-Nyakamubi!'

'And he always goes alone?'

'*Si-gi-di*, He who is equal to a thousand warriors, has no need of others!'

'I will go and watch the cattle being driven in too,' said Fairbrother, making to leave them. 'Do you think *Si-gi-di* will permit that?'

The herd boys could barely comprehend the notion that anyone might do such a thing without Shaka's express authority. But what did they know, who were not yet even *u-dibi* – and he, Fairbrother, a great warrior?

He left them and made his way (unobserved, he trusted) by every shallow fold of the veld. Even taking such precautions, in but a quarter of an hour he had reached Kwa-Nyakamubi, which was little more than a thorn-fenced enclosure, a hundred yards across, with a few huts for the chosen herd boys.

Shaka was sitting quite alone, except for two ancient attendants nearby, on a clay mound near the entrance to the byre, his red cloak wrapped about him, watching as the best of his cattle were driven in from the grazing ground beyond the little stream of Nyakamubi.

Fairbrother marvelled at Shaka's defencelessness. But who would dare try to discover if the praise-name *Si-gi-di* were without foundation? Did not the absence of guards tell all who might ponder on it that Shaka himself believed? And who, indeed, would challenge such a form as this? Even seated, Shaka was a colossus. In the *ndlunkulu* he had towered over them, long-shanked; but now Fairbrother saw that the stature came as much from the length of his back, ramrod straight, his shoulders square and broad.

He watched from the cover of an impala lily, not so much hiding as not revealing himself, while the cattle, lowing peaceably, tramped by, the herd boys dancing about them, conscious of Shaka's keen eyes on their endeavours, death the penalty if he found fault.

He heard voices behind him and to his right, a sort of march-singing, more praise-names for Shaka. He turned and saw five warriors of the Izi-Kwembu, one of the regiments from the north, the head-dress distinctive: the tail-feathers of the blue crane. But in the head-dress too was the red-lory feather, otherwise the preserve of the Fasimba. These were, indeed, warriors of especial bravery, the bringers of news from the campaign against Soshangane.

As custom prescribed, the warriors halted at six spears' length from their king, raised their *iklwa* and in unison gave the royal salute: '*Ba-ye-te! Nkosi!* . . . Hail, O Chief!'

Shaka remained seated, but raised both hands and motioned them to be at ease.

As one, they squatted, waiting to learn their king's pleasure. They might wear the red-lory feather, but the campaign was going ill; they did not expect that Shaka would heap praises on them.

Fairbrother strained to hear his reply. But Shaka spoke softly, seeming strangely unmoved. They appeared to be speaking with one another as equals, Shaka listening carefully, and respectfully, to their reports.

Not many yards beyond the mound on which they sat was a hedge, free-standing, unconnected with the byre, but plainly serving some purpose, for it was too straight to be made by Nature. Suddenly from behind it leapt Mbopa, angry, shouting. And Fairbrother supposed it was indeed its purpose – to conceal the royal guards, so that Shaka was not as defenceless as supposed.

Shaka turned, more curious than startled. Mbopa rushed at the warriors, waving his spear and cudgel. 'Cowards! Traitors! How dare you disturb *Si-gi-di* with your lying tales! Be off! Go to the guards and have them put you to death in the manner of felons!'

The Izi-Kwembu sprang to their feet.

Shaka seemed transfixed.

The warriors bolted.

But they bolted not towards the kraal, to death at the hands of the Fasimba; instead they ran north, an act of disobedience that only seemed to prove Mbopa's claim. He railed in front of his king, as if at the Izi-Kwembu still; as if . . . intoxicated. 'See, *Nkosi*! See how the cowards first lie to you and then defy you!'

And then, as though they were answering the cry of alarm, Dingane and Mhlangana sprang from behind the hedge and raced to Shaka's side.

Fairbrother froze: this was not the moment to be discovered skulking like the jackal.

He crouched lower as Mbopa's railing continued, turning to look for his line of retreat.

There was none but that would expose himself to Mbopa and the brothers.

He reached for his pistol, wondering how its one shot might be of best use (indeed *any* use).

Mbopa ceased his rant, and Shaka rose, as if from torpor.

Fairbrother's every muscle was tensed for flight.

And then came a cry like no other he'd heard. He froze, like Lot's wife turned to the pillar of salt.

Into Shaka's flank plunged Dingane's spear.

But the regal cloak deflected the point, so that instead it pierced his arm.

Shaka spun round.

Dingane thrust again, deep into his side.

Shaka reeled.

Mhlangana drove his spear into his breast.

Shaka threw his arms wide, and like a child betrayed, cried, 'It is you, sons of my father, who are killing me!'

Fairbrother pulled back the hammer of his pistol.

Shaka now stretched to his full height. The brothers shrank back in the astonishment of men who had inflicted mortal wounds to no effect. *Was* this chief immortal?

'What have I done, Dingane?' The voice was sorrowful, not angry. 'What have I done, Mhlangana, that you kill me thus? You think you will rule this country? I tell you, you will not, for I see the swallows coming. The white people have already arrived!'

The brothers stood rooted with horror.

Mbopa, who had watched as the adjudicator at a combat, stepped forward, and without a word, Brutus-like, thrust his spear beneath Shaka's ribs.

Yet still Shaka did not falter, even as blood poured from his mouth and the three body blows. He did not look at Mbopa, as if to deny he was worthy of remark. Instead, with all the majesty he could muster, he turned his back on them and began walking for the kraal.

The cloak slipped from his shoulders as if it were his life departing.

Only Mbopa followed.

A dozen paces, then as Shaka appeared to stumble, Mbopa quickened, and stabbed him twice more from behind.

Still Shaka did not fall. He turned, slowly, with a look of desolation. '*Hau! Nawe Mbopa ka Sitaya* . . . So, you too, Mbopa, son of Sitaya: you, too, are killing me . . .'

But Mbopa, as defiant as the brothers were hesitant, stood his ground. He had no doubts now of the mortality of this or any other king.

Without a sound, Shaka crumpled to his knees.

And for a full minute he remained upright, as if praying. Then the King of the Zulu fell forward, his face to the red earth, which he had reddened even more with the blood of countless warriors.

The assassins stood in watching silence. Fairbrother, certain he must be discovered, got to his belly and brought his pistol to the aim.

At length, when the spear wounds no longer bled, Mbopa spoke to the brothers – sharply, for they seemed paralysed. He raised his spear, gesturing towards the dragoons' encampment.

The brothers fled.

Mbopa now strode back to where Shaka's two ancient attendants crouched, terrified. They were witnesses – the only witnesses.

They did not flinch. If Shaka demanded their lives it was their duty to submit – and was it not Shaka's own chamberlain who took upon himself the king's mantle thus?

Fairbrother took careful aim. And then – iciest of calculations – he lowered the pistol.

The cudgel struck twice, and then the spear; and then there were no more witnesses to the death of *Si-gi-di*. He who was equal to a thousand warriors.

XVII

LAMENTATIONS

Later

'*Ku dilike intaba. Inkosi ye lizwe ishonile* – The mountain has fallen. The Lord of the World is dead!'

Rumour spread like flame along a trail of powder – a trail lit by Mbopa. He told of how the Izi-Kwembu had struck down the great Shaka.

Harem lilies and warriors alike fled the kraal, as if they would somehow be swallowed up in the great convulsion of the Earth that must follow the death of the Most High.

Fairbrother lay flat to the ground for what seemed an age, certain that in the frenzy, no foreign face could expect quarter. The shadows were long when at last he judged it safe to beat back to camp.

There he found Hervey and Somervile, oblivious of what had happened.

'Fairbrother?' said his friend, anxiously, seeing him dust-covered and greatly exercised.

'Shaka's dead. Murdered. Mbopa and the brothers.' He stumbled over the words, breathless. Hervey had not seen him so discomposed.

Somervile was at once agitated. 'You saw?'

'Everything. I thought I should not live to tell the tale.'

Hervey beckoned an orderly. 'Have the camp stand-to-arms,' he said, calmly.

'Who else saw?' asked Somervile.

'No one.'

'Damnation! Did you not try to prevent it?'

Fairbrother gave him a look of pity.

'Forgive me: I did not mean to imply . . . Tell me everything.'

When the account – a full and considered one – was finished, Hervey shook his head, and turned to Somervile. 'I'm sorry I doubted your trust in Pampata. He might be alive still.'

Somervile held up a hand. 'No. Mine is the responsibility. I told Pampata she would have our support, and I failed her.'

'We needn't fail her again. If we move at once we can have command of the kraal before last light.'

Somervile shook his head. 'Command?'

'Yes, command! We can apprehend the assassins!'

Somervile was calculating rapidly. 'That would present us with certain difficulties, do you not see? Dingane is heir; if we move against the kraal we shall become implicated in the plot.'

339

Hervey turned to Fairbrother. 'There's another heir, is there not? Mbane? Are his hands clean?'

'*Mpande*. No, he wasn't there with the other two. But Isaacs said he likes his pleasures in excess, did he not? He hardly sounds likely. There's Ngwadi – but he's illegitimate.'

He turned back to Somervile. 'Then what of this child of Shaka's? Is *he* not the rightful heir?'

'As I understand it,' replied Somervile, and sounding weary at his own incapability, 'the Zulu are not a people with settled precedent in these matters. More's the point: do you see them ruled by a boy? Who would be regent? Regency's a desperate enough affair in the most civilized of nations.'

Hervey pressed him for a conclusion. 'And so we look to our own defence, and withdraw to Port Natal as soon as may be?'

Somervile was still deep in thought, however.

When at last he broke silence, it was with a look that said he was resolved on something novel. 'Our own late regency was perhaps not entirely devoid of merit. Perhaps this is our opportunity to bring order to their benighted affairs, deliver them from error's chain.'

'You mean an *English* regency?'

'Why not? We have had such arrangements in India.'

Hervey cleared his throat. 'Forgive me, Somervile, but is that within your authority? Would the duke approve?'

'I have certain plenipotentiary powers . . . '

Hervey was still unconvinced. 'Even if that be so, how are we to find the child?'

Fairbrother, beginning to dust himself down, smiled grimly. 'I suspect that all we need do is follow Mbopa's trail, for he will be Herod-like.'

'Or statesmanlike? Himself as regent?'

'He might will it, Sir Eyre, but there's the little problem of his rank. There's Ngomane.'

Somervile nodded, conceding the point. Ngomane was chief minister, Mbopa merely chamberlain. 'He's at his kraal, did not Pampata say – Nonoti?'

'She did.'

'How far is it?'

Hervey took out his map. 'If this is at all faithful, nine or ten miles, but what the country is like, I cannot say.'

'Then we ought to send word there at once.'

Hervey agreed, but he was reluctant, still, to remain so much on the defensive. 'Might we try also to discover the state of affairs here, in the kraal?'

Somervile thought for a moment. 'Very well. We'll go at once.'

Hervey shook his head. 'That would be a needless risk. Fairbrother and I will go.'

Somervile looked faintly vexed at being once more excluded from a more active role in his own embassy, but was wise enough not to object. 'As you wish.' And then he turned again to Fairbrother, seeming to recollect something. 'What did they do with Shaka's body?'

Fairbrother frowned. 'I didn't observe, Sir Eyre. I confess that my head was in a hole.'

'Quite so,' he replied, chastened. 'But I think we must discover it. A king's obsequies should not lightly be set aside.'

They found Pampata kneeling by Shaka's side, alone, rocking to and fro, and moaning softly.

'This is Mbopa's work, I tell you,' she said without rising. 'It is as I foretold. Like the hyena, he circled, waiting.'

'You saw it, *Nkosazana*, madam, little chieftainess?' asked Fairbrother, gently.

She did not look at them, or move her head this way or that to signify her answer. 'I know it to be true. And then with those other dogs, Dingane and Mhlangana, he crept in for the kill when my lord was pulled down.'

How did she know this? Fairbrother pressed tenderly. 'Who has told you, *Nkosazana*?'

'My lord tells me.'

Hervey wanted to console her, as he would the widow of one of his own men. He crouched beside her, put an arm around her shoulders and lifted her to her feet, nodding to Fairbrother to cover the body – which he did with the bloody cloak. 'Come, *Nkosazana*. We shall bear him into the kraal.'

Fairbrother beckoned Serjeant Hardy and his six dragoons.

Hervey stood supporting her as they took up the body.

'*Nkosazana*,' began Fairbrother, judging it the moment that she would answer truly. 'Do you know where is Shaka's son?'

She understood. But her look of anxiety told him she had misunderstood his purpose. '*Nkosazana . . .*' He struggled to find the words. 'We wish to find the boy to make him chief under King George's protection.'

Pampata looked searchingly at him, and then at Hervey. She had trusted them, and yet her lord was dead. Yet what alternative was there? Dingane and Mhlangana would hunt down the child; they would hunt *her* down. Her peril could be no greater.

The dragoons bore Shaka's body with as much observance as they would one of their own officers, at first across the saddle, and then, as they neared the entrance of the kraal, on foot. They did so in part because their commanding officer rode with them, and Serjeant Hardy's sharp eye was on them, but also because Shaka's majesty somehow exerted a power even in death. And there was, too, the soldier's rough-hewn sympathy for the widow of the fallen warrior (if mingled with less worthy feelings).

The kraal was deserted, ghostly in its sudden emptiness. Night was fast falling; there would not be time to dig the traditional grave of a chieftain, to slaughter the customary black ox and wrap the body of her lord in its skin, but Pampata did not despair: instead she brought Shaka's most treasured cloak from the *isigodlo*, and dressed *Inkosi ye lizwe*, the Lord of the World, for the journey of his spirit to the place of his ancestors. And when she had done this, they went and found an empty grain pit, near the great council hut, and into the pit they reverently lowered the earthly remains of Shaka Zulu.

It was dark when they were finished. They sealed the grave with a stone and covered it with thorn bushes so that Mbopa and the brothers might not discover the last resting place of the king, and defile it. Yet although it was dark, Pampata would not leave the grave except by the most strenuous urging, and even then she was intent on making at once for the chief minister, Ngomane. Only with the gentlest persistence were Hervey and Fairbrother able to persuade her to come back to the encampment with them: there she could rest safely, they assured her, and then travel with them the next day, for Somervile himself intended going to Ngomane's kraal.

The camp stood-to-arms a full hour before first light. Every man knew what had happened, and expected – feared – the worst. Hervey himself had slept but little, doing the rounds of the picket twice before midnight and twice after. He did not know if the Zulu attacked at night, but he could take no risks. He did not believe that their burying Shaka had gone unseen, and it might serve Mbopa in implicating them in his death, if he had a mind to. In the febrile condition of the place, as Fairbrother had put it, Mbopa might have his warriors cast aside all that Shaka had taught, and throw themselves at once on these *izinkonjane*, these 'swallows'.

But morning came peacefully, if overcast. Hervey had lain with his telescope trained on the distant kraal from the first signs of daylight, and observed only stillness – no smoke of cooking fires, no singing, no calling of the herd boys. He could not recollect so complete a flight in Spain or in India, and wondered on the fear that wrought it; and the peril which fear of that degree threatened.

They breakfasted quickly – cold, just smoked cheese and rum. He had considered striking camp and quitting the hillside while it was dark, but he could not be certain that his patrols would detect Mbopa's men in the pitch black, and to be caught off balance so might have gone badly for them. And so he had decided instead to follow the Indian practice – *chota hazree*, 'little breakfast', then two hours' marching before an hour's off-saddling, a good mash of tea, and boiled bacon and biscuit.

They would divide into two parties. Somervile would go first to Ngomane's kraal, at Nonoti, and tell him what had happened (Pampata said they would find him willing to believe them, for the chief minister had always mistrusted Mbopa), and the other party would alert Ngwadi, Nandi's son, Shaka's best-loved half-brother.

Somervile had thoughts that Ngwadi might be

vice-regent, for there would be need of a native minister. And when Pampata revealed that Shaka's son, by her great rival Mbuzikaza, would be at Ngwadi's kraal, raised by a nurse in the greatest secrecy, he became certain of it. Pampata should not go, therefore, to the chief minister's kraal, but to Ngwadi's, escorted by Hervey: she knew the way (it was a hundred miles, perhaps more), and was confident of her welcome there.

This troubled Hervey at first. His prime duty was the safety of the lieutenant-governor. But by degrees he accepted that this did not require his being at Somervile's side at all times: Fairbrother would accompany him to Ngomane's kraal, and Fairbrother he trusted as himself. It was not, after all, hostile territory, except (perhaps) where Mbopa stood. But he did insist that the major part of the force, the Rifles and half the dragoons, would escort Somervile to Nonoti; Captain Brereton he would take with him to Ngwadi's kraal.

Somervile's party was first to move off. So eager was Somervile to leave, indeed, that he himself disassembled his field bed while his two servants folded up his tent. He wished to arrive at Ngomane's kraal before Mbopa or his news, although Pampata said that even if they galloped the ten miles to Nonoti, they could not be sure of it, for news, especially evil news, travelled fast in this country.

Hervey's party was delayed, however. Pampata had

first to be instructed – coaxed – into the saddle, and before that, accoutred in a manner more suitable for the journey (both for comfort and modesty). Johnson found her a pair of overalls, and a cape, but as they were making ready to leave, Pampata suddenly shrieked in dismay: she had left in the kraal the one thing that would reassure Ngwadi that she spoke the truth, for only death would have parted Shaka from it – the little toy spear with the red wooden shaft which Nandi had given him when a child. With a deal of gesture and pointing, she managed to make Hervey understand.

Reluctantly, he agreed to let her retrieve it, fretting that the sun was risen a good way further – half an hour and more, now, since Somervile's party had broken camp.

They formed column of twos – twenty-odd dragoons – and struck off, mounted, down the hill towards the kraal, Pampata's bat-horse on a lead rein in the charge of Farrier Rust.

At Shaka's private entrance to the *isigodlo*, in the outer fence, they halted. Hervey told Brereton to withdraw a hundred yards to the north and keep a sharp lookout over the kraal while he and Pampata went inside.

When the dragoons had withdrawn, the two slipped silently into the royal quarters. As they rounded the guard hut, Pampata gasped in delight: the *isigodlo* was covered in white blossom – a heavenly sign that her lord was favoured!

Hervey smiled, for not only was the blossom delightful, it was the first note of joy he had heard in Pampata.
She was a stranger, but her grief had touched him.

'I would see the resting place of *Nkosi*,' she said.

Hervey hesitated ... But he could not deny her one
last glimpse of the grave. He nodded.

He half expected the *ndlunkulu* to have been rifled, but
the great palace-hut was exactly as before. Pampata
quickly found the spear, and a string of beads that had
belonged to Nandi, but tears filled her eyes at the sight
of the bed of leopard skins on which she and her lord
had spent many a loving night.

'*Yiza*, come away,' said Hervey, softly, taking her arm.

Outside, Pampata braced herself, resolved to do what
she must. They hurried to the inner entrance of the
isigodlo, and thence for the grain pit.

But a sudden movement at the far side of the byre
made him push her roughly to the ground and flatten
himself beside her.

A cowherd, or a guard returning? '*Hlala!* Stay!' he
whispered.

He inched towards the nearest hut to spy from the
cover of its walls.

Pampata inched after him. Hervey tried to stop her,
but she struggled with his restraining hand, and with a
strength that took him aback.

'What is it you see?' she demanded, beneath her
breath.

He gave up the struggle, rising to his knees to get a clearer look across the enclosure.

Pampata leaned on his shoulders to see. 'Mbopa!' she gasped. 'The hyena returns!'

Hervey's blood ran cold. He watched, trying to slow his rapid breathing as Mbopa and his henchmen picked over the blossom-strewn ground.

'He wears red!' hissed Pampata, angrily gripping his shoulders.

Mbopa was a hundred yards off, but the red-lory feather at his neck was plain to see.

Pampata was now beside herself. 'He declares himself a chief, though he is nothing but a common dog – and a murderer!'

Hervey tried to calm her – *subdue* her – fearing she would run at Mbopa and decry him in front of the guards. He struggled to explain: 'We must . . . watch what he does. If he looked for Shaka's body and . . . could not find it, he . . . might think it is . . . concealed here.'

But her eyes burned. She made to rise.

He grabbed her by the shoulders, made her look at him, stared hard into her eyes to impress his meaning.

She gave up struggling. She understood. There was even something in her look which spoke of relief to be yielding. Here was someone she might trust, whereas all her own people had done was wail in despair.

He motioned for her to inch back.

But Mbopa's men were now hastening towards the *isigodlo*.

He pushed her to the ground again and flattened himself beside her.

They heard the warriors going in by the far opening in the hedge, not thirty yards from them – the bravado of those entering a forbidden place. He nodded to her; they crawled inside the hut.

But their line of escape was cut. They could only pray.

XVIII

PURSUIT

Minutes later

The Zulu ran in like hunting lions – from nowhere, with bewildering speed, pouncing, bringing down.

Brereton's right marker fell to a spear he did not even see, though a seasoned lance-corporal.

The dragoons, sitting at ease, smoking, exchanging the crack, were suddenly fumbling for sabre or carbine, too late to do other than desperately fend off the *iklwa*.

Zulu dashed in low, spears ripping open the bellies of the horses, demounting the wretched dragoons to be finished off by others that followed.

Private Hanks, enlisted but a year, fell under his trooper's dead weight and fought like the devil as two warriors taunted him with the *iklwa* point and feinted with their shields, before disembowelling him alive.

Corporal Connell, Brereton's coverman, spurred forward to the aid of his captain, managing to get between his charger on the offside and the taller of two spearmen. He drove his blade down hard – Cut Two – but the toughened cowhide shield took the edge. The Zulu sidestepped and thrust his *iklwa* into Connell's thigh. The corporal's sword arm swung full circle, and the sabre came down again to an exposed head. The Zulu fell instantly to his knees, blood bubbling from the cleft in his skull like water from a spring. Connell was only a length in front of Brereton as he reined hard left to deal with the other warrior – but too late, for Brereton had taken a spear in his left side, deep. The Zulu, in his surprise at bettering so braided an adversary, stepped back instead of turning to meet the coverman. Connell, sabre lofted again, made his third cut in as many seconds more, and sent the man to his maker. Dropping his reins, he grabbed Brereton to hold him in the saddle, but a third Zulu sprang from nowhere to drive his *iklwa* through Connell's spleen.

Cornet Petrie, new out of Eton and the only other officer, by sheer agility held off three jabbing spears for a quarter of a minute, until he too fell to their combined points.

Two dragoons, old hands, stood back-to-back as their horses thrashed on the ground, entrails spilling out like offal on a butcher's block. It took a full minute for four times their number to cut both men down.

One by one the rest of the dragoons fell. Not a shot was fired – for there was not a carbine primed. Private

Johnson, astride a Cape pony, holding Hervey's charger and his bat-horse twenty yards off, turned to make away, but a Zulu running like a gazelle caught them and lunged with his spear before he could get them into a gallop.

Johnson kicked out blindly, deflecting the point, which pierced his pony's flank instead. The startled mare and bat-horse bolted, but the charger stopped, the reins, looped round Johnson's wrist, jerking him clean from the saddle.

The Zulu pulled him to his knees roughly, raising his spear for the thrust to the heart. Suddenly the charger squealed, sprang forward and took off after the pony, dragging Johnson a hundred yards before both horses stopped. He scrambled to his feet, half stunned, swearing foully. He hauled Hervey's rifle from the saddle sleeve, checked there was a percussion cap in place, then dropped to one knee to take unsteady aim at the pursuing warrior.

The shot was ear-splitting. The bullet found its mark, a perfect mark, in the Zulu's breast.

'Bastard kaffirs!' spat Johnson. 'Bastard, bastard, bastards!'

He took the cartridge bag from the saddle and began reloading as he walked back towards the slaughter.

He fired three times – and three more Zulu fell. Only when he was too close to reload again did he perceive the danger, or that there was no dragoon still standing.

* * *

Hervey, hearing the first shot, had made to rise, but stopped himself just in time as warriors began running from the *isigodlo* in alarm.

One shot: what was Brereton *doing*?

And then three more.

But all he could do was wait – and trust to Brereton to deal with whatever it was.

They lay a long ten minutes. When at last he thought it safe enough, they began to crawl towards the inner line of huts. From here they were able to work their way, one hut to another, to the edge of the *isigodlo*, and thence dash, crouching, round its thorn fence to the serving-girls' entrance in the outer thorn fence on the far side of the kraal. They crawled on hands and knees for three hundred yards, and then another hundred, leopard-like, through the long, ungrazed grass just without the kraal, which was reserved for the serving-girls to gather flowers, to a bushy rise to the north-west. He reckoned he might be able to see the troop from here.

He peered above the waist-high grass, but could see nothing. What *was* Brereton doing? All he had told him to do was watch the kraal. Had he taken off in pursuit of Mbopa's men?

They crawled onto the forward slope, to a wild pear tree. He rose to his feet, out of sight of the kraal, to gain a clearer view.

He froze. His gut felt as if it had been torn open. Even

without his telescope he could see – Zulu, a hundred and more, stripping the dead like the peasants at Waterloo. Here and there a troop horse stood obligingly. The rest were vulture meat.

There would be no human survivors. This much he knew. And Johnson would be there. What could have happened that twenty men were overwhelmed, and but a few shots? If some had got away, where were they now? Why could they not show themselves? The Zulu could not touch them beyond a spear's throw. Why, in that case, had those who escaped not just retired out of range to fight back with the carbine? Even if Brereton had lost his head there was Serjeant Hardy . . . *No*; Hardy was with Somervile. He had insisted that Hardy go as first cover. But there was Connell . . .

He lowered himself to his forearms again, his face drained of all colour, his eyes misted. *Johnson* – his old friend, Georgiana's old friend, Henrietta's: he had not drawn a sabre or carbine in years. This was no sort of death for his old friend. It was no death for anyone. Not a soldier's death with but four shots. Had they been duped? Had the Zulu approached them under parley flag, and then turned on them treacherously? How could he know? How would he ever know, unless he caught Mbopa and made him speak the truth?

Pampata had also observed; and she saw his look. She pulled at his shoulder. 'Come.'

Slowly, reluctantly, but knowing that he must, he did

as Pampata bid, numb with the sense that a part of him had been torn away . . .

They were on their feet now, stumbling down a gulley towards a thicket of fig trees, Pampata leading. When they reached the bottom, a startled bush pig shot from the undergrowth, and between them, faster than Hervey could draw his sword or even sidestep. It jolted him awake like a carriage wheel in a pothole. He looked about, sabre in hand, as if wishing for an opponent with whom to test it, then turned for the cover of the fig trees, where Pampata was already concealing herself. Here he could think over his – their – predicament, see what actions lay open to them, decide his plan.

His first thoughts were whether Mbopa's men would be looking for them. Had he been observed with the half troop, before they had slipped into the kraal? If he had been, then Mbopa would soon discover that his body did not lie with the others. And what of Pampata? Would Mbopa know that she had come into the camp last night? He was thankful that her overalls and cape – mere functionals when she had put them on – served as some disguise. He concluded it was unlikely that Mbopa would suppose he was at large, but that his henchmen would be trying to find Pampata. That, indeed, was what she had said last night, that Mbopa would hunt her down – as he would Shaka's child?

But Pampata was not merely concealing herself; she

was plucking fruit, filling the pouch that hung at her waist. He asked her why she did this, for the figs were unripened, hard as iron, and she answered – as far as he understood her – that if they chewed the pith of the fig it would ward off sleep, and that they would have need of its fortification if they were to travel to Ngwadi's kraal.

This assumption, Ngwadi's kraal their destination, he balked at. Somervile had not too many hours' start on them, and if there were any loose horses they would likely as not be following, for horses had a sort of sixth, herding, sense. Perhaps he would be able to catch one of them. In any case, Somervile would stay a while at Nonoti, the chief minister's kraal. He and Pampata would be able to make the ten miles or so before dark, and he was sure Somervile would not risk a night march from Nonoti. And even if Somervile did press on to Ngwadi's kraal, without resting at Nonoti, then he and Pampata would at least have Ngomane's protection, a man they could trust.

Except he was not certain he *could* trust this chief minister. That Pampata did was reassuring, but it was not definitive. It was only natural that she should be seeking someone of her own tribe in whom to trust, for it was not enough for the white man alone to be her protector. And what would be the outcome if they were to go to Nonoti, finding that Somervile had left already? They would not know the success or otherwise of his embassy until it was too late. And so, reluctantly, like Pampata he concluded that the safest course was that which was most arduous – Ngwadi's kraal.

'How do you know the way?' he tried.

In truth, Pampata had no difficulty with his Xhosa, for what they had to speak of was so elementary that the words were almost the same as her Zulu. And her Zulu, once he had accustomed his ear to the pronunciation, was not so very difficult to follow – especially since she seemed to have infinite patience in making herself understood.

She replied that she knew every hill and stream, that she could take him there by night, even.

He studied her for a moment; a considerable moment. A hundred miles was a prodigious distance. But it was not such an impossible thing to believe, perhaps, for did he not know the Great Plain in Wiltshire as well? It was not a hundred miles – not even fifty – but its folds and ridges, which might look the same to a stranger's eye, were to him as the churches and statues of London were to a native of that place. *Yes*, he would trust her to lead him to Ngwadi's kraal. And if there were a moon as good as last night's, he might even trust her to lead him when it was dark. What perils an African night might bring, he had better not imagine.

XIX

DADEWETHU

Later

Not only did Pampata know the way – (she hesitated not
once in their first dozen miles) – she knew how to cross
ground. She avoided skylines, keeping lower than would
a warrior crossing the same country, for she expected
they would be followed, or even intercepted. She told
Hervey not to worry on this account, however, for she
would detect Mbopa's men long before they detected
them.

He believed her. She possessed something that com-
pelled belief. He made her show him their new line when
they reached a landmark on which they had just
marched, but beyond that he found himself following
her – and quite literally, for no matter how much he
quickened his pace, Pampata remained at least an arm's
length in front of him. They had no conversation:
Hervey scarce had breath to keep up (and he could not

claim the extra weight of sabre and pistol, for Pampata marched – half ran – with nothing on her feet). When they rested, just after midday, the sun hot, it was by a spring in a hollow on the side of a dry valley, and he marvelled at her hale condition.

She said they paused only for water, but Hervey insisted they remain longer. Three hours at a pace between walk and trot – he would certainly rest his troop horses after such a stretch. And he wanted to spy out the land lest they were being followed, or about to be intercepted. He wished he had his telescope.

But there was neither heat-haze nor mist to penetrate, and he was able to see as far as the lie of the land would allow – see the beasts of the field (there were surprisingly few), but no sign of Mbopa's men. No sign of human movement at all. Either they rested or else followed the same method of traversing the country, unseen. But why would they take any but the direct route? They had no need to follow their trail, for they surely knew the destination. No, he felt sure that if they were being followed they remained undetected still, their pursuers a comfortable distance behind them.

He felt hungry suddenly. How *would* they eat? They would be well enough today, but it would go hard with them tonight, an empty belly. It could be borne, but a second day and they would begin to feel fatigue. They might find ripe fruit, although it was not the season, except that here the seasons were not as they were in

England. Fruit, however unseasonal, would be better than nothing, for it would stop the colic (so long as they did not eat too much), but no amount of fruit was substitute for meat when it came to wind and limb, and he could not risk a shot to bring down game. But he had gone hungry before. It was a commonplace of the service: no commissary, however diligent, could keep an army in constant supply of fresh rations. And even the standby, biscuit, ran short from time to time. Before Waterloo he had had nothing in his belly for the best part of two days.

With few words, they resumed the trek in the direction of the sun, and slightly north. The veld before them was spring-green, less broken and scrub-covered than that which the party had first traversed on their march to Shaka's kraal, and spotted with brilliant patches of yellow, a flower he did not know, without distinction but its pleasing colour. Here and there was a splash of orange-red, the solitary fire lily, and he marked that there were now deer – antelope – grazing at some distance. But there were none of the *nyamakaza*, the wild beasts, that Johnson had been so keen to see.

Johnson . . . He felt sick in his gut at what had befallen him. They had been together so long. They had been friends; so many happy hours shared. He could not imagine being without his stoic cheeriness, which had so often prompted him to second, and useful, thoughts. He forced the picture from his mind.

* * *

Pampata's gait was unlike any Hervey had seen before. She had discarded the overalls (concealed them in a thorn bush), but she kept the cloak about her, though the day was warm. It was her high step that intrigued him: the warriors of both the Xhosa and the Zulu, in their loping march, kept the foot low, daisy-cutting, expending as little effort as possible, their weight alone seeming to carry them forward. And the exertion in Pampata's lower body was matched by inactivity in the upper part, for she neither swung her arms nor flexed her shoulders. Yet this curious action neither impeded nor fatigued her.

For much of the time he was able to observe the action clearly, for she kept her distance very decidedly. But then, after an hour's march ('march' was unquestionably the pace she maintained; indeed, what any regiment of the Line would admit was a *forced* march), she allowed him to close with her.

Could she maintain the pace for a hundred miles? Pampata led a life of some luxury in the *isigodlo*, at least in terms of what most Zulu enjoyed. She had not been reduced, as others he had seen, by frequent childbirth – by *any* childbirth, according to Isaacs (and who but Shaka would have dared to father a child by Pampata?). She was the superior in physique of any of the serving-girls, which was, he supposed, why Shaka had first singled her out. She was not in the least run to fat, and her legs were of good length and shape, permitting a long, even stride in spite of her high-stepping action. She had, indeed, impressed all of them at that first meeting by her form as well as her air of authority. But a hundred miles . . .

'Do you have a wife and children?'

Her breaking silence, thus, took him by surprise. He asked her to repeat her question.

'I ask if you have a wife. And children.' She spoke the words slower, and louder, exactly as Hervey had when he was obliged to repeat a question of some *ryot* who had neither English nor Hindoostani.

He thought he understood: *inkosikazi, umntwana* – wife, child – were the same in Xhosa. '*Yebo, Nkosazana* . . . I have a wife and daughter.'

He would have been able to add, with a little effort, that he had *had* a wife, who had died, and that his new wife, of but a few months, was the widow of his late commanding officer, but he saw no cause. Instead he waited to see what line of enquiry she would now take.

She took none, however. It was as if she had learned all that there was to know of him. Perhaps she intended only to be civil, as might a fellow traveller in England? And perhaps his unwillingness to say more than was strictly required in answer disposed her to think that he wished no association?

They continued a full half-hour in silence, making two more miles as the crow flies, before Pampata stopped suddenly and dropped to her haunches.

Hervey peered hard to see what had arrested her, shielding his eyes against the lowering sun.

'*Intshe*,' she said, quietly.

'*Intshe?*' He did not recognize the word.

But Pampata did not look fearful. On the contrary.

'*Intshe* . . . It is not the best of time, but there may be *amaqanda*.'

He now saw. How had he *not* seen so large a bird? And he understood: *intshe* – ostrich; *amaqanda* – eggs? Was it the breeding season?

For the next twenty minutes they stalked it: crouching, watching, crawling, dashing, just as he had done as a boy on the Great Plain, the thrill of finding the lark's nest . . . Until at last Pampata was sure, when she rose to her feet and strode purposefully towards a scraping in the earth, perhaps six feet across, in which were eight or nine eggs, some broken, some half buried.

Pampata evidently sensed his puzzlement. 'Many ostriches share the one nest,' she explained.

They rifled the giant clutch as rudely as any wild predator. Pampata discarded several without breaking them; Hervey took one, despite her protest.

He reeled at the stench when he broke it, and threw it as far as he could. Pampata laughed – the first time he had seen her do so.

She handed him another, nodding encouragingly. He drew his sword, wanting to make a better break than the other he had managed. He cracked it cleanly, opened it in two equal halves and gave it back to her. She handed him another, and he broke it the same way.

She let the white trickle away, so that the yolk occupied almost the whole of one half-shell. Despite his hunger, he saw it was no true waste: although there was less yolk than white compared with a hen's egg, he reckoned it was at least the equal of two dozen he would have found in the henhouse in Wiltshire.

They ate their fill.

By the time the shadows were lengthening – longer now than the umbrella thorns which cast them – and the birds of the veld, large and small, were beginning to roost, Hervey calculated they had made not far short of twenty miles. He could feel it in his bones. He had but an elementary knowledge of the human skeleton and its muscles, but he knew where and how a ride across country made its demands, and likewise how that distance on foot told. Pampata showed no sign of the exertion. She seemed, indeed, to be in some sort of trance – not of the kind the witch doctor induced with his potions and spells, as if the body were possessed by some spirit of another place, but instead the product of the most singular concentration of mind (such was her determined intent to reach the kraal of Shaka's beloved). She refused rest. She said they could walk for another two hours before all light was gone, and that in a further three there would be a good moon, and that as long as there were stars to see by, they could continue their march.

Shortly after two o'clock in the morning, Hervey now believing he must insist on rest, for his own as well as Pampata's sake, they came upon a small watercourse set about with lala palms. The moon slipped behind cloud as they stumbled over the thicker tussocks of grass. It had been slipping in and out for the best part of an hour, making the business of marching by the stars ever more difficult, but Pampata had not once faltered in either pace or direction.

Hervey thought this a good place to lie up a while. The shelter of trees was always a recommendation – the soldier's instinct for a roof over his head at night. Pampata was reluctant, however. Already they had startled the roosting birds, which made off with a good deal of noise; and water, she said, especially water at which there were trees, was favoured by the spirits of warriors who had gone home to their Maker. And by *nyamakaza*, wild beasts.

Hervey tried as best his Xhosa would allow to suggest that the spirits of the warriors would surely approve of their journey, knowing as they must of the murder of the greatest of them (perhaps even the spirit of Shaka himself would be watching them too). And as for *nyamakaza*, he was ready enough to put a ball into any that had the impudence to challenge them.

But it was pitch dark. Without a moon, under the lala palms, he could make out nothing of Pampata but an indistinct form. He had never been so strangely placed – at the will and capability of a native woman, and one whom he barely knew; yet he was her safeguard, too.

He was just able to see that she stooped to drink. Perhaps she would agree to rest here? He crouched beside her, cupping his hands and taking three good measures from the clear-tasting stream.

The challenge came silent and sudden. The blow pitched him onto all fours, stunned him. And then the snarl so loud, and the breath so hot.

Pampata screamed – but not in fear. She cursed, shrieked, spat, yelled.

The leopard made off as suddenly as it had struck, leaving Hervey grasping for his pistol but not knowing where to point it.

'Come!' hissed Pampata. 'We must leave this place.'

He would not gainsay her.

They stumbled on without moonlight for half an hour, the pain in his left shoulder growing. He could feel the blood down his back – not copious, more a trickle; but a wound nevertheless. How many of the leopard's claws had torn his flesh he could not know until morning, but he knew he had been lucky. In India, a leopard spelled death unless a covering bullet could stop it quickly; and he had no reason to suppose its African cousin was any less deadly.

Pampata knew they must rest. Hervey had not told her the leopard had drawn blood, but she could hear his breathing, and it was laboured. There was a break in the clouds ahead, and it would be good to be halted when the moon lit the veld again, for they would be able to see first, rather than be seen.

They sat down, Hervey supporting himself on his right hand. 'You were brave,' he said, simply.

'I was angry.'

'Why did the leopard go? Was he afraid of a woman's shouts?'

'He was afraid already, before he struck. Afraid we would take his place.'

Hervey wondered how she knew these things, how the king's favourite, the best-loved of the *isigodlo*, could be so versed in the lore of the wilderness. He tried to form the question, but he could not summon the words. And at that moment the moon slipped from behind its masking cloud, and lit the veld like an oil lamp brought into a darkened room.

They could see for two hundred yards, for it was flat and treeless. There were grazing animals, but he could not discern what they were. He looked about with all the intent of a scout who finds himself suddenly among the enemy, yet concealed.

Pampata had taken in the prospect at once – and it

bore no fears for her. But she saw that he rested on one hand, and knew at once the reason. She began examining the wound with her fingers. It spanned the whole of his shoulder blade.

'Only three – you are fortunate. But the leopard's claws are always unclean. You must have medicine.'

Hervey might have smiled. Where did she suppose they would find the surgeon?

She rose and walked off a little way. He watched her casting around, then bending, before returning with a handful of leaves.

'What is that?'

'*Umhlaba*,' she replied, pulling at his tunic so that he would slip his left arm from the sleeve.

He held her hand to his face so that he could smell the leaves: aloe – he was content.

She crushed them and dabbed the wound with the moist pulp, and he felt the balm at once.

'When the sun rises I will search for *ncwadi*,' she said, helping him put his arm back into the sleeve. 'And *inconi*.'

He knew neither word, but trusted in her remedy, for the aloe was already making the wound but an ache. '*Ngibonga kakhulu, Nkosazana* . . . Thank you, madam.'

'*Nami ngiyabonga, mfowethu* . . . I, too, thank you, my brother.'

Hervey could not but feel the warmth of that change in her salutation. '*Ngiyabonga*,' he repeated simply.

Pampata nodded. And then, in a little while, said, 'We must sleep.'

Hervey replied that first *she* should sleep, while he kept watch, and then he would wake her so that he in turn could rest. But Pampata objected. There was nothing here, in the middle of the wilderness, to keep watch on, she said. Besides, if a herd of wild beasts should choose to pass over them, they would hear them and feel the earth tremble, and wake therefore, long before they would see them. And if Mbopa's men were indeed following them, they could not do so when it was dark.

Hervey saw her reasoning, and said he was content. He took off his tunic once more, and made a pillow of it, offering one half to her. She laid down her head without a word. He, facing the opposite direction, laid down his, and, looking up at the stars as he had so many a time, thought for a fleeting moment of Georgiana, of how neglectful was his adventure, chosen or not, then closed his eyes and fell into a deeper sleep than he would have cared to own to.

Pampata woke him gently, with a hand to his sound shoulder. Hervey opened his eyes, and for once he did not instantly comprehend his situation, as invariably he comprehended in the field, alert at the first touch – Johnson's touch, more often than not. The stars had gone, the moon too, but the first fingers of light were stretching up from the eastern horizon, already seeming to bring warmth, and welcome.

He knew now where he was, and he shivered a little. The night had not been cold – not as cold as his first back at the Cape – but the ache in his shoulder was now more insistent, making him feel the need of a blanket. He raised himself on one hand again.

'*Ulale kamnandi na?*' It was what he had heard the Natal natives ask of him the morning after they had pitched camp ashore.

'Yes,' she replied – she had slept well. Had he?

He said – he thought he was saying – that he had slept so well that he could not believe it had been but the one night.

He began looking about, but keeping his eyes from the east and the growing glare of the breaking day. The veld was as peaceful as it had appeared by moonlight, not even much birdsong, nothing like the chorus that would have accompanied the break of an English day.

Pampata rose. 'Come,' she said, holding out a hand as if to help. 'We must find *ncwadi*.'

He got up by himself – stiff, but no more so than a hundred times before when he had risen unaided after a sodden night on cold ground. He breathed deep several times, as if the air had some restorative power – which it seemed indeed to have, as if it were somehow washed clean in the dark, silent hours, to begin again another day as pure as those which Adam himself had known.

It was no time for reverie. They had run, perhaps, a quarter of their course, and he supposed it would get no easier, and might very well get harder – much harder. He had not asked her: must they climb many hills, skirt many kraals, cross many rivers? Three times the distance still to go – the doubts began to press upon him.

They had been making tracks for an hour when Pampata at last saw what she was seeking, a small, un-distinguished plant which she at once began uprooting.

To Hervey, the *ncwadi*'s bulbous root looked unpromising, but Pampata crushed it first with her teeth, and then ground it in her hands – which she rubbed clean with the unwanted leaves – to make a dressing. Hervey removed his arm from the sleeve once more to let her apply the mulch. This time he felt only pain, however, for there was no balm in the root. Pampata told him it would make the wound clean, for the leopard's claws were always foul. Still, she insisted, they must find the *inconi*, for that could reverse any poison.

But not immediately, for when he had slipped his arm back into his tunic sleeve he saw – and with some astonishment – that she had in her hand an ostrich egg.

Pampata smiled: yes, she had concealed the egg.

He returned her smile as he drew his sabre. Her eyes were for the first time bright, and her mouth at ease. Her teeth, he marked, would have been the envy of many a lady of fashion.

He took the egg and gave the shell a sharp crack with the blade, edging as before around half its full circumference, allowing her then to pull it open in two perfectly equal parts. She drained off the white, just as she had with the others, and then pinched the yolk, dividing it between the two half-shells.

Thus they breakfasted: *hazree basar*, not *chota*, for although it was the first of the day, half a dozen hen's eggs were no small affair.

'Tea would complete our feast,' he said, before the thought reminded him painfully of Johnson, and he had to fight down the lump in his throat.

Pampata rose and held a hand to shade her eyes as she scoured the veld. Hervey knew better than to ask: he had seen how she picked the mark upon which they would march, and then examined the ground in between to choose her line of advance (there were as yet no prominent hills). She did so, indeed, with the skill of the dragoon-scout, and so far with entire success. He asked her on what she had fixed, and she pointed to a line of trees on the far, north-west horizon. How tall they were, he could not tell, but he could not suppose them great – perhaps palm. Whatever their height, he did not reckon them closer than a couple of leagues: the mark would see them through the next two hours at least.

But after only half an hour Pampata made a sudden diversion to a stony outcrop by what was evidently a dry waterhole. Hervey thought he knew why: an abundance of dark-green leaves, and brilliant red shrubs clustered with fruit the size of grapes.

A flock of small but equally colourful birds quit their gorging as they approached, and rabbits bolted to their burrows. He felt sorry, almost, for having disturbed them.

But Pampata waved him from his interest in the fruit, making a sign that could not be mistaken for anything but 'poison', and instead took herself to the outcrop, where she crouched and then beckoned him over. 'See, *inconi.*'

He could see nothing, nothing but the rock itself. How was that to heal his wound?

She pointed.

The white marks – streaks, patches – he had merely thought to be the colour of the rocks. Pampata shook her head. She began to explain, but he understood nothing. She pointed to the burrows, and made a motion with her fingers to suggest rapid movement – the rabbits running, perhaps – but still he could not see what she meant. Then she pointed between his legs and arched her hand towards the ground with a 'psss' sound, which ended with a girlish giggle as Hervey grasped her meaning.

So the white marks were rabbit urine; but he was none the wiser.

Pampata picked a broad, flat leaf from one of the

shrubs, motioned to his sabre and made a scraping gesture at the white patches.

Hervey drew his sword to oblige. Pampata was not
content until they had collected two teaspoons' worth.

He then removed his arm from the tunic sleeve for a
third time, and sat on a rock to await the application of
the white magic. He had no second thoughts about her
medicine, for he had learned an age ago, in India, how
effective native cures could be (and, besides, some of
what he had seen 'respectable' practitioners in England
do smacked of so much quackery). The aloe had eased
the pain to begin with, and although the *ncwadi* had
brought no relief, the wound hurt no more now than
before, which in his experience was unusual. What
manner of cure, then, would the *inconi* work? Horse
urine was an ammoniac, he knew; was the rock rabbit's?

Pampata wiped the wound clean of the *ncwadi* pulp.
Blood began again to ooze, though not so freely as
before. She let it fill the claw marks, dabbed at them with
the torn sleeve of Hervey's shirt, then pressed the linen
on the wound with the flat of her hand, and with increasing force until she was satisfied that the oozing would
not defeat her purpose.

For a full five minutes Hervey endured such a pain as
brought the most prodigious sweat to his brow.

She removed the linen, threw back her head and
poured the white powder into her mouth, which she had
filled with saliva.

Before he could ask her purpose – he now saw it was wholly impractical – she took his shoulders firmly in her hands, put her mouth to the wound, and squirted the milky astringent into the torn flesh.

Hervey was at once filled with admiration, and more – which he could not rightly determine. When she was finished, a new poultice of *ncwadi* applied and his arm eased carefully back into its sleeve, he turned to thank her. '*Ngibonga kakhulu, Nkosazana.*'

She made a face, as if to say it was nothing.

But Hervey would not have it. He took her wrists to express his earnest. '*Ngibonga kakhulu.*'

She gave a half smile of content, though of sadness too, unlike the earlier exchange, and rose. 'We have many miles to make today, *mfowethu.*'

He nodded. This was mere diversion; it gained them nothing in their true mission. But he could not let it pass without a proper expression of his esteem. He did what he had not done in many a year: he pulled a button from his tunic – not one of the black ones, but the silver dragoon button which he wore on the inside of his tunic-fall – he buffed it bright on the leg of his overalls, and presented it to her. '*Ngibonga kakhulu . . . dadewethu.*'

He had called her 'my sister', as she had called him 'my brother'.

Pampata took the token reverently.

XX

A SOLITARY DUTY

Earlier

Johnson had lain all day among the wild pear trees on
the little hill to the south-east of the kraal, with Molly
calmly pulling at the grass beside him. He had fastened
the reins to his swordbelt so that if he fell asleep she
would not break cover and reveal their hiding hole – or,
worse, take off and leave him in this wild and Godless
place.

She had not done so when the Zulu attacked. His Cape
pony and the bat-horse had bolted good and proper when
he had walked back towards the troop – on account,
doubtless, of the rifle fire – but Molly had stood her
ground, as a well-trained charger ought. And when he had
raced back to her pursued by more Zulu than
he could count, and vaulted half into the saddle, so that
he lay rather than sat astride, she had broken into the most
even of trots, allowing him to get his balance, and then the

reins and finally the stirrups. They had galloped, then, for the ridge on which the troop had camped, and when he had stopped shaking, and recovered his breath, and his wits (the instinct for flight displaced everything but brute strength), he had begun to take stock of the sorry situation.

From this position, he could see even better the fate that had befallen Captain Brereton's dragoons, and the certainty that none had escaped death. The Zulu were already stripping the bodies. But where Colonel 'Ervey was he had no notion – except that he was not among the dragoons below. Was he inside the kraal still? Had the Zulu woman given him away?

What was he supposed to do, now? What *could* he do?

First, he could make sure he wasn't caught. Even if the Zulus did have some of the troop horses, they wouldn't be able to catch him as long as he stayed mounted and Molly stayed sound. He would have to show himself, though, or how would Colonel 'Ervey know he was there? Could he keep riding round the kraal till Colonel 'Ervey saw him?

But what if he were a prisoner inside the kraal? Could he leave Molly tied up, hidden, and go into the kraal by himself? He had the rifle, after all. And when it was dark he ought to be able to get in somehow . . .

But he would have to look in every hut! And as soon as he fired the rifle, the whole of the kraal would stand-to, and then there would be no chance of getting out (there were only twenty or so cartridges left).

No, surely it would be better to keep looking for him outside. Colonel 'Ervey would know how to get out; he'd got out of worse places than here! Just as long as the Zulu woman hadn't given him away.

He reloaded the rifle and slipped it back into the saddle sleeve. 'Right, Molly, lass; we're gooin' lookin' for thi master!'

He had to think sharp again, however, for there were Zulus coming up the rise. Had they seen him (he thought he had kept his head down)? Were they after him, or just wanting to scour the camp ground?

He looked left, the way the rest of the troop had gone. Perhaps if he dropped back a bit, and headed in that direction, he would find somewhere to keep watch on the entrance which Colonel 'Ervey and the Zulu woman had gone through?

But there were Zulus over on the left, too. They looked like they were searching for him. Perhaps he ought to head back a little, the way they had come yesterday? Yes, that was the best course: if he got the other side of the hill behind him – only half a mile or so west – and then turned south for about a mile, he would come onto the queer-shaped hill they had stopped on to look at the kraal yesterday, and then from there he'd be able to see if there were any Zulus on the south side of the kraal, and if there weren't he could watch from there. He'd got Colonel 'Ervey's telescope after all.

He gave them the slip – bastard Zulus! Why didn't they

379

come at them fair instead of sneaking up like that? – and circled south, unseen. And from the queer-shaped hill he saw the clump of pear trees, and not a Zulu for half a mile and more. That would be the place to hide (Colonel 'Ervey wouldn't have said 'hide': he'd have said 'conceal themselves', but that didn't matter; just as long as nobody saw them).

He knew how the scouts did it. He may have been a groom for twenty years, but he knew a thing or two (and if he didn't, all he had to do was think what Colonel 'Ervey would do). He halted well short of the clump, in the open (but there was no other cover), and took out the telescope. He knew how to use it, except that even with Molly standing still it was difficult to find the trees through it, and then they were a bit of a blur.

He gave up after a while. But he'd have seen if there were Zulus among the trees, even blurred, because they'd have been moving – and there wasn't anything moving. He screwed up his bare eyes against the sun just to make sure. No – there were nothing.

The scouts used to dismount, and one of them would go forward and check a place on foot. But that was with another man covering him, and he hadn't got anyone. So ought he to dismount? No; he bloody well wasn't going to get down from Molly till he was certain there wasn't a Zulu in half a mile!

He slipped the rifle from its sleeve, pulled back the hammer, and edged Molly towards the clump of pear trees, as the sahibs did in India when they were hunting tiger.

There was nothing. Just wild pear trees, ten of them, and stunted little things, not like proper pear trees in England. In fact he wouldn't have known they were pear trees at all unless Old Bez – Corporal Bezuidenhuit – the Rifles' commissary, had told him. Not that they had come past this particular clump, but these were the same trees all right. Not that he needed to know. It wasn't even as if there were pears on them. He'd have to wait all summer for pears. Not that he felt like eating. Except that Old Bez had told him – warned him – about the *boomslang*, the snake that were so pois'nous that when it bit you, you didn't have time to say, 'God 'ave mercy', before you were dead. And this *boomslang* hung about in trees waiting for people to walk underneath, and then it dropped on top of you and you'd be dead. But it didn't like pear trees, said Old Bez, or some other sort of trees, which he couldn't remember now. But definitely not the pear tree. So here he could hide – conceal himself – with Molly and have a good scout of the ground with his – Colonel 'Ervey's – telescope, and then he could work out what best to do next.

He slid from the saddle and loosened the girth – he thought it was safe to, and Molly would have to have some grass in her or she'd get colic and then they'd be in trouble. They were in trouble already, but they'd be in real trouble with colic. And then he began thinking about the dragoons down there, with the vultures circling round. There was . . . He wasn't sure exactly *who* there was, because he'd been hammering a shoe back onto his pony right up until they mustered. There was Connell, because he was Captain Brereton's coverman that morning. He didn't like Connell much, but everybody said he was good at skill-at-arms, and riding school. And there must've been French, because he was Colonel 'Ervey's coverman, wasn't he? Poor old Frenchie. He were a gentleman really, but he didn't put on airs at all. He'd help anybody, in fact – write letters for them that didn't write an' all. And that new lad, Hanks, who'd thrown up when he'd had to drink rum from the piss-pot, which everybody had to do when they joined. And Mr Petrie, whose father had come to see him off, a nice old gentleman who'd shaken his hand and asked if he'd been at Waterloo, and gave him a sovereign when he'd said yes. He was a nice man, too, was Mr Petrie. He always smiled when he returned your salute; Colonel 'Ervey liked him as well, and said as he would make a good officer. It were a shame.

But he mustn't think about it now. The only thing he'd got to think about was watching for Colonel 'Ervey, and keeping himself out of sight.

So he watched: one hour, two, three – he'd no idea. The sun had moved a bit – he could see it every so often when there was a bit of thinning in the cloud – but he couldn't tell much from it; not like he would have been able to in England. And the Zulus kept coming and going, in and out of the kraal, more and more of them, and there was no sign at all of Colonel 'Ervey.

What if there were another opening, on the other side, and he'd been able to get out?

He couldn't just sit here – stand here, for he wasn't going to sit down and be eaten alive by ants, or crept up on by *boomslangs* if they'd fallen out of another sort of tree. He started to tighten Molly's girth.

He rode until the sun was fist height above the horizon. He tried showing himself as often as he could – so that Colonel 'Ervey could see him if he were lying low – but he had to keep backtracking, into dead ground, every time he saw a Zulu. And they were all over the place, and he wondered, if they saw him, whether they would think there was a whole troop of him, because he kept appearing in different places.

But he didn't see Colonel 'Ervey. Not a sign of him. Or the Zulu woman either – but it was difficult to tell because they all looked the same and because they didn't wear anything but grass skirts. But he'd know her if he saw her close up. She'd looked sad when he'd given her the overalls and the cape, and he'd noticed she looked like one of the girls in Stepney when he used to go for the things for the officers' house. She had nice eyes, and she didn't have those big lips like a lot of blackies did. In fact, if you put a dress on her she'd look better than a lot of the women you saw in the streets in London of an evening. In fact, if her hair were long, like a proper lady's was, she'd look like a proper lady – if she weren't black of course. But that didn't matter, really, because she was better looking than a lot of them, and she seemed nice. Except that she might've given Colonel 'Ervey away.

And so he rode back to the pear-tree clump the way he had come, and tried to think what else to do. He loosened Molly's girth again to let her pull at the grass, but he daresn't take her saddle off because they'd have to gallop like the blazes if the Zulus had followed them. He wasn't hungry. He'd drunk half the water in his canteen, but that was all right because it wasn't too hot, and he wasn't really thirsty. And there were plenty of streams he'd seen, but he hadn't wanted to dismount to fill his canteen again because if there were Zulus about they could be crouching in the grass, like the ones that got them this morning.

But he didn't know what to do. And it was going to get dark soon. He couldn't do anything when it was dark. Even if he could find his way to the kraal, how would he be able to get in? And how would he find his way round: there were so many huts? All he could do was wait until it was light again and then ride the way he'd gone today, and perhaps Colonel 'Ervey might have seen him and would be waiting for him to come back tomorrow.

And so now he would just have to wait until it *was* tomorrow. But first it was going to be night. He had never been by himself anywhere before at night. What would he have to do? He couldn't go to sleep. What would he sleep on? Not the ground; not by himself. And there were no sentries. There had to be sentries. He would have to be the sentry, all night.

When the night came it was darker than he'd ever known. He stood holding Molly's reins, short, pressed up against her. He had to put his cloak on, because it got cold as soon as the sun went down. And then the noises came – shrieking and snarling, hissing, hooting, whistling, rustling – and they went on all night, as if they were trying to frighten him out of the trees. And they nearly did. And all the time there could be Zulus creeping up on him, and he'd never know till there was a spear in his back. And it got so bad that he had to get into the saddle, although poor Molly had had to carry him all day.

And when it started to get light at last, he knew he had to stand to, so he got the rifle out of the sleeve again, and watched for all he was worth, shivering with the cold and not knowing if he'd see another living soul again that he knew. It wasn't as bad, though, now that he knew it would be light soon, except that now there were queer shadows moving about, and he knew that it wasn't anything but the way the sun came up, but he wasn't sure, because it could be Zulus not shadows, and they might even be using the shadows to creep up on him, because they were like wild animals really and they knew how to hunt.

When it was really light, and he could see there was nothing at all – just the long grass, and the kraal half a mile away – he started to feel better, because he'd stuck to his post all night and hadn't been too frit and run away, and he hadn't fallen asleep or done anything like that. Except that he'd been a burden on poor Molly. So now he got down and undid her girth again, and this time he unfastened the bit on one side of the bridle, and let her have a good length of rein so she could pull at the grass.

And now he was feeling hungry too, and he rummaged in one of the saddlebags, because he knew Colonel 'Ervey always had a few bits of things to eat (as *he* did too, but his pony had gone) – and there *were* some things to eat, some biltong and some corn cakes, and two hard-boiled eggs. He'd give Molly the corn cakes. She grabbed the first from him, and then the other two, and she nudged him for more when she'd done. He chewed a bit of biltong, but it made him want to drink, and he knew he'd have to be careful with the water just in case he couldn't get near any more till a lot later. The eggs were best. That's what he liked most of a morning, and Colonel 'Ervey always bought lots of eggs whenever he could and boiled them hard and kept them in his pocket or in the saddlebag, because old Mr Corporal Coates, his friend before he died, told him a long time ago, when he was a boy, before he joined the army, that he ought to take boiled eggs with him whenever he went on campaign, and he was always very good about sharing them with him.

He took out the telescope to have a good look round, but the glass was misted and it was a bit of time before he could dry it properly. But when he had, there was nothing – not even many Zulus about like yesterday. So he reckoned he ought to get moving soon, go round the way he had yesterday, show himself every so often – shout 'Colonel 'Ervey, sir!', even. Because the Zulus'd never be able to catch him on Molly, just so long as she didn't go lame – and there was no reason for her to go lame because she'd been hot-shod, proper, before they'd left Cape Town, and this ground wasn't nearly as hard as it was in England sometimes.

So he fastened the bridle again, and tightened up the girth, and rubbed her nose and said nice things to her – as he had all night, but now he could say them so's she'd be sure to hear – and got back into the saddle and set off to find Colonel 'Ervey.

But he saw no sign of him. He didn't call him, because it didn't seem right to – because the Zulus would hear, and they'd know then that Colonel 'Ervey was hiding somewhere, and would start looking for him. He showed himself once or twice – well, three times, really, if you counted the same place twice, there and back – but it just felt like he was waiting for a Zulu to come and throw a spear at him, and then he'd be no good for anything, and

certainly not to find Colonel 'Ervey. So after midday –
which he could tell because he'd noticed yesterday how
the shadows changed direction – he came back to the
pear-tree clump to work out what he'd do next.

The easiest thing would be to go back where they'd
landed. He'd be able to find his way all right. And he
might even find that Mr Isaacs, where they'd left him, if
he hadn't got better and gone back. But that wouldn't
really be what Colonel 'Ervey would do, was it, because
he wouldn't leave Mr Somervile by himself? He'd try to
catch up with him; that's what he'd try to do. That's what
he'd be *trying* to do, because he couldn't still be in yon
kraal or they'd be doing something that'd tell you they'd
got him – *bastard* Zulus!

But where had Mr Somervile gone? Nobody had told
him. All he knew was as they were going one way and
Colonel 'Ervey was going another. But he wouldn't want
to be going another way now, would he? He'd be wanting to catch up with Mr Somervile, and Captain
Fairbrother.

Yes, that was it – Captain Fairbrother. *He'd* know how
to find Colonel 'Ervey, even if he were in the kraal still.
He bet he could catch them up on Molly. And it wouldn't
be that hard, would it, to see where they'd gone, because
fifty horses couldn't not leave an easy trail to follow? So
if he set off now he'd be able to catch up with them in a
day or two. Except that he'd have to do sentry again by
himself at night, and he wasn't sure he could.

But what if Colonel 'Ervey wasn't doing that at all? What if the Zulus had killed him?

He sank to the ground, as if his legs turned slowly to jelly. And warm tears began trickling down his grimy cheeks.

XXI

THE WATERS THAT COVER THE EARTH

Afternoon

Hervey and Pampata stood staring at the Thukela in dismay and disbelief. In the morning they had crossed the Inonoti with barely twenty strides, the water not rising above Pampata's knees; but here the river was wider than Hervey could have thrown a spear, and looked deeper than his 'sister' could ford (he had learned already that she could not swim). Besides, the Thukela was in spate, its current stronger than he would have cared to tackle even on his own.

Pampata knew the cause. The Inonoti, she explained, was but a small river, rising from the ground not so very far from where they had crossed, whereas the great Thukela rose in the mountains – uKhalamba, the barrier of spears – many miles to the west. The clouds that had crossed their sky must have shed their water there in a great rain, *mvulankulu*, which the

Thukela had collected and now returned to the sea.

This was some comfort at least, for Hervey knew well enough that a spate river could fall as quickly as it rose. But he could not see how so much water could pass at such a speed without a great deal more behind it. He had watched the cloud for three days, and thought it unlikely there would be any let in the current before morning. With difficulty he asked her how deep was the Thukela when the waters subsided.

She pointed to her breastbone.

It was not encouraging: if she had to wade at that depth, it could take days before they might ford. And then a darker thought occurred. '*Ingwenya?*' he asked, pointing at the river.

Pampata shrugged, as if to say 'who knows?'

But if she had crossed the river before, she must surely know?

Her gestures indicated that she could not say one way or the other.

'How many times have you crossed the river?'

'*Kabila.*'

'*Twice?* Only twice?' How could she know the way to Ngwadi's kraal – a hundred miles – if she had crossed the Thukela but twice?

She understood him perfectly, and looked away. 'You will not come with me?'

He almost gasped at her determination. Instead he smiled. 'I will go with you.'

* * *

They spent an hour or so foraging, though without much success. Hervey had no great appetite for the creatures that crawled or slithered out of their path, though he could easily have caught one with his sabre, and there was no game to tempt him, even if he had thought it worth risking a shot – which he did not. He wondered if there were fish in the river, although how to catch them he did not put his mind to. They found some monkey orange, with their bitter fruit, but little else beyond the odd root that might have been enjoyable had they been able to boil it. Hervey was not hungry, though. The ostrich eggs had filled his stomach, and with a rich yolk as fortifying as red meat. He would not pine for bread and beef.

Instead they sat in the shade of a lala palm, watching the Thukela, resting and gathering their strength for the morning when the river would be lower. Hervey took off his boots as Pampata washed her feet in the river, then sat beside her to wash, and soothe, his own.

'*Qaphela – ingwenya*,' she said, with a cautionary laugh.

Beware the crocodiles: he took his feet out.

After a while he asked her about the rock rabbit, and how she had come to know the medicine in its urine. It was an ancient knowledge, she replied, taught her by her mother. All Zulu women knew of it, though not all of them could use it to advantage.

And then she smiled, as if at a happy memory of something in her distant past, her childhood. 'Do you know why the rock rabbit has no tail?' she asked, indeed quite childlike.

Hervey returned the smile, and shook his head.

It was a long story, made longer by frequent interruptions for the sake of clarification. 'At the newness of the land,' she began, 'animals did not have tails. All were happy except *ibhubesi*, the king of beasts, so one day he asked them to his court to receive presents that they might look more beautiful. All the animals went to the lion's court except the rock rabbits, who preferred to bask in the sun, although they still wished for their presents, and so asked the monkeys if they would bring them for them. The lion gave presents to all who came – presents of a tail – but being very old and his sight failing, he made many mistakes, giving, for example, the elephant a very small tail, but the squirrel a very long one. The monkeys took home their tails, wishing they were not so short, and those of the rock rabbits. But when they saw the rock rabbits they refused to give them up: "We shall attach them to our own," they said, "to make them longer." Since that day the rock rabbits have had no tail, but are no longer so lazy.'

Hervey lay back against the lala palm, hands behind his head, for all the world as if he were in the garden at Horningsham. The wound was now but a dull ache. He could take his ease. 'A charming story.'

'And one that has a lesson too,' added Pampata. 'Do not send another to do one's bidding.'

This Hervey managed to understand, but not without the need to open his eyes.

'Yes, sleep, *mfowethu*. I will watch for us both,' said Pampata, once the parable was done.

Hervey raised a hand slightly, in thanks, and closed his eyes again. But just as he was about to succumb, he snapped to and sat up as if he had heard a distant alarm.

'What is it, *mfowethu*?'

'Nothing, but I forget myself.' He got up, adjusting his sabre, and the pistol at his belt. 'I must go a little way back to see how things are. Stay here. I will return before the sun falls below that hill yonder.'

Pampata looked puzzled. 'Why do you not stay here, where we cannot be seen?'

He tried to explain. 'I am a soldier, *dadewethu*. I cannot only hide and wait.'

She bowed, understanding what impelled the warrior, if not always why. 'I will stay here, *mfowethu*.'

He backtracked for half a mile, until he came to a fold in the ground which would afford him a little elevation on the otherwise flat floodplain. He ascended cautiously, for he did not want to show himself, first crawling, and then rising to his knees, and only to full height when he was sure he had seen all there was to be seen from a crouch.

But the country was empty – empty of Zulu; he knew it teemed with other life, whether he could see it or not.

He sat down. He would stay sentinel here until dusk came, and only then return to Pampata and make fast for the night.

He turned his face to the sun, taking in its strength, watching, listening – trying not to think of what had happened, but of what was to come.

After an hour he saw the vultures. Or rather, he became aware of what they did, for there had been vultures overhead since early morning. They had come together, collected, flocked, whatever it was that vultures did when they no longer patrolled alone, to circle in a slow but purposeful way above a single point. And he could not be certain of it, but the circle seemed to be advancing, just perceptibly – exactly as he had observed before Umtata, when Fairbrother had first alerted him and they had thereby detected the advancing Zulu.

But how far away they were he couldn't tell. And it might signal nothing at all, for before Umtata the vultures had flown in a sort of extended line, the formation in which the Zulu had come on. This was different. All he could do was keep watch.

Half an hour passed. They were advancing, certainly (he could now make out the wings separately from the body). And all the time they had kept up the same routine of circling. If it were a stricken animal they were intent on, it would by now have gone to ground, would it not? Why would they keep post above the Zulu? But then, why had they kept post before Umtata?

And did the Zulu – if they *were* Zulu – follow their trail, his and Pampata's? What trail could two people make? He tried to calculate: how long would it be before they closed on the river? He could only do so by the vultures' appearance, how it was changing, a method he'd scarcely had any practice in. Perhaps a couple of hours?

He wondered if he should alert Pampata. But what could they do? They might, he suppose, put more distance behind them, beat up- or downstream, but they would leave a trail, if they had been doing so before, and then the Zulu would hasten. And was not this the surest place to cross the Thukela, she'd said? Pampata needed to sleep; she did not need to be woken and made more fearful, especially when he couldn't be certain there *were* Zulu out there. No, all he could do, again, was wait – and thank God for this searching light of the veld.

The first sighting sent a shiver down his spine. Now he had no choice but to rouse Pampata.

How many? They were still too distant to tell. Before Umtata there had been dust, a sure sign of numbers and speed, but it was not the season. How far? The plain was featureless, and this light so strong . . . two miles, three perhaps?

When first he had seen Matiwane's *impi* before Umtata, his blood had run cold. Yes, there had been many, many more of them than could be following them now, but at Umtata he had sat before his troop of dragoons and a whole company of rifles. If there were only a dozen – half a dozen – Zulu yonder, then his situation was even more perilous than then.

He had but an hour before they would find the two of them.

He got onto all fours (even two miles away, the Zulu might see him), and retreated into the dead ground which would allow him to steal away unobserved.

And then he froze. Three hundred yards, no more, as if from out of the earth: two scouts, eyes to the ground – following spoor? He dropped to his belly and began crawling for a lone thorn bush ten yards off to his left.

How could he not have seen them? Were there more as close?

What in God's name could he do? If he ran back to the river, where could they hide? If they tried to cross ... There was no time, even if the possibility.

All he could do was stop these two, and then take a chance of running with Pampata from the rest – upstream. No, *down* . . .

He could do it. He had pistol and sabre: the blade – and surprise – for the first, and the ball for the second. But if he used the pistol, the rest would at once quicken their pace, and their chance of escape would be even smaller. And he could not be certain of the pistol (there was not time to draw the charge and reload). How he wished for his percussion rifle!

No, he must take both with the sabre. He was

fortunate, though: he had a minute or so more to plan his ambuscade.

Nevertheless he opened the pistol's firing pan and blew out the powder, taking a new cartridge and making sure there was dry primer. If the fight were going against him he would have no option but to put a ball in one of them – and take the consequences.

The Zulu were young but wore the red neck feathers of the seasoned warrior. One was scarred heavily about the body. They came on side by side. Pity: it gave him no advantage, for if he attacked from a flank the one would screen the other – though it meant he would not face both at once. He must attack from a flank *and* behind, allowing him freedom to swing his sabre. He could first slice the spear arm of the nearer, gaining precious seconds to despatch the other, before turning back to finish off the first. They carried the short, not the war shield: that would help. All he needed was that they continue on their line, passing the thorn bush the way he expected.

Fifty yards off, they stopped suddenly. They began casting around. He could not think why (he and Pampata had not halted at all). One of them picked up something – so small he could not tell. What had they dropped – a button, a bead?

They looked about, pointed towards the river, exchanged words – a murmur to him, no more – and then resumed their advance, but at a cautious walk. His every muscle tensed; his gut churned like a water wheel (so hard he forgot the pain in his shoulder). They would search the thorn bush, he was certain: it was the only cover between here and the river.

They separated, one to pass either side. What choice had he now but the pistol?

The scarred warrior – the more seasoned of the two? – was coming left of the bush, his spear arm therefore closest.

Hervey took a last, deep breath, then sprang like a cock at set-to.

For all his caution the Zulu turned too late, Hervey's blade cleaving savagely through the flesh of his upper arm and shattering the bone.

He didn't wait to see its effect, turning on his heels to launch at the second while he yet had surprise.

The second, younger, looked afraid, eyes wide, though he still came on.

Hervey drew his pistol.

The Zulu faltered – he knew what a ball did – and Hervey rushed him with the point of the sabre.

He tried to parry with his shield, drawing his spear arm back. But in went the point – four inches, deadly.

Hervey withdrew, turned his wrist and sliced upwards and left to disarm him.

The Zulu dropped his spear and fell to his knees.

Hervey drove his sabre deep into his side to be certain.

It was a thrust too many. The other Zulu, spear now

in left hand, was on him like the leopard of the night.

But, left-handed, the spear had neither the force nor the precision of the real warrior's thrust. It pierced the cartridge case, not the kidneys. Hervey sidestepped and caught the Zulu without a guard. He drove in his sabre so deep he had to wrench it free. The warrior fell writhing like an eel out of water.

Hervey watched, panting, as blood ran to earth. Both Zulu had taken killing points; there was no need of *coups de grâce*. Yet it was a full minute before they lay still and he could trust to leave them.

What inexpert warriors they had been compared with those at Umtata! And they the scouts, supposedly the best. He need have little fear of the host which followed in their footsteps – if only they were not so many.

He braced himself. There was now, perhaps, but three quarters of an hour before the host would be upon them.

He ran as fast as he could, back to the lala palm where Pampata lay. 'Come,' he shouted, holding out a hand. 'Come, now!'

She rose, not alarmed but uncertain. 'What is it, *mfowethu*?'

'Mbopa!' he gasped, pulling at her arm.

She saw the blood running down his scabbard. 'Where do we go?'

'Across! Across the river!'

He pulled her to the water's edge. He looked at the Thukela's great width, the greatest river of the country of the Zulu (fifty yards across, one hundred, who could tell?), and at its great speed. Was there point, even, in taking off his boots?

And then, like the Children of Israel in the wilderness, their deliverance appeared as if by the hand of God – in the upper part of a fever tree, which bobbed towards them in the slacker water near the bank.

'There!' he cried, pointing.

But Pampata could not see deliverance. She could see only death – and this she was not yet ready to give herself up to.

Hervey saw, and her sudden fearfulness moved him the more. 'Come, *dadewethu*,' he said firmly. 'Trust me.'

She turned to him, trustingly.

He put an arm around her, and together they leapt for the saviour-branch.

They held fast to the sodden branches as the current took them midstream, whence the great cloudy rush of water swept them away from Mbopa's horde, like flotsam in a mill race – though east, away from Ngwadi's kraal. What creatures they shared the river with Hervey gave not a thought to, for the Thukela itself, in its angry flood, was a greater threat to life and limb than any crocodile's jaws.

But no ark of Noah's could have been a surer rescue than the fever tree. As the Thukela began swinging north, the velocity of the flood took the pair back towards the southern bank. Hervey would have been grateful for any landing, but then as suddenly as they had first been swept midstream, the river swung east again, and he and Pampata, like a billiard ball on and then off the cushion, were carried towards the north bank.

Not knowing how deep was the water even at the river's edge, for he could feel nothing beneath his feet, Hervey let go of the tree in faith, and grasped for the root of a lala palm projecting just far enough for him to reach with his left arm at fullest stretch.

The pain in his shoulder – whether by the leopard's claws or the great weight of water – almost made him let go. Pampata, who had not once struggled in their tumble downstream, content to place her life in the arms of this stranger whom she called brother, now saw what she must do, and with a strength that defied explanation pulled herself along his outstretched arm to the tree root. The weight that had pinned him now shed, and his right arm free at last, Hervey was able to hold on with both hands, and together they edged along the root to the bank, until at last they could drag themselves clear of the water – in utter exhaustion.

They lay a good while, side by side, without speaking. Hervey did not even open his eyes. Mbopa's men were a mile and more away; they might have been a hundred. They certainly could not know where he and Pampata were. And the sun's warmth was healing . . .

'*Ukhululekile?*' he asked at length.

He thought he asked if she were 'all right', if she were 'well'. He asked, however, if she were 'comfortable'.

Pampata had lost her cloak, but it was not cold lying on the ground, not in the warmth of the sun and the satisfaction of the escape. '*Ngikhona* ... I am there, *mfowethu.*'

She said it in a strange way: in a way that spoke of a threshold crossed.

Slowly, but very surely, as the afternoon sun replenished them, they sat up and looked about at their unexpected haven. Then, rising to their feet, they surveyed the Thukela, their saviour and (they prayed) now their guardian. They looked towards the country they must enter, a hillier, more broken country than hitherto. And then Pampata turned back to him, and pointed to his scabbard, the blood long washed away, and asked why it had run red.

He told her. And in telling her he felt ill at ease, for he had killed her fellow Zulu, for all that they would have killed both of them.

Pampata, too, seemed distracted. Her arms fell to her sides, and she gazed at him distantly.

He could not meet her gaze. Instead, he took off his tunic and offered it to her.

She thanked him, and said that she had no need, and that she could not wear the mantle of a warrior – that she was unworthy to wear it.

Hervey fumbled with his words, but managed to say that he had met no braver woman.

And in their incomprehension of each other's exact meaning, they resumed their journey, silent.

Two days and two nights they marched, sometimes wearily uphill, sometimes in a jogtrot which was easier than picking up one foot after the other. They encountered few men or boys, and only a handful of women. Even the beasts of the field hid themselves. When they did come across a herdsman, or a woman carrying water, there was no alarm – only curiosity at a woman travelling alone with so strange a thing as a man with a white face. Only once, when curiosity looked as if it might become a challenge, did Pampata have to show the little spear, and its effect was immediate and powerful; she could have possessed no better *laissez-passer*. And all whom they met were generous with what they carried – dried meat, honey, maize cakes, milk – so that both of them were able to journey without the declining strength which Hervey had earlier feared.

They crossed the Umhlatuzi with ease, as Pampata predicted they would. It was but a stream compared with the Thukela, for as she explained, it was not born of uKhahlamba, the barrier of spears. Like the Inonoti, it sprang – or rather, seeped – from the ground, just as blood from the finger at the prick of a thorn.

But although they had maize and meat, Hervey saw

that Pampata's gait was becoming uneven. She protested it was not, and would not let him speak of it, but in the afternoon of the third day, as they climbed to the plateau of Esi-Klebeni, Shaka's birthplace, she could no longer conceal her distress, and he grasped her arm, forcing her to halt.

When he knelt and took her feet, he could scarce believe she had been able to walk at all, for there were abrasions of every degree. She hung her head a while, as if despairing, before throwing it back defiantly and saying she would use the medicine of the *inyaga impi*, the war doctor, pointing at the green all about them. 'Here will be *u-joye*,' she said insistently, 'the warrior's relief.'

And so she limped painfully about the slopes of Esi-Klebeni until they found the medicinal shrub, and Hervey picked the dark green leaves which reminded him so much of his boyhood nettling, though they were much larger, and Pampata crushed them to a fine pulp between two stones, and then Hervey smoothed the poultice-pulp on the soles of her feet and between her toes, and laid her down so that the medicine could work its power.

She lay for an hour, no more, and during that time Hervey scouted for a mile along the slopes for any distant sign of Mbopa's men. But there was none. When Pampata rose and said she would continue, he told her there was no one following them – not, at least, within range of striking them unawares – and that they might lessen their speed. She bowed, but within half an hour she had resumed the pace of before. Only when a thick mist descended on the plateau did they slow, but it did not prevent their taking many a wrong turn, so that by nightfall he supposed they had made no more than half the true progress their efforts deserved.

Indeed, he was downcast, to a degree that overtook his resolution to think only of what lay ahead. No matter that the dragoons had been under Brereton's orders: they were his dragoons, his troop, Brereton merely having the temporary honour of command. He bore responsibility for their death, if only that he had not taken radical action in his doubts about Brereton's capacity for command. No one would blame him, of course (and certainly not formally); the system was the system. If Brereton was in command, then his was the responsibility. But he could not absolve himself so easily. And in Johnson's case, his was the responsibility alone. Johnson had been under his orders, not Brereton's.

There came a terrible, sick feeling in his gut. He could not care less *whose* was the responsibility: Johnson was dead, and that was the fact of it. His old dragoon-friend, as old a friend as Armstrong or Collins (and more intimate, in truth, for all the distance between their stations) had fallen to a Zulu spear, ill-equipped to parry on account of his long years of body-service. He ought to have been there with him. If he had been there with him, the Zulu would never have taken them by surprise.

* * *

And a shivery night it was – the numbing sense of failure which he sought in vain to suppress, and the damp, cold air of the uplands. He gave his tunic to Pampata, not without her protest, and steeled himself to the darkness, its chill and its demons. He would have lit a fire had he the means, for the mist was so thick that none but were as close as a dozen yards could have seen it. Fire warmed and cheered the spirits. He had wanted for fire many times – in Spain, in India; but always with his dragoons, so that without it they took consolation in their shared discomfort. And, in truth, he could not recollect so personal a desolation as this now.

They shivered all night, therefore, awake for the most part, lying back to back, contrary to all the customs of the Zulu: for Pampata knew she needed the warmth of her 'brother'.

Indeed, she had expected a greater warmth, for as a warrior who had slain a foe it was his right (indeed, it was his duty) to claim *sula izembe*, the ritual cleansing, the 'washing of the spear'.

Hervey did not know of *sula izembe*. All he knew was the instinct of one who had survived, and the potency which came of it. And yet with the bodies of two dozen dragoons in his mind's eye still, it was unthinkable.

XXII

A HANDFUL OF RIFLEMEN

Next day

Just before evening, the fourth day, as they crested another of the gentler slopes that gave shape to the low-lands beyond the high plateau of Esi-Klebeni, Pampata heaved a great sigh of joy. Pointing, she declared their triumph. 'There is kwaWambaza! There is Ngwadi's kraal!'

They stumbled the last mile, downhill, easier by far than the ascent but tempting them to more speed thereby, slipping, falling, staggering, and so painfully that Hervey tried to make Pampata stop, so that he could go on alone and bring back a horse, or her men-folk, to bear her in.

She would have none of it. She would not delay her mission one needless minute. And so Hervey relented, hopeful that the lookouts – his own dragoons, indeed – would soon spy their approach and send out relief.

But there was no relief. Only when they were a hundred yards from the kraal did anyone appear to notice their coming, and then only the herd boys playing at being *inkwebane*, cadets, jousting with toy spears like the one that Pampata carried. They rushed up to the two dust-covered strangers and danced about them uncertainly, half-fearful, until Pampata shot words at them like a flight of arrows, at which they fled, wide-eyed, towards the entrance of the kraal shouting that messengers of King Shaka were come to kwaWambaza.

The kraal was smaller than Dukuza, but in all other respects save one it appeared the same: for here were no trophies of death, no impalings, no human bones cast about casually as if to proclaim the chief's supreme power. There were a great number of cattle grazing, and the fields were in good cultivation. For all that the kraal's thorn fence was built in the same fashion as Shaka's, and the huts within were the same beehive shape, and the people looked the same and wore the same, it might have been another country. Here was a place of pastoral quiet, not a barracks of Shaka's restless war engine.

It was at once, therefore, a sight both of reassurance and alarm, for if Mbopa were to muster an *impi* of any strength (and for all that Hervey knew, the Fasimba were at his call), it would take warrior numbers and hardened skill to hold them off.

Out rushed Ngwadi, the clan elders – and Somervile. Hervey felt a second wave of relief at seeing his old friend. He braced his shoulders (they had been sloped in the same loping gait as Pampata's for days) and saluted. He had been without any headdress since the Thukela, but the open-handed salute was no less impressive. Ngwadi raised his ceremonial staff in acknowledgement and evident awe at what he knew was before him, and Somervile took off his straw hat as if he were presented at court.

'My dear friend,' he said, advancing on Hervey with a sense of the miracle. 'My dear old friend! I thought – I could not make myself believe other – that you were killed!'

And as he held out his hand, Hervey saw the moisture in his eyes.

'I very near was,' he replied, but recovering that air of composure required by the mask of command. 'Brereton is dead,' he added roughly, and then in an altogether softer tone: 'and Petrie, and the dragoons with him.'

'I know,' said Somervile, lowering his eyes. 'Your Private Johnson informed me.'

Hervey started. 'Johnson? *Informed* you? He is *here*?'

'He's at Nonoti still. He came two days after we left Dukuza. He refused to leave there until he had found you. Your serjeant-major threatened to clap him in irons, but he would not relent.'

Hervey's face was now a picture of the greatest relief and joy. 'It is the best of news, the very best!' he said, shaking his head in disbelief. 'What of Fairbrother?'

'He remains at Nonoti until we're sure what Mbopa's intentions are. What a capital fellow he is: Ngomane ate from his hand – put his guards under his orders, indeed!'

'And who came with you here?'

'Welsh and the Rifles.'

Several of Ngwadi's household had lifted up Pampata and begun carrying her towards the kraal. The chief himself now beckoned Somervile and his new-found friend to follow.

'A decent sort of man, I judge him,' said Somervile as they did his bidding. 'We have managed to converse. Welsh has been of use, too: he understands, if he doesn't much speak.'

Once they were inside the *ndlunkulu*, Ngwadi hovered about Pampata as if she had been his own sister. His serving-girls brought restoratives and lotions, and he questioned her gently, or rather, listened to her speak, about the events at Shaka's kraal.

The two old friends were therefore able to withdraw to the other side of the hut, where they were brought *tshwala* (beer), and sweetmeats to restore a man to his full vigour – or so the gestures of the serving-girls promised.

Somervile gave him a cheroot.

'Thank you. I would have given a king's ransom for this match last night,' said Hervey as he lit it. He blew a satisfyingly dense cloud of smoke towards the roof of the hut, and then turned earnestly to his old friend. 'We must speak about what you intend. Mbopa's men were hard on our heels, and I suspect them mere *voerlopers*. More will follow if he believes Ngwadi will challenge him – which he must believe, else why pursue Pampata thus?'

Somervile nodded as he got his own cheroot alight. 'When we reached Nonoti and told him what had happened, the chief minister declared himself at once against Mbopa, and Dingane and the others, and asked for our protection while he summoned all the *indune*. He has a sizeable guard, and said he could call on the warriors who had been stood down for the sowing. I judged they could match what Mbopa could muster immediately, so I instructed young Kemmis – excellent fellow, he! – to stay at Nonoti with half the dragoons to strengthen the old man's resolve. That allowed Fairbrother and the rest to go back to Dukuza to see if they could find you and learn what they could.'

'Then why did you come on here? And unescorted? A dozen riflemen only!'

Somervile attempted to look defiant, although he knew his offence. 'Because we had decided on the necessity of alerting Ngwadi, if you remember.'

Hervey frowned, and with some impatience. 'But the situation then changed materially. You had no right . . . with respect, to place your life in jeopardy so. And what in the name of heaven were Welsh and Fairbrother doing permitting it? And Collins, for that matter!'

Somervile held up a hand to stay his tirade. 'They are blameless, I assure you. Each of them – your admirable Serjeant-Major Collins, too – protested most vehemently, but in the end I ordered them to desist.'

Hervey shifted painfully, having allowed himself to lean on the wound too heavily. 'Somervile, my dear old friend, and again with the very greatest of respect, you are not entitled to issue orders in such a way. Theirs is the responsibility for your safeguard, and you cannot absolve them of it.'

The lieutenant-governor shook his head solemnly. 'I know it; I know it. But in truth I was so greatly affeard that you were . . . well, I thought it possible you might be captive, and I could not rest if I had done otherwise than I did.'

Hervey sighed. Somervile had divided into three the already divided little force, but he had done so to search for him, and at grave risk to himself. 'When did you come here? Is Ngwadi gathering his warriors?' he asked, almost softly.

'Yesterday, in the morning. Ngwadi was at once incensed by the news of Shaka's murder. He has sent messengers to all his kraals for the army to assemble. They are about five thousand, but they're stood down for the sowing. He says it will be a week before they can all assemble. And then he will march at once on Mbopa.'

'And what if Mbopa should come with his army before they are assembled? When is Fairbrother bidden here?'

413

'I ordered him to remain at Nonoti when he was come from Dukuza. Ngwadi will first march thither . . . What is the matter with your shoulder?'

Hervey began flexing it to relieve the ache. 'It is well enough – merely a brush with a leopard.'

'I will have my physician see it,' replied Somervile, rising.

'No, permit him finish first with Pampata's wounds; she is very ill worn.'

'I saw as much. A remarkable woman, I hazard.'

Hervey stubbed out the cheroot and made to rise. 'Somervile, she is one of the finest women I ever met.'

His old friend, for all his earlier self-absorption, heard the catch in Hervey's voice, and nodded warily. 'We may well have cause to honour her. I hope most earnestly that she is able to find this child of Shaka's.'

Hervey seemed now to brace himself, as if to throw off the lethargy that had been overcoming him since they entered the hut. 'See, my good friend, there's not a moment to lose. We must send a galloper to Nonoti and recall Fairbrother and the rest of the troop. *Here*, Ngwadi's kraal, is the pivot of your stratagem. Besides, fine fellow that Ngwadi may be, I am loath to place ourselves amid a thousand of his warriors, with but a handful of riflemen, when their world has been turned upside down with the death of Shaka. One rumour that we are ourselves implicated in his fall and I would not give a half-farthing for our continuing health.'

'You suppose it could come to that?'

Hervey sighed again. 'My old friend, I do not wish to sound pious, but I am a soldier: I cannot deal in suppositions, only possibilities.'

Somervile looked remarkably chastened. 'I forget myself.'

Hervey clapped him on the arm. 'No matter. Was it Serjeant Donkers I saw with those *inkwebane* as we came in?'

'It was. An excellent fellow, as are they all.'

'Then I shall send him to recall Fairbrother. And thereafter I believe we should give ourselves up to Pampata.'

'I concur,' said Somervile, more happily.

Hervey realized that perhaps he, too, forgot himself, for this much was polity not soldiery. 'With your leave?'

'By all means, Hervey. By all means,' replied his old friend, seeming to brace himself to the task. 'But first it is my object that the physician treat your wound. We cannot have a single sabre that is *hors de combat.*'

A shot woke him. Hervey sat bolt upright, for a split second trying to grasp the place and the cause. He had been in the deepest sleep, the security that was the kraal and ten riflemen inducing him to let go that which had kept him alert these last days.

A second shot. He sprang up, seizing his swordbelt and pistol. Then a third, and a fourth, and shouting –

the universal sound of alarm, no matter what the camp.

Outside the hut he found Corporal Cox. 'Sir! Kaffirs – dozens of 'em. They've killed the herd boys!'

Mbopa's men must have been pressing harder on their heels than he supposed. But the picket – four good shots – and the men of the kraal ought to be able to hold them. 'Very well. Keep up a good fire, Corp' Cox: best keep them guessing how many we are!'

He ran to Somervile's hut, finding him on his feet and priming his pistols. 'Mbopa's men, I think – the ones following our tracks. Fifty, no more, unless a second cohort were following.'

'Would you have one of the riflemen guard Pampata?' asked Somervile, anxious.

'I think not. I'll need every man. I think you must stand guard with her.'

'Very well. Where is Ngwadi?'

'I saw him making for the *sango*. I'll seek him out.'

Hervey saluted, turned and went back outside, shielding his eyes against the sun which was edging above the thorn fence of the cattle byre.

And then the rush of Mbopa's warriors – inside the kraal, like stampeding bulls, a great black wave, sweeping aside all in its path, a wall of spears and shields, wild cries, shots! How had they broken in?

He drew his sabre, raised his pistol and cocked it in one. He saw the riflemen left and right firing into the flanks of the wave, double-barrelled Westley-Richards, point-blank, a relentless, fearful toll. Ngwadi's men raced from the other side of the kraal, throwing themselves at the attackers without waiting to form, striking home with their spears, in turn falling to those of Mbopa's men.

Out came Somervile, pistols raised. He rushed to Hervey's side, and they stood, silent, waiting for the wave to reach them.

But the wave was losing its force. Urged on by Corporal Cox, the cattle guards had got the great thorn hurdle back across the *sango*. Those Zulu inside were on their own.

And with the inescapability of numbers and the superiority of powder, the rest was slaughter. Neither Hervey nor Somervile moved a foot: Ngwadi's men, pouring into the enclosure from every corner of the kraal, did the most terrible execution. Only once had Hervey to parry: a warrior, crazed by the bloodlust of the assault, and by the spear wounds to his chest and side, broke from the melee and ran at the two friends in a gesture of suicidal defiance.

'Mine!' Hervey rasped, like a shot facing driven birds. He levelled his pistol, the man ran on to it obligingly, and the ball broke open his chest in a gory splintering of bone.

Two minutes more and the business was done. Thirty-three of Mbopa's men lay dead – every warrior of his who had entered the kraal – a dozen of Ngwadi's men, and a score more for the *inyaga impi*, the war-surgeon.

'The devil!' said Somervile, at length. 'That should not have happened.'

'Indeed.' Hervey pushed his pistol into his swordbelt and returned his sabre. 'Quite an affair. But by no means unhelpful. Those fellows will have quite an opinion of themselves now,' he added, nodding to Ngwadi's men. 'And of their chief. You saw how he fought?'

'I did.' Somervile, as Hervey, had seen Ngwadi account for three men with his own spear.

'And Mbopa knows that the kraal can't be rushed, even when he creeps up by dark. Evidently he hadn't the men for a stronger attack. I believe time may be on our side.'

Corporal Cox came doubling. 'Kaffirs've bolted like rabbits, sir. Permission to follow 'em up?'

Hervey looked about the kraal. 'No, Corporal. Your zeal does you credit, but for once we must remain on our guard. I can't be certain that that's not what they want – having us come out into the open. By all means have a patrol look about – four men, not more, and no further than the maize.'

'Sir!' Cox doubled away to give the orders.

'He appears to be enjoying the work,' said Somervile, sounding faintly bemused.

'He's no doubt relishing his opportunity for command – and his survival,' replied Hervey drily. 'It's a powerful thing to discover you're on your feet at the end of your first fight. Don't you recall?'

Somervile, happy to be admitted to his friend's pantheon of fellow warriors, nodded. 'I do.'

'Come, then: let us see what manner of men Mbopa sent against us. We may learn something.'

Ngwadi's warriors were already stripping their enemies and bearing away their own fallen. Hervey stepped from body to body, crouching here and there to turn over a bloody corpse. He would not use his boot, as others did, for he was not yet sure that these Zulu had no claim on being God's creatures. And besides, Ngwadi's men were their kin: *they* might treat their enemies as they willed, but they might take exception to an outsider's doing so.

'Older men than I have seen hitherto, I would say.'

'Distinctly so,' agreed Somervile, peering at the heap of questionable humanity with the eye of a student of natural science. 'And what thereby do you infer?'

Hervey was examining the feet of one of them. He rose and shook his head. 'Shaka sent every *impi* but Ngwadi's against the Pondos and Soshangane, did he not, leaving just the usual guards at the kraals? Mbopa has evidently called out the veterans. Tough old veterans, judging from their condition.'

'Many more men at his disposal than we supposed, therefore. And the would-be *inkwebane* that Shaka recalled from the north?'

'I fear we must proceed on the assumption that they answer now to Mbopa. Pampata says that Shaka wanted them formed into a new *impi*, "the Bees". Upwards of a thousand – green-horned, but chasing the bubble reputation.'

'We must trust to your dragoons' speedy recall.'

Hervey inclined his head, the sign that he was not convinced. 'We may have to quit this place. We have the advantage of horses, that is all. Much as I admire Ngwadi, we have no obligation to him. My prime duty is your safe return.'

Somervile looked at his pistols, as if asking himself what he did here, a diplomatist not a soldier. 'I hope it shall not come to that. My mission would be altogether unaccomplished.'

'You would of course live to accomplish it another day,' countered Hervey.

'But the day may not be given me. Recollect that I am recalled to London.'

'*Carpe diem?*' said Hervey, with more than a hint of scepticism. 'But what pain in the seizing?'

Somervile frowned. 'You disappoint me, Hervey. "*Carpe diem, quam minimum credula postero.*" *Gather* the day, Hervey, not seize it.'

Hervey sighed. 'Somervile, we stand here with loaded pistols, and bodies lying all about us, like . . . *Medea*, and you declaim the finer points of Horace! I must respectfully remind you that I have a duty to discharge, and I intend discharging it.'

Somervile looked chastened once more. 'I would not stand in the way of duty, Hervey.'

'Come, then; let us leave these fellows to the sexton's work. I confess I was always discomfited by the evidence of victory.'

His friend nodded, acquiescing (though not, to his mind, in any scheme of quitting this place), before bending down to pick up a spear. 'I am not disposed as a rule to trophies, but the *iklwa* is indeed a singular weapon. I believe there would be profit in contemplating it.'

Hervey had not quite thought of it thus, but he was not averse to adding another memento of his trade to those he had acquired over the years. Georgiana would be intrigued by it at least (even if Kezia might recoil . . .). He stooped to prise the *iklwa* from the hand of the warrior who had intended death to him not many minutes before. 'At stand-to this evening I will ride out to see who is gathered; and likewise at dawn tomorrow. If there is a swarm of "bees" then I fear I shall insist we fly before we are stung to death.' He flexed the spear in his hand, wondering indeed if ever he would be able to show it to anyone.

Later, with Corporal Cox, he rode out from the kraal on his reconnaissance. He knew the ground he had trodden with Pampata well enough – all folds and hollows – and he did not reckon it safe to go much beyond a mile or so in that direction, for there were hiding places enough for a whole *impi*, and the fleetest of horses would have been hard-pressed to outpace a determined envelopment. He saw no sign of Mbopa's men, however, even whence they had attacked, and whither they had retreated. Neither saw he any sign in the rest of their circumnavigation of the kraal, and at a radius of a mile and a half. The ground in all directions, he discovered, was as unfavourable to the defenders as might be. He wondered how Ngwadi could have chosen such a place, for he would surely have understood the importance of ground (Matiwane's warriors, as he recalled, could make themselves invisible in what looked like the flattest country). And he rode back with his spirits sagging, knowing the initiative lay firmly with Mbopa, or whoever was his field commander. They could expect attack from any direction or several, and he could ill afford skirmishers out to break up the assault.

He reported his disquiet to Somervile, who asked simply if he had reconnoitred their line of withdrawal in the event that an attack went hard with them. Hervey told him he had (there was a line of thorn bushes, part of the cattle drove, which would give them cover by day and direction at night), and would have a rifleman stand by with the horses at the 'sally port'. He then asked what Somervile had learned of Shaka's child from Pampata.

Somervile expressed himself disappointed in this. 'She says the boy's been taken to a place called Mpapala, Ngwadi's father's kraal, a day and a half's march from here.'

'Safe, at least.'

'Oh, indeed so. And I would not hasten thither, for I think it would not profit us greatly to find the boy if Ngwadi is then defeated.'

'I understand. If the troop were here I would suggest we convey her there with an escort, out of harm's way, but . . .' Hervey would not divide his force any more.

'Exactly so. There is no option but to wait on their return . . . Did she tell you that Ngwadi himself knows of the boy, or his identity?'

'She did. Ngwadi knows both, but no one but Pampata knows of his knowledge. Ngwadi knows because Nandi confided in him her delight at having a grandchild.'

'I begin greatly to admire Pampata, you know, Hervey. She displays an admirable constancy that is most touching.'

Hervey raised his eyebrows at the dryness of his friend's appraisal.

'Oh, indeed she does,' Somervile insisted, misreading the gesture. 'And I might add that I have pity for her in her condition of bereavement.'

Hervey's mouth fell open. 'Somervile, you astonish me. Did you ever suppose her grief to be the less for her being . . . an *ingénue?*'

Somervile looked at him, puzzled. 'Hervey, are you quite well? Your sojourn has not left your faculties impaired?'

Hervey knew his old friend to be capable of studied

obtuseness, but on this occasion he had a very real fear that he was being entirely candid. 'Somervile, I may assure you, in the most certain of terms, that Pampata is as much a woman – more a woman, I might say – than many a one you would meet in London.'

Somervile studied the officer before him, the major of dragoons, lieutenant-colonel of mounted rifles, and thought to himself that this mission to Shaka, if no advantage of state proceeded from it, was worth it yet for the discovery of such sensibility – of such *appreciation* of humanity. He felt buoyed by it, indeed. He would prepare a paper on the Zulu; he would read it to the Royal Society at Somerset House. 'Capital, Hervey. Capital!'

All afternoon, men from the outlying kraals came into kwaWambaza. They carried with them spears and short shields, and bags of mealie cakes, the warrior's iron rations. Some appeared apprehensive, perhaps even resentful, for they had been stood down from military service for the season, and there was the late planting, which although a woman's work, required their supervision at least. The sight of white faces did nothing at first to allay that resentment, but Ngwadi greeted each of them with a fraternal warmth that soon converted them into willing warriors. And when the chief presented a man with his war shield, the property of the nation, Hervey observed how each appeared to take it as if it were some sacred trust. Whatever misgivings he and

Somervile had on seeing the first of this reluctant mobilization, they were soon dispelled. Or rather, they were displaced by anxiety at the actual rate of mobilization: by nightfall, there were not yet two hundred warriors under arms.

Hervey spoke with Pampata before dark. She looked immeasurably better for her repose. Her eyes, which had been almost closed in the exhaustion of the last miles, were wide and clear once more, and the dust of the veld was gone, her skin shining instead with the scented palm oil with which Ngwadi's serving-girls had anointed her. Hervey sat himself easily by her side while she made a necklace to replace the one she had lost at the Thukela.

'Are you well, *dadewethu*?'

'I am well, *mfowethu*.' She said it sadly, however. 'There was much killing this morning.'

'There was,' replied Hervey, as sadly but with resolution, and knowing there would be more. 'When Captain Fairbrother returns with more men, you must go to Mpapala and seek out Shaka's heir,' he said, as if telling her the detail of some small thing.

Pampata continued working at her necklace, her eyes remaining on the beads. 'And shall you come with me, *mfowethu*?'

She said it as if his replying 'no' might be some disappointment – or even a sign of faithlessness – to her.

'I must remain by the side of Somervile. That is my duty.'

425

She continued her beadwork without reply.

'But I will come to Mpapala as soon as Somervile wills it – when Mbopa's men are . . . slain.'

'There will be nothing more for me once I reach Mpapala, but I would see you there, *mfowethu*, before you return to where the white man lives.'

Hervey touched her arm. 'You may depend upon it.'

XXIII

MUCH KILLING

Next day, before first light

'Halt!'

The picket had come in at evening stand-to, slept a little, and an hour or so before first light, Corporal Cox and his three picked riflemen had slipped between the hurdle and the great thorn fence once more, out into darkness that had come with the setting of the moon.

'Who goes there?'

All four rifles were now at the aim, though there was nothing to be seen. Only the thud of hoofs gave them their direction.

'Captain Fairbrother and party,' came a voice from the bat blackness.

It could be no trick, but Corporal Cox stuck to the drill. There was always the chance that the Zulu might take advantage otherwise. 'Advance one and be recognized!'

The lead dragoon-scout dismounted and led his horse towards the unseen sentry. At five yards Cox could just make out his shape.

'Halt!'

'It's me: Pat McCarthy!'

'Come on, then, Pat,' replied Cox, keeping his voice low. 'How many of you?'

'The captain and nineteen more. No, twenty-one, counting the guides.'

'Call 'em in, then, Pat. I's'll count 'em.'

So began the lengthy procedure, while the other three riflemen kept the sharpest lookout – and cocked ears – for Zulu trying to follow them in.

Fairbrother, now come to the front of the column, was first into the kraal.

Hervey, standing with a torch by the thorn hurdle, could scarce believe it. 'My God, but you're a welcome sight, Fairbrother – or shall be when it's light!'

'*Hervey?* What . . .'

His astonishment was complete.

'Serjeant Donkers did not say I was here?'

'I haven't seen Donkers.'

'I sent him to Nonoti.'

'I came directly from Shaka's kraal. The herd boys told me Mbopa is making for here. A thousand warriors they said; but you know herd boys . . .'

Hervey didn't, but he knew Fairbrother. 'We can

muster, perhaps, three hundred. But say: how in the name of heaven did you find this place?'

'One of the herd boys, Ngwadi's clan. Not much short of a hundred miles, by my reckoning, and no more sign of tiring than the horses. We hardly checked, so good a moon was it. We managed to get a line on here before it set, and then went by the stars.'

'Remarkable. I should have been prodigiously proud to manage it myself. You saw nothing untoward?'

'Empty country. Even the game have fled. That of course means nothing, for if the Zulu want to conceal themselves . . .'

'Well,' said Hervey, clasping his friend's arm, 'let us not be too ready to imagine the worst, even if we must prepare for it. Let us have you fed and watered, and then after stand-down, a little rest. I'll have early need of your scouting.'

'You shall first have to wake me!'

'Depend upon it! And . . .' his voice changed, 'what of the dragoons at Dukuza?'

'Buried. We saw to that. And French read a few words over them. More seemly, I thought, than my doing so.'

Hervey nodded, which by the light of the torch Fairbrother took to be approval (in truth it was more a gesture of resignation). He wished no man dead in another's place, but he was relieved that French had not been with the others at Dukuza: a last-minute change of duty – the haphazard fortune of war.

The dragoons, for all their relief at finding haven, tramped in wearily. Hervey hailed each of them, all but a couple by name. Corporal McCarthy was last man.

'Good morning, sor!'

Hervey's spirits lifted. The old hands might still call McCarthy (who had first been an infantryman) the footiest dragoon on a horse, but his cheeriness in all circumstances was worth three sabres. 'Corporal McCarthy, there is no serjeant here. Would you be so good as to take local rank?'

'Local rank? I will, sor. Easy come, easy go!'

Hervey smiled. McCarthy's rank had come and gone throughout his service. It was just a pity – if he could think of it as mildly as mere pity – that Collins was at Nonoti still, and Wainwright at Cape Town. With those two he would have been certain of having men about him who would instinctively make the right decision (and, as God knew it, they had precious few men here to risk making anything but the right one).

While the nigh-exhausted dragoons were doing what they could to revive themselves and their troopers, Hervey handed his torch to one of Ngwadi's men, and slipped out of the kraal to accustom his eyes to the darkness once more. There was no real need of it: if there were Zulu out there, Corporal Cox's picket would detect them. But it helped him compose his mind to the trial ahead. And trial he knew there would be. The dragoons had seen nothing on their approach march, but as Fairbrother readily conceded, this might as easily mean the Zulu hid themselves. Yesterday, Mbopa's men had been here. Where were they now? They had had a sharp check, it was true – none, though, but that Mbopa could have expected with so small a number. Hervey was certain it had been a reconnaissance in force, to test the defences of the kraal, to make Ngwadi show his strength – or lack of it. He could only presume that reinforcements were indeed marching here at warrior-speed this very moment, as the herd boys said. And if they possessed the stamina of Fairbrother's guide, they might be here now.

Every man in the kraal was standing to his arms, whether spear, rifle or sabre. They were as secure as in any of the fortresses of Spain: firing the thorn stockade could not drive them out, for even if they had been ringed with flame, the kraal was large enough for them to form in the centre (and fire-blackened thorn was no easier to penetrate). Hervey had put Welsh in charge of the inner defences, for with the admirable Corporal Cox in command of the picket work, the riflemen had no need of an officer. Welsh could communicate well enough with Ngwadi's lieutenants. Need any of them venture from the kraal, therefore? His instinct told him they must: to allow Mbopa the initiative, when there was little hope of exterior relief, was to risk a surprise they would be ill-balanced to deal with.

He congratulated himself that he had, at least, timed things as well as he had, for as the assemblage was taking post, the first shafts of sunlight were broaching the eastern horizon. He slipped back inside the kraal, and the sentries made fast the hurdle.

Slowly the darkness gave way to shadows, and then to that curious, hovering half light in which there was no colour, only shapes and forms, and from this to morning, like a stage revealed. A glorious morning, as elemental as those he had known in Bengal, the scent of the land in the air, the essence of the country in one breath . . .

And then, as if he had blinked and another curtain had risen, there was the dread sight before him: five hundred yards away, no more, a long, black line stretching for half a mile, the right flank where the sun rose, the left on a hill just high enough to overlook the kraal. Hervey had Somervile's telescope, and standing on the platform from which the sentries observed, he swept the line.

The warriors stood by their shields – five hundred men, by his rapid reckoning. Even with the return of most his dragoons, now, they would have the devil of a job of it.

Somervile came striding, although Hervey had asked him to stay at his hut, so that in a sudden alarm there could be no confusion in finding him. 'Good God!' he gasped on seeing the host, standing stock-still except to check his pistols were still in his belt.

'Somervile, I asked you—'

Four shots rang out in quick succession, thick white smoke indicating where the picket lay, prone, at the edge of the mealie planting. Hervey took up his telescope again, forgetting his irritation.

'Well done, riflemen,' he exclaimed, their marksmanship exceptional. 'Three down, perhaps a fourth – I couldn't see all the line at once.' Nor was it just their marksmanship which inspired his esteem: it was their address, for he had given them no particular orders – and the senior of them but a 'chosen man'.

Another four shots – the second barrels.

'Upon my word, I never saw better shooting. Four hit, and almost next to each other!'

The line remained still.

In half a minute the picket fired again, and then the second barrels, and with equal accuracy.

Yet the line stood rooted.

'Corporal Cox!' bellowed Hervey, keen to seize the opportunity.

The corporal came doubling. 'Sir!'

'Take out *all* your riflemen. Get up the briskest fire. Drive them off their perch!'

'Ay, sir!'

'Can they do the trick, Hervey?' asked Somervile, sounding doubtful.

'I have no idea. But if yon black line stands obligingly it'll be a deal whittled down in ten minutes!'

If the line merely withdrew to cover, he would be content – but even if it began to advance he would take satisfaction, for he would have forced Mbopa's hand. The initiative was a damned fine thing to gain at the beginning of an affair thus!

The line stood for a quarter of an hour. Or rather, that part of it stood which was not knocked down by Corporal Cox and his riflemen. Hervey could scarcely believe that the Zulu held their ground against such accurate fire. He swept back and forward with his 'scope, trying to find some clue to their resolution. 'Boys, in all likelihood. The first courage.' He swore beneath his breath at Mbopa's cynical play with their inexperience.

The smoke had thickened to a dense fog on the right of the line of rifles, the sun not yet hot enough to disperse it.

Hervey suddenly stiffened. What if these Zulu were a decoy? He looked about for Ngwadi, seeing him standing just outside the *sango*, and hailed him. '*Nkosi*, your warriors, there and there,' (pointing to either flank of the firing line) '*ikhulu* . . . I need a hundred.'

Ngwadi had his men assembled in moments.

Hervey jumped from the platform and ran back to the horses, loosing the mare he had ridden the day before and vaulting astride.

Fairbrother and the dragoons were saddling up as fast as they could.

'Keep them out of sight till I call!' he shouted over his

shoulder, beckoning to Ngwadi to have him and his men follow as he galloped out.

'Hervey, what . . .' But all Somervile could do was watch as the press of warriors burst from the kraal, their chief at the head.

They beat Mbopa's men to the ground by a mere half-minute: for as if from out of the earth itself now sprang his best, the veterans, fifty and more on each flank, like a flash-flood. Without Ngwadi's men they would have overwhelmed the rifles in seconds.

Hervey galloped hard for the picket. In their determined sharpshooting they had not seen the peril on their flanks. 'Up, Rifles! Up! Up!' he bellowed hoarsely, as Ngwadi's men rushed to counter the veterans.

He managed somehow to get them to their feet. And then as they saw the trap they ran like the wind.

He only managed to rally them at the entrance to the kraal.

'Hervey, what happened there?' barked Somervile, now atop his horse.

'A deuced clever ruse. I should have seen it earlier. This ground is the devil!'

Corporal Cox had got his riflemen formed again, directing their fire on Mbopa's veterans, though the fight with Ngwadi's men was so entangled as to be a tricky thing for bullets.

'Those fellows, the Rifles: they looked as if they'd run

all morning!' gasped Somervile, his excited gelding pulling defiantly.

'Oh, they all do that at some time or other,' replied Hervey, impatiently, returning his sabre and trying to make out where Ngwadi was. 'The point is whether or not they'll rally. And they have. What are you *doing*?'

'Hervey, I can't sit on my backside while—'

But out from the kraal burst the rest of Ngwadi's warriors, eager for the fray.

'Christ! Get back! Get back!' yelled Hervey, turning his horse to try to halt them. 'Get back, damn you! Get back, I say!'

Even had he shouted in perfect Zulu they were in no mind to hear. There was battle without, their chief was in the midst of it, and no warrior could remain inside with his honour intact.

'I must see what they do!' declared Somervile, breathily.

'No, Somervile, I beg you would remain here. We may very well have to gallop for it. Where's Pampata?'

'I . . .'

Hervey cursed, and reined about.

Corporal French was there, his coverman once more, and exactly where a coverman ought to be, except that he had not been given much chance of it these past days. 'Corp' French, detail a dragoon to guard the Zulu woman!'

'*Which* Zulu woman, Colonel?'

'Pampata, damn it!'

French shook his head. 'Sir, I . . .'

Hervey realized. 'Captain Fairbrother knows.'

'Sir!'

French made back into the kraal.

Hervey now turned to see Ngwadi's men at last getting the better of the veterans – or at least holding them off. 'Corporal Cox, stand ready to retake your ground.'

'Sir!'

'I think, Somervile, that we may allow ourselves a little satisfaction,' said Hervey, his expression now eased.

'Not nearly as many of them as we feared,' agreed his old friend.

But scarcely had Hervey allowed himself that satisfaction when Mbopa revealed another hand. Half a mile to their right, on a low, grassy hill, a long line of warriors stood up, like the Guards at Waterloo, and let out a chilling *Huzu-u-u!* which carried to the kraal as if by a hundred speaking trumpets.

'The devil!' spat Hervey. 'What's his game?'

Corporal Cox at once had his riflemen form right to open a harassing fire.

'You mean why does he divide his force so?' asked Somervile, his gelding beginning to paw the ground impatiently.

'Yes. He showed five hundred to begin with, and then another hundred at least in that ruse to outflank the picket – and two hundred yonder, now. More than enough to break into the kraal if he used them all together.'

'Perhaps he fears our firearms?'

Hervey nodded, if uncertainly. 'He acts with caution; that much seems true. I wasn't of a mind to put great store by it, but those herd boys' "thousand warriors" looks not so wide of the mark. And if they're exactly correct, there's another two hundred or so which Mbopa's yet to commit.'

The riflemen began taking a toll, but at half a mile it was not heavy.

'A few whiffs of grapeshot would serve,' said Hervey, coldly, searching with his telescope for what he could learn of these new-shown warriors.

The line began advancing.

'I perceive another ploy!' Hervey looked about, weighing his options. The main body of Zulus, four or five hundred, stood motionless two furlongs off. What was left of the attempt to envelop the picket – twenty or so warriors – were making away as fast as they could, pursued by some of Ngwadi's men, although the chief had rallied the bulk of them in good order and was drawing them up to face the main body. There, things would be evenly matched. On the right, however, two hundred more of Mbopa's warriors would be closing with them in the space of ten minutes. It was not as he had wanted it – by far the greater part of the defenders' strength now outside the kraal, and perhaps two hundred more of

Mbopa's men yet to show. How would Mbopa use them?

The left flank was open; unwatched, even. He must at least post a couple of men to cover it. He could see that, inside the kraal, Welsh had fifty or so of Ngwadi's men in hand (and he would need them to guard the walls, so to speak), and the twenty dragoons stood ready. He had not wanted to show them until the last moment, when the sudden appearance of horses and sabres – and if necessary the carbine fire – would have their greatest effect. But the left flank . . .

'What to do, Hervey?' Fairbrother had come to his side, unbidden. He took in the situation at a glance.

Hervey was ever glad of his friend's knack of placing himself to advantage. 'See those fellows yonder?' He pointed to the advancing line.

Fairbrother nodded. It was all he needed.

Hervey would have directed a couple of dragoons to the left flank, but with only twenty, he decided on riflemen. 'Corporal Cox!'

'Sir!'

'Capital shooting. The dragoons will front them now. Keep up a supporting fire, but have two men go onto yonder flank' (he indicated the left) 'and keep a watch there.'

'Sir!'

'What would you have *me* do, Hervey?' demanded Somervile, his face red with the exertion of keeping his increasingly hard-to-hold gelding in hand.

In truth, Hervey was not much concerned what his old friend did, as long as he kept at arm's length from trouble. He sighed. 'Since you will not retire into the kraal—'

'I won't skulk in there while everyone else stands to arms out here! Infamous example!'

Hervey had to check his instinct to say that it would make not the slightest difference to any of them what example he set. 'Since you will not accept my principal advice, I must ask that you remain in this position and be ready at any moment to quit the place altogether.'

But Somervile was not to be persuaded. He ever liked the smell of powder and the shout of the captains, and, besides, the little prominence not a hundred yards to their left afforded as good a line of escape as it did a place of observation. He dug his spurs into his gelding's flanks.

Hervey cursed foully. He would now have to detach a dragoon as coverman. He turned to see how Fairbrother and the quarter troop were faring.

Thank God! They were mounted and making to leave as if riding out of barracks for exercise.

He turned back to see if the main body of Zulus was moving yet.

But in that space of seconds, all was overturned. Somervile, coming onto the knoll whence he would observe the field, blundered into half a dozen of Mbopa's veterans who had lain concealed for such a moment. His horse shied, he lost his balance and his pistol, and took the point of an *iklwa* in his leathered calf.

Hervey dug in his spurs as his old friend lashed about wildly with his sabre.

But it was Fairbrother who got there first. He drove straight between Somervile and the nearest spear, cutting viciously at what would have been the lethal hand.

The warriors reeled at the sudden, and unfamiliar, horse and blade. Two of them fell to the sabre's edge, and another to Somervile's second pistol.

Fairbrother's charger was disobliging, however, and circled large.

But Hervey had closed fast. He dropped the reins and drew his flintlock with his left hand, pulling back the hammer and firing into the face of a fourth warrior in one motion, his sabre cutting at the next. He put his horse at another, and the point finished the tumbled warrior.

The one remaining turned and ran. Hervey drew a second pistol, took angry aim, and brought him down at thirty yards.

'Somervile, you damned fool!' he bellowed as he turned, shaking with rage. 'You are *not* a soldier! Do as I say, for Christ's sake!'

Somervile looked thoroughly shaken. Indeed, he looked defeated.

'The kraal, now!'

'My dear Hervey,' he replied feebly, as if lost. 'I'm excessively grateful to you . . . and to you, Captain Fairbrother. I . . .'

Hervey cleared his throat. 'Forgive me; I spoke roughly. You fought like the devil.'

Corporal French had now joined them.

Hervey turned to him. 'Convey Sir Eyre to the kraal, if you please, Corp' French.'

'Colonel!'

'With your leave, Hervey?' asked Fairbrother, nodding towards the dragoons as they formed front midway to the advancing line of Zulus.

'By all means.' And then he smiled wryly. 'Not content with saving my life in this savage land, you save my reputation.'

Fairbrother returned the look of wryness in equal measure. 'I thank God I have only a reputation to *make*.' He touched his shako peak in salute and galloped off to the dragoons.

The two riflemen were doubling as best they could towards the scene of Somervile's blooding.

Hervey cantered up to them. 'You saw?'

'We did, sir,' they answered, breathing heavily.

'Yon little hill's a good place to see from. I'm sorry it's just the two of you, but we have at least cleared it!'

'Ay, sir. Very grateful on it we are,' they chirped, in the mordant humour of the battlefield.

As he returned their salutes and put his horse back into a canter, Hervey saw that the main body of Mbopa's force had begun advancing. He pulled up fifty yards in front of the *sango* to summon all the composure he could – not, for once, for the benefit of those who would derive encouragement from his mask of command, but for his own: he needed the clearest of heads to judge the action – to fight, or to make away. Ngwadi's warriors were beyond recall. They stood awaiting the charge of Mbopa's warriors with resolution and relish. If there were not so many more of Mbopa's Zulus now threatening their right flank, he would not have had to bring out the dragoons. And he could not withdraw his few riflemen – whose ammunition must now be depleted – for they were all he had left to cover his dash for escape with Somervile if the kraal looked like falling.

But for the steady crack of rifles – single, aimed shots – it was an eerily silent battlefield. Both the main body of Zulus and the two hundred on the flank advanced without battle cries or sound of any sort. Here before him, indeed, was a battlefield the like of Sparta, or Judea . . .

'Colonel Hervey, sir?'

French was back at his side.

Hervey smiled at the reassurance of a familiar face. 'Corp' French?'

'That Pampata, sir. Strong-willed is she. Young Toyne was detailed to cover her, but she's got herself her own little escort of warriors.'

Hervey shook his head. He could picture it well enough.

'And I missed being where I was meant to be again, sir – in that melee, I mean.'

'You did, Corp' French, but I perceive your sabre will soon be wanted,' replied Hervey, sighing, nodding towards Mbopa's host.

And even as he pointed, the numbers grew: as if to overawe Ngwadi's cohort at the very moment they needed their greatest resolve, three hundred more warriors rose up from behind the ridge, ready to hurl themselves down the slope and tip the balance of the fight. 'So now we see his design!'

'Ay, sir,' said French, grimly. He drew his sabre.

In half a minute more the eerie silence was gone. Now it was the clash of close battle.

And in but five minutes, the mathematics began telling, Ngwadi's line inching back.

Hervey spurred towards the riflemen. 'Corp' Cox, about face and extend! Enfilade if you please!'

Eight rifles against many hundred spears: a drop in the ocean – but what else to do?

Five minutes' enfilade fire, perhaps more, the shots finding their mark, but to no decisive effect.

'Down to ten rounds apiece, sir!' shouted Cox.

Hervey screwed up his courage for the decision. It was time. They could do no more. 'Very well, Corp' Cox. Form at the entrance to the kraal!'

He turned anxiously to see how were the dragoons.

He wished he'd kept Bugle Roddis by his side: now was the time to recall them too. 'Corp' French, tell Captain Fairbrother to break for the kraal!'

'Sir!'

Hervey reined round to make his own way back – at the trot so as not to dismay the riflemen.

He did not see Pampata at once. She stood in front of her warrior escort, just behind the melee, four-square as if in a trance, Shaka's toy spear in hand. When he did see, his blood ran cold.

He turned to make for her.

Ngwadi's line broke suddenly, overwhelmed like the wall of a dyke by a monstrous wave.

Mbopa's men poured through, and on at the solitary figure of Shaka's widow and her escort.

Pampata raised the toy spear high as they lunged.

Hervey galloped at them furiously.

But one spear and then another ripped open her belly.

And she fell to her knees, and cried defiantly, above all the noise of the battle: '*U-Shaka!*'

XXIV

THE SERVICE OF THE STATE

Cape Town, a month later

'I fear it will not serve well for you, Hervey, and I am very sorry for it. I have written in the strongest possible terms to the Colonies Office, absolving you of all blame in the affair, but it is most unfortunate that Huskisson has seen fit to leave the government. You will know Sir George Murray better than do I, but I do not count on his support as I did on Huskisson's. I fear daily for a dismissal. There's an Indiaman coming in on the tide even now!'

Hervey, for all his dismay – anger, even – at the late events in Natal, could not but pity his old friend's situation, especially now he had lost his best supporter in Whitehall, though even had there been a telegraph line from the Colonies Office to the Cape there could scarcely have been a dismissal communicated so fast. 'You acted as you saw best in the King's interest,' he replied firmly.

'Things might easily have gone our way. Fortune was not smiling on us that day.'

It was true, except that Fortune was not ultimately against them: they had made their escape from kwaWambaza, when few others – Ngwadi included – had done so.

'But now there is a chief on that throne who is ill disposed to us. For all that we know, Dingane may be gathering his strength even now.'

'I think it unlikely,' said Hervey, taking his coffee and moving to a chair by the open west window of the lieutenant-governor's office. 'It was in part Shaka's prolonged war-making that sowed the seeds of his fall. Dingane will likely as not wish a period of peace to consolidate his succession. It is, after all, a precarious one.'

Somervile rose from his desk and limped to the sideboard to replenish his cup. 'Your appreciation of the situation would do credit to a diplomatist. I wish only that my essay as a warrior had been as acute.'

'I think you chastise yourself unfairly. The warrior's trade is a difficult one even for the most practised. I never had a harder fight than at kwaWambaza.'

Somervile took a sip of his coffee, and stifled a sigh. 'The warrior's trade, as you reduce it thus, is not slaying, but being slain. That is why our nation – I might add, the world – honours the warrior, because he holds his life at the service of the state.'

'Perhaps "King" rather than "state" might be more . . . lyrical?'

'Do not dismiss the notion lightly, Hervey. You placed your life at the service of the nation, and I fear the nation will not repay you.'

Hervey half frowned. 'I have generally settled for penury in that direction in the past – as have we all in the service. Beggars in red, Somervile.' He knew, though, that in recent weeks Somervile had placed his own life in the service of the King, but that his old friend believed he would not now see the gilded appointment in Canada which Huskisson had promised him.

'I am especially sorry that . . . Shaka's favourite,' (he had noticed that Somervile had not been able to pronounce Pampata's name since kwaWambaza) 'should have perished, and in such a brute way.'

Hervey turned his head to the window. He had been trying for a month to put away both the fact and the image of her death. 'It is very hard not to think of this country as but one enormous brute place. I confess I will be well pleased to leave this fairest cape, for all its sunsets and sunrises.'

'And your dragoons?'

'They will not be mine for much longer . . . But, yes, they too are glad to be recalled. Though we leave behind a good few of them in the ground.'

Somervile knew that there were as many buried from natural causes as by hostile hand, but he honoured them just the same. 'How shall you proceed in the case of Captain Brereton?' he asked, his brow lined.

Hervey turned his head back. 'With recourse to the cardinal virtues.'

'The Platonic virtues, I trust you mean; not the Patristic excrescence.'

Hervey suppressed a smile. 'Indeed.'

'And to which of the two appropriate virtues shall you have recourse: prudence or justice?'

'Prudence.'

'The only one for which experience is required.'

'Just so.'

'And Brereton will therefore be placed in the pantheon of regimental heroes.'

'I see no offence against God or man in that.'

'No. Nor do I.'

'I must see to it, though, that Fairbrother has his laurels – and Collins too. It does not bear thinking how events might have been without their admirable address.'

'Admirable, admirable.' Somervile took his chair once more. 'And, I might add, you have made a very great ally in Colonel Smith. His despatch – if mine does not – makes clear your own peerless service.'

Hervey nodded, obliged.

Somervile heaved a considerable sigh. 'And so, you will take Friday's packet and be in London in a month. And I, meanwhile, shall await the new governor . . . and my fate.'

Hervey rose, and began making to leave, glad at least that he would be going to *meet* his fate, as a soldier ought, rather than awaiting it as his poor old friend must.

As he rose, he remembered the letter from Kezia, in his pocket; it had come that morning by one of the Indiamen, much delayed, and he had still not opened it. 'Well, we all dine together tonight, do we not? That is no occasion for low spirits. I shall take my leave until then.' He held up the letter. 'Matters to be addressed ... Canada, and all.'

An hour or so later he had attended to his most pressing correspondence. He picked up the sheets of paper and began reading them over. His account of events in Natal was – even he recognized – flat in the extreme, but he had no wish to trouble Kezia with details in which she would scarce be interested, and he certainly would give no account which included the sanguinary particulars. All of it she would be able to read, no doubt, in the pages of *The Times*, if she wished, for the official despatches now seemed to find their way into print with alarming speed.

He lingered over the final page, wondering about both its contents and manner of expression:

> *And now, my dearest wife, I return to the subject of*
> *the lieutenant-colonelcy of the 81st. Events here, of*
> *which I have only been able to give but a very*

*incomplete account, have led me to the settled
conclusion that I must take the commission. In doing
so I know it to be contrary to your wish, and that you
have every good reason to set your face against it,
Canada being a place of some primitive society yet,
and I therefore can neither insist upon your
accompanying me nor even hope for a change of heart,
for I see that such would be unconducive to your music
and therefore to your happiness. I shall therefore bear
the deprivation for as long as needs be, in the sure
hope that it will not be excessively long, and that we
shall soon be reunited in a station more agreeable to
you.*

He laid down the sheet, and groaned. What other way
might he express himself? He rose, and paced about the
room. Ought he perhaps not to write at all? Should he
wait until he was back in London to explain? But the
sloop-of-war left on tomorrow's tide, and would likely
make the passage a week and more faster than would his
packet. There was no excuse not to take the
opportunity to write, and if he *were* to write, there was
no excuse not to disclose his settled resolve. Besides,
there were letters for Georgiana and his family, and
others (one, even, for Kat); it was insupportable that
there should not be one for his wife too.

He sat down at his writing table once more, scratched
a few signatory lines, and placed down the sheet to dry.

He would now change into undress uniform and go to the hospital to see how were his sick dragoons (he still thought of them as his, even though he would soon be taking off his blue coat for good). Some had been most grievously sick by the time they had made it back to Port Natal.

Fairbrother, dressed for dinner in plain clothes, had arrived ahead of his time at the castle, hoping to be able to read some of the commercial intelligence which he supposed the newly arrived Indiaman had brought. He sat comfortably at ease in a small ante-room perusing the shipping news in *Lloyd's List*, enjoying a cigar and a large measure of whiskey and soda.

The door opened. 'Captain Fairbrother, sahib, there is an officer come from England who claims an acquaintance, sahib.'

Fairbrother turned his head languidly. 'Upon my word, Howard!' He rose and held out a hand, which he preferred to bowing.

Lord John Howard took it, smiling broadly. 'My dear fellow, how very good it is to see you!'

'What brings you here?' asked Fairbrother, not able at all to conceal his astonishment, for Hervey had said many times that Howard was tethered by chain to the Horse Guards.

'Exactly speaking, the *Empire*, an Indiaman. We came in this afternoon. My business . . . well, I have news for our mutual friend that I would tell him myself. *And* I wished to take leave of the Horse Guards for a few months and see a little something of where we fling far our gallant troops. I hoped, indeed, to ride with you both on one of your frontier sojourns!'

Fairbrother smiled ruefully. 'I think I may say – I speak for myself, of course – that the frontier holds no immediate call upon our time.'

Lord John Howard looked both disappointed and puzzled.

Jaswant returned with a tray.

'Take a little whiskey and sit you down, and I'll explain myself better.'

Howard took a great deal of whiskey and a very little soda, and settled comfortably into a low chair.

'But first tell me, if you would, what is this news of Hervey's that tempts you from the drawing rooms of London?' Fairbrother took a long draw on his cigar, hardly supposing that Howard would oblige him with an answer, for all the whiskey-generosity.

But he was wrong. Howard did not feel himself at all bound by confidentiality, since the news was entirely official. 'Here,' he said, producing a piece of folded paper from a pocket.

Fairbrother took hold of it, intrigued. He sat back in his chair and looked Howard steadily in the eye. 'It is nothing that Hervey would have me know from his own lips?'

Howard shook his head and took a good sip of his whiskey.

Fairbrother unfolded the paper, and read:

> *His Majesty is pleased to approve the Commander-in-Chief's desire that the under-named officers be promoted Major-General.*
>
> *Colonel Stamford Blakeborough*
> *Lieutenant-Colonel The Earl of Holderness*
>
> *(Signed) Willingham*
> *Asst. Private Secr.y*

He frowned, and folded it again. 'Upon my word, Howard, this is hardly calculated to be pleasing to our friend. He had a regard for Hol'ness, but I should scarce suppose it ran to thinking him fit for such a promotion! And *this* brings you to the Cape?'

Howard held up a hand enigmatically.

'Come, man! Or is it . . . Ah, I see. The Sixth is now up for purchase!'

Howard shook his head.

'But why should the commander-in-chief wish to promote a man who has fits at the least provocation? I suppose he does not know of them, of course. And that business on manoeuvres at Windsor . . . all Hervey's doing, the success that night. Hol'ness had a fit in the middle of the river and Hervey took over the whole affair – *and* swore everyone to secrecy!'

'I don't doubt it. Indeed, I knew of it. And so did the commander-in-chief. Bushels don't *always* conceal lights, you know.'

'Then what—'

'The Duke of Wellington himself wrote to Lord Hill and requested that Hol'ness be placed on the major-generals' list to be appointed lieutenant-governor of the Duchy of Lancaster, and since the Duchy appointments are in the prime minister's gift ... I fancy the duke imagines Lord Hol'ness will not disgrace the court. Lady Hol'ness is, of course, in waiting to the Princess Victoria.'

'Well,' said Fairbrother, blowing out a great deal of smoke. 'It all astonishes me.'

'You are not inclined to know why the duke favours Hol'ness?'

'If you are able to tell me, I have no objection in knowing.'

Howard smiled, and took another good measure of whiskey. 'It would seem that the duke attended a concert of music in the summer, and was much delighted by the play-ing and singing of a certain lady.'

'I understand the duke is fond of music, yes. And I fancy you will tell me the lady was a handsome one.'

'The lady was, word has it, Lady Lankester – that is, Mrs Matthew Hervey.'

Fairbrother's eyes widened. '*Indeed?*'

'At supper afterwards, apparently, the duke asked after Hervey, and she informed him that he was to be gazetted to the infantry in Canada on return from the Cape, and that she was much disappointed in this, and—'

Fairbrother sat upright. 'You don't mean that the duke wished to create a vacancy in the Sixth by promoting the lieutenant-colonel?'

'I have been unable to think of any other explanation. And, in its way, it is a perfectly proper thing. It certainly serves!' Howard took another sip of his whiskey, and smiled contentedly. 'Evidently Mrs Hervey plays the pianoforte with a good deal of passion.'

Fairbrother sat back in his chair. 'You mistake the matter, Howard. I have heard Kezia Hervey play the pianoforte. She does so with a great deal of anger, not passion.'

Howard looked rather taken aback. 'I am not best qualified to judge these things. But a happy outcome nevertheless.'

Fairbrother sat up again, frowning. 'But see; how anyway does this help? The Cavalry's changing hands for twenty thousand and more – far beyond Hervey's means!'

'Lord Hill has the discretion to appoint without purchase. He does so in Hervey's case.'

Fairbrother rose at once, with the keenest expression of pleasure, and pulled the bell-rope.

The khansamah came.

'Be so good, Jaswant, as to send at once for Colonel Hervey-sahib. It is most imperative.'

For the next quarter of an hour they sat in happy contemplation of the news from the Horse Guards, so that when Hervey did come – from out of his bath and hastily dressed in plain clothes – the two good acquaintances were thoroughly fuelled with excellent malt and equally good cheer.

'Howard! What a deucedly fine surprise!' Hervey clapped both hands on his old friend's shoulders, thoroughly disposed now to being as cheery as they.

'My dear Hervey, I bring you the most excellent news. So excellent, indeed, I could not forbear to bring it in person rather than send it. You are to have the Sixth, and without purchase! At the special bidding of the duke!'

Hervey was all astonishment. 'The duke?'

'Ay. His doing. The details we may leave until later. And Lord Hill ordered that it be without purchase.'

Hervey continued to shake his head. 'I can scarce believe it.'

'That a man doesn't get his deserts? You served both the duke *and* Lord Hill admirably in their time.'

'So say you, but—'

'And, I may say, I bring for your celebration a basket of Monsieur Moët's best champagne. From the duke's own cellar, indeed!'

Hervey stared at his old friend, even more incredulous.

'Well, not, that is, at his express request. But he did

leave behind a good many dozen when he left the Horse Guards.'

'Loot!' declared Fairbrother, vastly amused. 'But I fancy it was only that which the duke himself looted from Bonaparte's cellar when he took prize of Paris?'

'Just so, and therefore it is booty not loot,' declared Lord John Howard, very decidedly.

Fairbrother groaned. 'Staff officers! Jesuits in gold braid!' He raised his glass. 'But, my most excellent friend, Colonel Hervey, whether it be loot or booty, I propose a toast to you: "To the warrior the spoils!"'

THE END

HISTORICAL AFTERNOTE

Sources for the history of the Shakan period are mainly oral. This does not mean they are inherently unreliable, but it does mean, of course, that it is not possible to re-examine them. The white traders at Port Natal (Durban) wrote journals and letters, but since there were no white witnesses to Shaka's assassination and the immediate aftermath, there is no contemporary written account. The oral history is strong and consistent, however. It appears that Mbopa's scratch army of Izi-Yendane ('mop heads'), cattle guards, veterans, and the newly formed 'Bees' regiment of youths, was cobbled together remarkably quickly. Somehow Mbopa persuaded them that they were marching to avenge Shaka, who had been murdered at the hands of an 'evil relative in the north' – Ngwadi. Ngwadi was indeed the only chief whose clan warriors had not been impressed for the campaign against Soshangane.

Pampata certainly made her epic journey, a hundred miles at least, and alone except for the first half when a youth accompanied her (at some stage he fell out, too weary to go on), for there were separate reports of her progress by village elders whom she encountered. On each occasion Shaka's toy spear proved her *laissez-passer*. Ngwadi had no time to muster all his warriors, however. It appears that initially he mounted a strong defence of his kraal, beating off the first assault of Izi-Yendane, but Mbopa brought the 'Bees' forward, and, fired with vengeance and youthful courage, these hurled themselves at the stockade. Seeing he was outnumbered, Ngwadi withdrew with all his womenfolk and children to the calf byre in the middle of the cattle enclosure.

Ngwadi's last stand is recounted as one of the heroic episodes of Zulu history. He personally is said to have killed eight of his attackers before succumbing to the *iklwa* with all his household. At this point, Pampata may have taken her own life – with Shaka's toy spear, as one tradition has it. Whether she took her own life or not, the story goes that as she died, her last cry was, indeed, '*U-Shaka!*'

Dingane assumed the throne, promptly murdering his half-brother Mhlangana, as well as Mbopa and anyone else whose loyalties were in question. There was a brief period of peace in Zululand (and favourable contacts with the settlement at Port Natal) but Dingane soon became as paranoid and brutal as Shaka, though without his brother's other qualities. Relations with the settlers at Port Natal deteriorated, not least because of the increasing numbers of Zulu refugees that sought sanctuary there. Three times, the settlers had to evacuate the port whilst Dingane's warriors sacked the place.

In 1837, the 'swallows' of whom Shaka had warned finally appeared in Natal – the *Voortrekkers*, Cape Dutch farmers and merchants at odds with the Colonial administration. The first party, led by Pieter Uys, tried to negotiate with Dingane to occupy the empty land south of the Thukela (Tugela) River. But they could not cross the flooded river, so a shouted conversation ensued between the trekkers and some warriors on the far bank. As a result, the trekkers came away believing they were free to settle the land. In fact, Dingane had already given the land to a missionary from Port Natal. A few months later, another party under Pieter Retief did see Dingane who requested that, as a sign of good will, some cattle be recovered from a local chief who had stolen them. Retief recovered the cattle, together with some guns and horses which he had no intention of giving Dingane.

In February 1838, Retief and a hundred trekkers paid Dingane a visit to return the cattle and ratify the treaty giving the trekkers the land south of the Tugela. Dingane surprised the party and dragged them off to his hill of execution, kwaMatiwane, where they were put to death. He then sent 10,000 warriors to destroy the Voortrekkers in the Drakensberg foothills. On the night of 16 February 1838, 500 trekkers were killed. Dingane had underestimated the number of wagons that had crossed the Drakensberg mountains, however, and several camps were untouched. Ten months later, the trekkers wreaked revenge at Blood River, where 460 men defeated a force of 10,000 Zulus at almost no cost. The trekkers tried then to seize Dingane but he fled, burning his kraal.

Some months later, Mpande, Dingane's half-brother (so fat and slothful that Dingane – as others – believed him harmless, and who had thereby escaped the fate of the other half-brothers), defected to the trekkers. His general, Nongalaza, defeated Dingane at the battle of Magongo Hills, forcing him to flee to Swaziland where he was killed by his own warriors. Mpande was installed as king of the Zulus, and reigned with surprising success for more than thirty years.

Long before Mpande's death, however, a power struggle developed between two of his sons – Cetshwayo and Mbuyazi – which was settled in 1856 when Cetshwayo defeated Mbuyazi at the bloody battle of Ndondakusuka, in which 23,000 warriors perished. After Mpande's death in 1872, Cetshwayo revived and reconstructed the Zulu army. By this time, however, the encroachment of both the Boers and British in the south meant a series of border disputes which came to a head in 1878 when the discovery of diamonds in South Africa (though further west) forced the British to take a new look at the independent African nations. An ultimatum, which many historians on both sides believe could never have been fulfilled, and was really an excuse for war, was handed to the Zulus in December 1878. A month later, three columns of British troops under Lord Chelmsford marched into Zululand. So began the first Anglo-Zulu War, whose battles of Isandlwana, Rorke's Drift and Ulundi have passed into legend.

But that is a generation, and more, from Hervey and his comrades at Shaka's kraal. So where will the new commanding officer of His Majesty's 6th Light Dragoons find himself in the next instalment of these cavalry tales? We must wait and see. Indeed, we must wait a little longer than usual: twice as long, in fact, for the eleventh book in the series will be published – *Deo volente* – in two years' time, not one. Then, I trust, loyal and patient readers will be rewarded with a story of that singular, glorious, never-to-be-repeated thing: taking command of a regiment of the British Army.

THE DUKE OF WELLINGTON'S CAVALRY

AN EXPLANATORY NOTE

Here is a picture – a very incomplete one – of the cavalry in the Duke of Wellington's day. The picture remained the same, with but minor changes, until after the Crimean War nearly half a century later.

Like the infantry, the cavalry was organized in regiments. Each had a colonel as titular head, usually a very senior officer (in the case of the 10th Light Dragoons, for instance, it was the Prince of Wales; in the case of the fictional 6th Light Dragoons it was first the Earl of Sussex and then Lord George Irvine, both lieutenant generals) who kept a fatherly if distant eye on things, in particular the appointment of officers. The actual command of the regiment was exercised by a lieutenant-colonel. He had a major as his second in command (or 'senior major' as he was known in the Sixth and other regiments), an adjutant who was usually commissioned from the ranks, a regimental serjeant-major (RSM) and various other 'specialist' staff.

A cavalry regiment comprised a number of troops identified by a letter (A Troop, B Troop, etc.), each of a hundred or so men commanded by a captain, though in practice the troops were usually under strength. The number of troops in a regiment varied depending on where it was stationed; in Spain, for instance, at the height of the war, there were eight.

The captain was assisted by two or three subaltern officers – lieutenants and cornets (second-lieutenants) – and a troop serjeant-major, who before 1811 was known as a quartermaster (QM). After 1811 a regimental quartermaster was established to supervise supply and quartering (accommodation) for the regiment as a whole – men and horses. There was also a riding-master (RM), like the QM usually commissioned from the ranks ('the ranks' referred to everyone who was not a commissioned officer, in other words RSM and below). With his staff of rough-riders (a rough was an unbroken remount, a replacement horse) the RM was responsible for training recruits both human and equine.

Troops were sometimes paired in squadrons, numbered First, Second, Third (and occasionally Fourth). On grand reviews in the eighteenth century the colonel would command the first squadron, the lieutenant-colonel the second, and the major the third, each squadron bearing an identifying *guidon*, a silk banner – similar to the infantry battalion's *colours*. By the time of the Peninsular War, however, guidons were no longer carried mounted in the field, and the squadron was commanded by the senior of the two troop leaders (captains).

A troop or squadron leader, as well indeed as the commanding officer, would give his orders in the field by voice and through his trumpeter. His words of command were either carried along the line by the sheer power of his voice, or were repeated by the troop officers, or in the case of the commanding officer were relayed by the adjutant ('gallopers' and aides-de-camp performed the same function for general officers). The trumpet was often used for repeating an order and to recall or signal scattered troops. The commanding officer and each captain had his own trumpeter, who was traditionally mounted on a grey, and they were trained by the trumpet-major (who, incidentally, was traditionally responsible for administering floggings).

The lowest rank was private man. In a muster roll, for instance, he was entered as 'Private John Smith'; he was addressed by all ranks, however, simply as 'Smith'. In the Sixth and regiments like them he would be referred to as a dragoon. The practice of referring to him as a trooper came much later; the cavalry rank 'trooper' only replaced 'private' officially after the First World War. In Wellington's day, a trooper was the man's horse – troop horse; an officer's horse was known as a charger (which he had to buy for himself – two of them at least – along with all his uniform and equipment).

A dragoon, a private soldier, would hope in time to be promoted corporal, and he would then be addressed as, say, 'Corporal Smith' by all ranks. The rank of lance-corporal, or in some regiments 'chosen man', was not yet properly established, though it was used unofficially. In due course a corporal might be promoted sergeant (with a 'j' in the Sixth and other regiments) and perhaps serjeant-major. The best of these non-commissioned officers (NCOs – every rank from corporal to RSM, i.e. between private and cornet, since warrant rank was not yet properly established), if he survived long enough, would hope to be promoted RSM, and would then be addressed by the officers as 'Mr Smith' (like the subaltern officers), or by subordinates as 'Sir'. In time the RSM might be commissioned as a lieutenant to be adjutant, QM or RM.

All ranks (i.e. private men, NCOs and officers) were armed with a sword, called in the cavalry a sabre (the lance was not introduced until after Waterloo), and in the early years of the Napoleonic wars with two pistols. Other ranks (all ranks less the officers) also carried a carbine, which was a short musket, handier for mounted work.

And of course there were the horses. The purchase of these was a regimental responsibility, unless on active service, and the quality varied with the depth of the lieutenant-colonel's pockets. Each troop had a farrier, trained by the farrier-major, responsible to the captain for the shoeing of every horse in the troop, and to the veterinary surgeon for the troop horses' health. Hard feed (oats, barley, etc.) and forage (hay, or cut grass – 'green forage') were the serjeant-major's responsibility along with other practical details such as the condition of saddlery, allocation of routine duties and, par excellence, discipline.

Although the cavalry often worked independently, sending detachments on escort duty, patrols and pickets, regiments were usually grouped into brigades of three or more, commanded by a brigadier who was a full colonel or major general (brigadier at this time was an appointment not a rank), with a brigade-major as his staff officer. Brigades could in turn be grouped into divisions (most spectacularly in the retreat to Corunna under the command of that quintessential cavalry general Lord Uxbridge, later Marquess of Anglesey) or attached to an infantry division or to a corps of two or more divisions. The cavalry were prized for their flexibility, though Wellington complained that they were too frequently unmanageable in the field, with the habit of 'galloping at everything'.

The independent-mindedness of cavalry officers had in part to do with the manner of their commissioning. The cavalry (and the infantry) were the responsibility of the commander-in-chief – for most of the period of these cavalry tales the Duke of York, whose headquarters were at the Horse Guards in Whitehall. On the other hand, the artillery, engineers and other technical services were the responsibility of the Master General of the Ordnance, whose 'explosives authority' gave him a seat in the Cabinet. To make matters even more complicated, the commissariat and transport were the direct responsibility of the Treasury.

Officers of the MGO's arms were appointed to their commissions without purchase and promoted on seniority and merit. Those of the cavalry and infantry, with a few exceptions, purchased their commissions and promotion. They actually paid several thousand pounds for the privilege of serving. When it came to their turn on the seniority list, they bought promotion to the next higher rank, which in practice meant selling their present rank through the regimental agents to someone else and paying the difference in price for the higher one. In fact a rich and influential officer did not need to bide his time on the seniority list: he could offer an officer in another regiment more than the going rate for his rank – called paying overprice. The exception was during active service, when the death of an officer meant that the vacancy passed without purchase to the next regimental officer on the seniority list. Hence the officers' black-humoured toast, 'To a bloody war and a sickly season!'

The iniquities of the purchase system are obvious, principally in the widespread abuse of the supposedly strict and fair rules. The advantages are less so, but they were nonetheless significant (space precludes a worthwhile discussion of the purchase system here, and I commend instead the essay in the first volume of the Marquess of Anglesey's *History of the British Cavalry*). There is no doubt, however, that with so many men under arms, England (which in Wellington's time was shorthand for the United Kingdom of Great Britain and Ireland) was on the whole well served by it.

It did mean, though, that men such as Matthew Hervey, a son of the vicarage, of the minor gentry – the backbone of Wellington's officer corps – who had little private money, had to watch while others less capable and experienced than they overtook them in the promotion stakes. There were promotions for meritorious service occasionally, but the opportunities were few even in so large an army, and when peace came to Europe in 1815 the opportunities became even rarer.

This, then, is the army in which Matthew Hervey is making his way – a slow, sometimes disheartening progress, but with the advantage of knowing that he serves among friends who face the same odds, and with NCOs with whom he has, so to speak, grown up. The strength of the army was this regimental system, because the regiment was largely self-supporting and self-healing. It remains so today. It is threatened more than ever before, however. For who that has not served in a regiment, directly or indirectly, can truly appreciate its strength? Certainly not the Treasury, and, I begin to doubt, even 'the War Office'.

Acknowledgements

The abbot, librarian and brethren of
Pluscarden Abbey, Moray.

MATTHEW PAULINUS HERVEY

BORN: 1791, second son of the Reverend Thomas Hervey, Vicar of Horningsham in Wiltshire, and of Mrs. Hervey; one sister, Elizabeth.

EDUCATED: Shrewsbury School (praepostor)

MARRIED: 1817 to Lady Henrietta Lindsay, ward of the Marquess of Bath (deceased 1818). 1828 to Lady Ivo Lankester, widow of Lieutenant-Colonel Sir Ivo Lankester, Bart, lately commanding 6th Light Dragoons.

CHILDREN: a daughter, Georgiana, born 1818.

MILITARY HISTORY:

1808: commissioned cornet by purchase in His Majesty's 6th Light Dragoons (Princess Caroline's Own).

1809~14: served Portugal and Spain; evacuated with army at ✕ Corunna, 1809, returned with regiment to Lisbon that year: Present at numerous battles and actions including ✕ Talavera, ✕ Badajoz, ✕ Salamanca, ✕ Vitoria.

1814: present at ✕ Toulouse; wounded. Lieutenant.

1814~15: served Ireland, present at ✕ Waterloo, and in Paris with army of occupation.

1815: Additional ADC to the Duke of Wellington (acting captain); despatched for special duty in Bengal.

1816: saw service against Pindarees and Nizam of Hyderabad's forces; returned to regimental duty. Brevet captain; brevet major.

1818: saw service in Canada; briefly seconded to US forces, Michigan Territory; resigned commission.

1819: reinstated, 6th Light Dragoons; captain.

1820~26: served Bengal; saw active service in ✕ Ava (wounded severely); present at ✕ Siege of Bhurtpore; brevet major.

1826~27: detached service in Portugal.

1827: in temporary command of 6th Light Dragoons, major; in command of detachment of 6th Light Dragoons at the Cape Colony; seconded to raise Corps of Cape Mounted Rifles; acting lieutenant-colonel; ✕ Umtata River; wounded.

1828: home leave.

AN INTERVIEW WITH
ALLAN MALLINSON

In *Warrior*, Matthew Hervey finds himself back in South Africa. What drew you to South Africa, and what in particular made you think that this was a place where you could situate two novels?

You have to march towards the sound of the guns, and in the mid 1820s the sound was in South Africa. The trouble was with the Xhosa and other tribes – generally referred to at the time as Kaffirs – who were cattle rustling for the most part, but it worried the authorities because there had been two bitter 'Kaffir wars' within recent memory. In *Company of Spears* the action is set against this background of frontier skirmishing, in which Hervey and his men run up against a marauding Zulu force at the Umtata River. In fact, whether there were Zulus at the battle of Umtata River is disputed: some historians insist that they were an independent renegade group – all of which I explain in the afternote to the story. But the whole point is that no one really knows for sure because Zulu history at that time was not written down: the Zulu simply had no technique of writing. Partly because of this, I felt that there was unusual latitude to insert Hervey and his men into real history. I had known for many years of the murder of Shaka, and always believed that there was a good story to be written about it, but it was not until I began the real research that I discovered just how rich a vein of adventure there was to tap into. The epic of Pampata's flight and the climactic battle at her father's kraal seemed to me to be positively Wagnerian.

The other attraction of South Africa was, of course, that it was a place that Hervey had been to before. The Cape, and Natal – Zululand – is a colourful setting in terms of geography, flora and fauna, without being 'exotic' in the Indian sense, and readers may perhaps observe that in neither *Company of Spears* nor *Warrior* are Hervey and his associates charged by elephants, hunted by lions, savaged by crocodiles or bitten by snakes, for that would be perilously close to cliché – if not an excess of it. And so the only 'encounter' is with a leopard, in the night, unseen, over in a flash – and the glimpses of other fauna are more mundane, like the weasel, or of birds. It is much the same in *Prester John*, the first novel set in Africa that I read (at fourteen).

One of the special features of *Warrior* is its detailed depiction of Zulu history. Was it an easy subject to research?

As I said, Zulu history is oral, and therefore depends on transcriptions of stories retold over the generations. The first of these were recorded in the late nineteenth century, but over the years there have been exploitative accounts – especially lurid – with an eye to commercial success. In 2001, some time before I began researching for my own Hervey Zulu tales – and before I knew about Google and AbeBooks – while killing a couple of hours before the grounds at Glyndebourne opened to admit pre-opera picknickers, I came across two books in a second-hand bookshop in Lewes by two South African historians (the best things frequently happen by accident). First was an account published in 1964 of the life of Dingane, Shaka's usurper, by Peter Becker, director of Bantu studies at the Institute of South African Languages. Even more apt was the second, however; a biography of Shaka published in 1955 by E A Ritter, the son of a Natal magistrate, who grew up with the Zulu at the turn of the nineteenth century. It seemed to me that here was as faithful an account of Shaka's life and the habits of the Zulu at that time as any to be found. And then a little later, while browsing the dusty shelves of my favourite library – the Royal Institute of Defence Studies in Whitehall – I came across a 1973 PhD thesis from the university of Port Elizabeth by John Burridge Scott, entitled *The British Soldier on the Eastern Cape Frontier 1800-1850*. Such things are gifts from the gods!

And then when I came to write the books after the obvious 'field work', I retired to my study in the Highlands of Scotland – like John Buchan – with pen and paper. Once the first draft was complete, I had intended leaving my Highland fastness and taking the sleeper train from Aberdeen to London to discuss the technical details of language and one or two other things with the dons at the School of Oriental and African Studies, but the gods suddenly bore me even more gifts. After the day's writing I had taken to repairing to the fireside comforts (it was midwinter) of the splendid Castle Hotel, former dower house of the dukes of Gordon, up-river on the edge of nearby Huntly. Here I could enjoy a glass or two of decent claret and the Castle's excellent venison stew. The owner's wife, who was South African, liked to employ foreigners, and one evening a tall, slim and strikingly handsome black girl in her late twenties brought me my stew. 'Where are you from?' I asked hopefully. 'East London,' she replied. I almost held my breath as I asked, 'Which East London?' I received the reply I

476

had wanted. 'So you are Xhosa?' I asked, clearly with a note of doubt in my voice, for she laughed and said, 'Yes.' And thus it was that in the wilds of Banffshire in the depths of winter I had found my Xhosan – and by extension Zulu – interlocutor.

One of the many pleasures of the Hervey novels is re-meeting characters from previous novels. Hervey's friend Fairbrother is particularly interesting in this respect. Is he drawn from history or your imagination?

The master/slave progeny was, of course, always a feature of plantation life, but in the southern states of America, usually within a couple of generations, all trace of the white genes had disappeared. In the Caribbean, however, things were not so cut and dried. When I was a young officer I spent some time in Jamaica training with the Jamaica Regiment, where I met a number of officers with 'cafe au lait' complexions – handsome, well-made men who were very much at home in the field. But Fairbrother is an educated man as well as being extraordinarily good in the field. When I was at theological college in the 1960s I met a young curate – Ewen Ratteray – who had trained at Codrington College in Barbados, and I was much taken by his learning and his measured way of speaking (he is now the Right Reverend Ewen Ratteray, Bishop of Bermuda – the first black priest to hold that appointment). Fairbrother is, I suppose, a conflation of the men I met during that formative time. But the important thing is that while he has the attributes of an insider, he is an outsider. So too in many ways is Hervey, and that may account for their mutual attraction. And I think we shall see more of Fairbrother, for close male friendship in the army is tricky:

there is always the matter of relative seniority to take into account. Fairbrother's semi-detachment from the army allows Hervey to speak to him in an entirely different way from that in which he would be obliged to speak to a fellow officer, who by definition would always be either his subordinate or his superior.

You started writing while still serving in the Army. Did this inform your vision for the Matthew Hervey series?

Let me put it this way: I could not have written the series (and so far there are only ten books – a million words!) without having been a soldier for a substantial period. I have been lucky in my service: I have seen a good deal of service 'in the field', as they say, and also in Whitehall. At the Staff College you find that if you can write, your card is marked: officers are needed in the MoD who can write policy papers and briefs for senior officers and officials, but when you are told you are going to the MoD you groan, because there is always the fear that you'll never be let out. Actually, I enjoyed my first tour in the MoD – as a young major – in particular, for I discovered that a well-turned phrase could have a powerful effect, and it was here that I undoubtedly honed my writing skills. In addition, during the forty-five minute railway journey home each evening from Waterloo, I re-read *Hornblower*, and I think, in retrospect, that 'it all began here', but without my knowing it. The other advantage of serving in Whitehall, and later in the diplomatic world, is that you are at the interface of politics, policy and practice, and you see human nature at its best and its worst. In a sense, everything I write about I have experienced – except the historical context, of course.

You are currently taking a break from Hervey, and are writing a non-fiction book. Can you tell us about this, and when we might expect to see it in the shops?

The idea is very simple: what has made the army what it is today? The answer is people and events. My non-fiction is called therefore *The Making of the British Army*, with the additional tag *From the English Civil War to the War on Terror* – which indicates the historical range, I hope. It is a narrative and commentary on the people and events that have shaped the modern army, and is aimed at readers who do not perhaps know the extent of the army's history but are drawn to it by what they see and hear today of the army in Iraq and Afghanistan. *Deo volente*, it will be published on 10 September (2009).

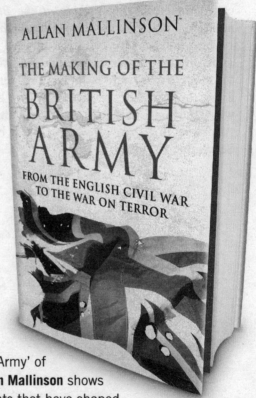